ARZONO PUBLISHING PRESENTS

THE 2021 ANNUAL

ARZONO Publishing Presents The 2021 Annual:
An Anthology of Short Stories & Poetry

Print Edition

Copyright © 2021

Cover Design by Jonas Steger of Fantasy and Coffee Design
www.fantasyandcoffee.com

Catalog in Publication Data Held by the Library of Congress

ISBN: 978-0-9968088-4-2

Dedication

This anthology is dedicated to the many writers who submitted this year and trusted me yet again to uplift, support, and get the words that follow this page out to the rest of the world. With over 200 submissions, it was a most difficult year turning so many away, but I do believe we have an absolutely epic Annual for 2021. I also dedicate this work, the time I've put into it, and the hope and love I've poured into this project to my family. This past year has brought our world more challenges than we could have ever imagined, and my personal world is no different. I, like many in these troubling times, have lost much as a result of lockdown, mental health, and love lost. No matter the challenges ahead, I urge our world to hold onto hope in abundance of love.

Thank you for supporting my publishing house and the amazing writers inside these pages.

Stella Samuel

April 2021

Table of Contents

Short Stories

Poetry

Acknowledgments   346

Short Stories

Mark Jabaut

Mark Jabaut is a playwright and author who lives in Webster NY with his wife Nancy. Mark's play IN THE TERRITORIES, originally developed via Geva Theatre's Regional Writers Workshop and Festival of New Theatre, premiered in May 2014 at The Sea Change Theatre in Beverly, MA. His 2015 Rochester Key Bank Fringe Festival entry, THE BRIDGE CLUB OF DEATH, went on to be featured at an End of Life Symposium at SUNY Broome County and is listed with the National Issues Forum for those who wish to host similar events. Mark also had entries in subsequent Fringe Festivals, THE HATCHET MAN, DAMAGED BEASTS and COLMA!. Mark has authored several short plays performed by The Geriactors, a local troupe of elderly performers. Mark's fiction has been published in a local Rochester magazine, POST, as well as The Ozone Park Journal, SmokeLong Quarterly, Spank the Carp, Uproar and Defenestration.

We Ran Up

It is Monday, and Kenyon sits in a vinyl chair in the waiting room, squeezing his eyes shut and trying not to vomit. Saliva keeps forming in his mouth, pooling around his molars, and it has a metallic taste he doesn't like. He swallows it and breathes in deeply through his nose like they taught him.

"Do you have someone coming for you, Kenyon?" Through his tight face—eyes pinched, throat rigid, nostrils flared—he recognizes the voice of Jen, one of his favorites. He loosens up a little and opens his eyes.

"Yeah, my buddy is coming to get me," he says. "Thanks."

Jen pats him on the shoulder and goes back toward the lab. He watches her ass with little interest.

Kenyon closes his eyes again and leans his head back against the wall. He pictures the battle that is being waged inside him.

Mondays and Thursdays. He dreads those days. The rest of the week is no picnic, but Mondays and Thursdays bite the big one.

***

The first soggy thud confuses Kenyon. The buildings have not fallen yet; that future is still unimaginable. He is outside, having been sent back down the stairwell to find the command center, as their communications aren't working. The rest of his crew are still going up, over seventy floors to climb.

He turns around to locate the source of the noise, and something splats loudly onto the sidewalk not fifteen feet away. He stares for a moment, unable to tell what it is. It is some nonsensical thing, a special effects mistake from a movie studio. And then he sees it for what it is. It is a woman. A woman has fallen from one of the tower's windows and has landed in a messy heap. Then, he sees the source of the first soggy thud and can somehow tell that it was a man, although it only looks vaguely human.

Kenyon moves away from the base of the building to avoid being hit, and from his new vantage point, it looks like people are jumping from the tower on purpose. He dismisses this as a trick of the light—they are too far away to be sure, and no one would jump from the seventy-fifth floor of a building, even if it was burning.

***

Six months ago, they found an obstruction in Kenyon's colon. Big deal, he had said, so I'll eat less meat. The doctor had not laughed, and after a flurry of tests, they told him he had colon cancer. And bladder cancer. And lung cancer. He was a cancer-growing farm, like those mushroom kits: Kids, Grow Mushrooms in your Basement!

They couldn't say with any certainty where the cancer had originated, but it had metastasized and spread through his body like wildfire, roaring through his bloodstream and lymph system, hungry for new organs to burn.

Metastasized. It is the scariest word of the twenty-first century. The M-word.

It is so sad it's almost funny. In order to fight the cancer cells, which apparently have nothing better to do than reproduce inside his formerly rockin' body like they were horny rabbits, the doctors have to inject poisons into him. Poison to fight the poison. He is almost surprised they don't just inject him with more cancer and let the cells fight it out amongst themselves.

***

Ever since he was a kid, Kenyon has scribbled notes to himself, thoughts, descriptions of people he sees on the street. He takes a small notebook with him wherever he goes, even to the station house. The guys think he's writing poetry in it; maybe he is, of a sort. They call him Shakespeare; they call him Emily Dickinson. "Can I get you a cup of coffee, Ms. Dickinson?"

He loves these guys. He would give his life for them, as they would for him. He knows it. They all know it. It is what bonds them together closer than a family.

That's why it nearly breaks his heart when he is sent back down the stairwell to the command post. He wants to be with his brothers, running up the stairs two at a time. But someone has to go. His bad luck.

Everyone has been cleared away from the landing zone, as some are calling it. The Impact Zone. Kenyon watches as another person—long hair, it might be a woman—accelerates toward the pavement. A lesson from high school physics pops into his head: When drag force is equal to the gravity force, acceleration becomes zero. It's called terminal velocity.

It must be god-awful hot up there, to make someone jump.

Kenyon can't watch them anymore and tries to focus on the flames roiling out of the windows high above. Black smoke and orange flames, paper, and other sorts of debris fluttering softly downward. His boys are running toward that. He wishes he were with them; he wishes them luck.

***

There is some sort of a lawsuit, Kenyon has heard, brought against the city by a group of sick emergency responders, like himself. An action for all the illness resulting from first responders breathing the dust from the collapse. He's not sure what the point is. His medical bills are paid by the union. What else matters? He imagines the litigants are just angry. A nice fat settlement might make them feel better, if they live long enough to see it.

He is thinking about this at home, which is a small apartment on the lower east side. He used to have a bigger place, a nicer place, but since the divorce, this is all he can afford. It's basically a kitchen, a bedroom and a tiny bathroom—shower stall, no tub. He spends all his spare time in the kitchen, which is funny, because the last thing he ever feels like doing is eating. There's a table there, though, where he can sit and read the paper and sip a coffee.

The docs are always begging him to eat. They tell him his body needs fuel to help fight the cancer as well as the cure. But his appetite, which used to seduce him into eating up to three sausage-and-sauce sandwiches at a sitting, has deserted him. He does what he can.

Kenyon opens a drawer in a small table and withdraws a rolled-up baggie. He gives it a small shake, and it unfurls in all its plastic glory to reveal three buds of what his buddy's nephew described as outrageous ganja. He twists off a little piece, tacky and herbal, and drops it into a metal pipe, also supplied by the same nephew. He lights the pipe and draws the smoke into his lungs.

Some semblance of his appetite returns with the effects of the weed, and he scrounges around in the kitchen cabinets for some food, settling on a can of store-brand chicken noodle soup, a box of Ritz crackers, and a sticky jar of peanut butter.

***

Most of the time, he wears sweats to the lab, what he calls the lab. The cancer treatment center. He slips on old Converse high-tops with the laces loose and, depending on the weather, either a t-shirt or a sweatshirt. Sometimes they're even clean. If he's feeling particularly perky, he wears a Giants jersey. Generally, however, he just doesn't have the energy to care about what he looks like. None of the nurses seem to mind.

There is a mirror on the wall just inside the door of the waiting room. Kenyon can't figure out why they would put a mirror there. It pisses him off. Every time he walks by, he has to catch a glimpse of himself as the circus freak he is now. He used to be muscular and in shape. Now what he sees when he passes the mirror is a frightening collection of bones and angles, hollow eyes, thinning hair. Blotchy skin and pale lips. Dead man walkin'.

He forgives the staff at the clinic for the mirror. They've probably never thought of it—of what that reflection does to him and every other patient who enters.

He laughs at himself for his vanity. He used to think he was pretty hot, a lady's man. Now he would be happy to look like a zombie if he could be sure he would be alive next spring.

That strikes him as funny, too. He already looks like a zombie.

***

On the rare times that Kenyon allows himself to think about that day, he mostly pictures the dust. The dust was everywhere. It filled the remaining buildings and the streets; it blotted out the sun. He turns away when he sees the footage on the television.

When he thinks about it, he thinks about what that dust was made of. The debris of the buildings, of course, crushed by gravity into tiny, breathable particles. And everything inside the buildings. The desks, the lamps, the carpeting, the filing cabinets and the urinals, the gray cubicles and the expensive artwork, the fichus trees, and exit signs and coffee mugs.

And people. When the buildings fell, almost everything was ground down and converted to powder, to dust. They didn't find very many bodies, the rescue teams and corpse dogs. Why was that? Because all of those people, the ones who didn't jump, had been processed into a fine dust. A fine, breathable dust.

Kenyon accepts this as fact, although he has never heard anyone speak of it. He knows, more than he knows anything else, the dust that had flowed down over the city like a tidal wave was made up of the last earthly remains of most of the victims, all mixed together with each other and with the concrete and porcelain and wood.

The molecular essence of bankers, lawyers, secretaries, and janitors had all combined to coat Kenyon's tongue, and the roof of his mouth, and his nasal passages, and had settled in his lungs. These people, these murder victims, in some way, still exist inside him. It makes him wonder if maybe the cancer is not some invading force but an outgrowth of all the lost souls pooled within him.

He is legion.

***

On Thursdays, the nurses seem livelier than usual. Kenyon guesses it is because the weekend is coming. They are good people. It makes him happy that they have things to look forward to.

Kenyon stopped looking forward to anything months ago.

The nurses pretend like he is still good-looking. They flirt with him and say things like, "If I were only single." He wonders if they can see the real him beneath all the illness, the strong, vibrant Kenyon that used to like to toss a football and was captain of his high school rugby team. He knows they don't realize how much their playfulness hurts.

13

Everyone at the center is super extra positive. They're always coaching the patients about beating the cancer and asking Kenyon what he's going to do when he's better, and it's all said with exclamation points. The right attitude is important, they say. Kenyon smiles and plays the game with them, but he has told himself the truth. He's not getting out of this. Or rather, he is, but not in a way the staff is excited about.

***

Visualize the chemo doing its work. This is the advice of the morbidly obese chemo tech who gives him his treatment. His name is Lowell.

Kenyon visualizes. What has he got to lose? He sees the dark mass in his colon, a throbbing collection of cells and pus and god-knows-what-else. It is evil. It is the enemy. And then he sees the chemicals pouring into his body like cancer-seeking missiles, driving through his bloodstream and pounding into the cancer. He is imagining this so hard he can almost feel the percussive thumps of the impacts.

He sees the special chemo sauce enveloping the cancer in his bladder and smothering it, sees the healing poison seeping into his lungs to attack the spots located there. He sees all of this happening in full-color Cinemascope, CGI-enhanced, like a super-powered lovechild of Spielberg and Lucas.

When he opens his eyes, however, he is still stuck in the treatment room, tubes attached, machines whispering softly, and he is still the same dying guy.

***

Another Thursday, and Kenyon is in the chemo room. He's wearing his boxers and a hospital gown, which feels like it's three sizes too big. He feels small in it, reduced. He knows all these gowns are big and blousy, but he still has the impression that he is slowly being pared down to a bare minimum. Soon he will disappear inside one of these gowns. He is light as a feather.

The doc comes in and confirms what Kenyon is feeling.

"You've lost three pounds since Monday," he says. "Try to drink some milkshakes."

"Okay," says Kenyon.

Then the chemo begins and is every bit as enjoyable as it always is.

Later, in the waiting room again, Jen pauses to say have a good weekend. Kenyon tells her not to do anything he wouldn't do. Jen dutifully laughs.

"See you Monday," she says.

"I don't know," says Kenyon. "I might not make it in Monday."

"Really?" says Jen, looking concerned. "You shouldn't skip. Did you run that past Dr. James?"

"Don't worry," says Kenyon. "I won't let anyone poison me but you guys."

"Oh, you," says Jen. She laughs and goes back to the treatment room.

***

When the South Tower collapses, it is like watching a sci-fi movie. There is no way it can be real. Kenyon stares, open-mouthed, as the building slow-motions downward into a mushroom cloud of dust.

He is frozen. There's no training for anything like this. In no fevered imagination did this scenario ever take hold. It is beyond the scope of all experience.

Kenyon hears screaming and fervently hopes it is not coming from him. He's not sure, though—the world has just become hell. There is no up, no down. Just light-obliterating dust.

What finally gets him to move is the realization that the South Tower was his tower. That was where his crew was, in that stairwell. Where he was supposed to be.

He rushes off into the oncoming brown cloud.

***

Friday is spent huddled within a squall of nausea and lethargy. He can barely open his eyes to watch television. Saturday is not much better, though Kenyon finds himself able to read for short spurts between trips to the bathroom to throw up. This is the typical two-day period immediately following chemo.

Sunday is day three, however. It is the only day three in his schedule when his body can feel at least partially poison-free. This particular Sunday gets things rolling with dazzling sunlight streaming in through his one window and painting the kitchen gold. He has not seen a morning as pretty as this in a long time.

Kenyon decides to make this morning his. He finishes his coffee and quickly dresses. Then, he grabs his notebook and pulls a six-pack of Bud from the refrigerator and shoves it into a brown paper bag. Then he's out the door.

The subway is half-empty; it takes him to Coney Island. He walks along the littered sidewalk toward the beach, not sure where the energy is coming from. He's usually exhausted just walking from the street into the treatment center.

He reaches the beach, sweating a little but not hurting anywhere. He kicks off his sneakers and sits to pull off his socks, leaving them in a small huddle at the edge of a parking lot. Then he steps barefoot into the sand.

The surface of the sand has been warmed by the sun, but just beneath it is cool and soothing. Kenyon digs his toes in as he walks. He finds a smooth spot and sits down and takes the six-pack out of the bag and sets

15

it in the sand next to him. He looks around him; there is no one else here except some raucous seagulls.

He opens his notebook and begins to write.

***

Grit is filling his eyes and his nostrils, and Kenyon is forced to breathe through his mouth, so now there is sand and dust between his teeth. He is chewing the South Tower. Then, he remembers he is wearing his self-contained breathing apparatus, and he pulls the face mask on and feels the raw oxygen hit his lungs. In the brown gloom, however, he still can't see where he is going, and he stumbles into something hard and metal. It is a car. He is in the street, but which street, and which direction he is facing, he has no idea.

Kenyon wanders through the false dusk. Occasionally, someone runs past him or staggers into him and then bounces away. There are currents in the dust; it is like walking underwater.

At last, he finds himself in a group of city police, and he walks with them toward clearer air. When they are free of the worst of the dust, he takes his face mask off and looks back toward where they were. The South Tower is gone. It is impossible.

***

Kenyon finishes writing and sets the notebook in the sand. He has finished two of the beers while he wrote, and he is feeling quite tipsy. Tipsy enough.

He used to be a more-than-competent drinker, downing six-packs like this one in record time. Since the illness, though, he has lost his skills. Two beers—he would be embarrassed if anyone other than the gulls were watching.

Kenyon has dressed for the day—clean blue jeans and a nice sport shirt. The kind of outfit he would have worn on a date long ago. He stands up with a grunt and feels a little dizzy with the sudden change in altitude. He shakes this off and tears off one more beer from its plastic mooring. Then, he sets the remnants of the six-pack on top of his notebook, open to the page he was writing in, and walks toward the ocean. The sand has gotten warmer since he first arrived.

When his toes first hit the water, he almost squeals like a little girl—it is colder than he had expected. He opens the can of Bud, puts it to his mouth, and tips it skyward, chugging as much as he can. Then he pours the rest into the sand.

With his lost brothers in his memory, Kenyon walks out into the soft surf.

***

We Ran Up

We ran up
Against the heavy current.
While all the rest were running down
We ran up.

Armored and enabled
Hearts pumping our heavy blood
Our knees popping audibly
In the cavernous stairwell.

We were not afraid
Or if we were, we hid it
One person in danger
Was reason enough.

Whether we succeeded
Or died trying
Was beyond imagining.
We ran up.

Sandy Stuckless

Born on the Canadian East Coast, Sandy R. Stuckless now lives in the 'big city' with his wife, two teenage children, and two cats. When Sandy isn't writing fantasy, sci-fi, paranormal, or anything else his twisted mind can conjure, he can be found at his day job in the traffic management systems industry.

In his downtime, Sandy can either be found watching the game with a plate of chicken wings, or during the summer, traveling the province of Ontario in his travel trailer searching for a good burger and craft beer. His love for hiking, camping, and being outdoors keeps him on the move avoiding confined spaces at all costs.

Sandy strives to one day see his name on the spine of a book on a bookstore bookshelf.

Sandy's publishing credits to date include: *Redemption's Beacon* (Toronto Prose Mill, 2017), *Date Night* (Cloaked Press, 2018), *Unfollowed* (Cloaked Press, 2019), *Fear the Moon* (The 2020 Annual, Elizabeth River Press & Arzono Publishing) and *Hot Under the Collar* (Self-published, 2020).

Dead, Sort Of

Johnny gaped at me from his front porch, speechless and pale-faced for a long moment. "Quinn? What the—Hold on, you died."

"Yeah, well, it didn't stick."

Johnny scrubbed his eyes with his fists, then patted me on the cheeks and forehead to make sure I was real. "What do you mean, it didn't stick?"

"Paperwork. Apparently, someone screwed it up. Good thing they hadn't stuffed me into a pine box yet."

Johnny grunted. "Ain't that always the case? Can't even die without red tape getting in the way." He shuffled to the side to let me into the front hall of his swank townhouse. "You better come in. I need a drink. Or a CT scan."

"You think you're freaking out. You should've seen the funeral tech wheeling me to the embalming room." I shed my jacket and hung it on the coat hook next to the door. "After he stopped screaming, I suspect he went to change his underwear."

"So, what do you do next?"

We moved to the sitting room where I plopped down on a soft leather sofa. "Well, I'm not going looking for the bloody stuff, if that's what you're asking. I got a date tonight that I don't aim to miss."

"You talked to Ashley? Damn, dude. You don't waste any time."

"She took one look at me and fainted. When she came to, she slapped me. I think the imprint she left on my face convinced her. I'm going to ask her, Johnny. Even had the ring picked out before I croaked. I should've done it a long time ago. She deserves it."

Johnny retrieved a bottle and two tumblers from the liquor cabinet. "Yes, she does, but she loves you and was willing to wait. Glad to see you finally come to your senses. Even if you had to die to do it."

"You still have the keys to the Mustang? I need it for tonight. I was leaving it to you in the will. I know you adore that car."

"Yeah, of course. Your baby's in the garage. Ashley loves that car as much as you do. If you're popping the question, you might as well do it in style." He disappeared from the room for a moment before coming back with the keys. "You got time for a drink first, right? I mean, it's not every day your best friend is resurrected. Can you walk on water yet? How's Moses doin'?"

I chuckled and shook my head. Johnny, ever the smartass, even in a moment of utter shock. "Just pour the drinks, ya bloody clown."

Johnny poured two fingers of bourbon into a tumbler and handed it over. He slid into a leather recliner across from me. "I gotta say, man. This is blowing my mind. I watched them pull the plug. You flatlined and everything."

"I don't know what to tell you. One minute I was heading for the light. The next, everything went black, and I woke up on a prep table in a funeral home. You think it's weird for you. How do you think I feel? I'm losing my shit here."

Johnny raised his glass in a toast. "Well, I'm glad they got this one wrong."

I downed the bourbon. Whoever 'they' were, I hope they never find the mistake. "I'd love to stay and chat, but I have an appointment with my lawyer. Apparently, being dead is reason enough to freeze your bank accounts. I can't get any cash until after the will is read."

Johnny slid a couple hundred bucks from his wallet across the table. "Ain't that a bitch? Even when you're dead, the government and the banks screw you."

"The good news is there's enough empirical evidence—" I gestured at myself, "that I am, in fact, not dead."

"Good luck with that. The government doesn't like to admit mistakes and takes forever to undo them."

Johnny followed me to the door. I turned back to him as I pulled my jacket up over my shoulders. "Listen, if anyone comes around asking about me, you haven't seen me. Have a feeling I'm not done with this whole dead thing yet."

I grabbed a latte from my favorite coffee shop. Hey, being dead made me appreciate the finer things in life. When I returned to the car, I wasn't alone. Hot coffee sloshed down my shirt when the stranger cleared his throat. I almost had to add new underwear to the day's shopping list.

"Awful skittish, aren't you, son? I suppose I'd be too if I were you."

I sipped on what coffee I had left, mostly to keep from throttling the stranger in my passenger seat. "You're lucky none of that spilled on the upholstery. Who the hell are you, anyway? What are you doing in my car?"

"Is that any way to talk to your pops?" the weirdo replied with faux hurt.

"My pops died in prison. I barely knew him."

"Right on both counts, for which you have my most sincere apologies. Listen, I'd love to hang out and hash out old times, but my time is short. Like, minutes short. They don't give us much time off the leash."

I tried unsuccessfully to deny my sense of familiarity with this man. "How the hell did you get into my car?"

"Don't be dense, son. I'm dead, remember. Mortal boundaries don't apply to me."

"What do you want?"

"Just to deliver a message. You're supposed to be dead." He held up his hand, stopping the question on my lips. "No, don't ask. We don't have time. Besides, they didn't tell me where you were going. The point is someone screwed up, and they'll stop at nothing to fix it."

"They can try," I said defiantly. "And who exactly are 'they'?"

"Angels, son, and you can't fight them. Eventually, they will win. Three will visit you. I don't know when, where, or what they'll say. I suggest you listen to them."

"Is that all?"

"No, that's not all. Others will try to get to you too. Soul Hunters, who'll want you to collect for them."

I raked my hands through my tangled hair. This day was only getting weirder. "What's a Soul Hunter? Collect what?"

"They're after souls, Quinn. They're usually serial killers and terrorists, but they'll use anyone willing to take a life without remorse."

"So, someone like you?"

"Touché. I deserved that. I should tell you, however, that I know what I'm talking about. Listen to me, son. You don't want anything to do with them. Promise me you'll turn them away."

Fear dripped from my father's voice. True fear. But this second chance was too good to pass up. There was a woman I intended to make my wife, and we were going to live happily ever after, white picket fence and everything. "I'll think about it."

"About what I expected you'd say. I know I haven't been much to you, but I'd hoped you'd give me the benefit of the doubt. You'll be okay as long as you use your head."

My father's specter faded from the car, leaving me in complete silence. Well, except for the mess going through my head. Was any of that real, or a product of a stressful day? I rubbed my hands over my face and drew in a couple deep breaths. Nothing I could do about it. The death certificate and my bank accounts, however, still awaited.

I parked outside Porter and Associates Law downtown and took the elevator to the twenty-sixth floor. Hopefully, they still had all the paperwork. Why couldn't these big-wig firms ever get offices on the ground floor? A second person occupied the elevator, side-eyeing me with a slimy smirk. "Is there something I can do for you?"

"You're Mister Quinn Nichols, yes?"

An eerie chill washed over me. Please don't say an angel. Please don't say an angel. "Who wants to know?"

"I am the Angel of Reason. Your father told you I'd be visiting."

Well, crap...

"There has been some misunderstanding. You see, Mr. Nichols, you are, in fact, supposed to be dead. A terrible mistake at Intake sent you back, and I am here to collect you. If you'll just come along, we can avoid any unnecessary aggravation."

Both of us got off the elevator on twenty-six and cut right towards Porter and Associates. My heart thudded. "Oh, no. You had your chance. This is my second chance, and I aim to make the most of it."

The stranger linked his hands behind his back. "I'm afraid that's not how it works, Mr. Nichols. Once the proper... paperwork... shall we say, has been completed, your time here is finished."

"Any way I can speak to customer service? I should get some credit for your clerical error. Maybe a six-month free trial."

"If you make this difficult, Mr. Nichols, it will be painful for you. We take these matters quite seriously."

I pushed on the frosted glass door with the black lettering etched on it. Thankfully, Mr. Porter didn't have a client at the moment. The color drained from his face when he saw me. "Mr. Nichols? Is that really you? I didn't believe Liz when she said you called. I must say. You're looking pretty good for a dead guy."

"Yeah, I thought the same thing. Seems the hospital mixed up the death certificates. Listen, is there any way we can hold off on will reading and stuff for the time being? I should be able to get this straightened out in a day or two."

Mr. Porter shuffled some papers into a pile and set them aside. "I don't see why not. Seeing as you're not actually dead."

"I also need my bank accounts released. I have plans for tonight and need some cash."

"Of course. I'll have Liz take care of it right away."

The Angel of Reason still lingered outside of the lawyer's offices. "You mentioned a second chance, Mr. Nichols," he said, as he fell in beside me on the way to the elevator. "What exactly would you do with it? From my understanding, you have squandered much of what you have been given. You've lived your life selfishly."

"I have a couple things in mind, but I'm open to suggestions. Maybe I'll wait to see what the Soul Hunters have to offer."

The angel's face turned into a scowl. "Do not joke about things you do not understand. The Soul Hunters are not to be trifled with. Once you collect the first one, there is no saving you."

The elevator door opened, and we both stepped inside. "That's your problem."

"Please, Mr. Nichols. This is highly irregular."

"Not my problem. You guys messed up. That's on you."

"If I go back without you, they will just give you another heart attack and take you that way. Or, if you are particularly obstinate, they will give you cancer and draw it out painfully. Is that what you really want? I'd much prefer this go as seamlessly as possible."

"Tell me something," I said. "If I were to go with you right now, am I going upstairs or downstairs?"

"I'm afraid I don't have that information. I am only the Angel of Reason. I am an escort, nothing more. All of that is sorted after your initial intake."

"Yeah… Not an enticing offer. I think I'll just stay here. There's someone I need to see."

"You will only hurt her more, you know. She doesn't fully believe she has you back. If you pursue this, she will be devastated when we take you again."

I grabbed a fistful of the angel's jacket. "If I find out you've approached her at all, we'll find out if angels really are immortal."

He placed his fingertip against my chest, and it was like I touched a live wire. The shock exploding through my body threw me against the elevator wall. Everything hurt. I couldn't move.

"Examine your life and ask yourself honestly if you are actually worth saving."

The angel's words hit below the belt, but the images running through my mind supported them. A kid in a baseball uniform holding his hat out for a donation. I walked by without missing a step. Somehow, I knew that the baseball team no longer existed.

Several more images flashed through my mind. A single mother trying to wrangle her unruly kids and groceries into the car, an old man with a flat on the side of the road. Opportunities to make even the slightest difference, all ignored. "Make it stop."

The angel crouched over my supine form. "I suggest when the Angel of Insistence comes to collect you, you go with him." He got off the elevator on the third floor.

By the time I reached the ground floor, the painful shock had worn off. I stumbled out to the Mustang and sat behind the wheel for a few minutes to gather my wits. I'd be damned if those bastards were going to intimidate me. Perhaps I was a bit selfish in my younger years. As if I was the only one. Their guilt trips wouldn't deter me. This was my chance to do things differently.

I left the downtown high-rise, but instead of going to the department store, I went the opposite direction, to the first shelter that needed volunteers. Maybe if I showed them I was trying, they'd let me stay.

"Do you need a bed for the night?" a lady in a red smock asked.

She must've misunderstood my ratty t-shirt and ripped jeans. Not exactly the dressed for success look I usually went for. "No. I saw your sign out front. I'm here to help."

For the next two hours, I ladled chicken noodle soup into foam bowls. I'd never experienced the level of gratitude shown by the recipients before. Like that one bowl of soup changed their lives. That hit me in the gut. Maybe that angel had a point.

The kitchen supervisor approached me after the last bowl had been handed out. "You were a big help. Thank you. Will you come back tomorrow?"

"That's my hope. If everything works out."

My next stop on this Resurrection Tour was my favorite clothiers near the lawyer's. This second chance called for a new outfit to take my baby out for dinner. I knew exactly what I wanted. On my way to the cashier with the designer jeans, tan shoes, and blue overcoat, a stranger fell in beside me. I felt a chill, like someone had just walked over my grave.

"Mr. Nichols."

"Let me guess. The Angel of Insistence? I have to come with you right now or else I'm going to catch cancer."

The stranger laughed. A menacing sort of cackle reserved for Bond villains and crooked politicians. "No. I am a little more liberal than my sanctimonious cousins."

Jesus, he even talked like a politician. "You're a Soul Hunter. I figured I'd be talking to you sooner or later. You're all like a bunch of leeches. You latch on and don't let go."

"Now, now, Mr. Nichols. I'm offended. We don't like wasting opportunities."

I muscled my way around the demon. "I'm not interested. I have better things to do than be a pawn in your little holy game."

"But you haven't heard my offer yet."

"Save your breath."

"Don't you want to marry Ashley? I can ensure that happens."

I stopped in my tracks, my whole body going stiff. If my hands had been empty, they would've clenched. The Soul Hunter had his hands folded behind his back when I faced him. He looked like a businessman trying to close a deal. I guess, in a way, he was. "That sounded a lot like a threat. I don't take kindly to threats."

"I like to think of it more as, shall we say, proper incentive. I'm sure the other one made it clear, you don't have much choice. It's them or us. I can make your life very comfortable. Or very uncomfortable."

I stepped in close to the Soul Hunter. "Listen here, buddy. Take your proper incentive and stuff it up your ass. Don't come near me again."

The stranger offered another greasy smile. He patted me on the cheek as if he were some mafia don praising one of his wise guys. "I'll give you some time to think about it. Consider wisely, Mr. Nichols." He walked away, leaving me with all the chills.

A sharp pain stabbed through my temple. The department store disappeared, replaced by a luxurious home on a large piece of property. A Land Rover and a Mercedes sat in front of the three-car garage. In the back, a boy and a girl frolicked in the pool while Ashley kept a close watch from a deck chair. Damn, she was sexy.

The vision faded, and the department store returned. That was what my life could be if I accepted the Soul Hunter's offer. It was all an illusion. Smoke and mirrors hiding sinister magic.

I sat the clothes down on the counter and reached for my wallet. My phone buzzed in the other pocket. The call display said 'Johnny.' That got the hairs on the back of my neck twitching. I hit the 'Answer' button. "Talk to me, John-Boy."

"Yeah, so, before you freak out, I want you to know that I'm okay."

"What happened?"

"It was the weirdest thing. Tire blew on the freeway. Put me into the center median. Couple broken ribs and a dislocated shoulder, but I can still kick your ass."

"Jesus Christ, man!"

"Hey now. I said no freakin' out."

"Alright. Where are you? I'll pick you up."

"You'll do no such thing. I told you I'm fine, and I've already called my old man. You have a proposal to get ready for. I'll let you know when they have me patched up."

Johnny was right. I couldn't help him, and he sounded none the worse for wear. Me, on the other hand? I was in a world of trouble unless I found a way to defend myself. It had been a long time since I walked around armed, but I was fully legal, and if that's what it took to keep these crazies at bay, so be it.

Less than two minutes after hanging up from Johnny, my phone buzzed again. Porter and Associates. This couldn't be good. "Hello."

"Mr. Nichols, this is Liz from Mr. Porter's office. I'm afraid I have some bad news. We were in the middle of uploading the request to lift the injunction on your accounts when our system suffered a catastrophic failure. The paperwork is gone, and there's not enough time to resubmit."

My head spun as Liz explained things. None of this was a coincidence. First Johnny, now this. Either that angel or the Soul Hunter were messing with my business. That settled it. If they wanted to play hardball, so would I.

They either left me alone, or they'd find out why I was named top marksman in my class.

"Mr. Porter has authorized your access to our accounts until the mess is cleared up. Whatever you need, just have them send us the bill."

"Thank you. I'm about to purchase some new clothes for a special event tonight."

"Of course. We'll take care of it. Just give them our name. Anything else?"

"Yeah, now that you mention it. I'll need a little cash for the same special event."

"Absolutely. Will five thousand be enough?"

I almost laughed. "Yeah, I think that will do."

"I'll leave it downstairs with the front desk."

I gave the cashier the info for Porter and Associates and left with my purchases. The Soul Hunter was nowhere to be seen. I doubt he'd gone far, though. Like a dog to a bone, that one. I tossed the bag of clothes on the Mustang's back seat and started towards Pierre's Barbershop a block away. The fresh air on the walk would do me some good.

I weaved among others enjoying the pleasant day, not really paying attention to faces. Until one particular gentleman refused to move out of my way. "You don't look like the Soul Hunter that threatened me in the department store, so I'm guessing you're this Angel of Insistence here to threaten me. Am I close?"

The angel huffed. "My colleague said you'd be difficult. I'd hoped he was exaggerating."

"I'll tell you what I told him. This is your screw up. I'm not going anywhere."

The angel grabbed me by the elbow and directed me off the sidewalk. "Let me make this perfectly clear. You don't have a choice. Not one. Zero. You can come with me now sensibly, or I can make a scene. Would you like to test how much pain I can cause you?"

"That's a bit beneath one of your position, isn't it?"

"We may be angels, but we are not delicate. We can get our hands dirty if need be. Do you know how many souls we ferry through the gates every day? We don't have time for obstinate children."

I stuffed my hands in my pocket and leaned against the side of the building. "So, why not just take me then? Why are you even talking to me if I have no choice?"

"Your body has to die. We can't take you until that happens. If you agree to go, we can do this in a quiet, private setting and make it relatively painless. Or we can commit coldblooded murder. Obviously, we frown upon that particular method."

"What if we approach this a different way? Is there a way to give you a dead guy that isn't me? What if there's something I can do that fulfills your paperwork while leaving me free to live the rest of my life?"

"I do not like what you're implying, Mr. Nichols. We do not make trades in matters like this. We have a very specific criteria."

"I'm not suggesting I murder someone for you. Jesus, I'm not a monster. Is there something I can do, like a good deed or something that will buy me some time? I already served a shelter uptown. I'll do more, if it'll help."

The angel's brow furrowed, and he leaned in close to me. "Are you trying to bribe an angel, Mr. Nichols? That will reflect poorly on your file which, according to my colleague, is not a pillar of virtue."

"Not a bribe. A trade. I'll do whatever you want in exchange to remain among the living."

The angel paused for a moment and stroked his chin. "You mistake me for a Soul Hunter. Even if I was willing, I don't have the authority."

"Well, why don't you go get your supervisor and maybe they'll be able to help me. Now, if you'll excuse me, I have a date to prepare for."

I thought I was home free at least for a couple hours and could enjoy my haircut in peace, but no. Half an hour after I left him on the sidewalk, the angel entered the barbershop right in the middle of my straight razor shave. "Couldn't let me have a few minutes to enjoy a shave and haircut, could you?"

"Unfortunately, this is a time sensitive matter. My superiors have agreed to let you stay in exchange for someone you love."

Pierre's straight razor almost slit my throat as I bolted upright. For a fleeting moment, I wondered if that was the angel's intent. "You sadistic bastards. Who?"

"You must choose. You have until sundown tonight to make up your mind. If not, the Angel of Compromise will choose when he comes tonight." He pressed his fingertip against my forehead. "Just something for you to keep in mind as you consider."

"What was that all about?" Pierre asked.

"Nothing," I stammered and settled back in the chair. "Just finish the shave."

I closed my eyes and tried to forget the angel, but once again the images started. My Mustang speeding down a country road with two occupants. I assumed it was me and Ashley, but the angle changed, and it wasn't me at all. Johnny had one hand draped over the steering wheel and the other resting on Ashley's thigh. They both wore wedding rings.

Something wasn't right here. Ashley would never agree to marry Johnny. Or would she? If I were dead, she'd have no reason not to. Never in a million years did I believe my two closest friends would betray me in such a way.

The image faded, leaving me anxious and angry. The angel's ultimatum stole the last bit of joy I had over avoiding death. Ashley and Johnny had been my family since I was eighteen. How could I choose one of them to take my place in the afterlife? I clamped my jaw against the anger. I knew exactly what the angels were doing. Giving me an impossible decision so I'd go back with them.

There had to be some higher authority I could appeal to. Maybe the church across from Pierre's shop could help me. I'd never been the religious type, but what the hell? What did I have to lose? Maybe my father was up for another short visit.

The church was empty, but knowing what I did now, all sorts of spirits likely watched me. And condemned me. Candles burned on both sides of the altar and the aroma of incense filled the air. I sat in a pew at the back, still uncomfortable about the whole thing. The visit from my father and the two angels shook me, I wasn't ashamed to admit.

"Well," I said, as I fixed my stare on the Jesus caricature on the cross. "Any advice?"

Obviously, I got no answer. Not sure what I expected coming in here, anyway. Not like the wooden savior could tell me if my best friend and soon-to-be fiancé would end up as man and wife.

If I had to be completely honest with myself, there were worse possible outcomes. They both could end up in miserable relationships, and truthfully, they were much easier to haunt if they were in one spot.

I enjoyed the peaceful silence for a few minutes longer. I had a feeling there wouldn't be much of it in the near future. "Probably should say some kind of prayer since I'm here. I used to be a non-believer, you know," I said to the wooden Christ. "Sorry. Nothing personal. Probably why I'm in this mess to begin with. Just figured if you were real, you could've helped out in my life a little bit. Probably not the way that works, huh?"

As I stood to leave, the door blew open with a cold gust of wind. The flickering candles on the altar went out, deepening the shadows. Despite that, I could almost see the crucifix staring back at me. At that point, I was certain someone or something was looking into my soul. "You want me to give them my blessing and go with the angels, don't you?" I stepped towards the altar, drawing my shoulders up. "Well, what if I choose not to do that? What if I choose the Soul Hunter and my marriage? I deserve it."

Another gust of wind buffeted me. I didn't know how to interpret it. Coming in here hadn't offered me the peaceful reflection I'd hoped.

I stopped off at my apartment to change into my new clothes and to strap my Beretta in the shoulder holster. I almost second guessed myself and put the gun back in the lockbox. This was supposed to be the happiest night of my life. I really didn't want to shoot anyone. I left the apartment with the pistol still strapped to my torso.

Another car pulled up my driveway, and the Soul Hunter from the department store got out. His face had the same oily grin from earlier. "I thought I told you to stay away from me."

"And I told you, you didn't have a choice. I was hopeful your friend's accident would've been enough to convince you, but I guess I overestimated."

"You did that? You bastard. I'll kill you."

"Let's agree to not make pointless threats, shall we? I have no desire to hurt your friends, but I do have need of a Soul Hunter. So, what's it going to be?"

I let my jacket fall open, revealing the loaded pistol under my left arm. "I'll tell you what it's going to be. I'm going to get into my car here, and I'm going to visit a nice jeweler. I have a ring to buy. If I see you, I'll shoot you."

"I have a better idea. I just received a new contract. You're going to fulfill it, or I'm going to kill your best friend." He got back into his car and drove off. I didn't even have a chance to react.

The air rushed from my body, and I staggered against the side of the Mustang. Something told me this lunatic was serious, but I couldn't allow him to hurt Johnny. If that meant someone else had to die, so be it.

I returned to the church, not knowing where else to go. I didn't sit in the back this time. I went straight to the altar and knelt before the cross. "You have to help me," I begged. "The Soul Hunters have found me and want me to fulfill a contract. If I don't, they're going to kill Johnny."

"That's quite the dilemma."

I nearly crapped my pants and knocked over the lit candle stand next to me. This guy wasn't there when I came in. "You're angel number three, aren't you? The Angel of Compromise, I believe the other one said. I'm supposed to tell you who's taking my place."

The angel slid down the pew to allow me to sit. "You've really made a mess of things, haven't you? You should've listened the first time we came to you."

"Would you, if our positions had been reversed?"

"I suppose not, but still, we have a problem, and you have a choice to make."

"I realize I have not lived a very virtuous life. I have some regrets, like the billions of other living people. I can't change things if I'm dead."

"You were supposed to realize these things before you died, not after. I'm not sure there's anything I can do at this point."

"Let's start with stopping the Soul Hunter. I don't want to kill anyone."

"The good thing about contracts is they all have a clause. You're not actually obligated until you collect your first soul. That should buy us some time. I'll stall your recall until we figure out the target. Go about your business for now and don't do anything stupid. Well, any more than usual anyway." He traced the crucifix on my forehead. "Just something to consider if you decide to use that pistol inside your jacket."

I knew what was coming. Every time one of these creatures touched me, the visions started. The sharp pain in my temples returned. The vision it brought turned by stomach. Ashley, lying dead in a pool of her own blood, a single gunshot wound to the heart.

That had to be a lie. Nothing on heaven or earth could make me shoot her. I'd shoot myself first. The angel was trying to scare me. Admittedly, he was succeeding.

The angel was gone by the time I reached the bottom of the church steps. I had about an hour to go three blocks uptown to pick up the ring and make it back here to meet Ashley for dinner, with a quick stop off at the lawyer's to pick up the cash I needed.

The ring I had picked out still sat in the case, sparkling as beautiful as the woman who would wear it.

"That's a nice one. Ashley will love it."

I tried not to react to my father's sudden appearance but wasn't sure I quite accomplished it. Thankfully, no one else was around to notice.

The jeweler, a young lady who knew diamonds better than anyone I knew, wandered over. "Mister Nichols. I'd hoped we'd see you again. Are you still interested in the same piece?"

"I am. Can you have it polished and boxed, please? I'll be needing it for tonight."

"Of course. It'll just be a few minutes."

"Can anyone else see you?" I whispered after the jeweler walked away with the ring.

"No. You know all that guardian angel mumbo jumbo? It's all true. The folks upstairs weren't going to let me in unless I took this little job watching your back."

My eyes darted back and forth. No one else seemed to notice my unusual conversation. "You're doing a bang-up job so far. Would a little effort while you were living have killed you? Do you have any idea what it's like living life as an orphan?"

"I'm sorry, son. You seemed to have done well enough without me. Unfortunately, we don't have time to discuss this further."

"What do you want then? If you've been watching, you know what's going on."

"There're some things the angels and the Soul Hunters don't want you to know. You can hurt them. While they're on the mortal plane, they are vulnerable to the same threats humans are. Except, they don't die. They just get recalled."

"Great," I hissed. "My only way out of this is either killing an angel or another person. Can't I just splash some holy water on them or something?"

My father stared at me flatly. "Be sure you get them through the heart. They're like vampires that way."

"Why didn't you tell me this the first time you came to me? You said I couldn't fight them."

"I thought you'd have sense enough to listen to me. If you had gone with the angels, we could both have crossed over and been at peace. Now, we're all scrambling to clean up the mess."

"I don't need anyone to clean up my mess. I just need everyone to leave me alone."

"Yeah, that's not going to happen. This needs a conclusion. Soon."

"Okay. I'll figure something out. Thanks for the heads up."

My father faded from view again. One thing was for sure. If I didn't end up dead again today, I was going to end up insane. The jeweler returned with the ring, and after paying her, I almost ran from the store.

I found an empty bench in the parkette halfway between the jewelry store and the restaurant. The engagement ring weighed in my hand like a cement block as I turned it over. I wanted to slip this on Ashley's finger so badly, wanted to kiss her when she said yes. Neither of those things was likely to happen, though. In the end, my father was right. I couldn't fight this. I had to go back with the angels. Killing someone wasn't going to save my life, even if I lived.

I strolled up to the restaurant with sweaty palms, trembling like a frightened child. This should have been happy nerves, but it wasn't. Maybe the angels would let me be Johnny and Ashley's guardian angel. Probably not. I'd just rattle the cupboards while they were in bed together.

"Reservation for Nichols," I croaked at the maître d'.

"Ah yes, for two," he said. "The lovely young lady is already waiting for you. Right this way, sir."

We approached the table, and my jaw dropped a little. Ashley was gorgeous in her black spaghetti-strap dress. Her hair was pinned up and wavy. She looked every bit the princess I envisioned. She stood, and I embraced her, savoring her kiss a little longer than usual. I wanted to remember that feeling when I died.

Dinner started quietly. Wine and finger foods were served. I picked at the breaded calamari but had very little appetite.

Ashley reached across the table and squeezed my hand. "Are you okay? You seem distracted."

I inhaled deeply. I had to do it. It was now or never. "I have to tell you something, Ashley. Something you may not believe, but is important, nonetheless."

Her beautiful smile faltered. "I don't understand. You're scaring me."

"You know how everyone thought I died?" Every word felt forced through a thick veil. "Well, I did, but I wasn't supposed to be sent back."

The color drained from her perfect face. "What are you saying?"

"I can't stay, Ashley. My time is over no matter how badly I want to deny it."

"No, Quinn," Ashley begged. "Don't do this. I just got you back. I can't lose you again." Tears welled in the corners of her eyes.

"It's the right thing to do, Ash. I don't belong here. Johnny does." I put the open ring box on the table in front of her. "Make him happy. You have my blessing."

She sat back in her chair, and the tears fell. "What? I'm not going to marry Johnny. I want to marry you."

"Hearing you say that makes me the happiest man alive. I can go knowing you love me."

A gentleman walked by on his way back from the bathroom. Something zapped inside me, like static discharge from a carpet. He was my target.

I tracked the man back to his table where he sat across from a lovely young lady. Her eyes lit up when he sat down. Was he doing the same thing I was here for tonight? I felt my legs push down to stand. No, I wasn't going to commit murder to save my own life. If the Soul Hunter wanted this one, he'd have to do the collecting.

"What's the matter?" Ashley demanded. "You look like you've seen a ghost."

"You're not far off the mark." I did stand then. "I'll be right back. I need some air."

Outside on the sidewalk, several people mingled about. Across the street, patrons enjoyed drinks on the patio of another establishment.

A chill raced through me when I saw the angel approach. I'd hoped for a little more time with Ashley before they came for me, but there was no putting it off any longer. I spun to go back inside to say my goodbyes and came face to face with the Soul Hunter. I wasn't expecting him to show up at the same time.

"Why is the mark not dead?"

"I'm not killing anyone for you. I'm going with the angels. Find yourself another stooge."

"I told you what would happen if you refused me."

"Leave Johnny out of this. He's not involved."

"Johnny? Oh no, my good man. I'm not collecting Johnny." He gazed at the restaurant door.

Ashley. "You sonofabitch. Leave her alone." I went for the gun under my jacket.

The Soul Hunter grabbed my wrist with one hand and my throat with the other. He lifted me off the sidewalk, like the Incredible Hulk in a tailored suit. "I am not playing anymore. I am going inside to collect your girlfriend. You can watch, if you like."

I fought to breathe, but his fingers were like vice grips. A little more pressure and he'd crush my larynx. Spots danced in front of my eyes. It looked like I was going with the angels after all.

"Unhand him, demon," the angel said behind me. "He belongs to us."

The Soul Hunter threw me against the side of the restaurant. "I think not. He has agreed to collect and is now in breach of contract."

"The contract has yet to be filled. There is no breach."

"Only a matter of time, angel. Only a matter of time."

The angel pitched forward, slapping his hand against the Soul Hunter's face. The ear-splitting shriek rattled the windows and attracted the attention of those close by. No one intervened. Lucky them.

The Soul Hunter jammed his thumb into the angel's eye. "I'm going to send you back to your masters in pieces, peon." He darted inside the restaurant, followed closely by the angel.

I staggered after them, pulling the gun from its holster along the way. I grabbed the maître d' by his lapels. "Get everyone out of this place now."

"I don't understand, sir. What's happening?"

"Those two are going to kill each other and anyone that gets in their way. Trust me, you don't want that."

Inside, tables splintered, and fine china smashed. Orbs of pure white and black slammed against each other as the angel and demon clashed. They were between Ashley and I, with no way for me to get to her.

I held the gun out in front of me with my finger on the trigger. No. I couldn't. Ashley was still back there. What if I missed? The third angel's image stuck firmly in my mind.

A chair flew over my head, smashing through the large window facing the sidewalk. The battle moved back toward the kitchen, giving me an opportunity to move deeper into the restaurant. I still couldn't see Ashley or the mark.

"Ashley," I screamed. "Where are you?" I might as well have screamed into a hurricane for all the good it did.

I heard the 'whoosh' of flammable material igniting an instant before the heat wave hit. Within seconds, flames had snaked out of the kitchen and crawled up the dining room walls. The restaurant had nearly emptied, but neither Ashley nor the mark was among the escapees. I pushed toward the back corner where our table had been.

This was how the angels were going to take me. Dying in a fire I practically caused was how they'd fix their paperwork error. It didn't matter as long as Ashley made it out alive.

Movement near the bathroom caught my eye. Ashley. She probably went after I stepped outside. Sweat poured down my face as fire raged around me. I wasn't going anywhere without her.

I pushed deeper into the restaurant, holding my arm over my head. Ashley lay on the floor in the bathroom corridor entrance. Her skin glistened with perspiration, and she wasn't moving. The angel and Soul Hunter were still in here somewhere, hopefully finishing each other off.

I felt Ashley's neck. She still had a pulse. I could still save her. I rolled her over onto my shoulders and crawled toward the exit. Well, what I thought was the exit. As we inched our way out, the smoke thickening with each passing second, we came up against another lump on the floor. It was my mark.

I didn't bother checking for a pulse. I grabbed him by the collar and dragged him along with us. I coughed against the smoke, every breath a fight for clean air. There was a small amount of relief when I spotted the bright beams of light slashing through the darkness.

"Hey," I called out. "Over here."

I collapsed to the floor and didn't feel the hands lift Ashley from my back or the ones that carried me out. When I regained my senses, I was in the back of an ambulance with an oxygen mask strapped to my face. I tore it off, snapping the straps.

"Take it easy, sir," the EMT said. "You have some smoke inhalation."

"I'm fine," I said and climbed out the back of the ambulance. Several others sat in a half circle around the burning restaurant. I found Ashley in the one next to mine.

She looked up at me, tears in her eyes. "I thought I'd never see you again."

"I'm sorry, Ash," I replied. "I screwed everything up. I even lost the ring."

She held up her left hand. "You mean this ring? I don't care if I'm married to you for five minutes or fifty years. I just want to be your wife."

An EMT came around the corner, except it wasn't an EMT. It was the first of my three angels. Right. I still had that one wrinkle to iron out. "I'm ready to go with you now."

"Yes, I suppose you are. Had to make it interesting though, didn't you?"

"The angel and the Soul Hunter?"

"Both recalled. You won't have to worry about them anymore."

"You know what I realized?" I said. "I don't have to save the whole world. I just have to save someone's. Pretty sure I've done that. I can go in peace."

The angel grinned widely as well. "It seems, Mr. Nichols, that your paperwork has gone missing. Highly irregular. We must return to investigate." He tipped his ball cap at me. "Until we meet again."

"Take your time," I called as he retreated up the sidewalk.

Terry Conrad

Terry Conrad is an accountant from Atlanta, who also has a background in counseling, education, and auditing. He is also the author of three books - *Illusion of Grandeur*, about an apocalyptic-minded cult attempting to invoke Armageddon; *Fugue*, about an accused serial killer attempting to remember his involvement in a series of murders halfway across the country; and most recently, a political thriller about the dangers of resisting the status quo in Washington, *The Idealist*. Terry's *Illusion of Grandeur* was a quarterfinalist in the 2010 Amazon Breakthrough Novel Award, a contest that drew 10,000 entries.

His newest work, *The Asset*, is a preview for a series of forthcoming books revolving around its main characters, FBI Agent Angel Reznik and Jason, her slightly more homicidal friend. Delving into the dark world of human trafficking, the series seeks not only to entertain readers but also hopes to shed light on the ever-present danger that threatens women and children daily.

The Asset

1

Jason pulled the garrote tight around the man's neck until he could see it begin to cut his skin. The more the man struggled and attempted to wrestle control from him, the tighter Jason pulled.

His desperation palpable, the besieged man reached blindly for any object he could find. He was losing the battle, and maybe his life.

"Sit down in that goddamn chair now!" Jason barked.

He pulled even tighter to hammer home his demand.

"I'm…gonna…f…ff…fffuck you up!" he managed to spit out.

"You aren't doing a fucking thing, Jeffrey Tatum Lydell."

Lydell said nothing, stunned that his unknown assailant knew who he was.

Jason looked around the kitchen for a way to hold the garrote in place while he handcuffed his prisoner. When he saw what he needed, he dragged Lydell backward in the chair and pulled him over to the cabinets.

Using his elbow to open a low hanging cabinet door, he was able to position himself on the inside, pinning his prey's back against the front. Pulling down as hard as he could, he quickly closed the door again, locking the garrote handles on the inside.

To keep Lydell from standing, he kicked at his kneecap, then spun and chopped at his neck. With his back holding the cabinet door in place, Jason reached to the side of his belt for the handcuffs and slapped them on Lydell's right wrist, arching his other arm behind his back, eventually cuffing his left, as well.

The prisoner was now struggling to breathe, so Jason gave him a minute before beginning his interrogation. To keep him from kicking out, his feet were now cuffed, too. Then Jason pulled him back up into the chair.

"Are you ready to talk?" he whispered into Lydell's ear from behind.

"I'm not talking to you, bitch! You can believe that!"

"Gotta be honest. I don't. Before we're done here, you're going to tell me everything I want to know."

Haggard, he cracked a smile as he stared back at his tormentor.

"How'd you find me?"

"That was the easy part. After I made a deal with Emir, he gave you up rather quickly."

Lydell laughed out loud.

"There's no way you got Emir to give me up! I'm his fucking supplier!"

"He isn't buying anymore," Jason said flatly.

"Bullshit!" his captive said with a laugh.

"Sorry, but it's true."

The certainty in Jason's voice stopped the dance. The man in the chair was now stone-faced and seemingly ready to bargain.

"Did you kill him? After he told you where I was?"

It was the interrogator's turn to laugh.

"The only thing you should be worried about is whether I'm going to kill you."

Still in shock, Lydell tried to process it all.

There was no way his captor could have found him in the middle of nowhere without help, and Emir was one of the very few who knew exactly where he was.

Moreover, something seemed familiar about his assailant. He couldn't quite place it, but he felt he knew him. By the time it came to him, Jason had already seen it in his eyes.

"You recognize me now, don't you?"

"You're different now."

"You mean I'm not a scared little child anymore."

The captive stared his tormentor down but didn't respond. Jason imagined this piece of shit was reliving the past in his twisted mind, but he had more important things to accomplish right now.

"Where is Wren? How do I find him? How about the others? Jeremy? Tommy? Marcus? Where are they?"

"Ah, so you know their names now. I see you paid attention. So that's what this is all about. A revenge tour. What are you going to do? You gonna get us all? What good does it do me then if you're going to just kill me after I talk? Seems I'm better off not tellin' you shit, 'cuz I got information you need me alive for."

The smirk on his face set Jason off. Lydell had always been the one with the upper hand. But now, his victim finally had enough. He reached for Lydell's pants and boxers, yanking them off and around his handcuffed ankles.

"Now, that's what I'm talking about! You were just missing me this whole time! I knew you just needed a piece of my—"

He froze as he finally saw what Jason grabbed from the island countertop: a large, serrated steak knife.

He headed straight for him with it, his face full of rage.

He raised the knife over his head with two hands and then stabbed downwards at full force. Lydell screamed out, though no one was there to hear it.

A moment later, he looked down and saw that the blade was wedged deep in the wooden chair, just millimeters from his manhood.

Insanity dripped from the sweat pouring off Jason's face. Lydell could smell it as he leaned in towards him.

"I have other options, don't I?"

"F...Fffuck! You're crazy!"

"Tell me what I want to know. Now!"

Lydell talked.

He told Jason everything he needed to know: names, addresses, and how to contact them online.

It had never occurred to him that the little child he had broken could ever come back so strong, but he had. Lydell had underestimated him, and now he was reaping what he'd sown.

"What are you going to do now?" he asked in desperation.

Jason held the knife in his hand and stroked the backside of the blade gently as he thought about his next move. In front of him sat one of the men who destroyed his childhood, crushed his innocence, and stole any chance of a normal life. The asshole was at his mercy.

"Maybe it's time I told the authorities. Turned you in. I have a friend I could call."

"Yeah, yeah, that's a great idea," the prisoner responded eagerly.

Jason pulled out his phone and pushed the speed dial button. After a short conversation, he hung up. Angel was on her way.

Lydell appeared relieved. Someone was coming. Someone was coming to save him from this crazed animal who'd nearly chopped his dick off. He would live to see another day, and it didn't matter if it was in prison at this point. He was happy to be alive.

Jason stared intently at his captive, pondering his options. He began to reconsider whether he was making the right choice by turning his abuser in.

"No," he said sternly.

"What? What are you talking about?"

"No," he repeated defiantly. "I'm not letting you get away with what you did to me!"

"I won't be getting away with anything. You're turning me in!"

"That's not good enough! That doesn't begin to be good enough for what you did to me! For what you did to the others!"

Jason grabbed the knife and plunged it into Lydell's chest, all the way to the hilt. Blood splattered everywhere, the corpse now staring back at him in shock and horror.

"Hell isn't even enough," Jason finally said with a final look at his victim.

After the initial shock wore off, he realized he only had a short time before Angel showed up. He had work to do first, so he started by searching the house for an electric shaver which he found in the upstairs bathroom.

Next, he looked for paper and a marker but couldn't find them anywhere. He'd have to improvise. Then came the computer, which he found upstairs, and predictably, there was a camera on a tripod in the bedroom. He trembled at the sight of it but brought everything downstairs.

Jason set up the camera to face Lydell's body and began recording. Without showing his face, he made sure that the dead man could be seen clearly, as well as the stab wound and the blood on his shirt.

Since there was no paper or marker anywhere to be found, his prey would become the canvas. He quickly removed Lydell's shirt, turned him around, and shaved his back. Using the blood from his wounds, he dipped his finger in it like a calligraphist and spelled out the message which he would email to the others in the form of a video: W-H-O- -I-S- -N-E-X-T-?

By the time he was finished washing his hands, he slumped to the floor, back to the wall. It was then that Angel appeared and saw the knife in his hand and the blood covering his fingers.

2

"What the hell did you do?" screamed Angel.

Blood was everywhere, and a panic began to envelop her. Jason was comatose and clearly not present in this moment. Something had to be done, and quickly, with other agents arriving at any moment.

Angel knew cleaning up a crime scene would not be possible, so she would have to stage it to look like she and Jason had been attacked. She needed Jason's help, though. He had to be awake for this.

A hard slap to his face did the trick.

"Get up, goddammit. Others are coming."

Jason looked around at the macabre scene around him and rose to his feet. Realizing he didn't have much time, he went to the video camera and took what he needed to complete the next phase of his operation.

"Jason, why didn't you stick to our plan?"

"It was never really my plan."

"Jason, I'm a Federal Agent. Being involved in this could ruin my career."

"I guess you could just not be involved if it bothers you that much."

"You know I can't just walk away from this…" She paused and cast her eyes downward. "I prefer justice to be a prison cell, not a fucking hole in the ground."

Jason laughed at the irony.

"I know you can't just walk away, for the same reason I can't just walk away. They all deserve to die. You can't tell me that's not true. Besides, you've been an accessory from the beginning. Now stop fighting and help me find them. We don't have much time."

Jason rushed towards the door initially but then backtracked to the dead man on the floor. He was searching for something in his pockets, and when he pulled out the keys, he gave himself a little cheer and then continued out of the cabin. Angel followed reluctantly.

Outside, Jason took a left past Angel's vehicle and circled around to the back. Off in the distance, he could see the marker, just like he remembered from all those years ago.

Angel was having difficulty keeping up, but she had him within her sights and followed behind. Angel knew what he was trying to do but wondered whether it was better to wait and let the FBI discover it instead.

"Can we just wait a minute and talk about things here?" she yelled out.

Jason turned and looked at her.

"What the hell do you mean? We don't need another plan. They're right here."

Jason pointed at what looked like an iron water pump in the middle of a large sea of overgrown wheat. He gestured towards it as if the next step was obvious.

"Let's let the reinforcements find it and focus on us. What are we supposed to do when they get here? We need to clean up a little or make it look like we were attacked and had no option but to kill Lydell."

Jason came back towards Angel and grabbed her firmly by the hands, pulling her towards the old pump.

"It won't be hard to come up with something to tell them. You're smart. You'll think of something. But they'll never find this. It's too far from the house and well hidden. Besides, I'll be gone before they get here. I promise."

"How are you going to manage that?"

"I guarantee you there'll be no trace of me by the time they arrive. You can tell them you were in a struggle with him and had no choice but to kill him. They'll believe you, especially if they see what you've found."

Angel wasn't liking this one bit, but it seemed to be Jason's way. He always acted first and left her to clean up the mess. The routine was growing old, but she acquiesced. She always did for him.

As they approached the marker, memories began to flood back to Angel. Although she knew what they would find in the middle of the field, she wasn't sure whether she could stomach reliving the past. She stopped and let Jason carry on with it.

Jason reached the old blue pump. He pumped the handle of the weathered device, but instead of water, he began to see the opening under the matted floor covered with dirt and crop. He pumped harder until it opened enough that he could wedge his hands in and move the enormous door.

Angel stepped out of the way and let Jason, who was very strong, slide the oversized covering to the side. Beneath it, he saw the familiar wooden stairs leading to the bunker below. He wasn't waiting for Angel. He was going down. Down into the abyss he once called home.

3

Jason groped for the cord that would light up the cellar and eventually found it. The makeshift dungeon, with numerous rooms, expanded to about 3,000 square feet. It was quite impressive to those who were unfortunate enough to have seen it.

Jason walked through the staging room first and saw the whipping post, as well as a seemingly infinite array of torture and sex devices, hung from hooks on the wall. There were also a myriad of cameras set up to catch multiple angles of action and a large server to match the array of computers and monitors.

He looked at the different screens, each representing a different cell in the underground prison, with children occupying two-thirds of the rooms. He estimated about 20 in all. He'd have to move quickly to free them.

Jason pulled the keys he'd found and fumbled through them until he discovered the ones he needed. He began unlocking the cages and then the shackles on the 12 girls and 10 boys, aged 5 to 22 years old, cowering in the corners. He urged them out and led them towards their escape from hell.

Some were reluctant, the intense fear paralyzing them, but in the end, they all climbed out of what would either have been their slaughterhouse or the first step in a harrowing journey from one monster to another.

After Jason emerged, he said to Angel, "Get them to safety. I've got to go."

"You know I will."

With that, Jason was gone.

Angel turned to the children, who had no clue what was happening or what they should do next.

"I'm Agent Reznik," she said. "I'm with the FBI. I know you might be scared, but I have some friends that are coming soon, and we're going to get you all to safety."

A little girl raised her hand meekly and stepped forward.

"Are you okay?"

Another older girl soon asked the same question with concern on her face.

Angel looked perplexed at first but then remembered the blood all over her shoes and jacket sleeve. Shit, this was a problem she didn't have time to deal with. It was why she didn't want Jason to free the kids first, though she understood his reasons.

"I'm fine," she replied with a little laugh. "But the bad man is not. He won't hurt you anymore, I promise."

"Did you kill him?" asked one of the boys. He seemed a little too eager with his inquisition.

"No, no, I didn't kill him."

The older girl, who seemed rather bright, asked the one question Angel was hoping not to hear.

"Was it, was it the one who set us free then?" she asked hesitantly.

Shit! I knew this was going to be a problem. Dammit, Jason!

"I know my friend let you out of the cages and helped you all escape, but we must never talk about him again. Especially to the people who are coming here soon. They must never know he was here, okay? He could be in big trouble if you tell anyone, and we don't want that, right? He helped you, and now it's your turn to help him, okay? It'll be our little secret…"

Angel was growing more nervous now. She hoped they would keep quiet and not complicate things even more.

The group nodded. They were grateful for their salvation. She had to hope that would be enough.

As she guided the kids back towards the cabin, she couldn't help but notice a young girl in the back. She hadn't said a word while the others were talking with her and had avoided eye contact with everyone. Angel knew what she had experienced and couldn't help but see herself in the little child. Her heart broke for her.

Within ten minutes, the other agents arrived. By then, Angel had moved the children back towards the cabin and her car. She had looked inside for some blankets to keep them warm while they waited and tried to clean up whatever evidence she could manage, knowing it was likely not enough. She was going to have some serious explaining to do.

Four others arrived on the scene, including her boss, Supervisory Special Agent Anton Brooks, Senior Special Agent Frank Treore, and two newer Field Agents named Benjamin Lad and Marcus Renbach. They were as surprised to see the children as they were to see the blood on Angel's clothing.

"Lad, take the kids with you and call for more back-up," Brooks instructed. "Renbach, get your things. You two, follow me."

He looked sharply at Angel.

"I take it you didn't wait for us as ordered?"

"No, I did not, sir," she responded. "I heard a scream, and so I entered the cabin. It was one of the kids. I felt I had no choice."

Brooks motioned for Treore and Angel to stay put before entering the cabin. Renbach finally joined them, handing each a pair of booties and gloves to put on before going in.

As they proceeded, Treore muttered under his breath, just audible enough for Angel to hear, "Gloves are a waste for you since you already fucked up the crime scene, right?"

Angel was used to hearing comments like that from Treore, whose opinion of her couldn't be any lower, but this time it was the sneer that rubbed her the wrong way. She hoped his hostility wouldn't turn into suspicion.

It didn't take long for the others to find Lydell's dead body beyond the furniture strewn about the blood-soaked floors and walls.

Renbach got closer and examined the corpse, making observations as he did.

"Ligature marks on the neck. Possibly a garrote of some kind. Did anyone see anything like that laying on the ground on the way back here?"

The assemblage shook their heads, so he continued.

"He was hacked up pretty bad…"

"Is that your professional opinion?" cracked Treore. "He was hacked up pretty bad?"

He could be a real asshole sometimes. A stern look from Brooks shut him up quickly, though.

The young agent was hoping to be a technician, and Brooks knew the learning process had to begin sometime. Renbach continued.

"Looks like he was stabbed maybe thirty times, which would indicate that it was deeply personal for the assailant."

Treore rolled his eyes out of Brooks' sight but so that Angel could see. Brooks turned his attention now to Angel.

"Tell me what happened here. Start from the beginning and don't leave anything out."

"I entered the cabin after hearing the scream. The door was closed but unlocked. Since the sound came from the back of the cabin, I figured there would be no one in the front room, and I was correct. I made my way to the back through the kitchen, which was already a disaster by the time I got to it.

"I got to the room we're standing in now and saw him with one of the children. He was already bloodied and in bad shape, but he came after me with the knife."

"So, you stabbed him thirty times?" Treore asked.

"No, he had already been stabbed multiple times prior to me getting there. He actually had pulled the knife out of one of the stomach wounds when he came after me with it."

"Wait, are you saying the child stabbed him all those times?" snapped Treore. "Look at those goddamn wounds. There's no way a kid is doing that. Which one was in the room when you got here?"

The inquisition had begun.

"No, I'm not saying the girl did it to him either, but I did see her in the room with the man at the time. Someone could have left after hearing me come in."

Angel knew she was digging her grave, but there wasn't any other way to spin this. There was no way any of the kids could've done it. Since she was not going to offer herself as a sacrificial lamb, it had to be someone else.

"Maybe he had a partner, and it went south. I don't know."

"Okay," Brooks interjected. "What happened next? And why didn't you just shoot him?"

"I was trying to get the kid out of there, but she was reluctant. I was distracted. He rushed me and got on me before I had a chance to react. He knocked my gun to the floor and tried to stab me with the knife, but I fought back. He was already weak because of his wounds, so it wasn't hard. I knocked the knife over there and watched him die right where you see him now."

"And the blood all over your jacket?"

"From when he knocked me to the ground. The sleeve is from when he was on top of me, just basic transfer, and there was already blood on the floor, which is why my back is covered in it."

Brooks stared intently at Angel for what seemed like an eternity, then studied the room some more. Angel believed he was retracing the events of her story to see if they were believable or not.

After several tense minutes of silence, he asked which child outside had witnessed what had happened.

"I'll show you," Angel said, knowing full well who she was going to choose. Having witnessed first-hand the trauma of abuse, she knew which of the children would be most likely to talk about it afterwards and which ones wouldn't say a thing, perhaps not even for years.

***

Back at the field office, Angel went through a more thorough debriefing and later had her wrist slapped for acting impulsively and against orders. It would hurt her career in the short-term, but she felt she'd answered enough questions just well enough to conceal Jason from them.

Agents would later scour the entire compound for more evidence of the killer, but she knew it would come to nothing if they believed her story. For the most part, she was right, but Frank Treore was going to be trouble.

4

A meeting was called the following day involving over 2,000 men from across the globe. It was set up online over the dark web through a streaming platform that all of them had used on a daily basis.

Although they often communicated amongst themselves, never before had a meeting been called involving the entire group at once. Each of them knew it must be important, but none could say for certain what it was all about.

The meeting was called by Emir, who always wore a colorful keffiyeh which covered his entire face, except his eyes. Before the proceedings began, there were many side discussions taking place, mostly related to business transactions among the various members. As Emir appeared on screen, visible to all, a silence immediately fell upon them.

"I've gathered all of you here today," he began, his Middle Eastern accent barely traceable, "to discuss the message that was sent yesterday on our platform."

No one in the assemblage said a word, but a look of concern was now etched on their faces.

Emir continued, "Our network has been compromised, and one of our members has been removed from this life."

At this news, a low murmur began to emanate. It was quelled immediately as Emir raised his voice.

"Silence! The threat made was real. The answer to 'Who is next?' could be any one of you, so you must be ready. Business must not be interrupted."

A high-ranking member of the group raised his hand to ask the question on everyone's mind.

"Do we know anything at all about who's behind this?"

"I do not know who the threat is," lied Emir, "or what it is they're after. Our lost member was from America, but that does not mean any of you are safe. Be on guard. Assets pass among us all, no matter where you are from, so exercise extreme caution."

"Are you saying this was a former asset?"

Emir paused before answering carefully. "Maybe a former asset; maybe law enforcement. Either way, we must not ignore this. Spread this message to everyone below you in the chain. The threat is real and is imminent."

***

Jason and Angel met in their usual secure and isolated spot, a rundown warehouse abandoned for nearly a decade. It was one of many in the desolated area, but it held particular significance for both of them.

As with most conversations between them, no one could know it occurred.

"What are you planning now?" Angel began, exasperated.

"They all have to go. You know that."

Angel sighed.

"You know where I'm at with this. We've had this fucking discussion before."

"And yet you continue to help me," Jason retorted. "I don't understand why you would hesitate at this point."

Angel held out her hands and shrugged her shoulders mockingly.

"Look, I'll be careful," Jason said. "I'm not going to put your precious career at risk. I need your resources. You know that."

"You've put my career at risk already, and you know that. Some of my colleagues already suspect me. You're not there, Jason. You don't see the looks I get from some of them."

"Fine, I'll be more careful going forward."

"You get caught, then I get caught," she responded, gesturing with her finger for emphasis. "So, who's your next target?"

"Wren."

"Wren? Are you kidding me?"

"No, I'm serious."

"What happened to being more careful?"

"I will be."

"Going after him? It's fucking suicide."

"So, are you saying he's off limits? He should get away with everything he did to us?"

"No, I'm not saying that at all. But he's the most difficult one to get to. Why not start with someone easier and work your way up the ladder?"

"Are you hesitating because of your career? You little chicken-shit."

"Hey!" she exclaimed. "If it wasn't for my connections, we wouldn't be able to do any of this. Maybe you need to take my career more seriously, too. Without it, I can't help you. You know, I could refuse to help you now if I wanted to."

Jason laughed.

"Yeah. Sure, you could."

"I could!" she insisted.

"Fine. I have the money to find other resources."

Angel began to realize she wasn't going to win this argument. Hell, even if she backed out of everything, she could still end up being exposed.

Fuck it, she thought. It was better to be involved and keep an eye on his impulsive behavior than to let him roam freely, untethered. But Wren would have to wait.

"Look, you know I'm on your side, always. I'm just trying to keep us safe. You do get that, right?"

"Yes, I do."

"Then can you please give me the courtesy of having my back, too? I'm not saying we don't go after Wren. I'm just saying let's not poke the bear right off the bat. Let's work our way up to him. If we rush into getting him first and fail, then no one else gets what they deserve. Low-hanging fruit first. That's all I'm saying."

Jason thought for what seemed an eternity. Angel knew he wanted Wren badly, but the planning had to be extensive, and even then, success was far from guaranteed. She hoped he would consider the smarter course of action for once.

"Fine," he conceded. "Who do you suggest then? Tommy? Jeremy? Marcus?"

"Marcus is a little more high profile than the others. He should be right before Wren. Either Tommy or Jeremy, take your pick."

"I guess it doesn't matter. They'll both be waiting on us."

"What the hell do you mean by that?"

"I sent a message on the network."

"You did what?"

Angel paced the room with her hands on her head, mouth agape. She couldn't believe how reckless he'd been.

"How could you do this? They're going to come after us!"

"Relax. They don't know who we are."

"But one of them does know, Jason."

"He won't say a thing."

"How do you know?"

Jason laughed again.

"Trust me on this one."

"It doesn't matter. The word is out. They're all going to be on high alert. Christ, Jason, why? Why did you do it?"

"It wasn't to make you angry, Angel. I did it because I wanted them all to experience the same fear that we felt every day. The fear of knowing that death was coming for them, and it could happen at any time."

5

Jason moved quickly and quietly around the back of the property. Tommy's residence was in a quiet suburban, upscale neighborhood outside of Atlanta. He was doing well for himself financially.

Darkly clad, Jason was nearly invisible as he approached the fencing along the backyard. Foliage was abundant on both sides of the barrier, which not only provided cover but afforded an easy entry.

After climbing a tall tree high enough to be able to see over the six-foot fence, he pulled out his night vision binoculars and scanned the area inside.

Although his vision was slightly impaired by the shrubbery, the house was only 200 yards from where he was perched, and some of the windows were visible. The lights were on in the kitchen and dining room. The rest of the house was dormant.

Tommy opened the fridge and took something out, bringing it over to the microwave.

Jason smiled.

This might be easier than I thought, he told himself.

Having cased the house for two days, he knew there was a dog and an internal security system, but neither of those would be a problem; he had planned ahead.

With help from Angel, a blackout would occur for the entire neighborhood at precisely midnight. It was the middle of the week, and most of the residents would be asleep. By the time the power company arrived, the task at hand would be complete.

Jason pulled out a gas mask from his backpack and put it on. A specially made headband allowed him to slip the night vision goggles over it and work hands-free.

Next, he pulled out two canisters containing remifentanil and carfentanil, two derivatives of the drug fentanyl that were infamously used in the Moscow theater hostage crisis as an incapacitating agent decades before. He checked their condition and put them back in the bag. Jason was amazed by what could be found for sale on the dark web, as long as you had the money.

The appointed time was now approaching, and he readied himself by moving to the back corner of the house.

Picking up a rock sitting in the yard, he broke a window in the back room the moment the lights went out, then ran to the far side where the rear entrance was. It would be easier to break in knowing exactly where Tommy and his dog would be.

He quickly picked the lock on the door and entered, closing the inlet behind him. Moving as quietly as he could, he made his way towards the back room, where the broken window lay in pieces.

He threw a canister inside, releasing the gas into the room and stood back, weapon in hand. No movement came from the room, though, so he took a look inside.

Tommy's Doberman pinscher lay motionless on the floor, but his master was nowhere in sight. Jason understood why when he heard the click behind his right ear.

"Drop the fucking gun, now!" Tommy shouted.

Jason complied slowly but didn't turn around.

"On your knees, motherfucker!"

Jason hesitated, plotting his next move. He knew Tommy could only see dimly with the lights out, but for now, he still had the advantage. There was no way he could pull out the other canister. It was too risky. What he needed was a distraction, and it came in the voice of a little girl who cried out from another room.

"Daddy!" she wailed.

It was enough to turn his attention ever so slightly. Jason dipped and kicked the left kneecap while simultaneously striking the radial nerve, causing Tommy to drop his gun. Jason kicked it out of reach and picked up his Glock.

Just as he was about to pull the trigger, the lights came back on. It was time for Tommy to see who was going to take his life, so Jason removed the gas mask and goggles.

"You?" Tommy questioned.

"That's right, it's me."

"Look, I didn't touch you. It's not me that you want to kill."

"Oh yes, it's you I want. You were very much involved in ruining my life."

Suddenly, a girl of about six years ran into the room straight towards Tommy and in the line of fire, her desperate mother running in not far behind.

"Don't hurt my daddy!" she cried.

Fuck! Jason screamed inside his head.

Things were getting messier by the minute. Jason reached his free hand back into his bag, keeping a steady eye on his prey, and managed to pull out a zip tie.

"You," he said, with a gesture toward the mother. "Put this on him. Bind his hands behind his back."

The woman complied, despite the complication of Tommy's broken kneecap, and within a minute, he was no longer a threat.

"Please don't hurt us!" his wife pleaded. "You can take anything you want, just please don't hurt us!"

Tommy, who had been silent for some time, finally spoke.

"This isn't a robbery, honey. This is an execution."

His statement was met with the reaction he hoped it would be, hysterics. Using his family to play on the killer's conscience might be his only hope.

Jason was beginning to rethink his strategy. If he killed Tommy, it couldn't be in front of his family. Now that his wife and child had seen his face, they could identify him to the authorities. He could just shoot them and leave no witnesses, but they were innocent, with the exception of being fooled by Tommy.

Then, a new idea came to mind. He turned again to his intended target.

"I'll let you live if you tell them what you did to me."

Jason could see Tommy begin to squirm, so he let him think about it for a minute, all the while reveling in the thought of Tommy's perfect life falling away from him.

"Time's up. Live or die? If you lie about anything, you die. It's that simple. I want them to know who you really are."

"I'm an accountant," he said flatly.

Jason laughed.

"A half-truth is the same as a lie. Try again and do better."

"I work for an organization that sells people to other people..."

"More specific," Jason urged, pointing the gun towards Tommy's genitals.

"I work for men that kidnap and sell children and young adults as sex slaves!" he blurted out. "I'm their accountant. I handle all the transactions and launder the money so that they don't get caught."

The horror could immediately be seen on his wife's face, and she grabbed the little girl, pulling her away from her father. The girl may not have fully understood what was going on, but Jason was content in the knowledge that he was actually saving her life.

Tommy's wife began to move towards the front room as if to leave with her daughter, but Jason waved the gun in their direction.

"Not yet. I'll let you go, but you need to stick around until I'm ready to go. I've got one more thing for you to do for me," he said, looking again at Tommy.

Jason directed the woman to assist in getting her husband up off the floor. He led his captives towards the study, where the family computer was located. On the way, he shut the door to the bedroom where the dog remained asleep.

After navigating to the website he wanted, Jason placed a quick call to a friend and wrote down a series of numbers on a nearby pad of paper. He thanked the person on the other end of the line and directed his attention back to Tommy.

"Show me where I need to go to move the money," he demanded.

"Are you kidding me?"

Jason pointed the gun squarely at his temple.

"I don't know. Does it look like I'm kidding?"

"If I do what you want, they'll kill me. I might as well just let you shoot me now. What difference does it make?"

"The difference is whether your family gets to walk away or not. Besides, if you talk, at least you'll have a running start."

"These men have connections everywhere. I can't hide from them."

Jason shrugged.

"You lie with the Devil, you're gonna get burned. Tell you what—how about I let you move some money for yourself, too? How does five million sound? I'm sure you could go off the grid with that kind of cash."

Tommy thought about it some more. Given little choice, he relented.

He told Jason how to log in to the bank accounts and watched as they were drained. Finally, the last five million was deposited into Tommy's offshore holding company.

"There, are you happy now? Can you let us go?"

"I'm letting them go, but you're not going anywhere until they're safe. After everything you've done, they're not staying with you."

He turned toward Jason's wife.

"Don't go to your neighbors and wake them up. I want to see you get in that car outside. Drive to the police station. Tell them what he's done and get as far away from him as you can. Don't ever look back."

Jason knew it was risky letting them leave. They could go for help as soon as they were clear and probably would.

In the end, he decided, it didn't matter. His work was nearly complete. He took the woman's cell phone and ushered them out the door.

After they left, he turned to his prisoner and said, "Time to go, Tommy Boy. I'd say good luck to you, but well, I hope they find you and do far worse to you than I had planned this evening."

"They'll find you, too. No one gets away with stealing billions of dollars. Especially from them."

"You're forgetting that I know who they are. I was passed around so many times that I've been to the top of the pyramid, and yet somehow, I've survived."

"You won't survive this."

Jason pointed his Glock at the side of Tommy's head and pulled the trigger.

"I'll take my chances."

Carol Gieg

Carol Gieg is a poet and author. Her memoir, *TBI-To Be Injured-Surviving and Thriving after a Brain Injury,* is well researched and offers practical exercises for maintenance of brain function, as well as inspiration and hope for those who have been brain injured.

She composes Prose and Poetry with Purpose. Her writing of immersion into the natural world, and engagement in the creative process, seeks to inspire hope and recovery in those burdened by homelessness, disenfranchisement, bias, disability, or being cognitively compromised.

Carol's poetry has been featured in the *American Chronic Pain Association's Chronicle,* the *Benicia Herald,* and many anthologies. Her poetry and prose have been featured on OZCAT RADIO.

Carol now lives in Benicia with her husband, Luis.

Healing Through Tradition

Ana was worried about her sister. Ever since the death of Maria's closest friend, Teresa, Maria had closeted herself in a bedroom at her mother's house, like a snail drawing into its shell.

The girls had always been close. Maria's mother was pregnant at the same time as Teresa's. They gave birth to the girls within a few weeks of each other. Teresa and Maria had been inseparable throughout childhood, adolescence, and as young adults. During latency, they talked about the "crushes" they had on boys who were decidedly "really, really cute!" They agreed about how annoying their little sisters and brothers were.

Both girls learned quickly. They helped each other with homework, and when they began putting words into sentences, they created stories which were always about the two of them and their adventures (imagined or not).

When they reached adolescence, two things had not changed since their childhoods. Younger sisters and brothers were still annoying.

"Right! But at least everyone knows that we're taking care of them now as women, not just as older sisters!" Maria crowed.

The other topic deemed worthy of intimate, confidential chat was still boys. However, additional descriptors were added to the list of desirable traits required, in order to establish their preferences.

"What do you think of Marco, Teresa?"

"Yeah, he is super good looking and so cool! And he's really popular!"

Teresa eventually moved to Mexico City in order to achieve her goal of graduating from a university. Nevertheless, Maria opted to remain in their village. Teresa was one of the few in her high school class who applied for and was granted a scholarship. Eventually, she completed an undergraduate degree in business with a specialization in marketing. Soon after that, she landed a job which satisfied these interests.

Even though Maria and Teresa no longer saw each other on a daily basis, they kept in touch by phone and FaceTime, as well as sent birthday cards and the occasional letter.

"At least I can keep track of what's going on in your life this way!" Teresa laughed. Maria agreed, though halfheartedly.

Several months after Teresa's new job started, Maria called and asked, "So, are you seeing anyone yet?"

"No, there was this one guy, I have to admit. His name was Mark, but it was only about sex for him, definitely not boyfriend material. Fortunately, I found that out soon enough." Teresa breathed a sigh of relief.

"How could you be so sure?" Maria asked.

"Oh, you know, he never spent the night. Sometimes, he was late or didn't even show up when we agreed to meet. I'd call him, and he'd apologize over and over... until I caved."

"Well, good thing you didn't waste too much time on him." Maria agreed.

"What about you, Maria—any fish on the line?" Teresa asked.

"No, not in my neck of the woods, but I haven't given up all hope!" Maria giggled.

As young women looking back, they agreed that their fondest memory from adolescence was the same. Without question, it was their respective "quinceañera." Each helped the other plan for this celebration, which took place when a girl turned fifteen. A time-honored Mexican tradition, this rite of passage marked a transition from childhood into adulthood. The entire community was invited to acknowledge this change in status.

Preparation was a lengthy and sometimes arduous process. Godparents often shouldered responsibility for footing the bill, as was the case for both Teresa and Maria.

"My godparents really outdid themselves!" Teresa reminisced, then added, "You know it's as much about the parents as it is about us! Mom's status in the community is so important to her." She paused, then added, "But, everyone knows that about Mom, anyway. They still love her, don't you think so?"

"Of course, they do!" Maria reassured her.

Teresa added, "Juan and Lizabet were just great. They've always been there for us, whatever the situation."

"Well, I'll say! They spent the most I've ever heard of. But even though my godparents weren't as wealthy as yours, they did a pretty good job too, didn't they? After all, we both enjoyed ourselves to the max at mine too!"

"How could we possibly not have?" Teresa asked. "Our mothers, friends, and relatives did such a good job of keeping everything organized. They all put so much time and effort into it and always checked with us about the details before deciding anything."

"Yep, and you and I made sure that all of the gifts were just what we wanted. Remember that list we put together?" Maria asked.

"I do. We weren't exactly subtle, but at least we were honest about it! I mean, we deserved them, didn't we? After all, we made it through childhood and came out the other side still in one piece!" She laughed.

"We just wanted to be sure we got ones which emphasized that our roles had changed, greedy though we were! Such a long list we put together!" Maria added.

Their list had included champagne glasses, cake servers, iPhones, watches, clothes, and makeup. Each gift accented their maturity.

Teresa thought for a moment, then said, "It wasn't until the ceremony that I realized how important the religious gifts were—the medal and scepter, the copy of the Bible and the crosses —in terms of what it means to be a woman."

They decided that money and status alone could never fully have accounted for the significance of that time in their lives. Maria and Teresa were elated to be the centers of attention (up to and culminating in that single day). The quinceañera memory served to bond them even closer.

"My dress was absolutely gorgeous!" Teresa clapped her hands.

"I still have mine," Maria told her. "Remember it had so many layers of chiffon that I almost flew away!"

The ceremonies began with a Catholic mass. Both young women were given medals, which were traditional signs of loyalty and commitment to God. Maria and Teresa were blessed by the priest.

"My favorite part was when my Dad replaced my flat shoes that the kids wore with high heels worn by mature women."

Though critical when younger of the traditions their Mexican culture treasured, through sharing memories, Maria and Teresa developed a new respect for this important part of who they were. Over time, as they matured, they felt the draw of their native culture, so community-based, compassionate, and empathic.

Teresa met some other students while at the University who felt the same, now valuing the closeness of their community and the support gleaned from that connection.

As a result, Teresa tried to return home as much as possible to celebrate significant events in the lives of both her family and friends.

One day, Teresa got word from her mother that her sister had just given birth to a child destined to be the first of the next generation in the family. This hallmark was notable not only for Teresa's family but for all who would gather at their home to celebrate.

Teresa had already talked with her boss (who coincidentally was also Latino) about this impending event. He was very understanding, and despite her relatively recent arrival to the company, he allowed that she would be able to take a few days off when she needed it. So, when the time came, Teresa packed her bags and headed for home. She looked forward to seeing her family and friends. But most of all, she wanted to spend some time with Maria.

A large contingent from the village to her family to commemorate both the birth and christening. Everyone seemed to have a good time, and even Teresa's mother was pleased with the outcome.

When a week had passed, Teresa knew it was time for her to return to the city. She decided to drive back over the ridge road, a narrow and winding route which the locals had aptly named "El Serpiente" (the Snake). Though this decision added an hour to the journey, the seldom traveled route provided breathtaking views of the valley and villages below. Unfortunately, that choice proved to be a fatal one.

Hours later, Teresa's body was discovered by a farmer heading into the city to deliver fresh produce. Suddenly, he spied skid marks and followed them to Teresa's mangled car off to the side of the road. It appeared Teresa had been going too fast, had taken a sharp turn and, to avoid spinning off the road, she'd turned too sharply, miscalculated the angle and collided directly into a tree. By the time the ambulance arrived, it was too late. The EMTs lifted her body into the ambulance, after trying fruitlessly to resuscitate her. They returned to the village and delivered the tragic news.

Maria learned about it all from her sister. It was then that Maria sequestered herself in her mother's spare bedroom. Ana visited daily and was updated by her mother about Maria.

"Oh, Ana, I know she was up all night. I heard her pacing back-and-forth in her room."

"Has she eaten anything today?" Ana would ask.

"Hardly anything, and only because I begged her to," her mother explained.

Though everyone initially encouraged Maria, another several weeks passed before she began to show meager signs of her previously positive personality. She occasionally joined her friends for a cup of coffee in the neighborhood café and visited one or two of them briefly at their homes. Ana and her mother breathed a sigh of relief, cautiously allowing themselves to believe in a full recovery.

Soon, however, they regretted having felt that Maria's rosy disposition had returned. Maria swore she could feel Teresa's pain and anguish and quickly returned to her previously demonstrated isolation and grieving.

Finally, Ana consulted with a small group of older women in the community who were well respected and revered for their wisdom. Teresa's grandmother, Maria's grandmother, and great Aunt Sophie gathered to discuss the issue. They agreed to become involved and planned what was best to do at that point.

By then it was October, the time when "Día de los Muertos" (Day of the Dead) took place.

This day was dedicated to honor the deceased and was a time when the memory of those lost was shared amongst friends and family members. The celebration took place both at home and in the cemeteries on November 1 and 2nd. The multi-day holiday afforded the chance to pray for and remember those who had died. Dia de Los Muertos was commonly portrayed as a day of celebration, rather than of mourning.

Maria's grandmother asked, "Remember the day when we talked about the soul of my little grandson who was lost in the traffic accident? That loss was almost the end of my daughter. It was hard for the rest of us, but losing her Danielito was almost more than she could bear."

"Yes, and when my sister's husband died at such a young age from cancer, it really did help to talk about him and remember his spirit on November 1 that year," added Teresa's grandmother.

After talking a bit longer, they agreed that each of them would provide some things they considered necessary on Dia de los Muertos at the celebration. They talked amongst themselves about how they would encourage Maria and make sure she understood the full meaning and importance of this day.

Teresa's grandmother was to provide traditional food and fresh flowers. She made "Pan de Muertos" (Bread for the Dead) baked into shapes of skulls and human figures.

Teresa's great Aunt Sophie was to bring candles, fragrant incense, religious images, soft drinks and "aguardiente" (white lightening liquor) to the Dia de los Muertos celebration.

Maria's grandmother said, "Let's not forget the water, so important since the returning souls are thirsty after their long journey back. You remember that's because it's such a main support of our lives."

Teresa's grandmother added, "We can explain all of this to Maria. This is certainly the most significant loss in her young life, and I think once she better understands, she will be able to pull together some personal items which were important to both of them, using ours as examples."

The three women decided to go to the house and were welcomed by Maria's mother and ushered to Maria's room.

"Maria, it's your Aunt Sophie, your grandmother, and Teresa's grandmother. Please open the door. We want to talk to you."

"No, but thank you anyway. I really don't want to see anyone right now," was the response.

"Well, honey, we're not going to leave until we have a chance to talk with you about Teresa." Aunt Sophie tried to convince her.

After five more minutes of pleading with her, Maria finally opened the door and stepped aside. She crossed to the far side of the room and sat down facing the concerned women.

"Maria, we know how much Teresa meant to you. We're missing her too." Teresa's grandmother continued. "But, honey, this is the time and place to honor her. We know that she can hear us and the love we are sending out to her. We have to celebrate that death is just another phase of life and that she will be able to live on as long as we treasure memories of her."

Maria's Aunt Sophie delivered the next part of their message. "Maria, we are going to help her know we are remembering her as she was when she was still with us. If we can do this for her (as well as ourselves), she will remain with us forever. The shrine we create for her will contain items in it which remind us of her, to be placed at her home. She will be satisfied and grateful because we are thinking of her after she's gone."

Once the women had finished explaining and encouraging Maria, Aunt Sophie concluded with, "Here are some things we've collected for her. All we ask is that you add some of your own."

One at a time, each of them came forward and set one or two small items on the bedside table next to Maria, later to be placed in an altar with several levels ("ofreda") standing in the living room of Teresa's home. This included baby shoes, a few toys, many nosegays, a shallow bowl of water, some salt, flowers, and a picture of Teresa taken at the celebration of her sister's baby.

"Maria, we will take these things to Teresa's mother for the ofreda. Please add things which remind you of Teresa. We know you'll feel better if you do," they urged her.

Maria thought carefully, then turned to her closet. Opening the door, she reached for her diary, filled with stories of the adventures she had shared throughout her life with Teresa. She placed these on the bed amongst the other memorabilia, then turned to the women and said, "This has helped some. I always had some idea of what this day meant but never as fully as I do now. Thank you; I feel like she's a little closer at least. I am certain that I can add more eventually."

They collected their items and embraced her gently, knowing that, if they showed too much enthusiasm, she might withdraw again.

"Maria, we're so glad you understand. What we've done will help Teresa to stay with us and to live forever in our memories."

They left the room, saying that they would return to see her over the next few days and wished her well until then.

Once they'd left, Maria began searching around the room for other items she wanted to add to the altar. She found the first letter Maria had sent to her after Teresa went to Mexico City. She'd saved a few others as well, sharing secrets only the other could fully appreciate. Next, she added some of the books they'd exchanged: Gabrielle Garcia Marquez's *100 years of Solitude*, Laura Esquivel's *Like Water for Chocolate*, Julia Alvarez's *How the Garcia Girls Lost their Accents*, and their favorite, *The Crazed Woman Inside Me* by Rosa Montero. She found a bottle of Teresa's favorite nail polish and lip gloss, then finished off with a picture of her and Maria laughing and waving at the camera on the Tulum beach, an hour's drive from Cancun.

As the weeks past, Maria thought about all she had learned. She began eating a bit more food and occasionally went out for a short walk.

One day after sleeping well for the first time in months, she left the house and headed straight for Teresa's family's home. She carried with her the items she had collected at home.

When Teresa's mother answered the door, Maria asked her for several items from Teresa's room, then added these to the altar.

By the next year at Dia de los Muertos, Maria's nightmares had ceased, and her mood had shifted, so that she was once again enjoying time with her friends and was pursuing her own education. She was in love with a man she had known all her life. Aunt Sophie and the grandmothers considered this to be a sure sign that Maria was moving on with her life.

Maria never again was able to think of Teresa without grieving. But the grief was balanced by an equal measure of gratitude. She cherished the memory of Teresa, now certain that, in doing so, Teresa would always be with her.

Jay Waitkus

Jay Waitkus is a freelance writer based in South Florida. He has worked as a reporter for numerous publications, including *The South Florida Sun-Sentinel, The Palm Beach Post, The Miami Herald, The Daily Voice, The Real Daily,* and *The South Florida Business Journal.* He is also the author of the crime novels *In the Depths of Shadows* and *Dividing line,* as well as several short stories and eBooks.

The Waif

The sky above was ashen gray, as it had been throughout the region for nearly seven years.

Her brief journey from Ugarit behind her, the pretty young maiden padded in bare feet up the cobblestone walkway to the castle outside of Latakia. She stopped for a moment and looked up at the portentous structure, its impregnable walls half-covered in ivy.

Eager to do what she came to, she knocked intensely on the enormous oak door before her. Eventually, she could hear the sound of boots tromping toward the entranceway from inside. The inlet creaked open, and with a look, she felt certain she'd finally reached her objective.

The thin, rough-hewn man in shabby attire was disheveled and blurry-eyed at first, like he'd been awakened from a great slumber brought about by physical exertion or far too much to drink.

His expression grew more pronounced, though, upon a glance at his visitor, her almond-shaped blue eyes and angelic, slightly impish, face the only things visible behind her hooded robe.

The rest, he tried to surmise, tracing the vague outline of her body behind the covering, quickly concluding, correctly in fact, that her beauty was rare and unspoiled.

A surge of lust overtook the middle-aged ruffian, and he instinctively pushed back the unruly mat of dark black hair that had wadded up at the top of his head. Offering his guest a salacious grin with a mangled, gap-toothed mouth, he resolved she would be his, and soon.

"May I help you?" he asked her innocuously.

"I hope so, sir," she said sweetly, offering an innocent, shy-looking smile. "I've come from the realm of King Danel on my way north and have need of room and board for the evening. Of course, I can pay you for—"

"No need," the man responded. "My home is always open to weary travelers."

"Thank you. That's very kind."

"Not at all, my dear," he said, standing aside to let her enter. "How many others shall I expect?"

"Why, none," she said, sounding a little confused.

"None?"

"Does that create a difficulty?"

"Of course not," he said with delight. "I confess, though, that I am a little surprised."

"Why, sir?"

"A young woman traveling alone through large areas of wilderness and knocking on a stranger's door?"

"Yes, I realize how that must seem. I confess, though, that I was not properly made to understand the dangers of the terrain nor the potential rigors of the journey. When I saw your beautiful estate, I thanked El for rescuing me. And you, of course, sir, for your forbearance and hospitality."

"Not at all," he said. "May I ask whose acquaintance I have the pleasure of making?"

"My name is Paghat," she replied matter-of-factly. She searched his eyes for a trace of recognition, but none seemed to be forthcoming.

"I'm Yatpan," the man said, confirming what she sought to know.

Every instinct urged her forward, but she fought them in hopes of getting the answers she wanted first.

With a welcoming gesture, the master of the castle led the young woman down the long corridor into the banquet hall. The large table, which had room for thirty people, was filled from one end to the other with the finest meats, cheeses, fruits, and wines available. Paghat was taken aback.

"Yes, I know," Yatpan said. "My needs are well taken care of."

"Forgive me for saying so, but you must have a lot of servants."

"Nothing of the kind. In fact, the only one who lives here is me."

"But how could all of this be prepared without—"

"Please, sit," he said. "Eat. You'll have to forgive me. I receive so few visitors, I sometimes take for granted the privileges I enjoy here."

"Privileges?" she asked, taking a small bite of a pear.

"Indeed. In fact, this castle is not properly mine, in the strictest sense."

"Not yours, sir?"

"A gift, in fact. Nothing more. And endless provisions, too, that seem to appear from nowhere. Payment, one might say, for a job well done. That being said, those I assist have the good sense to recognize the depths of my devotion. Clearly, I'm rewarded accordingly."

"I don't think I understand."

"Actually, you may. Especially if you're from Ugarit."

"What do you mean?"

"How long have you lived there?"

"Why, all of my life."

"Then, as young as you are, you must at least be old enough to remember when King Danel's fortunes turned."

"Of course, sir. The day Prince Aqhat died."

"Yes, a tragedy, that. He was a man of barely twenty."

"It was terrible for everyone. Not just the royal family but the people in the kingdom, too."

"I've heard the stories. That Aqhat's death brought drought and famine to the entire realm. But how could the events be related?"

"They couldn't," she said. "No one can make any sense of it."

"Yet they are connected, aren't they?"

"If so, no one understands why."

"I do."

"You, sir?"

"Would you like to hear a story, Paghat? As a Ugarite, I think you'll appreciate it."

She paused for a moment, a look of deep concern washing over her.

"All right," she said reluctantly.

"The circumstances of the prince's death were brought about at a feast not unlike this one."

"Yes, there was a royal banquet the day before. The whole city was talking about it."

"But you don't know who attended, do you?"

"The rulers of Tyre were there. Everyone knew that."

"No, my dear, I'm not referring to them. In fact, I'm referring to only one guest in particular, who the prince made the mistake of offending."

"Who?"

"Prepare yourself for my answer. Your inclination will be to dismiss it."

"All-right. Who did the prince offend?"

"Anat."

And with that, Paghat burst out laughing.

"The war goddess?"

"The same."

"A grand joke, sir. I confess you had me fooled."

"No ruse, milady. Anat appeared to the prince."

"You actually mean this!"

"I do, indeed."

"But why?"

"He had something she wanted. A gift, they say, from the famous craftsman, Kothar-wa-Khasis."

"Who is also believed to be a god."

"I have no reason to doubt it."

"What did the prince have that she wanted so badly?"

"A bow made of solid gold. She was willing to trade for it, and handsomely, but he rejected everything she offered."

"With all due respect, sir, the prince was killed by a hawk during a hunting trip. It's common knowledge in the city."

"I'm sure it is. But how difficult would it be for the war goddess to arrange that?"

"It wouldn't, I suppose. If I believed it."

"I speak the truth."

"But how would you know this?"

"You've already seen what I know. You're in the midst of it. The estate, the castle, the provisions. A thousand-fold more than any commoner in a thousand other realms. They're nothing but trinkets to my benefactor. Or benefactress, as the case may be."

"Anat is your benefactress?"

"She is indeed. As a point of fact, I believe she's delivered something else to me on this very day. And I mean to take it now."

He rose from his chair with menace.

Paghat's face remained expressionless, though, to Yatpan's utter dismay.

"Did you hear what I said, milady?"

"Indeed. Do you wish me to run?"

"I mean to claim you. And to dispose of you when I'm finished. So yes, dear, running would be most appropriate for you now."

"I've heard that," she said. "I was told that's what you like."

Yatpan stood there seething, then attempted to speak again.

"Are you mad?" he asked incredulously.

"Far from it, milord. But I don't believe you finished your story. You said that Anat arranged for the prince's murder, but you left out an important detail. You never mentioned the name of the real killer."

"The only murder you need worry about is your own!"

He sprang toward her but was taken down hard with a leg sweep that seemed to be almost effortless. His intended victim didn't even trouble herself enough to leave her chair.

"Please," she beckoned, "let's finish our discussion."

Stunned and injured, the rogue could only grimace as he lay on the concrete floor.

"Let me see if I can reach the conclusion by myself," she said, finally standing and turning toward him. "The hawk that killed Prince Aqhat was you, transformed by the war goddess to do her bidding. The life that you've been enjoying these many years is precisely what you said: payment in full for services rendered."

"Who are you?" Yatpan gasped.

"A fair question," she replied, her voice now resonating with confidence, superiority even, far removed from the dulcet tone of the timid waif she'd pretended to be before. "Forgive the deception, Yatpan, but I needed to be sure my information was accurate. Now that I am, we can finish this."

"Who are you?" he demanded again, rising unsteadily back to his feet.

"Let me show you," she said.

And with that, Paghat unfastened the chord at the waistline of her robe, sliding effortlessly out of the garment. Her rich blond hair emerged from behind the hood, falling around her shoulders and spilling down her back.

The first thing Yatpan saw was her headband. Forged of white gold, it bore the insignia of the House of Danel.

"No," he whispered, an icy chill running down his spine.

"Yes, villain. Justice has come for you today, in the form of the crown princess of Ugarit, sister of the fallen Aqhat, and daughter of Great King Danel. With his full knowledge and blessing, I may add."

Yatpan's heart was in his throat. Paghat, who had clearly been taught to fight, had arrived in Latakia prepared for battle.

Her gleaming white armor was striking, both in its functionality and capacity for distraction.

Though her neckline, shoulders, and midriff were uncovered, a steel chest piece cupped over her bosom. The strap that held it in place wrapped horizontally around her sides below the axillae and across the middle of her naked back. The top half of her arms were exposed, as well, but metal bands below the bend at the elbows protected her forearms and wrists.

Her panties extended downward to her groin area in a perfectly formed V-shape. To the left of the beltline was the scabbard that contained her sword. The top of her legs remained bare, but another set of steel bands beneath the kneecaps kept her calves and ankles well-covered.

The result was an ensemble allowing Paghat a full range of motion to strike, while providing her a modicum of protection.

Momentarily distracted by her beauty, even in his terrified state, Yatpan narrowly avoided decapitation as the princess drew her weapon and took a vicious swipe at the side of his neck. He turned and fled, upending a chair behind him in a feeble effort to slow her down.

Sweat began to fly from his brow as he raced toward the armory. Paghat kept him in her sights as she pursued him, her steps light and purposeful.

Yatpan entered the cavernous room and ran to the back, hastily grabbing a large sparth from the assortment of bladed weapons mounted on the wall. He turned toward his assailant with nary a second to spare, using the ax to block another strike that surely would have destroyed him.

His effort, though, merely delayed the inevitable, for Paghat wielded her sword as well as any warrior that had ever come before. With a seething hatred now given way to an outpouring of unbridled rage, she unleashed a furious barrage against her foe, easily knocking the ax from his hands.

A final swipe caught Yatpan on the chest as he tried to recoil, the devastating flesh wound leaving the mercenary laying in a pool of his own blood. He tried to crawl but couldn't even move. Paghat now stood above him, the battle all but won.

"Any final words, villain?"

"Please, please," he stammered, but the princess only smiled.

"I'll show you every bit of the mercy you extended to my brother and undoubtedly countless others."

She raised the sword above her head and prepared to deliver the deathblow, but then a new presence entered the fray.

"Stop!" demanded a voice from the corner of the armory. Paghat whirled but saw nothing at all.

The smell of perfume then filled the chamber, and a small plume of smoke gathered in the air.

Paghat watched the scene unfold before her. As the fog began to dissipate, she could make out the form of a woman emerging from its depths. A few moments later, the veil had lifted, and the princess stood face-to-face with her.

The raven-haired beauty smiled gleefully. She loved making an entrance. Clad all in black, with a form-fitting sleeveless mini dress, thigh-high boots, and gloves extending to her elbow, she looked Paghat over with the most piercing green eyes the young warrior had ever seen.

"Hello, your highness," the sorceress said. "It's good to meet you at last."

"Anat, I take it," the princess replied.

"Indeed. I've been watching your exchange with Yatpan here. I'm very impressed with the ease in which you dispatched him."

"Kill her!" the fallen man cried with an anguished howl.

"Silence, dog!" Anat responded, and Yatpan meekly obeyed.

"I'm glad to meet you too, witch," Paghat chimed in. "After all, your pathetic servant was merely the instrument of my brother's demise. His real killer now stands before me."

"Be careful, young one. My forbearance has its limits."

"As Aqhat could no doubt attest to. If he was here."

"You humans are fascinating creatures. Reckless, foolish, and frail, yet with a capacity to love one another so deeply. Intriguing."

"I'm not here to be studied by you. I came to pay a debt. Since killing you is impossible, unfortunately, either strike me down, or stand aside and let Yatpan and I finish our business."

The war goddess stood unmoving, but a pensive look came across her face.

"Suppose," she said, "there was another way?"

"There is no other way," the princess replied. "You've taken everything from me. My brother, the realm, and my father's heart along with it. I've resolved to do whatever is necessary to seek redress, insofar as it's even possible. All that leaves me is Yatpan. One of us will not leave here alive."

"As I said, reckless. Dramatic, though, I'll grant you that. But tell me, before you force me to snuff out your life, what harm is there in hearing what I have to offer?"

"Ah yes, one of Anat's heralded offers. Like the ones you made to Aqhat before you murdered him. And over what? A bow. A bow! Tell me, war goddess, what in your history suggests that I should listen to a single word that passes from your lips?"

For a moment, Anat said nothing but then looked at the princess severely.

"The fact that I can grant you the one thing your heart truly desires: the restoration of your brother's life."

"You lie!"

"You doubt my power?"

"I doubt your sincerity. Why would you come to me with this after seven years?"

"Perhaps I needed some time to reflect."

"While Aqhat lay cold in the ground, and the kingdom lay in ruins."

"You humans have such a limited conception of time. I suppose it's understandable, though, given your absurdly short lifespan. Still, your brother would be in the prime of his life were he reborn. Your father is still alive and would welcome his son's return. And what of King Danel's subjects? Are they not worth considering what I propose?"

Paghat did not respond.

"Good," Anat said. "I'm heartened to see you're capable of putting your anger aside, if only for a moment."

"Why do you make this offer?" the princess asked evenly. "You're not going to tell me you feel guilty for the accursed deed?"

"Gods don't deal in guilt, my dear. Perhaps, though, I do feel some sympathy for you. Perhaps it's only pity. What difference does it make, if it gives you what you want?"

"It doesn't," she retorted. "What do you propose?"

"The decision to bring your brother back is not one that I make lightly. Indeed, there will be a cost. A small portion of my power will be gone forever. Still, I extend you the offer."

"And what do you want in return? I have no golden bow to give you. As you're no doubt aware, it was destroyed in the attack."

"Yes, a pity that. It was truly a fine piece of craftsmanship. Kothar outdid himself."

"So, what do you want?"

"I ask you only this: abandon your quest of vengeance and leave my servant in peace. By sparing Yatpan, the prince will live, as well."

"Oh, thank you, thank you," Yatpan murmured from the floor.

"Silence!" she ordered again.

Paghat glanced back at the pathetic mercenary, then turned to Anat, perplexed.

"Who is he to you," she asked, "that he'd be worth a part of your power?"

The sorceress, too, gazed down at her fallen champion.

"He's no one," she responded. "Another minion, whose value is rapidly dwindling. Still, the scales must be balanced. A life for a life. In exchange for Yatpan, I offer you your brother back. And with his rebirth, the end of the drought and famine that have plagued your father's realm."

"But what does Aqhat have to do with—"

"Your sibling is far more powerful than anyone is aware. And so are you, in fact. Perhaps you could find out together. But the decision is yours alone."

Paghat paused for a moment, weighing Anat's potential for treachery against what she claimed to be offering.

"All right," the princess said. "I accept your terms."

Unknown to Paghat, though, Yatpan, despite his injuries, had recovered enough of his faculties for a final, desperate move. Rising from the ground abruptly and grabbing the ax, he lunged toward the princess from behind her, raising the weapon to strike.

"No!" the war goddess exclaimed.

With a wave of her hand, Yatpan fell dead.

For the first time since arriving at the castle, Paghat appeared visibly shaken.

"Why?" she asked, beginning to sob.

"My rewards to my servants are manifold. But disobedience is never tolerated. In attacking you after we'd struck our bargain, Yatpan outlived his usefulness."

"And now, without him, our deal is voided, isn't it? Aqhat remains in the ground, and the people in the realm continue to suffer. If a life for a life is what you demand, take mine, so the rest may be spared!"

Anat looked at the brave young woman, more intrigued than ever. Her anger aside, everything Paghat had done had indeed been motivated by love.

Though loathe to admit it, a twinge of regret came over the war goddess for all she'd set in motion.

"Your offer is rejected," she said. "Our original bargain remains intact."

"I don't understand," said the princess, wiping away a tear. "I thought you told me—"

"You pledged not to kill Yatpan, and you didn't. I did. Appropriate enough. He was mine to do with as I pleased."

"And Aqhat?"

"Return to the field where your brother died. I have no doubt you know it well. Even as we speak, his life forces begin to gather. By the time you reach him, he will be physically restored. By tomorrow, he will be as you remember him, his mind and spirit fully intact."

Paghat paused for a moment, unsure of what to say. Thanking Anat after all the suffering she'd caused would hardly have been appropriate. But if what she said was true, the sorceress had at least returned what she'd stolen, and in doing so, made a measure of restitution.

"Your mission is finished," Anat said. "Go."

With a nod, Paghat turned and left, walking the length of the corridor and exiting the door at the front. Once outside, her eyes were again drawn skyward. The ashen haze that had hung over the region in perpetuity since Aqhat's passing was now beginning to lift, the first rays of sunlight she had seen in seven years peering through the cracks in the clouds.

The dark skies would return in the days ahead but only long enough to bring her people the rains they desperately longed for.

Reaching the bottom of the cobblestone road, Paghat strode toward the adjacent field leading back to Ugarit. The lush grass was warm beneath her feet. Taking a final glance at the castle, she turned and headed for home.

With so much time already lost, she hadn't a moment to waste. Her pace began to quicken, her heart full at the prospect of reuniting with her brother and the restoration of fortune to her father's realm.

Ewa Gerald Onyebuchi

Ewa Gerald Onyebuchi is a writer based in Nigeria. He writes both short stories and poetry. Some of his works have been published on brittle paper, nantygreens.com, bengaluru review, zenspen.com, latunespublishers.com, Whimsicalpoets, and elsewhere. His poem, Mother Nature Ill, won Instagram-based 2020 Evolving Landscapes Competition.

Forms of Grief

Arinze Okafor was sprawled on the floor while something thick and white lathered his mouth where flies started to gather for a feast around.

From afar, one might think he was dead until coming closer to discover the heaving of his chest and the sizzling of his breath like a snake. With a closer look, the redness in his eyes, the bulged rim around them already slackened, would be quite visibly shocking. The dried scale-like appearance of each side and below his eyes proved he had been crying profusely not too long ago.

But don't think it odd for a person of his status, a grown ass man to be crying, as though he were a woman grieving the loss of a child. Not at all.

For his was a grief, like a wound, that just wouldn't heal despite the therapy he'd undergone. Sometimes it stuck in his throat like a lump, so no matter how many bottles of whiskey he gulped down, the grief didn't dissolve. Other times, it took the form of a scar, sleeping on his chest, and regardless of how hard he scrubbed his body, each time he took a shower, it refused to fall off. And there were those times, more often than not, he wore his grief like a cloth, torn and leaking on all sides, utterly visible before every eye.

He willed himself to his feet. His leg hit the empty whiskey bottle with a thin neck and fat, round bottom like a child suffering Kwashiorkor, forcing it to dance from side to side until equilibrium was achieved. It was his sixth bottle and a miracle this one didn't join the rest in death. He'd bought all six from a supermarket downtown. A young lady, the cashier, had attended to his bills.

"Having a party tonight?" she asked, counting the bottles of whiskey before standing them carefully inside the small, brown carton.

He smiled. But the smile wasn't in any way a direct answer to her question. Yet, it was a waning smile. If only she knew he was going home to soak himself in whiskey, just maybe, his grief would finally drown away.

He staggered towards the door, over the shards of brown glass, the ones his rage and bitterness had beckoned him, minutes ago, to destroy on the wall from across where he laid. How his steps, which were far from being gingerly, failed to make contact with a single shard of glass, surprised him given he was drunk. He hesitated at the door, then made a sharp turn. Staring at the fragments scattered all over the floor, he gave a loud belch and yawn, and his mouth curved in a smirk.

You want to kill me. Ah-ah, I'm smarter than all of you put together. He gave a shrill voice to his thought, and the echo flew around in the house. Then he staggered on.

First, he made his way to a room, which used to be his children's. The room was empty, not a bed in place, nor the two pink bicycles he bought for his girls, not a single trace of clothing or hairbrush littered on the floor, not the kind of toys they liked to play with, not a single picture of them. He had had everything moved out three weeks ago into his new house at Abuja, the one Katherine Ala, his wife to be, had handpicked from a catalogue she got from an agent. While the rest like the chairs, dining table, curtains were sold since the new house had fresh, breathtaking furniture and other interior decor. This house had been sold already. Still, he was only here, the last time, to reconnect with the past and to say goodbye to the memories the house contained, memories that had haunted him all these years.

Initially, Katherine didn't want him to bring any of his belongings to the new house, but he was adamant. So, she let him. There was nothing she could have done to prevent it. But they both agreed those things would be kept in the warehouse, far away from the main building. She didn't want him to start brooding over the past once they were husband and wife.

***

Arinze had come to one of the biggest shopping malls in Lagos to buy a few household items. Standing there like a tree, perplexed, wondering where what he came for was in this gigantic mall. Katherine, who had been staring at him for a moment, hurried to the rescue, as if she had read the confusion on his face. He was wearing a tight, black t-shirt with blue jeans, car keys swirling in his hand. The pair of white sneakers on his feet wore beautiful patterns.

"Excuse me, may I help you? What is it you are looking for?" she inquired.

He couldn't have failed to notice the exceptional elegance to her appearance. He would have been blind not to see how gorgeously black she looked in that red dress which sucked up her entire body, revealing her small breasts and full curves. Employing her right hand, she trailed her long, rich mass of satin, black wig—which was already cladding her face from being seen—as in a slow-motion picture. Damn, she was hot! So, he had to make a loud impression. A lasting one.

"I'm looking for the food section. Need some groceries," he said, trying not to look too much at her. He kept fiddling with the keys.

She stared briefly at him. She said, "Follow me."

He complied.

She led him up a flight of shiny stairs to a large room adorned with a variety of fruits, veggies, and other perishables, well-sealed from contamination. But she didn't leave immediately, given that she was the gregarious type. Soon they were thrown into an aura of chitchat, even though Arinze hadn't planned to start any conversation.

He was awed the instant she said she was the owner of the mall because she was young and stunning. "Wow!" was all he managed to say. Numbers were exchanged.

Those long midnight calls began between them—he calling her sweet pet names, and she blushing over the phone. A date became inevitable. Thereafter, a relationship sprung forth.

***

This time he was in her mall, sitting across from her at the large desk, not as one who came to buy things but as her lover. She was talking so much about the wedding and the plans already put in place and how she couldn't wait to be his wife, all while flipping through a big book in her hand. But he only listened in mute reverie, wondering how he was able to open himself again, how she managed to bring to life what he thought had died recently—that thing called love. Perhaps it was her smile, not just her perfect body, that endeared her to him. Or that air of humility and generosity she carried about regardless of her rich and sophisticated background: her father was a Senator and her mother a Professor at the University of Ibadan. Or it was the way she endured him all through their one-year-old relationship: those nights, while on a date, cutting her mid-sentence, he talked about his late wife and children with every ounce of undeniable attachment that forced jealousy to run down her spine; or sometimes when they made love, his late wife laid on the bed beside them, becoming an inevitable guest, a stimulant, that ladder to a rewarding climax, as he moaned her name from his loins.

A security guard appeared just by the glassy entrance door, saluting customers (done in a theatrical way), as they strolled in. He was always anticipating a tip from a good Samaritan.

"Honey, what do you think about this? I know it's just the perfect house for us. Don't worry about the mall. My younger sister will be in charge," she said, holding out the catalogue of beautiful houses in Galadima, Abuja, to him.

He took the book from her, ran his eyes across, and nodded. "Anything just to make you happy, my love," he replied with a smile.

He was happy; she was happy. Actually, he was not. He hadn't been, but she was not the reason for this. She knew all along about this sadness, this grief he carried about him. And yet, it didn't deter her from going on with the wedding plans. The wedding was in two weeks. And sometimes, she was apprehensive he might wake up one morning and call it off, although he hadn't shown any clear sign of that.

She decided to say something in a bid to slice off the silence that hung in the air between them like a threat, something that sounded both strange and funny to her; and her laughter popped out faintly, so girly. Stealing a cursory glance off his face, she feared it wouldn't arouse the same feeling in him. But to her amazement, he laughed, flaunted the laugh in a way that attracted eyes to them, and she wasn't perturbed in the slightest form. In fact, this left a reassuring smile, that feeling of ownership, that he was still her man, the one she fell madly in love with.

The night Katherine suggested the idea of them moving to Abuja, the night he had proposed to her, they were in a restaurant having dinner.

"Honey, I want us to relocate to Abuja. Please let's leave this State. Maybe that way you would heal faster. You know... so that the memories would stop coming and hurting you," she stated after screaming, 'He proposed, he proposed,' before everyone present. She had waited for this moment.

Gulping down a half-filled glass of water, he cleared his throat as if to say something, but he didn't. He just stared at her, rudely, with his mouth hanging open. He was wondering what to tell her. He was used to Lagos, the air, the traffic, and all. If he said no to her request, it would dampen her spirit. He knew this. But a part of him wanted to leave Lagos, to let go of the memories, to embrace this new life with her; but another, that other part, still held on strongly to the hem of the past.

"No problem, my love. I only want your happiness," he said, finally, after a brief silence.

***

He had lived all his life in Lagos. He was born and bred in Lagos, Oshodi precisely. And as an only child, his late parents had lavished him with so much love. They had both been lecturers at the University of Lagos, which he later attended.

Their deaths reached him while he was in school. Professor Rotimi, a friend to his parents, had called him on the phone one afternoon. From his tone, it sounded like an emergency. Indeed, it was an emergency! So, he ran out of the hostel to his office, located at the faculty of Science.

"Arinze, you have to be strong for what I am going to tell you," Prof said.

"Yes sir," Arinze replied. But his heart was racing.

"I got a call that the plane your parents boarded from Europe, where they attended a one-week conference, crashed on getting to Nigeria. I'm sorry, they are..."

"They are what, sir?" he cried.

"Please, be calm, you are a man. I'm sorry... your parents are dead."

Suddenly his blood ran cold. Tears poured down his eyes. His body became stiff. It took a while for him to regain himself, to give mouth to the pain on his inside. Then he shouted. "Hey! It's not possible." And fell off the chair to the floor. Prof came over to console him.

Nevertheless, his career was not truncated. His studies continued because his late parents had been wise enough to will some properties and huge amounts of money in his name. And Prof tried to look out for him.

Lagos was where he first met the love of his life, got married to her, the marriage was consummated with two beautiful girls. Everything was all right. They had what seemed to be an enviable family until that unfortunate day. And everything was snatched before his eyes. All of it. And his mother-in-law, who had, at some point, accused him of using her daughter and granddaughters for rituals to increase his wealth even though she knew exactly how they had died.

***

With an unsteady gait, he paced around the room touching the pink walls. He paused, his gaze fell on a few tiny letters scribbled on the wall, and began to weep. That was Ada's handwriting when she was in primary one. She used to try out every new handwriting learnt from school.

"Daddy, I want to become a writer, just like Chimamanda, when I grow up," she said one time he returned from work—although exhausted—he still assisted with their homeworks while their mother busied herself at the kitchen.

"And, Dad, I will become a pilot too. I will take you and Mum, and we will travel the world together," Uloma quipped.

"No problem, my beautiful girls. You can be just anything you want to be," he assured with a smile.

The moment he couldn't bear it, he moved out of the room, shutting the door behind him. He entered another room, wider than the former. The master bedroom. He had told Kate he wanted to spend some alone time here, in this empty house. He needed some space to think things through, and finally, decide to let go of the past. To forget that horrible incident. It was time to move on, to learn to love again. To trust again.

His restless eyes darted around, as if searching for something. Yet he had no clue what it was. Had no clue an old portrait laid carelessly on the floor until he almost crashed on it. Picking it up, he couldn't stop gazing at it. He was stunned, though there was nothing left in the house. Immediately, tears bulged out of his eyes, and he broke down. It was a wedding picture of him and Elizabeth.

Arinze and Elizabeth were married for ten years. She was his first love. They dated while at the University. After their graduation, he proposed to her.

She accepted. They got married. They had two daughters—Ada and Uloma.

That early morning, he kissed his wife as he made for the bathroom. While she hurried to the kitchen. Ada and Uloma were still asleep.

Breakfast was ready at the dining—toast bread and butter with tea. Elizabeth appeared in the living room, from the kitchen, with a glass of water.

"And hope my darling is enjoying the food," she said, dropping the cup on the tray before him.

"For sure. Why won't I? And who's the best cook in the world?" the gayness in his tone unclothed.

"Mua! Mrs Elizabeth Okafor!" she cooed.

"Ada! Uloma!" she began to call out, but no reply. The girls were snoring quietly in their room.

"Allow them to sleep a little longer. You know yesterday was so hectic for them, for all of us, after the evening outing."

"Baby, you are spoiling these girls so. And it's seven already, on a Monday morning. They should be up by now for school," she said after gazing at the clock. She started to scrape the crumbs of bread from the table into the ceramic tray as soon as he finished eating.

"What did you say the time is again?"

"Seven."

"Gush! I am so fucking late for work."

"Watch it! No 'f' word, babes."

"Oops! I'm sorry. See you when I return. I love you." He kissed her again before taking his leave.

"I love you too. Bye!"

***

No sooner had he arrived and settled in his office than the call wired in. It could have been an hour, maybe, or two.

The caller, a masculine voice, reported.

"Is this Mr Arinze Okafor?'"

Arinze replied appropriately.

"I am calling from Lagos teaching hospital where your wife and two daughters have been confirmed dead. I'm sorry. It was a ghastly car accident. They had lost a lot of blood even before they were rushed in. I would like for you to come over to the hospital so..."

The phone crawled from his hand to the floor.

He screamed and collapsed on the floor in his office. He was the senior manager of Atteco Roof and Tiles company limited.

The scream gathered a handful of staff into his office, trying to fan him back to consciousness. Someone brought a glass of water for him, as he

77

narrated the awful report. He wanted to go over to the hospital at once, to identify the bodies, but they stopped him.

"You are in no shape to go to the hospital right now, Mr Arinze. Maybe later," Adams Otedola, the CEO, insisted.

Later that day, he went to the hospital and found his wife and two daughters covered with white linens. There they were, cold and lifeless, laying on different beds, about to be wheeled to the morgue. He dropped to his knees, held his mouth in a bid to stifle the urge to scream again, hot tears poured from his eyes.

His stomach gave a distress call. He rushed to the toilet to puke out everything he had eaten and drank that evening. On the tiled floor beside the toilet, he laid until sleep washed over his eyes.

***

The following morning, he awoke to a bout of pain banging in his head. But it jaded the moment he took some pills. He felt lighter, freer, after taking a cold bath. He was no longer wearing the ring from his previous marriage. He had it flushed down the toilet the previous night. Katherine had complained about it, presenting it in the form of a plea to him.

Now, his mind was made up; he was ready to walk down the aisle again to begin a new life with her, one he sensed was promising. He knew Elizabeth would have, more than anything in this world, wanted this for him—his happiness. As he stood gazing at the mirror plastered to the wall of the bathroom, he imagined her beautiful, caramel face popping up right in front of him. She was nudging him to let her go, to let Ada and Uloma go. To embrace love again.

Suddenly his instincts pulled him to where his phone sat in his trousers pocket. Ten missed calls. All from Kate. He looked closer and found a text message beneath the missed calls.

Good morning, love. Trust you had a splendid night. Where are you? Remember we agreed to go shopping together for the wedding gown. I'm waiting for you at my place. Please call me ASAP. A love emoji.

He smiled when he finished reading the text, and said to himself, almost aloud: *I love you too.*

Meg Paonessa

Meg Paonessa is a Professor of Creative Writing at North Central College in Illinois. Her work earned her the *Hayden's Fairy Review* 25th *Anniversary Award*, Honorable Mention in the 2020 *NYC Midnight Short Story Contest*, and has appeared in *The Adirondack Review, PANK, fwriction : review, Camera Obscura, Scary Mommy,* and elsewhere. Her chapbook, "The Great Reimagining of Greenletter Avenue," is due out June 2021. Visit her at megpaonessa.com.

My Mother, The Psychic

My mother's a psychic. I hate this for two reasons. One, because when she's asked to go to women's birthday parties and sit around reading their palms, people laugh at her and call her a fake, and sometimes, she does fake it, just to make them all like her. I hate that. The second reason I hate that my mom is a psychic is because she's psychic. She knows all about me, sometimes even before I do, and I can't stand her knowing all about me, sometimes even before I do. Especially when I'm pretending to die so Tisha won't leave us.

We get a lot of stupid people knocking on our door, asking for readings. Drunks too. It doesn't help that we live across the street from a bar. You've got to watch out for these people, my mom says. They tend to have very unbalanced temperaments. She used to make us leave her alone in the front room when she had clients but, after one particular client, she stopped protesting when we'd sneak into the kitchen to listen and soon, we were able to walk out and even use the toilet while she was telling people about themselves. I get a lot of strange looks from clients who don't expect to see children lying about when they come up our stairs, but I think it makes them watch their language.

Being psychic isn't hereditary. Kids at school tease me about reading their fortunes and pass me fake tarot cards hidden in folded notes, and I keep trying to tell them I wasn't blessed with any of my mom's gifts, but they don't understand. They just think it's funny. Nancy Maytown didn't think it was funny after I told her about her puppy getting hit by a car on the first Saturday after the next full moon, though. I thought it was funny. Until her mom called my mom and yelled about God and devils and dying and just plain awful mean stuff, and I could tell it really hurt my mom's feelings that I pretended to be psychic like her and ended up turning her into a big ole joke. She told Mrs. Maytown that she didn't see anything about Nancy's puppy dying for at least six moons and not to worry, but Mrs. Maytown took offense to that for some reason and hung up the phone real rude like.

Tisha hates that mom's a psychic too, but for different reasons. She's always siding with the birthday party ladies, saying mom shouldn't be so public with her gifts. I keep asking her what the point of being a psychic is if you're not gonna tell people what's up, but Tisha just gets all red in the face and tells me I'm too young to get anything. I'm not too young to know she shouldn't be running away from home when she's only 15 just cause mom's a psychic—but there's no reasoning with her. This is why I'm pretending to die.

Two nights ago, at the PTA meeting at school, my mom got this really strong vibe coming from Mrs. Coheen. She told me she tried not to say anything since Tisha's been so mad at her lately, but it was like all the stars in the sky aligned, and Mrs. Coheen came straight over to her and asked how my mom was doing. Mom just had to read her. Turns out Mrs. Coheen's #1 chakra was all out of whack and, considering that's your sex parts chakra, and they were at a PTA meeting, my mom got all flustered and tried to shut off her head. But then, *bang*, Mrs. Coheen came right out with a big ole smile and asked how her aura looked. So, my mom just said the first thing that popped into her head, which was, "How's Gerald doing? Everything ok?" And Mrs. Coheen lost it. Turns out Gerald isn't *Mr.* Coheen, if you catch my drift. Poor mom. She was just nervous because of Tisha.

I sat mom right down in the kitchen when she got home from the meeting and made her some chamomile tea to calm her nerves. She looked sad all over and near tears. When Tisha came in, I poured another cup of tea and rubbed my mom's shoulders as we rehashed the whole story for Tisha. This time, the real tears really did come. I hugged my mom real big and tight and encouraged her for a good couple of minutes until she was okay again. Then, I told her Tisha and I would get ready for bed, and everything would be alright in the morning.

I climbed into bed pretty tired after all that comforting. I thought Tisha was a little rude for shutting her door so loudly when she finally went to bed, but it wasn't until I woke up an hour later and made out that Tisha was on another one of her rampages that I realized she had actually meant to slam her door real loud. She was screaming about how embarrassed she'd be at school the next day and *how could you this* and *how could you that* all in front of her friend's parents. It was pretty dramatic. She took up the usual chorus line, "I want to go and live with Aunt May in Connecticut!" And then I heard something that shocked me onto my deathbed. My mom said, "Ok."

So, I decided not ever to get out of my bed until Tisha comes in and apologizes and promises never to leave. I have to use the bathroom, obviously, every once in a while, but I make sure to run there like I'm in the throes of vomiting and make a whole lot of noise while I sit on the toilet to pee. I'm a pretty good actress. I mean, my mom definitely knows what's going on, but maybe that's not all that bad. She can keep a secret.

I can tell it's working on Tisha, too, me about to die. She's been in to see me twice today. Problem is, I don't know how to tell her my sickness is directly connected to her plans to run away. I'm thinking I may need to persuade my mom to help out with this situation. I figure she could tell

Tisha she has a *feeling* that the two of us have connected sadnesses, and without one another, we'll both be unhappy for*ever*. It could work. I'll definitely have to up the amount of moaning I've been doing, just to make sure she understands the dire situation we are in.

Eventually, my mom comes in to bring me a tray full of food. She could probably tell I'm starving in here. She sits on the edge of my bed and rubs my toes, waiting for me to finish. I may not be a psychic, but it *feels* like she has something on her mind.

"Leigh," she says, "I know you're really upset about Tisha going to visit Aunt May."

I nod with my mouth full, unable to fully explain how it's not so much a visit as an abandonment.

"I think, though, it may be a really good thing for her to do right now."

I can hear the doubt in my mom's voice as she speaks. I put my pretend sickness on the back burner for a second 'cause I can tell she needs someone to think this over with.

"I don't think it'd be a good idea at all, Mom," I say.

"Honey," my mom says. I know then she's already made up her mind, and I'm not going to like what I'm about to hear. "Tisha isn't like you and me," she says. She's rehearsed this, I can tell. "She doesn't want to live like we do."

"So. Tough luck for her. We're family."

"Some people don't like the truth always pushed in their faces." This, I think to myself, is coming out of left field. I figure she's back to thinking about Jerry, my dad. But this was no time to rehash the past.

"Tisha's only fifteen, Mom," I say.

"She'll like Aunt May. It'll give her some perspective. She's completely lost, Leigh. Her third eye is totally shut."

I can't very well deny this third eye stuff; anyone can tell Tisha isn't happy where she is, but I don't like admitting to the idea.

So, then Tisha comes in and sits down with my mom at the end of my bed, looking at the blue carpet and fidgeting with her stubby hands.

"This is something I need to do, Leigh. It's not like I won't miss you a ton—" She looks up at me briefly but probably can't take the laser beam scowl I'm aiming directly at her third eye.

My mom pats Tisha's back, and for once, Tisha doesn't squirm away like she usually does.

I know she's leaving. I get this helpless feeling all over. So, I do what any ten-year-old girl would do in this situation; I throw an enormous tantrum.

"You're so selfish, Tisha! What did Mom and I ever do to you! We're family. We're supposed to love one another and STAY TOGETHER!"

Through ghastly sobs and streams of snot running down my upper lip, I ask Tisha why she has to leave, and my mom gets up and grabs the box of Kleenex from the bathroom and brings it back for me. Tisha starts crying too, saying no one understands her, but that just makes me more mad. I mean, Mom's a psychic. She's understands her all the time!

I look to my mom for help but can't get past seeing her as a traitor to the cause. She's allowing this to happen, after all.

"It was just a stupid PTA meeting, Tisha!"

My mom hugs me to her even though I don't want to be hugged, which makes me cry even harder. She says it's more than just the meeting mishap behind all this. She says she knows everything is going to be fine, and Tisha won't be gone forever. I look at Tisha when mom predicts this, and I don't think she even blinks at the fortune. She probably doesn't have the heart to protest. *Good*, I think, *you can't escape forever.*

I cry myself into a daze of sleepiness on the bed with my mom and Tisha there, and when I hear my mom tell her to go and pack a bag, I wake up mad and cry myself to sleep all over again. Tisha must really hate living with us if she can get through all my dying and crying stuff and still want to go.

In the morning, Tisha comes back in to say goodbye. I've already begun my grieving process, so when she mumbles something about love and missing me, I pretend she's dead to me and don't respond. I kind of regret not listening better now that she's gone. But, when Tisha makes it to La Guardia, Aunt May has her call home to say she's gotten in all right, and I can tell she's a little sad by the soft way she speaks into the phone. I decide to forgive her. I mean, seriously, if Mom says she'll be back, I guess eventually it will happen. My only worry is that when my dad left, my mom said he'd come back too—and look how that's turned out.

Mark Blickley

Mark Blickley is from the Bronx, NY and a proud member of the Dramatists Guild and PEN American Center. He is the author of the story collection *Sacred Misfit* (Red Hen Press). His multi-genre collaborations with artist Amy Bassin include *Weathered Reports: Trump Surrogate Quotes from the Underground* (Moira Books) and the text-based artbook, *Dream Streams* (Clare Songbirds Publishing House). His videos, *Speaking in Bootongue* and *Widow's Peek: The Kiss of Death,* represented the United States in the 2020 year-long international world tour of *Time Is Love: Universal Feelings: Myths & Conjunctions,* organized by esteemed African curator, Kisito Assangni.

Root 66

When I was alive, my favorite joke to tell was the one about the woman who was arrested at a cemetery for peeing in public on her husband's grave. When the arresting cop said she must have really hated him, the woman was shocked. "Hate him? I was crazy about him. I'm just crying from the place I miss him most."

Yeah, I know. The joke's vulgar and silly. But guess what? It always cracks me up when telling it, and truth be told, most people at least giggle, if not outright belly laugh. So, if it offends you, get over it.

My name's Craig Luzinsky, and I recently died at age 66 of what my liberal lesbian daughter calls Covfefe-19. Zoe's a smartass, but I don't blame my President. I blame China. Both my parents died at 66, though four years apart. Who's to say I wouldn't have bit the big one at age 66, anyway? I did have diabetes. To quote my favorite President about the hundreds of thousand recent American deaths, "It is what it is." Not wearing a mask or social distancing didn't kill me; it was my heartbreak over the loss of my God-given right to protest those fascist restrictions that did me in.

I am honored to have my favorite leader's signature on my Presidential Memorial Certificate, issued by the sitting Commander-in-Chief to all veterans who died with an Honorable Discharge. God knows what my lefty daughter will do with that noble document. Hope he won re-election.

I'm a Navy veteran with three years submarine service. I earned my dolphins and am proud to be called a Bubblehead, the Navy nickname for sailors who serve on underwater boats. My wish was to be buried in a National Veteran's Cemetery, lying in proud solidarity with my military brothers, although I don't have much use for those Air Force vets who consider themselves military. Most of them were a bunch of wusses, except for the combat pilots. Or if not planted in a military cemetery, I wanted to be cremated (the VA pays) with burial at sea, a proper end for a Cold War warrior.

Neither of my requests were honored. Here's a tip for those of you still walking above ground—avoid seriously pissing off your kids for long swatches of time. I was estranged from three of my four kids, and as luck would have it, the only child who continued to have contact with me was my self-proclaimed "progressive" youngest child, Zoe. I have her to thank for the horrible place I am in today. I can only dream of being buried in a proper graveyard where anyone who feels the need could piss on my grave if they want. I learned in the Navy that urine is sterile.

Every night, the news would run sob stories about how all we Kung Flu victims on respirators have to die alone, without the comfort of family beside them. For Christsakes, we're all born alone, and we all die alone. Suck it up. Who needs a bunch of "loved ones" crowding around your bed, gawking down out at you as you rattle out a final breath and lose control of your bowels? Give me a break. They pay people to clean up that kind of mess.

Zoe and her angry, what she calls "wife," would often visit and argue current events with me. I think I did an admirable job defending myself, as they usually stormed out of my apartment, speechless. I may have won those battles with Zoe and her girlfriend, but damned if they didn't win the war. My environmentally zealot daughter is turning me into a tree. And believe me, it couldn't be further from a green peace. It's humiliating.

Zoe had me stuffed into this biodegradable plastic pod that looks like a giant egg. To fit me inside, I was placed into a fetal position. You believe that? A powerful, manly person like me going out like some helpless naked baby. Hope she's enjoying her last laugh at my expense.

Here's her plan: As my burial pod disintegrates, the surrounding soil gets nutrients from my decaying body, and the tree sapling they planted above me begins to take root. I'm so lucky to have died in one of the 33 States that allows this burial mockery of patriotic, God-fearing men like me who served this nation. I went from a proud former First-Class Petty Officer to a goddamn eternal tree-hugger.

I must be planted in some kind of left-wing pod forest cemetery because there are a bunch of other people down here, and we are all connected in some kind of crowded, twisted network. Most of them look like brown and beige freaks, but some of the women are still pretty hot, though I could do without the smell of our evaporating gasses. In a weird way, it reminds me of being close quartered in a below ground submarine.

A pleasant surprise is how really sweet it can get down here, an added treat for a former diabetic. Every root pumps out a sugar hormone into other roots that often leaves me feeling like a young sailor on shore leave. I did get upset at first when other guys were pumping me full of sugar and not just the ladies, but it's executed with such organized harmony, I can't help but admire its military-like precision. Sue me.

Don't get me wrong. This place is no hippy-dippy paradise like my daughter probably believes it to be. Actually, Zoe's not such a bad kid. She's just mixed up. I don't really buy that she buried me in a fetal position to humiliate me. She probably figured it was something joyful. I used to get tired of her always asking me, "Pops, don't you feel any joy or passion? What gets you excited or curious?" I told her I haven't felt any of those things since her mother died.

When I was a young sailor, I used to eat magic mushrooms with my buddies. I liked them very much, especially all the intense, colorful visions during sex. But the fungi down here (that's what they like to be called), these mushrooms are truly magical. In between my sugar rushes, I get crackling jolts of electricity from this internet of shrooms. These flashes of energy pinpoint exactly how we're feeling. Trust me, it's not euphoria and bliss pulsing in and out of my body. It's most often a melting anger alongside cackling surges of fear.

We are all wired.

And uncertain.

Yet none of us are alone.

Zach Murphy

Zach Murphy is a Hawaii-born writer with a background in cinema. His stories appear in *Reed Magazine*, *Ginosko Literary Journal*, *The Coachella Review*, *Mystery Tribune*, *Ruminate*, *Ellipsis Zine*, *Wilderness House Literary Review*, and *Flash: The International Short-Short Story Magazine*. His debut chapbook "Tiny Universes" is available via Selcouth Station Press. He lives with his wonderful wife Kelly in St. Paul, Minnesota.

437 Wilton Street (A Brick Story)

Charlie's wistful heart tingles as he pulls up to 437 Wilton Street, the apartment building from his childhood. Everything is gone but the skeleton of a structure and the echoes of Charlie's memories. You can board up the windows, but you can't cross out the souls that once occupied the walls.

Every Saturday night, the entire block would light up with a Fourth of July jubilance. Dueling music speakers battled to steal the humid air at full volume. The Ramones shouted to the rooftop. Bruce Springsteen crooned to the moon. And Sam Cooke sang to the heavens.

Out in the street, Rich used to show off his candy red Mustang. Rich thought he was a lot cooler than he actually was. His hair grease looked like a mixture of egg yolks and cement. Charlie hasn't forgotten the time that Rich revved up his ride in front of the whole neighborhood, only to blow the engine. As everybody laughed, Rich's face blushed redder than his broken car.

Shawn was the tallest human that Charlie had ever seen. He dribbled the basketball on the bubblegum-stained concrete like he had the world in his hands. He never did make it to the pros, though. But he did become a pro of another kind. Charlie hadn't heard about Shawn in years until the day a familiar voice spoke through the television. It was a commercial for a landscaping business—aptly named Shawn's Professional Landscaping.

Charlie wished that he were older. Then, maybe he might've gotten noticed by his first crush, Henrietta. He'd often daydream about her curly hair, sparkly lip gloss, and mysterious eyes. Sometimes when Charlie passed by her door, he'd hear loud yelling and harsh bangs. Wherever she is now, he hopes that she's safe and happy.

TJ always treated Charlie like a little brother. He'd even give him extra cash for snacks every single week. Charlie always admired TJ's bright red Nike shoes. One day, TJ got arrested by the cops in front of Charlie's very own eyes. It turned out TJ was selling a certain kind of product, and it wasn't chocolates.

Charlie's grandma cooked the most delicious spaghetti. It smelled like love. The sauce was made from fresh tomatoes she grew on the building's rooftop. Charlie still thinks of her sweet smile with the missing front tooth and the big, dark moles on her cheeks. The cancer eventually got to her. When she was put to rest, Charlie was forced to go into a new home. But it wasn't really a home. The memories from that place are the ones that Charlie permanently boarded up in his mind.

After snapping out of his trance, Charlie picks up a decrepit brown brick from the building and sets it on the passenger side floor of his pristine Cadillac. When he arrives back at his quaint house in a quiet neighborhood, he places the brick in the soil of his tomato garden and smiles.

CW Booth

From a young age, story-telling has been a passion of mine. I not only enjoy creating fictional tales, but I am also passionate about telling other people's stories in order to create a deeper understanding of the human condition. As a result of this, I studied journalism and now work as a radio producer at a children's radio station in Cape Town, South Africa, where I guide children in sharing their own stories. My own fictional stories tend to feature elements of sci-fi, dystopian fiction, magical realism, and the surreal. Aside from writing, I am also an avid reader and hiker - I enjoy spending time in nature with my nose in a book. Travelling and living in many countries over the last 6 years - including Japan and the UK - has broadened my horizons and allowed me insight into various perspectives around the world, informing my writing of fictional tales.

The African Black Eagle

The African Black Eagle took flight. Dropping like a stone from one of the crumbling buildings, before spreading its wings and riding the thermals. The bird flew straight through the hollowed out floor—twisting and turning to avoid the rusted beams that stuck out at all angles. Its dark black feathers and white lines almost glinting in the sunlight as they spread out against the dull red of rust.

Matthew, a young boy with dark skin and short black hair, stared up at the bird with his mouth half hanging open. He'd never seen anything so breathtaking in his entire life. He was surprised that something so majestic and graceful could still exist in the outside world. He twirled the gears of his goggles to get a closer look at the creature as it glided through the air.

A sharp whistle from Matthew's father drew his attention away from the black eagle as it landed on the top-most rafters of a derelict skyscraper—its eyes catching sight of the boy as he ran towards his father.

The deserted city of Old Cape Town stretched out around Matthew as his boots crunched on dry dirt and dust. A gigantic flat mountain dominated his view, making the surrounding run-down buildings appear minuscule in size.

The city had stood empty for the past sixty years as catastrophic weather conditions and rising sea levels had left the land barren, forcing its surviving citizens to adopt a new type of city—a new city that could withstand whatever Mother Nature threw at them, one that was hidden from view.

Matthew helped his father heave a boulder pierced with various iron rods—a now precious metal that could only be harvested from dilapidated buildings. It was the boy's first excursion into the city as a Hauler: workers who brave the harsh environment to scavenge for valuable and rare resources.

As he stood in the back of a battered pick-up truck with sweat pouring down his brow, Matthew glanced back up, searching for the dark wings that had kept him captivated mere moments ago. The bird had once again taken flight, soaring down for a closer look at the strange creatures known as man.

A fierce wind blew and slammed the eagle into a jagged metal beam.

But that wasn't just a mere gust of wind. It was an indicator of another devastating storm. In the distance, an ominous cloud of dust and sand loomed—being driven forward by harsh winds that whipped over the bone-dry landscape towards Matthew and the other Haulers.

A shout of panic came from his father as he climbed into the back of the truck with his son, banging on the roof as a signal to the driver. The old pick-up sparked to life, its maglev wheels forcing the car a few centimetres off the ground. The truck hovered for a brief moment before zooming forward—propelled by the magnetic force of the mid-century roads.

Matthew looked back at the powerful dust storm now heading their way. His eyes scanned the horizon, hoping to see a sign of the bird. A tiny pinprick of black showed him that the eagle had woken and was trying to out-fly the storm. His heart pounding, Matthew urged the bird to move faster. All the while, the truck raced towards New Cape Town—a city hidden within a mountain.

As they neared the foot of the tallest mountain peak, an entryway slammed open, allowing the racing truck to enter before slamming shut. At the last possible second, Matthew caught sight of a dark shape zipping under the closing door and flying up to the rafters.

From its perch near the high ceiling, the sharp eyes of the eagle saw the result of modern man's work: a vast tunnel making its way through the mountain with artificial UV lights acting as realistically as the sun.

The bird cocked its head to the side and saw cosy, compact houses lining the length of the tunnel and disappearing into the hazy distance. A hive of humans buzzed around their manicured gardens—all of which flourished due to the grace of horticulture. No fences separated the houses as citizens mowed their tiny lawns, tended to their vegetable patches, and went about their business under the artificial sun. Flowing water ran down the walls behind the houses—the aquifer was doing well.

Smiling with relief, Matthew hopped out of the pick-up, trying to make out the dark creature that had flown up to the rafters. He had a feeling that this could very well be the last bird of its kind in existence—and he was relieved that it was safe and sound in his city. His father called out to him for help, but Matthew's attention was elsewhere. Placing his hands on his hips, the young boy nodded at the bird and turned away. And even though it might have been his imagination, Matthew could have sworn that the eagle nodded back.

Stella Samuel

Stella Samuel is a women's fiction author whose credits include her novel *34 Seconds,* a short story compilation, *Stories South of The Sun,* as well as several short fiction pieces published in various literary magazines. Stella has been an Alliance of Independent Authors Author member since 2016 and earned her BFA in Creative Writing for Entertainment from Full Sail University, graduating valedictorian. As sole owner of ARZONO Publishing, Stella strives to uplift new writers and help authors create and build their portfolios. With the release of *The 2020 Annual,* she embarked on an annual adventure bringing authors and poets together. When she is not busy publishing and writing fiction or screenplays, Stella freelances for agencies and other authors, offering editing services and coaching. She's also created, developed, and taught a children's writing class for elementary and middle-grade children. Writing or not, Stella is often poolside with her chocolate lab and a notebook.

Lara & Lisa

Few had life figured out quite like Lara Hanson did. She'd lived and loved to the fullest and had let go of pain like water running from the tip of the umbrella above her head as she stood at the bus stop on Tremont Street in Boston. Walking away this time broke Lara. Her brittle soul cracked beneath the three university hoodies she'd grabbed from their closet before snatching Lisa's umbrella from the stand they'd kept by the front door. Her half-smile turned to a frown as she touched the velvety inside of the first hoodie, the only one she wanted of the three she piled on in a fit of rage... no, in a world of pain moments before leaving the old Brownstone on Montgomery. It still smelled like Lisa. Her cologne, the one that irritated Lara when they first started dating, had become the same scent she yearned for as she left their home, the pets they'd shared, and the loving touches she'd dreamed of her entire life.

Fear.

It's what stopped her from moving. Lara, lover of life, embracer of emotion, the woman who had it all together for all the world to see, stood in the freezing spring rain frozen in absolute fear. Four buses paused in front of her, doors open wide, waiting for adventure or simply carrying the passengers of Tremont and Dartmouth to their destinations. Lara didn't have a destination. Fear does that. All-encompassing fear stops everything except a beating heart, and that was the only thing Lara wanted to stop. She had no destination. At least, not one she could arrive by on a MBTA bus.

Her destination was a future alone. Only, she didn't know just how to get there. Lost. Frozen. Incomplete. Questioning. Frozen—literally, even wrapped in three hoodies, and figuratively. Without Lisa, Lara wasn't sure she knew how to accomplish even the basics... life, water, air, smiles, laughter... they all eluded her, instinct taking over as the world turned on its axis and water fell from the sky covering her tear-stained cheeks and mascara lined eyes.

She stood at that bus stop on Tremont Street searching for someone, anyone, who could tell her exactly where she was and where she needed to be. In desperate need of a guide to give her the map to get there, she only noticed no one bothering to offer her guidance, a hug, or even a tissue, for whatever good that would do in the pouring rain. Passersby approached as each new bus stopped. They got on, and those who got off, walked away in the icy cold downpour, eager to reach their destinations. Pushed, poked by strangers' briefcases, rolling bags, elbows, Lara stood her ground. Those were the only human contacts she faced in the three hours she stood in the rain.

Bus after bus stopped. She watched as the 10 stopped in front of her. The doors opened, the driver shielding her face from the wind and rain rushing in, as Lara stood, stoic on the sidewalk unable to decide to stay or go. Brookline wasn't her solution. Maybe she'd wait for the 501, then take the redline back home. Not her South End home, back to her parents, the ones who told her moving Lisa into her brownstone five years ago wasn't the brightest idea. She didn't get on any bus that stopped. There was no bus to take her back home to life with Lisa, the life she loved, yearned to live but needed to leave. The 501 paused without a single passenger getting on or off, then rode off again, flinging dirty road water onto her soaked clothes. Lara stepped back and sat on the wet bench. There would be no more buses, at least not ones that would take her anywhere she needed to or wanted to go. She was her destination.

Just how does one find oneself, anyway?

How did she get to this space? The one where a single scented hoodie was her saving grace, and her faded smirk from under a now stolen umbrella the only definition of herself.

Lara had found herself before. When she left Cambridge, without going far, and came out to her disapproving family. Sure, they loved her. They welcomed girlfriends over the years, even with introductions as their daughter's friend or roommate. They gave Lisa gifts at every holiday and invited her to family celebrations. Before Lisa, she found herself in South End with a small startup company at Copley Square with enough money to buy her first place. She was stressed, poor, and without a girlfriend because she never had the time while dealing with what a disappointment she was to her family, running to an expensive side of Boston, and building a career, for what her measly job was worth. Lara put on a great face to the world. She had her shit together. She was out and proud. She was a homeowner. She had a career. From the outside, she was confident, sexy, and smart. On the inside, Lara, who'd fronted a well-put-together life, was completely broken. Now she was shattered.

***

Lara and Lisa had almost always been... even when they weren't. Lisa said for all the years they'd loved one another, she'd looked for Lara in every person she'd ever met. Every woman she'd dated. Every person who'd crossed her path. Every friend she'd trusted. Living life with pieces of the perfect woman for her, Lisa settled here and there for something good, then better, then this will do. Until on a whim, on a hot summer day, Lisa ran into Lara. Literally, ran into her, spilling iced coffee down both their shirts.

"Hey! Whoa!" Lara shouted as she stepped away from the coffee kiosk on Garrison Street.

Too late, Lisa, jogging and tangled in something, probably her own two feet, tumbled, caught her footing, then crashed, hitting Lara's elbow knocking the large freshly brewed ice cold coffee onto her chest. With an instinctive response, Lara brought the cold drink away from her chest right onto Lisa, leaving them both soaked in coffee and an empty cup rolling down the street.

"I am so sorry," Lisa said as the world seemingly stopped around them.

They each assessed the damage and laughed at the other, cutting through the awkwardness.

The world hadn't stopped for long. "Get outta the road!" They didn't see who'd said the words, but both felt a cool breeze as a delivery bike rode past them.

Lisa reached out her hand and took Lara's helping her up the curb, safe and out of traffic. "I was running... well, jogging, I'm not really a runner. It's just a word I like to use, running. Actually, old ladies with walkers could probably pass me, so I'm not even sure jogging is the correct term either. Anyway, look at me ramble. I'm not sure what was in the crosswalk, but I got tangled in something and almost went down." Lisa looked closely at Lara.

Lara laughed, the left side of her smile peaking upward, just in a small, sweet corner of her mouth.

"I—I'm still rambling. I'm sorry. Can I buy you another coffee?"

The smirk Lara spent a lifetime perfecting widened into a broad smile. "You know..." she started. "I can smell coffee on us both, and I think I'm good now. I could use a new shirt, though. And maybe some breakfast." She pointed to a souvenir shop across the same crosswalk Lisa spilled out of. Next to it, Lenny's Bagels. "How about I get us shirts, and you buy breakfast?"

Lisa stammered. "Umm..." She looked from Lara to the shops, then to the crosswalk and back at Lara. "I'd love that," she finally said. "Yeah. I'd really love that."

The two walked in silence across the crosswalk. Lara stopped and picked up a coiled wire about eight feet long, a tangled mess.

"This is your culprit," Lara said, holding up the long wire, twisting it into a ball, and dropping it into a nearby trash bin.

"I wouldn't be surprised if I wasn't even near that thing. I could fall just because gravity isn't my friend," Lisa said.

"Well, it sounds like you need better friends. I'm Lara."

"Lisa. It's nice to run into you. I mean it's nice to meet you... well, running into you wasn't so bad. Looks like I'm getting a new shirt out of the deal."

"And I'm getting breakfast. The jalapeño bagel with spicy Sriracha cream cheese." Lara playfully smacked her lips.

"And an iced coffee. I owe you another coffee."

"Don't get too excited about your new shirt. I'm buying." Lara held the souvenir shop's door open for Lisa. "So, I get to pick your new stylin' t-shirt." She flashed that sexy half-smirk again.

Lisa pierced her lips together. That smirk—the hottest thing since... well, ever. "Okay. Let's see what they have."

"It's on," Lara said, laughing.

Twenty minutes and two souvenir t-shirts later, Lara and Lisa sat at a booth in Lenny's with a spicy bagel in front of Lara and a sweet bagel in front of Lisa.

"Patience is not a virtue; being legendary is," Lisa said as she read the text on Lara's new shirt.

"Don't you forget it! It's a shame they didn't have any really embarrassing shirts, but the spilled coffee graphic on yours is perfect. We already had shirts with coffee, but that one looks better on you."

Lisa looked down at her shirt with a coffee cup on its side and coffee dripping almost eloquently down the front before wrapping around the side to a tiny cat licking its paws next to a cup of creamer not spilled. She smiled. "It is goofy."

"I think you're probably quite goofy. Am I right?" Lara asked.

Lisa nodded. "You know me so well already."

Conversation about careers flowed with ease. Lara lived and worked near Copley Square, where Lisa worked in non-profit helping abused children, and Lisa lived in Cambridge, where Lara's family lived, and took the redline and two buses to work each day. They sat for three hours in what would later become their favorite bagel shop and place to eat before Lara said she needed to go and let her new puppy outside for a walk.

Their conversation had taken them to pet talk. Lisa had an old cat, one who'd been with her for every break-up since high school. Lara confessed she'd never had a pet, and on a whim rescued a puppy her neighbor found in a drainage ditch just outside of Springfield on a business trip a few weeks before.

"I don't know anything about dogs. I don't know what kind of puppy she is. She's sweet and silly, kind of like you. And she's a handful, probably like you." Lara laughed and flashed her sexy smirk but didn't give Lisa a chance to reply. "She's all black with a white bow tie. Seriously, the only white spot on her is around her neck, and it looks like a bow tie. So, I named her Bowie."

"Cute. I like David Bowie," Lisa said. "So, there's that if no one gets the bow tie reference. Or if she grows, and it no longer looks like a bow tie."

"If she grows! I don't even know what kind of dog she is. What if I have a Great Dane on my hands?" Lara tossed her head back and sighed. "What have I gotten myself into with a puppy?"

"I know a bit about dogs. I can come take a look at her and either calm you down or teach her how to sit her butt on your couch with all fours on the floor."

Lara laughed. "They can do that?"

"Well, Danes can. Beagles, not so much. I'm not yet convinced you know the difference." Lisa balled up her napkin and slid her plate to the edge of the table.

"Well, we're close. If you'd like to come by and meet Bowie, I could use any puppy expertise I can get."

Bowie turned out to be a mutt. A little bit of Australian Shepard, maybe a little bit of Cocker Spaniel. The good news for both Lara and Lisa, Bowie wasn't a Great Dane and never grew over thirty pounds.

Their first meeting turned into breakfast, quality puppy training time, lunch and a beer on Lara's patio that overlooked a beautiful urban garden, and one quiet kiss at Lara's front door.

"We need to work on her jumping," Lara said as Bowie jumped on them both. Lara's right hand pressed firmly against the back of Lisa's head, holding them both in place after their first kiss.

***

Lara and Lisa were living together within a few months, completely in love and ecstatic to spend every spare moment together. Unlike the other women each of them had dated, both women felt they had specially been made for one another. As such, Lara was happy, fulfilled, and completely in love with Lisa, Bowie, and the old cat who clearly didn't feel the same for either Lara or Bowie. Overall, life was beautifully amazing.

Lara continued her mundane role at the startup that had hired her to turn things around before they shut down. It was a high-pressure position and completely out of her skill set. Lara had the drive needed to turn the company around, but she didn't know the industry well enough to have the confidence.

Lisa jogged every morning, tripping in life rather than in crosswalks. Several years into Lisa's career helping others, a political nightmare forced the closing of the center Lisa had poured her time into. Completely confident she and her team were not responsible for the events that unfolded before them affecting hundreds of children and families, she eventually lost everything. Without her job, without a sense of purpose, and lost in South End with only their dog and Lara to lean on, Lisa faced an old familiar battle. In the midst of her fourth week of unemployment, Lisa's funk turned dark. It was the week Lara learned the most about the woman she loved but, clearly, didn't know at all.

***

The freezing rain lifted as a cold wind picked up. Fewer passengers arrived at the bus stop as mid-day approached. Her outer layer wet and her core shaking, Lara turned left on Tremont, leaving Dartmouth behind. If her destination was herself, she wasn't getting there by bus. Home would be the best place to find herself, but home was Lisa and Bowie and an old cat who didn't like her. Home was the wedding that wasn't.

Her cold spring walk led Lara to the Charles River Esplanade, Lisa's favorite jogging spot. Trading the cold metal bus stop bench for a wooden park bench, Lara sat and stared at the water, numb from the cold and from the pain. Boston had always been home. Leaving wasn't an option. And being so close to everything she loved—and lost—wasn't either.

Today, with the freezing rain, a city still closed from a harsh winter, and a lover no longer, wasn't a good day for a wedding. It had been planned. It had been dropped. Forgotten. Push to the side.

Lara didn't bother stopping the tears.

Did Lisa wonder what would have been? If only she'd talked...

Toes in the sand and laughter rippling through the crowd.

Tacos on the bar and drinks passed among many. Their many. Friends, lovers, family celebrating the only love meant to be. Did she miss the breeze on her skin, Lara's thumb on her smirk, their hands touching, fingers intertwined?

Did Lisa know... today they were to say the words that tied their individual ropes into the knot that would keep them safe, together, for all time?

Did she remember? The days of silliness and laughter, of connection and touching. The evenings of long talks and tears, yearning for more, begging the sun to stay behind the horizon where life waited for them to join again.

Not a moment had passed in the years since planning their day of I do, I will, and I promise, did Lara ever think they wouldn't make it. Never a day passed when she imagined not touching Lisa's lips, her crooked smile in front of everyone they loved.

Alone in the cold, wet from tears and rain, ice freezing her heart, mind, body, and spirit, Lara spoke out loud. No one was around to hear. She wanted to scream. As loud as her voice could carry, she wanted nothing more than to let out every hurt her body bottled up inside. Frozen in fear again, she only spoke softly.

"The exact moment my soul touched yours isn't one I can pinpoint. The day I touched your arm? Maybe. Physical touch translated to metaphysical being? I'm not sure. The precise moment I fell in love with you... that I remember."

***

Lara had dated women before, but none as vibrant as Lisa. As goofy as Lisa. As silly or fun as Lisa. None who could wear a ball gown and dance the night away at a fundraising event and roll her long hair in to a messy bun and play soccer the next morning with the neighborhood kids.

Standing from the park bench to move her body and build warmth was instinctive, not purposeful. Freezing rain turned to a light snow. She thought back to that early day just before Thanksgiving when everything she loved crashed down right in her lap without rhyme or reason. Without purpose.

That day, back in November, Lisa came home in tears and spilled information of a new friendship to Lara. No relationship. No affair. Just a lost woman Lara had ignored while building her career and turning the startup company that hired her years before into something amazing, something that she did all alone in a time of economic strife, when otherwise, the company may have shut its doors... in a time when Lisa and Lara may have lost their home.

The walks were all Lisa had shared with her. She'd walked with this woman every day for three months in her darkest days. Lara had no idea why Lisa's days were so dark, why she'd lost her purpose, or even what her purpose was. Lara was busy—with purpose, with a job that paid their bills while Lisa walked around town with another woman.

From there, nothing was the same. Lisa stopped her morning runs with Bowie and spiraled downward again, only worse. Wedding plans stopped. Talking ceased. Even Bowie grew depressed as the worst winter in history settled over Boston. Before the end of January, the city was closed with the third storm in seven days situating itself over Boston, where it also spiraled in hurricane-like formation, calling Boston home for three days. City officials asked everyone to hunker down and stay home unless they were essential. Empty streets piled with snow remained open for emergency vehicles to pass, but overall, like Lisa and Lara, the city was left alone to deal within the confines of its challenges and boundaries.

Valentine's Day came and went, and though the city opened again, neither Lisa nor Lara headed out to celebrate love in any fashion. Barely speaking became comfort for them both. Lara missed Lisa, and they were with one another each day. She missed herself. Winter's hold on the city didn't help Lisa's job search. On top of a poor economy, small businesses faced the harshest times anyone could remember. Rejection after rejection reminded Lisa of just how unworthy she was. Lisa not communicating reminded Lara just how unlovable she was. Just like her father used to say before his belt came off or when he kicked her out for being gay.

Winter started to let up its hold on the city. A warm spring day with sunshine brought Lisa and Lara hope, but not together. Separately, they dealt with their problems. Lisa took a few temp jobs to bring some money in. Lara was promoted twice since she'd helped develop the app that changed her company for better. Rumors among the staff were that she'd be offered a partnership in the company.

Two more spring storms hit, leaving Lisa and Lara homebound again. Close, yet separate. The second storm, hitting on March 30th, quickly turned to rain, making everything slick. The city vowed not to shut down again but asked everyone to remain cautious. By April, Lara was done. Scared. For her safety and for Lisa's.

The last thing Lara said to her lover, the woman she wanted to marry today, Lisa ignored.

"If you don't want me to, I won't say it again. But... before then, please know this: When you close your eyes tonight and ask sleep to take you to a safe place, you are loved; from the deepest spaces in my soul, you are loved. Tell me your boundaries but remember mine, too. My love has no limits when it comes to you. My love for you is endless. I don't need to tell you every day. I hope you feel it to your core. And before you tell me I am no longer allowed to tell you the words out loud, please... for the love of everything we've ever faced together, for the vulnerability that dies on the surface of our lips, for the emotions we've buried for the sake of sanity, soak up these words before I can no longer say them to you... I love you."

It was over. Lisa was gone. Lara knew it yet didn't want to face it. Some relationships can be saved. Some people cannot.

Lisa ignored Lara's pleas. Lara ignored the political scandal that ended Lisa's career and, ultimately, their relationship. In one moment, one swift passing of time, Lara's world shifted forever. Angry that Lisa ignored her sentiment of safety and love, Lara walked right out the front door. Taking ten deep breaths wasn't quite enough to ease her hurt. Never giving up, she walked to the coffee shop and grabbed two coffees to go with a plan of going home and talking. She'd take the day off work, give her entire team the day off so no one bothered her, and she'd spend the cold, icy spring day, the day they'd planned to marry, listening, talking, and loving her partner.

It never crossed her mind that that opportunity would pass her by forever.

***

Bidding farewell to the Charles River Esplanade, to Boston, to a life well lived, Lara pulled her phone out of her pocket, well-hidden and protected from the earlier downpour in her second hoodie layer. She flipped the phone in her cold hands as she walked back to Montgomery Street. She'd have to sell. The cat could stay with the house. He never liked her anyway. Bowie would be devastated.

BOWIE!

Breaking into a sprint, Lara slipped on ice three times, falling hard once. Frozen streets meant few witnesses. Lara laid on the cold ground laughing, thinking of how Lisa would have laughed at her. She would have given Lara a hand to help her up, then fallen herself. That's one thing Lisa did well and often. Fall. Gravity was never her friend.

"Why?" Lara cried. Shoving down the pain, holding in the scream, she scrambled back to her feet. She had to get to Bowie.

As she turned onto the street she'd called home since she left her parents' house in Cambridge after deciding to always be true to herself, she touched one button on her phone and held it up to her ear.

"I need to report a suicide." At the last word of the sentence she'd planned on saying out loud all day, Lara, the woman who had it all together and lost it all trying to keep it together, broke down and screamed. As she opened her front door, Bowie ran to greet her, her paws and left side wet with the two coffee drinks she'd brought home earlier and dropped next to Lisa's body.

"It's back to just us, Bowie. I don't know how to live without her. I don't understand what happened to her. To us. I don't know what to do." She buried her face in Bowie's neck, breathing in her fur, which smelled like her lover.

Lisa's body lie on the bathroom floor next to their closet, the only place Lara found comfort because of the hoodies Lisa left behind.

Everything she'd shoved down came out. As tears. As sobs. As never-ending screams. Her neighbors opened their doors to a frozen, wintry afternoon. Sirens wailed in the distance.

How could she find herself when she was to exist now without the best love she'd ever known?

David B. Barnes

David B. Barnes was born in Cedar Rapids, Iowa and was raised in Asheville, North Carolina. He graduated from the University of North Carolina at Asheville in 1971 and became a patrol officer with the Asheville Police Department soon after. In 1973, he was accepted as a Special Agent for the N.C. State Bureau of Investigation. He retired from the NCSBI in 2001.

In 1988, Barnes began a Master of Liberal Arts degree at UNCA but had to stop before completing the program. In 2017, at the insistence of his wife, he reapplied with the request that his last four courses be focused on creative writing.

Upon graduation with his MLA degree in December of 2019, he began writing short stories for possible publication. *Crosscut*, about a marijuana dealer was his first published piece. It was followed by several more over the next year and into 2021.

Most of his work centers on those who are ignored in our society. *The Mouse, Lost* and *It's just a Start* have been published, and soon, *Paulie's Unpaid Debt* will follow. He has written a few stories that have fly-fishing in the mountains of North Carolina as their setting.

Barnes lives in Western North Carolina with his wife and 13-year-old Lab, Crew.

As he writes about those who are criminals or under noticed by society, he makes no judgments. He simply tells a story.

Battle on the Little Snowbird

On a mild October Monday, I took a day off for a confrontation with Bob. He and I were going to do battle, not the skirmishes of the last months. This was serious business.

***

I was raised in the Western North Carolina mountains and spent hours in the woods walking alongside streams and creeks. These creeks can be narrow enough to step across or wider than a city street. The water can meander downstream or thunder over rocks and rocky cliffs making stunning waterfalls. Sometimes, the water races over smaller rocks causing riffles, giving rainbow, brown, and speckled trout a place to flourish. As I walked the stream banks, I enjoyed the sounds and the deep, pungent smells of the forest. During spring and summer, laurel and rhododendron compete with chigger weed and cardinal flower for attention. The wildflowers are gone in the fall, but smells of galax and skunk goldenrod linger. Distant campfires add to this mix most times of the year.

When I was a teenager, fast water erased most of the anxiety many of us felt. My imagination conjured visions of the Cherokee walking the paths I found deep in the woods. I sometimes found dry stack walls, gray rock stacked with no mortar, that at one time surrounded apple orchards of settlers. Often, a reminder of past life would rise from the leafy earth in the form of an old chimney. Always these walls and chimneys were within easy reach of such streams. I wondered if the Cherokee and others who lived here thought of the streams the same way I did.

As my adult life eased along, I added fly fishing to my walks near the fast water. One cannot seriously use flies to attempt to catch trout and think of anything else. If a mind wanders, there's rhododendron, laurel, and other vegetation lining the water's edge that will catch errant fly line and remind the angler to pay attention to the task at hand.

***

A little over a year ago, Bob and I had our first encounter. I was sitting on a rock at the edge of a riffle on The Little Snowbird in Graham County, North Carolina. The weather was warm for late September. The shade of trees alongside the creek was still substantial. There were hints of fall in the yellow leaves of tulip poplar, reddish tint of dogwood, and gold of hickory. Some of the younger oaks and walnut trees were also beginning their color changes indicating surrender to winter. I had been walking in the stream, casting, mending line, and catching little. A large rock streamside offered a bit of sunlight and a place to relax. The shaft of gold light upset the cool feeling of the shade of the streamside trees, providing me a bit of warmth while I took a break to light my pipe.

As I lit the charring light, my eyes naturally drifted to the woods on the other side of The Little Snowbird. Initially, my attention was focused on how the area had begun to recover from a recent forest fire. It hadn't been bad as these things sometimes are but bad enough to see scarring and new growth.

What the heck was that? At the bottom of my line of sight, I thought there was a flash of silver and gold in the water. I sat upright with a start.

If that was a trout, it was huge. If that was a trout, it was resting where a big brown should be. But that wasn't a brown. That was a big rainbow trout, a huge rainbow.

I stared at the edge of the stream. I could just make out where water had carved a kind of cave, or shelf, under a large rock on the other side of the stream. The water flowing by this shelf was smooth. It was a steady flow, like water in a lake. But out just a bit and upstream about six feet was a large rock that caused the stream to split. While the side nearest the bank was flowing calmly, the opposite side was fast water, running down a couple of rocky outcroppings similar to mini waterfalls. The fast water then transitioned to slightly slower, shallower water called riffles.

Bigger trout stayed in the deeper edges of the riffles. They had no need to compete with the smaller fish. Bigger and smarter meant they hid behind rocks, under leafy overhangs, or at the edge of stream banks. Smarter meant harder to catch.

I maintained my position, left leg flat; right leg bent at the knee; left hand on the rock; my left arm was straight and maintained the third part of this lopsided tripod. This monster would see movement on my part. He would know I was watching. He would know why.

I slowly puffed on my pipe, all the while staring at the water's edge on the far bank. A red-headed woodpecker banging a dead pine on the bank didn't distract me. At my sight's edge, I saw squirrels playing tag and cardinals watching me from deep inside a stand of burn scarred Balsams. But I focused on the water. After what must have been an hour, I saw the big guy three more times. I wouldn't try today. I would be back though.

A week later, I returned. The water in this part of the high country is as clear as the finest glass where it flows smoothly. In the fast water, the edges are clear, but the main run is full of water being jostled by rocks and mixing with air. It becomes opaque just for that time it interacts with the rocks and the downward race of the streambed. I was going to fish the fast side of the rock above the big trout's lair. I was wearing felt bottom boots so I wouldn't slip on the streambed rocks.

After approaching the stream, I figured I was about five feet below the big trout. Staying in the shadow of an overhanging White Pine, I flip cast the dry fly, tippet, and fly line past the rock and into the flow of the water. This would bring the fly past the big rock with the fast running water and into the slower pool near the undercut bank, arriving just outside the closest riffle.

The fly landed perfectly. I mended line keeping it tight. It rushed through the small waterfall. I almost lost sight of it in the roiling water. Then it popped out and slowed down. The stream was running quickly, but the water was deep and smooth.

Suddenly, I saw a splash of water, and the line took off toward the shelf under the bank.

Good Lord Almighty, he took it. I've got him!

I shoved the rod up and pointed it to the heavens. I pulled in line, ignoring the reel, just letting it drop to the water as I pulled inch after inch toward me. The trout fought hard as he realized he had been fooled and was now in danger. He jumped clear of the water twice. Each time, he flipped his tail toward the tippet and snapped his head back and forth. The second time, he rose from the water as though he were a ballistic missile. He came straight up from a deep pool. As he rose, he turned to look at me. At the apex of his jump, two things happened within milliseconds of each other. He flashed his side to me showing the bright red cheek of a huge wild rainbow. The red was brighter than a cardinal. Then he slashed his tail toward the tippet I'd been keeping so very tight. Using his tail, he snapped the tippet in two, and he was gone. It was really just as well because I had neglected to set the hook. Still, it was maddening.

I'm a grown man and hadn't thrown a real temper tantrum in ages. I threw one right then. I cussed and looked at the heavens, asking aloud, "Why?... why damn it!"

Of course, no answer came, and I slowly calmed down. I climbed out of the water and sat down on the rock that served as the roof of the big trout's lair.

I pulled my pipe out of the inside of my vest and lit the tobacco. I knew he wasn't going to be tempted to take another fly today. As I slowly calmed down, a thought came to me. That fish needs a name. I rested my back against the rock and puffed away. All the time, my gaze was looking at the bright blue sky and then the darkness of the burned woods. Here and there, shades of green were climbing from the earth as the trees and bushes continued their recovery. What name would be worthy?

It came to me as I watched a red tailed hawk circling and screeching. A good friend of mine had passed away suddenly. He was the outdoorsmen's outdoorsman. I'm calling that rainbow Bob.

Over the next months, I tried to catch Bob a dozen times. Sometimes I couldn't tell if he was still in that spot or not. I'd cast and get no movement. Just when I thought he was gone I'd see a flash from the little cave and a tug on my line only to see him scurry back to safety after spitting the fly. When I thought he was gone, I was sad. When I knew he was there and wouldn't take the offered fly or wouldn't move at all, I yelled at him that he was a coward or that he was doing this just to irritate me.

I know all of this sounds strange. But if you've never had a Moby Dick issue in your life, there's no way to understand. Take it from me. It was exasperating.

So, on this fine October morning, I drove purposefully to my favorite pull off on The Little Snowbird. It took me a good three hours to get there, and all the way over I planned my assault on Bob. A number 12 Elk Hair Caddis fly would be my first attempt. I'd been using various sizes of Royal Wulff dry flies to this point.

I pulled over at my spot; put on my vest, waders, and felt bottom boots. I made certain to have my pipe, matches, and tobacco in a waterproof bag. I adjusted my brimmed hat and tied my fly, tippet, and leader to the fly line. I started walking, holding the fly rod handle, so the rod trailed and wouldn't readily get hung in the brush. The closer I got, the faster I could hear my heartbeat. By the time I got to the stream's edge, I had to sit and calm down. After ten or fifteen minutes, I stood and prepared for battle.

This part of the adventure demanded a cautious approach. I knew if Bob didn't take the fly in a few casts, I'd have to wait before trying again. If he saw me, he wouldn't take it at all. For this first try, I didn't dare get into the water. I cast from the bank over the top of Bob's cave. Nothing happened. Usually when Bob was this way, I just left and fished upstream; not today. I sat with my back to a half burned hickory tree, loaded my pipe, lit it, and relaxed.

An hour later, I decided to step into The Little Snowbird and cast upstream right into the water on the calmer side of the big rock. The fly hit the water and floated nicely. I kept mending line to keep everything tight. I could see the fly clearly, the bright tan of the fly against dark brown of the stream bottom. It floated within inches of where I thought Bob would be.

Bob attacked that fly as though he were furious with it. He suddenly realized what had happened and began a run. Upstream he went. I went with him, pulling in line. Downstream he ran. He tried to break the line on some rocks, but I was ready for that trick and got him to deeper water. We fought like enemies for half an hour. Bob finally showed signs of tiring. I was pretty sure I had won. My battle was soon to be over.

A strange sadness fell around me. All the times I tried to catch Bob, there was never a thought of what came next. It had always been about the competition between him and me. What was I going to do now?

As the seconds passed, I knew he was too tired to continue. He was a big trout. What a trophy to hang on the wall in my office. Those bright red cheeks were something I'd never seen before. People would see him there on the wall and ask all kinds of questions. What a conversation starter he'd be.

I pulled him closer and saw his tired eyes and his slowly moving body. He had given up.

As I got Bob near my net, I began talking to him quietly.

"Bob, you are one hell of a fighter. You and I have had some of the best times for the better part of a year. Each time we competed against one another, I learned something new about fishing. Did you have any idea that you're a teacher? Did you have any idea how badly I wanted to catch you? What the heck are we gonna do now?"

As I pulled the line bringing him closer to the net, I made my decision. Bob never went into the net. That would have been demeaning for such a fine opponent. I flipped the fly from his mouth and turned Bob around so he could see his cave. At first, he moved very little. He was getting his bearings and maybe wondering what was going on. Then a flash of his tail, and he was gone.

I still come to the big rock over top of Bob's cave. Bob might still be there, or he may be gone now. I sit on the rock, smoke my pipe, and remember the battle and the skirmishes that came before. Memories are far better than a trophy hanging on a wall.

Tom Larsen

Tom Larsen has been writing fiction for twenty-five years, and his work has appeared in *Newsday*, *New Millennium Writing*, *Best American Mystery Stories*, *Raritan*, *Puerto del sol* and the *LA Review*. His novels "Flawed" and "Into the Fire" are available on Amazon. Mr. Larsen just signed a two-book deal with Dark Edge publishing and his novel "Going South" will be released this summer.

DARK AND STORMY NIGHT

It was summer when he finally showed up. Larry worked the night shift then, and Nicole was still a baby. Gina was at the kitchen window watching raindrops plink the puddles when she heard a rumble outside the front door. She knew right away it was him, though she could never say how. There were always cars idling in the street at night, boyfriends of neighborhood girls giving it one last shot, suburban kids copping a bag. They cursed too much and laughed too loud, and their flashers kept her up at night.

This was different, she could tell by the sound. This one moved down the street at a crawl, and as it paused outside her door, she saw a match flare inside. Her first impulse was to grab Nicole and run, but something held her to the spot. She watched the headlights sweep across the yard as he turned into the driveway. Instead of stopping at the garage, he pulled the car behind the house, killed the lights and the motor, and sat listening to the radio. Basie, she thought, or one of those swing bands he favored. A sound she hadn't heard in years.

When he got out, Gina's heart was pounding so loud she could hear it. He circled to the front of the car and opened the hood. She could see rain roll off and over his back as he fiddled inside. Whatever was wrong, he fixed it quickly then stood staring up at the back of the house, still tall and rangy in leather jacket, jeans and work boots.

Six years since she'd heard a word.

She opened the door before he could knock.

"Hey, Gina. It's me, Pete. How's my girl?"

"I'm not your girl."

He had an answer for this. She could see it in his face. But the words wouldn't come and instead he just stood there blinking into the rain.

"I'm in a fix, kid."

"You go to hell."

"I got you something." He pulled a small box from his jacket and handed it to her. Good N Plenty's, half empty.

"Jeepers, thanks, Dad." She turned and tossed it in the trash.

"It's short notice, baby. Hell hounds are on my trail."

"Where's Corrine?"

"Back in Florida with her mom." He shrugged. "I guess she couldn't hack it anymore."

The news didn't hit like it should have. Corrine was the reason he'd left them flat, and Gina always prayed she'd get fat or die. From the time she was a girl until it didn't matter anymore.

"You can't stay here."

"Is that what you think? Gina, honey, you got nothing to worry about. I just want to see my grandchild. Then I'll be on my way."

She'd let him stand there until he was soaked, doorknob warming to her hand, steam rising from the hood of the car. This was nothing like she thought it would be.

"Look, Gina, I know you don't want anything to do with me. I used to think someday I'd make it all up to you. I don't know. When you're young, you believe anything's possible. You know what I'm saying?"

"I learned a long time ago to leave it alone."

He glanced away, following the taillights of a passing car.

"OK. I guess I always had an unrealistic view of life. I can understand why you hate me."

"Hate you? I don't even know you."

Just the way she'd always rehearsed it, studying her reflection in the mirror for the perfect look. Proud and contemptuous, the glib tone to cut to the quick.

"Yeah, well, it's probably just as well."

Gina just looked at him.

"How is she? The baby?"

"She's asleep. Thunder had her up half the night."

"I'd be grateful if you'd let me in for a minute."

"I told you to go to hell." She pushed the door shut, and that was that.

Except he wouldn't leave, wouldn't even get back in the car. For over an hour, he sat on the stoop, letting the rain pour down on him. She watched from upstairs, biting hard on her lip to keep it together. Seeing him stirred up memories she'd kept buried for years. Not forgotten but sealed off in a part of her heart she'd put off limits. The night he showed up in a limo full of presents. God only knows where they came from, a portable TV for her and a tricycle for Bette, a diamond pendant and earrings for their mom. They'd driven to the shore that very night, passing through those sleepy Jersey towns like desperados, hitting the boardwalk just as the sun was rising. The police picked him up the next day at their beachfront hotel. Her mom pawned the jewels for the cab ride home.

So long since she'd let herself drag it all up, but time had failed to dim the image. Her recollections of him were as worn and dog-eared as an old paperback.

"It's not the feds I'm worried about. They're like elephants. You can hear them coming a mile away."

"I don't want to hear this, OK?" She was still angry with herself for letting him in.

"Sorry baby," he gave her that crow's feet grin. "Tell me about your husband. Does he know about me?"

"He knows you ran off. The rest doesn't really bear mentioning."

He laughed. "You always did have that sledgehammer touch."

"Larry's a good man who loves his wife and kid. End of story."

"What about you? Do you love him?"

Leave it to Pete to ask the one question she couldn't answer. What she had with Larry was good, but she'd seen love burn as hot as fire.

"Larry and me are doing fine."

"I should shove off before he comes home."

"He doesn't get off for a few hours yet." She poured him more coffee. "I thought you wanted to see your granddaughter."

"More than anything in this world."

"How'd you find out about her?"

He took a single bent Camel from his shirt pocket and rolled it straight on the table.

"I looked up your sister when I was on the coast. I told her I was coming here."

"Bette didn't say anything to me."

"I made her promise not to. I figured the less time you had to think about it, the less likely you were to shoot me."

"I'm partial to knives, actually."

Again, the grin. "Bette said you had a hard time of it. With the baby, I mean."

"Yeah, well, they come into the world kicking and screaming. If they knew what was out here, they'd think twice about it."

"You can't really mean that."

"You can't smoke in here."

She led him down the hall to the baby's room. Nicole lay sleeping on her stomach with her hands balled in tiny fists. He reached down to touch her head.

"So much hair for such a new baby."

"She gets that from Larry's side. That and her temperament."

"What does she get from you?"

"Fear of thunder. I don't know, flatulence?"

"Your mom used to swear she never once broke wind. She claimed she didn't even have an asshole until she married me."

Gina had to laugh and laughing made her think of what this must look like. Three generations of Perkins in the same room. It had never occurred to her that this could happen, and now that it had, she could feel the tug of kinship, sweet and unbearably sad. He was running out of time or he wouldn't be here.

"I'd wake her, but there'd be hell to pay."

"That's fine. I just want to look."

He stroked the side of the baby's face, running his finger from cheek to jaw line. Gina couldn't help herself. She moved up close and brought her hands to his shoulders. Pete was all skin and bone compared to Larry. Lowering her head to his back, she breathed him in, leather and smoke, the flesh of her flesh. It was all too much for her. She was already crying when he turned and took her in his arms. Folded her away just like a real dad.

"Baby, don't," he whispered in her ear.

"I can't help thinking it could have been like this," she sobbed into his jacket. "I just want to hear you say it could have been like this. Please."

"Gina honey, you're killing me."

"SAY IT, DAMMIT!" She broke away, pounding his chest like a B movie spitfire. Pete twisted away from her, stumbled off a few steps, then crumpled to a heap on the floor. He lay gasping on his side, and she could see the blood through his open jacket.

"OH MY GOD! YOU'RE HURT!" she shrieked.

He rolled to his knees and hugged himself against the pain. His face was pale and sweaty, and she was certain he'd die right there on the spot. Instead, he pulled himself up slowly by the baby's crib and turned to her with his right hand raised.

"It's not as bad as it looks." His grin faded to a grimace. "No more hitting, OK?"

She did what she could for him, cleaned the wound, then closed it up with a box of butterfly Band-Aids she found in the bathroom. He'd wanted her to stitch him, but her hands were too shaky, and her stomach wasn't up to it. Pete sat at the table talking non-stop while she dressed him with Pampers and wads of duct tape.

"Who knows where they come from? I've known some bad boys, but these guys are murder. I thought he was just a card cheat."

"What guys?"

"Skip tracers. They contract out to bail bondsmen for a percentage. Do yourself a favor, baby, don't ever jump bail."

"Here, hold this." She handed him the scissors and worked the tape over his shoulder. "You should be in a hospital."

"I must be losing my feel for people. Back in the day, I would have smelled him out in a crowd. Thing is, he had intellect. The man read Gaddis, for Christ sake!"

"You knew him?"

"We ran a high stakes game in Reno. He beat the bushes, and I fleeced the bunnies. He knew he had me anytime, so he rode it out."

"So, he's a crook too?"

"He's a bounty hunter. Mostly they're ex-cops or mercenaries. A hell of a thing to do for a living."

"Do they work with the police?"

"Not if they can help it. They might serve notice, but they don't carry a badge, and they don't need a warrant."

"How much you owe?"

"Enough to make it worth their while. But it's not like you can just pay them back." He pulled the bloody shirt back on and leaned forward in his chair. "There's no negotiating, believe me. And they're not like cops. They love what they do."

"Maybe you should turn yourself in."

"I've been tempted, if only to cut them out of the deal."

She stuffed the scraps of tape and diaper in a plastic bag and crossed the kitchen to the trash bin.

"Don't." He reached out his hand. "I'll take that with me when I leave."

"You're hurt pretty bad, Pete. You need a doctor."

"Got one waiting for me down in Knoxville. His eyes aren't what they used to be, but he still takes my health insurance."

She knelt by his side, took his hand, and held it to her face. Might be she'd never see him again, and she wanted to take in as much as she could. She touched his fingers to her own cheek, then turned his hand from front to back. The knuckles of his thumbs were swollen with arthritis, but his nails were clean and freshly manicured.

"Stay the night. I'll tell Larry you're an old cousin or something. I don't think you'll make it to Knoxville."

"I appreciate it, honey. Thing is, these guys have eyes and ears where you'd never expect. I'm OK as long as I keep moving."

"You don't think they'll come here, do you?"

"Nobody knows I have family. I go by different names. Before I left Reno, I made a few calls to an old pal in Tahoe. With any luck, they'll be dropping in to see him."

"Gee thanks, old pal."

"I meant that figuratively." He gave her a wink.

She made him breakfast, scrambled eggs and bacon done crisp the way she knew he liked it. Her mother had never been much of a cook, and she left the kitchen work to her daughters as soon as they were able. Gina remembered making breakfast for Pete and his cronies. She'd get up early and arrange everything on the counter, then watch cartoons until she heard them pull up outside. She'd make cheese omelets or French toast with orange juice and plenty of strong coffee. The men shoveled in all she could make, plying her with praise and proposals of marriage. They may have been crooks, but they treated her like a queen, and there were always a few bucks on the table when they were through. Sometimes they'd sing to her, doo wop harmonies from when they were boys or one of a half dozen drinking songs, a morning serenade that would carry her through the whole day. Then they'd leave in a swirl of laughter and cigarette smoke, pulling away with horns honking, long after the other dads had gone to work. When she thought of him, she thought of mornings. When he left, just the skillet could bring her to tears.

"Was Bette glad to see you?"

"Hard to say. I know she was surprised."

"What's her place like. I've never been there."

"Nice place. Her hubby's rolling in it. Funny thing is, I did some work for his father back in the seventies. He had a few shipments go bad on the docks, and he needed them to disappear."

"But she met Jack at Cal."

"What can I tell you? It's a small world, kid."

She thought back to the globe he gave her one Christmas, black oceans and green continents with a pin sticking right out of New Jersey. Shit was coming from everyplace now.

"So what, you've been living out west?" she asked him.

"Nah, the coast doesn't suit me. Too much sun makes a man simple."

"This thing in Reno. When did it happen?"

"We left there over a week ago. He waited until Chicago to make the bust. Had me handcuffed to a motel television, so I picked the lock. About this time yesterday it was. That's another thing. I gotta get rid of that car."

"You took his car?"

"It's a rental. I'll drop it off in Knoxville after I see the doc."

"What did you do to him? The bounty hunter."

"He'll be alright. Too bad, though. We could have cleaned up in Branford. The kid had some class."

While she did the dishes, he studied a map, tracing his route with a yellow highlight pen. Outside, the rain had stopped, and the sky was turning gray. The car in the yard looked cold and forlorn and it pained her to think it was down to this for him, a stolen car, a vague destination. She saw his reflection in the window as he came up behind her, and she knew she would always look for him there.

"You're right, Gina. It could have been like this." He kissed the top of her head. "I got my share of regrets, that's for sure."

She turned and looked him in the face. "Will I ever see you again?"

"Honey, there's no doubt about it."

Lightning flashed outside the window, and a loud crack of thunder shook the dishes in the drainboard. She slipped past Pete to check on the baby. Nicole was looking straight up at the ceiling, gurgling on a mouthful of fingers. More thunder rolled right over top of them, breaking off somewhere to the west. Still, Nicole did not cry. Gina couldn't know it, but years would pass before she'd see her baby cry again. And then only when they buried her Grampa Pete.

She picked up Nicole and wrapped her in a blanket. The baby's smile seemed to light up the room. Gina searched her daughter's face for signs of crow's feet, but the baby's skin was as smooth as satin. Lightning flashed as they made their way up the hallway. When they got to the kitchen, he was just driving off.

Cynthia Stock

Throughout my forty-year nursing career, I pursued writing through UT Dallas, SMU, The Writer's Garret, and Writing Workshops Dallas.

My short stories have appeared in *Memoryhouse*, *Shark Reef*, the *I Am Strength* anthology, Lunch Ticket's a-la-carte site, and HerStry. Most recently *The Manifest-Station* accepted a piece of my CNF. My first novel, **The Final Harvest of Judah Woodbine** was published in 2014. My nursing memoir, *Clocked Out: A Nurse's Life After Hours*, is a work in progress.

At sixty-nine, I pursue reinvention.

The Father-Daughter Dance

I dipped my hand into the water and pulled back until my thumb grazed my thigh like Dad taught me. My body surged forward. I kicked twice to maintain momentum as my arm arced through the air like the wing of a gull. Dip. Pull. Glide. Kick. Arc. I heard Dad's voice in the mantra, coaching me decades ago to finish one full lap. I made time for this before I caught the plane to see Dad, not knowing it would be the last swim before he died.

At 3 a.m., I knocked the phone off the nightstand in a mad scramble to answer the kind of call that comes at that hour. An empty wine glass and a copy of *When Breath Becomes Air*, defiled by dog-eared pages, accompanied the phone's free fall onto the pile of scrubs I wore to work that day. Don't hang up. Don't hang up. Snarled in the sheets, I found the phone. My hands jittered.

Before I managed to say, "Hello," a professional, anonymous voice, took charge of the conversation. I'd made innumerable calls like this; I did not like being on this end of the conversation.

"First of all, don't panic. I'm your dad's nurse at New London Memorial. He's okay right now. Are you The Swimmer? Your mom told me since his surgery, he calls you The Swimmer."

"I'm Lily, his daughter. What's wrong?" I sat up, my mind and heart in overdrive.

The nurse's voice softened. "I know it's late, but your dad was so agitated. He kept saying 'The Swimmer' over and over. I thought it might calm him to hear your voice. I'm in his room."

Three months earlier, my parents flew from Connecticut to check out my new life in Texas. I cried when I saw Dad. "He looks so old," I whispered to Mom.

His hair glistened, short, spiked, and white. Bones sculpted harsh angles in his previously well-rounded face. The way his eyes roved uncontrollably made me wonder what he saw that made him so afraid. With time, we learned something more virulent than aging devoured his energy and cognition.

"I'm going to hold the phone up to his ear," the nurse said.

I tried not to cry and held back the words I wanted to scream. Stay with me. How many times had I snorted with disdain when I heard the same directive uttered to a wounded victim or fellow officer on an episode of *Law and Order*? No words changed Fate. Life or death happened regardless of prayers or bargains struck with omnipotent beings. Stay with me.

"Dad, it's me. Everything's okay. As soon as I can fix my schedule, I'm coming." I mashed the phone against my face as if that would make things clearer, as if he could smell me and sense my urgency.

The nurse's voice, hollow now, coached Dad to speak. "Do you want to try and say something? I can tell by your face you know it's Lily." Sheets rustled and something knocked and scraped the phone.

"N-n-need The Swimmer." A huge sigh escaped, the cost of his effort.

"Did you hear him?"

"Put the phone by his ear one more time." I counted ten seconds and pictured the nurse's hands nestling the phone between the pillow and his cheek. "Dad, I'm coming."

I packed blue jeans, t-shirts, running shoes, and shorts. If I couldn't swim to de-stress, I always found a place to run. An oversized t-shirt cushioned my meager beauty supplies and other essentials. Kalanithi's book fit into my oversized purse. I looked around my room and wanted to remember each thing in its own place. I tapped the top of the bobble-head nurse Mom gave me for graduation and repositioned the ceramic nurse angel holding the Serenity Prayer etched in glass, a Christmas gift, also from Mom. "Good-bye." I sensed change in my future.

My index finger hovered over my bookshelves until I found a worn gold paper spine, The Little Golden Book of The Wizard of Oz.

Dad taught me to read using the now dilapidated treasure. With my body curled against his, my human hammock, he read the story and deliberately skipped words until I corrected him. He'd wait until I pointed at the word and sounded it out. Eventually I read the story to him from cover to cover.

Twenty-six years old and I still had both my Barbie dolls, my favorite stuffed bear, and all the letters my different boyfriends sent me. Dad and I were cut from the same mold. He hid a box with every birthday card I ever gave him in his workshop. One Christmas, he bribed me into going to a pro-football game with him so he wouldn't be alone by promising to let me wrap him in tinsel and take a picture. He kept the picture with his cards.

I tucked the Golden book in my suitcase.

***

I figured now that Lily worked in a hospital, my stench, sweat with a hint of mold like a well-worn tennis shoe, wouldn't bother her. I wanted to die but couldn't tell anyone. The sentence formed, then fragmented into a mess of puzzle pieces tossed in a box, leaving my mouth a wasteland. Broken connections. Sometimes. It takes me. A while. To find. The Words. I needed Lily. She, who propelled me through the frozen tundra of my marriage, would fix this, too.

My wife, Janine, fulfilled her obligatory marital duties. She played her roles well. For a business gala, she stunned my colleagues in a stove pipe dress of splashy sunflowers against a green background. The dress complemented the unique shade of her red hair. Every Sunday, she set formal place settings for a plentiful, but bland evening meal. The almond scent of cookies she hand-pressed onto baking sheets symbolized Christmas. After Lily was born, Janine performed all the required tasks. She performed care without caring. I soothed Lily's skin when the eczema drove her to tears. I ran her bath and washed her hair until, just like that, Lily insisted she was too old for such nonsense. Janine lurked at the periphery of our family. She watched but didn't engage. She buried her love as if it would betray her.

The headaches began months ago, and I thought, "Jesus, man, you've got to tone down those power-lunches and those all-night sessions of bridge and bourbon."

The day my best friend pulled a chair up to my desk for lunch, and I couldn't say his name, I knew I was in trouble. I pretended to straighten my desk and appraised the man before me. His curly black hair receded, leaving his bald pate aglow in the fluorescent lights. Brown eyes shone through black wire frame glasses. His nose, a perfect line, flared if something excited him about work or football or his family. The New York accent and the pasta fazool he always brought for lunch saved me. Amusing, intelligent, Italian. His name was Joe. I mastered the art of stalling. My brain linked style quirks, body type, task performance, and tone of voice come up with the names of guys I'd known for decades. For a time, disease fostered brilliance, until it neared its end game.

Within weeks, I couldn't even retrieve the names of those I loved. I never spoke my mother's name again. Rose. A big woman. Taller than all her brothers. She taught herself math by counting on her fingers. She fled the farm and landed a job as a cashier in a department store. She made German pastries from scratch, yeast, and cinnamon her trademark perfume. I could see her and smell her and taste the memory of her desserts, but when I tried to say "Rose," my brain played Scrabble with the letters and her name came out "The Strong One." I dared not try to say "Lily" fearing I couldn't manage my own daughter's name.

"Mid-life crisis," diagnosed the first doctor. He scribbled on the prescription pad. Valium. "Job stress. Receiving a pink slip after devoting your best years to a corporate behemoth can do that to you."

Good point, Doc.

Some expensive test Lily learned about in nursing school found the tumor. After the surgery, the doctor explained a glio-blast-it-all-to-hell-something grew like crabgrass in my brain. The microscopic invader rooted and destroyed. Expressive aphasia. I knew everything I used to know. My thoughts no longer had an efficient outlet. Now I wasted away until my dentures jiggled on my shrinking gums. Fetid saliva dried and laced a path down the side of my mouth. A tube in my bladder drained beer colored pee into a clear plastic bag. Lily. Get here.

***

I dreaded visiting Dad. I hadn't seen him since his surgery. Mom acted like the surgery was Dad's greatest human failing, a crime that needed to be kept secret.

"It's private," she would say.

A nurse for three years, I still conjured the sweet, yet foul, bouquet seeping from the shallow breath of the first patient who died under my care. It taught me the human body revealed death's presence without words, as clearly as lines on the palm of the hand portend a life story to a fortune teller. I knew empty eyes stared from a flaccid body. The slow leak of life infected the air with a signature smell, fermented and stale and subtly repugnant, an odor that made you want to cover your mouth when you inhaled.

I peered into the room. Dad's body barely filled half the narrow, metal-framed hospital bed. The cancer downsized his once robust physique.

Prior to his surgery, I saw Dad vulnerable only once. My first summer home from college, I lost my job as a lifeguard after mouthing off to my supervisor when he commented on my ass. Dad supported my income-ending assertiveness. He and I shared an intolerance of arrogance and misogyny. Days without purpose transformed hours into eons. Dad, as an official "starter" for NCAA swimming meets, received an invitation to a sports banquet recognizing local athletes.

"Come on," he said. "Go with me. It will be fun." He grabbed my shoulders the way he did the day I left for college. Playful, yet commanding. His touch communicated a plea.

I never asked why he didn't take Mom or why she didn't volunteer to go. Nor did I question his desperation. I knew a lot of the athletes, even dreamed I might score at least one date that summer. "Sure."

The banquet took place on a revitalized river boat. We boarded. I trailed behind while Dad shook hands and made small talk with sports officials and local coaches. I recognized many of the boys, marveling at bodies transitioning to manhood. Broad shoulders, trim hips, creased slacks, their feet no longer bare and tanned or housed in flip-flops, but with business-formal, polished shoes.

I smoothed the fabric of my carefully selected dress over hips as slim as most of the young men. I longed for the state I usually fought, invisibility, until I realized these boys might not recognize me in clothes. They had only seen me in the second skin of my racing suit. The river splashed smelly, brown water against the hull of the boat. No throwing myself overboard.

"Dad. I'm gonna sit right here." From a table for two at the entryway, I could see, but not be seen.

Dad nodded. To my surprise, he walked back and sat down with me. I stopped watching the boys-men and watched Dad. He scanned the room. When a swimmer named Randall Budde walked by, Dad extended his hand. "Hey Budde." After all the years Dad stood at the side of the pool, dedicated to getting a race started with precision, he merited a perfunctory three-second handshake.

"How are ya'?" A swirl of air followed Randall as he and some of his friends rushed past Dad to the tables up front.

Dad propped his elbows on the table and clasped his hands. I noticed his out-of-style black framed glasses. An ink mark from a pen streaked up from his pocket. The family crest on his pinkie ring was almost worn away. His survey of the room lost its focus. I didn't just see a light go out in his eyes. His whole being dimmed. Distress wormed through my body and wiggled in protest of something more discomfiting than the cheap folding chair on which I sat. I looked away and felt sorry for my Dad. The center of my universe. Ignored. Diminished. He knew it.

When he avoided eye contact with me and toyed with his ring, we silently shared an understanding. Those young men had moved on. Someday, I would too. I would leave behind the smell of the popcorn he made in a dented Revere Ware pan and the sight of him turning a steak on his Weber Grill with snow flurries powdering his head. I would leave behind the one person who made it clear I could be anything. I wished I never agreed to go with Dad.

I stepped toward the hospital bed.

***

The day I taught her to swim, God let me find her name. I know her name. L. It starts with L. She stood on the edge of the pool. Fearless. Ten stubby toes curled over the rough concrete edge. She nailed me with a look that said, "I trust you."

"Come on, Lily girl." There. I found it.

Lily swung her arms back. A grin revealed small pearls of teeth. She hesitated. I counted three, four, five seconds before she started to swing her arms up to the sky. She squatted. I watched the muscles in her thighs tense and thrust, propelling her into the air and over the water. I had no intention of catching her. I knew she would swim.

Lily bobbed in the water. She flailed but shooed me away when I reached for her. The water distorted the pumping of her legs. She sculled with her hands and hovered with her head well above the surface. "What now?" Drops of water shimmied and sparkled in her hair.

"Come here," I said and reached out a hand. Lily grabbed it. I pulled her to me until she floated horizontal in the water across one of my arms. "Show me."

Lily mimicked the strokes she'd watched me take and started to kick. Her body took off. I let my arm fall away. Lily swam for the wall. She became one with the water. I watched her hand grip the gutter.

She threw her head back and yelled. "I. Can. Swim."

The next time we went swimming, Lily tugged on my hand. "Teach me to jump off the board."

I freestyled to the middle of the pool and tread water in the shadow of the lowest board. "Do it the same way you did when you jumped from the side. I'm right here." It was my turn to pump my legs and hold my arms up. Silence. Thump. Thump. Thump. Lily took a running start.

"Eeeeee!"

The diving board dipped less than an inch from her weight. A fireball of red nylon, Lily in her new racing suit, flew over my head. Her body created a crater in the surface. The sun bejeweled the eruption of water. I grabbed onto the board and dangled by one arm. My stomach lurched; my testicles shriveled. A lifetime passed before her head appeared.

"That was great," she shouted.

Lily didn't look for me. She raced to the side of the pool, climbed out, and stood in line at the board.

I retreated to a lounge chair and watched. Repetition convinced me she would be okay, whether I watched or not. I pretended to read the newspaper.

After one jump, Lily took her time surfacing. A muscled, pubescent boy cannon-balled into the water. He landed right where I expected Lily to come up. I leapt to my feet and sprinted to the pool. Every worst-case scenario entered my head. I imagined the silence, the toxic stillness of life without Lily, without her signature little girl smell of cherry cough drops and baby shampoo. Her voice ripped through the air.

"You idiot. You're supposed to watch for the diver in front of you. That's the rule." She slapped the water and splashed the boy as she scolded him.

That's my girl.

"Sorry," the boy mumbled.

The two swam to the side of the pool. Lily arrived first and clamored up the stepladder. Sun-painted skin radiated a startling golden sheen. Her chubby body and domineering little girl voice let me peek into the future and glimpse Lily, the woman.

My girl strokes my head, not trying to iron the wrinkles out like she did when she was young. Her fingers flutter across my forehead in one smooth motion.

When she touches me, I understand the way dust feels when it rains down and settles on treasured, neglected possessions.

Now that she's working, Lily doesn't swim like she did in college. She swims for exercise, and the smell of chlorine lingers on her like The Strong One's cinnamon.

In competition, Lily would climb onto the starting blocks, look over her competition, and shake out her arms. I loved her long, sinewy swimmer's muscles. She performed the same ritual every race. After throwing her towel onto a chair behind the block, she sucked in a breath of air and exhaled through pursed lips. With her toes curled and clenching the edge of the starting block, Lily poised for the gunshot. Bang.

Lily flew off the block, a graceful arrow slicing the water with hardly a splash. Once she broke the surface, her arms churned. Her legs kicked with the rhythm of a right-sided breather. She tore through the water as if chased by demons. My girl.

***

I watched Dad and waited for proof of life. It came, a whispered "pah" as he exhaled. Air whipped through open hospital windows. The curtain between the beds snapped and fluttered like an angry ghost.

When I was little, Dad chased me through a white forest of sheets pinned to a metal tree, branches of thin wire, wooden clothespins the only nuts it would bear.

"If those sheets touch the ground, you'll both be doing the laundry for a month," Mom hollered from the kitchen window.

Dad winked and growled. The sheets shielded us. Dad stalked me, the monster clamoring after the prey. I darted in and out of my make-believe world.

Dad loved to play games with me. For Ping-Pong, Dad built a standard table that filled one room of the basement. He taught me the basics. We volleyed easily until I got a feeling for the weight of the paddle and how to control the ball. He was patient, but I knew he itched for real competition.

Dad let me win an occasional game to keep me interested. I assumed other dads played sports with their daughters. I never asked myself what Mom did while we played. I never heard her in the kitchen at the top of the stairs. She never indulged in a game. Dad and I populated our own exclusive playground. He expected maximum performance. I had to deliver.

One day, I rocketed a serve Dad couldn't return. Our volleys ran for minutes on end. Sweat dribbled down his neck. If I scored, he moaned. I flexed my legs, waiting for his serve. I was on fire. Dad's face gloated when the game ended.

"I didn't let you win that one. You earned it."

I recognized the pride in his voice.

I pushed aside the curtain as I neared the bed. "Dad." I wasn't in the basement anymore.

***

I heard Lily call to me. The pressure in my head and the pain medicine slurred the word, "Daaaad." I wanted to answer. I understood the pain of silence.

When she was fifteen, Lily stopped talking to me for a month. It happened during the year her mother and I sent her away to train for the Olympic Trials. My lean, blond-headed, smart, and moody, heart-on-her-sleeve daughter dared to leave the safety of her known world. I thought I was having a heart attack from the pain bursting in my chest.

"You don't have to go," I blubbered.

Janine remained silent, satisfied in a way I'd seen when she finished a "to-do" list. I couldn't let Lily leave without saying something she'd remember. "You look so good." Not "I'm going to miss you" or "I love you." Such a fool. I blamed myself for her departure. All the games. All the pushing. All the celebration when she succeeded.

Away from home, Lily fell apart. She attended swimming practice twice a day and maintained her grades. But on the phone, her voice sounded lifeless. She admitted she'd gained some weight and couldn't sleep.

Powerless from the miles between us, I threatened my girl. "If you don't straighten up, I'll fly out there myself and bring you home." I never wanted her to go. But. I. Never. Went. To. Get. Her. Lily. Her name is Lily. Isn't it?

After that, every time Lily called home, she refused to speak to me. I'd orbit around the phone by my wife's ear, listening to muffled tones.

"Does she want to talk to me?" I'd mouth.

Janine shook her head "no."

My moments of joy with Lily forgotten, I relived every mistake I'd made. I regretted the day I offered no sympathy when we raced bicycles onto our gravel driveway. In her effort to beat me, Lily fell and skidded in the rocks, shearing the skin on her legs. Red beads gathered along the skin tears. Grit freckled her leg. She picked up her bike. Her red face belied her effort to hold back tears.

"I was going too fast."

I should have hugged her. Instead, I bragged that she didn't cry.

Holding the phone to my ear, Janine ordered Lily to speak to me. The absolute silence sickened me. I couldn't even hear her breathe. Bile crowded my throat. "Lily?"

***

"Dad?" My voice is hushed but steady.

When I was fifteen, I didn't talk to my dad for a month. I don't remember why, but I wielded the cruel power of silence and felt righteous. I left home to train for the Olympic Trials. I asked myself why any parent would send a child away. What mother wouldn't want to share puberty and boyfriends and secrets with her daughter? Who would my Dad play with when I was gone?

At the airport the day I left, Dad hovered around me. He read the departure schedule again and again and stroked his chin between a thumb and forefinger. His splayed hand settled on the small of my back. I coveted his touch. I waited for him to say something, something I wanted to hear but couldn't say myself.

"You're so grown up." A look of shock spread over his face, as if until he spoke those words aloud, it never occurred to him. His eyes brimmed. His mouth pressed into the trembling seam.

"I love you, Dad. I'll make you proud." Make me stay. I wanted him to be selfish, but Dad let me go. I couldn't tell him I didn't want to leave. He should have known. Our inability to ask for what we wanted punished us both.

I walked in on Mom sitting next to Dad's bed reading.

"I hope you don't mind I borrowed your book?" She held up the Kalanithi. "I love this quote you marked. People will say great things about him, once he's gone. This is not exactly light reading."

"It helps me at work. In my job there's recovery, and there's survival. It helps families to know the difference." In three sentences, I told my Mom more about my work, and myself, than I had in three years. "Why don't you take a break? I'll sit with Dad."

With Mom off to the cafeteria, I began to make up for the month I lost those years ago. I rambled about John, the boy who took me for a ride on his motorcycle and Russ the marine who took me for walks and the miles and miles and miles I swam until my fingertips turned to pink raisins and my back looked more muscled than a football player's. One month of stupid things, the minutiae of a teen-aged girl's life. Through my words, I hoped Dad would see it all.

***

I listened to my girl describe her days away. She enjoyed freedoms she didn't realize I would have denied her. How monotonous the swimming must have become for someone like Lily, thank god her name keeps coming to me, who immersed herself in so many things. Inside I cringed and laughed, mourned, and celebrated everything I'd missed.

Lily came home from her year away on the cusp of adulthood. She'd stand with a hand on each hip, accenting her new curves. If I'd start to talk, she'd cross her arms and make it clear she was no longer receptive to my truths. Home turned into a battleground.

We faced off in front of the fireplace, yelling and shaking our fists. I saw a younger, female version of myself, stubborn and more-than-likely arguing for the sake of discussion. Politics? Drugs? Sexuality? It didn't matter. In the past, Lily retreated when her emotions reached a point where she would lose control or displease. No longer. Our verbal sparring escalated.

Lily leaned toward me, cursed me, and gestured with an extended middle finger for emphasis.

There Lily stood, a stranger in frayed cut-offs and a faded t-shirt with some distorted cartoon character marching beneath "Keep on Truckin'." Anger personified. The white pockets hung below the edge of her jeans and lured my gaze to her muscular thighs. Her words sucker punched me. This outlander, struggling with her identity, hid my real daughter, the one I captured in a picture, my little girl in a pink bonnet amid a cluster of daffodils. I stammered. "W-w-well, screw you."

***

It became routine to walk alone down the hospital corridor to Dad's room. The nurses acknowledged me as "one of their own" and promised me time alone with Dad. Mom sipped coffee in the waiting room. My presence seemed to absolve her of facing the horror of Dad's condition.

I paced around Dad's bed. Starting at his bedside table, I trudged a "U" shaped path. The nurses' call bell sat at the top of the bed, coiled like a snake ready to strike but out of reach. A denture cup with its top flipped up, empty for the moment, seemed to yawn with anticipation of what it would eventually receive. In a few steps, I curved around the end of the bed, stopped, and stared at Dad. One of his hands rested on his forehead as if in salute to his pain. The time that passed between each of his breaths suggested time, itself, could not be bothered moving forward. I watched. I counted. I stood, a statue in a sepulcher of silence, a part of me as near death as my father.

When Dad finally took another breath, I waited for the next one. And the next. I wished I could cry or scream or hurt someone. I pushed my emotions into my mental safe room, hoping courage and self-control would keep reality at bay. Silver slivers from voluptuous gray clouds streaked the windows.

I remember the same kind of rain slicked back Dad's thinning hair the night I came home late from a date with a young man I'd picked up at summer school. Dad never met him. My date drove around the horse-shoe shaped lane to my house. The glare of the headlights ignited the watery rivulets of Dad's raincoat as he stomped along the side of the road.

"Do you know who that guy is?" my date asked. He slowed the car. "Who the hell would be out in this?"

"It's my dad." I shrugged. "Stop the car." I jumped out, leaving the passenger door ajar. Water soaked my hair and teased its way down my neck. Dad marched up to me. Steam swirled above his head. Water beaded on his glasses.

"Dad. What are you doing out here?" I felt the mix of rain and mascara trickle down my cheeks. My dress stuck to me like one of my swimming suits. "I left a note." I waited. Dad started to take off his coat. "Stop. I don't want it. Talk to me. I'm a big girl." I heard a car door slam. Tires jettisoned pebbles as the car pulled away. I felt relieved. This drama needed no witness.

"At least let me cover you." Dad opened his coat. "Lily, parents are a sorry lot. We want our children to grow up. But we, no, I am so afraid to let you go out into this world." His body quaked. He stifled a sob.

I lunged and tried to shove him. He stood rock solid. "You let me go once when I didn't want to go. You threatened to come get me. You didn't. Why didn't you come?" I'd be damned if I'd back away. The ragged grimace of Dad's face told me I felled him with the keen blade of my rant. I stepped in to hold him up.

We hugged, cloistered in his raincoat. Dad felt cold. Remorse set in for the hurt I had inflicted. United in our odd embrace, we swayed in the rain, a father-daughter dance. The downpour seemed more a shelter than a storm.

I let my hand skim over the fuzz growing back on one side of Dad's scalp. I touched the horse-shoe shaped scar behind his right ear with one finger. His upper denture peeked from between his lips in a macabre smirk. My hand shook as I slipped my index finger between his lips. I hooked it along the hard resin gum line of the plate and pulled. Strings of saliva hung between it and Dad's mouth. I wrapped Dad's teeth in Kleenex and put them in the denture cup on the bedside table. "I'm sorry, Dad, but you could swallow these." It was easier to be a pragmatic nurse than a grieving daughter.

The moment Lily removed my dentures, I knew. With a simple gesture, she spoke truth. She dried her hands on her clothes and burrowed them under the sheet to find mine. Before I got sick, dry skin on my palms prickled and scratched. One of the nurses slathers me in lotion every night.

Lily sandwiches the new softness of my hand between hers. She kneads my palm with her thumb. My little girl is crying. Don't cry, Lily.

I can't believe Dad's bear paw of a hand. Soft. Not one hang nail. Not one callus. The worry wrinkles between his eyebrows gone. His sunken cheeks glow smooth and clean shaven. A wet sound gurgles in the back of his throat.

Suddenly I'm six or seven. I find abandoned baby rabbits in our backyard and drag Dad to the nest of writhing pink creatures. "Can we keep them?" I beg. "We can feed them with doll bottles. I'll do it myself." I tug on his arm. "Please."

Dad squats. He gathers my hands in his. "Lily, either their mother abandoned them, or a hawk carried her off. They'll die no matter what." Dad saunters off to the garage. I run into the house, crushed.

Standing at the back door, I look out. Dad holds a shovel. His body quivers like a heat mirage. His muscled figure lifts the shovel and pounds the ground. Once. Twice. I lose count and plug my ears with my fingers. Nothing mutes the sound. Thunk. Thunk. I run into the house and hide in my closet. When I emerge from my mourning, Dad tells me he buried the bunnies in a box beneath the willow tree. I make three crosses out of pipe cleaners to mark the graves.

***

"Dad? What can I do?"

I order my eyes open. They flutter. Up. Down. Open. Shut. Open. I see my Lily, hair a blaze of blonde, eyes that are mine, a chin she inherited from her grandfather. I focus my energy on the last functioning remnant of my speech center. I bargain with a power I discounted for a lifetime and beg to be allowed to let Lily know I am present. I barely manage to lift my head off the pillow. I tilt my chin to my chest. I look at her and snapshot the face I won't see again. My tongue presses against the top of my mouth. Sounds emerge. "The Swimmer." I say, "It's great." My head falls back. She came. Now. I. Can. Go. "Oz."

Dad's last word cues me. I pull a chair next to his bed and pull out The Little Golden Book of The Wizard of Oz. "Long ago, a little girl named Dorothy lived on a farm in Kansas…." When I turn the page, it falls away and flutters to the ground. I close the book and throw it in the trash. I bow and press my forehead against his hand.

I grab the extra pillow from the foot of the bed, hug it, and bury my face in it. Tears dampen the batting. Bending, bending, my back tenses. I shadow Dad's face with the pillow. A sour smell overpowers peppermint mouthwash. It wafts up my nose. I kiss Dad on the lips, a chaste kiss, his warmth a final surprise.

"Great things will be said." I press the pillow against his face. My hands feel the contours of his chin and brow. His hands barely lift off the bed. He manages to pat my hip twice. His legs thrash, then settle more quickly than I expect. His head never moves. It is my twenty-fifth birthday. I fluff his pillow and straighten his head. His lips curl over his toothless gums. I place the call near his hand, ever the good nurse.

Weeks later, I drive down an asphalt road once comprised of dirt and pebbles. I pull the car onto the grassy shoulder. The past and present compete.

When I was ten, Dad drove us down the same road. The tires set off dust devils and shot rocks into the high grass. We arrived at a sparkling lake where people milled around folding tables. "You're going to do an open water swim," he announced. One table displayed awards for the race. "10 and under" was etched into a large sterling silver bowl.

Common sense kept me swimming near the rope that marked a half-mile. When a huge snapping turtle's head broke the surface five feet from me, I took off. My arms stretched over the water, dipped in, and pulled. My legs kicked up a storm of white water. To my surprise, I took that bowl home.

From the seat of my car, I watch the sun dapple the water. My cell phone makes the sound of a train whistle to announce a text. I read: "We need to talk about your Dad. Call me. Mom." I turn off my phone and shove it into the glove box.

The water beckons. I set the bowl on the shoreline and test the water. It's cool but tolerable given the heat of the day. Holding the bowl with both hands, I wade in up to my knees. The water teases my skin. I raise the bowl over my head and spill the ashes. White and gray dusts my arms and hair and face. I heave the bowl as far as it will go and start to swim. Dip. Pull. Glide. Kick. Arc.

Gary Campanella

Gary Campanella first remembers screaming when his sister's hair caught fire as she leaned over a jack-o-lantern to see the candle inside. He was three and she was two, and they were sitting at the kitchen table of the small apartment their parents rented in Springfield, MA. They were alone in the room, but their father raced in and smothered the flames against his bare chest. Gary was given credit for saving her life, something he reminds her about every Halloween, just before she reminds him that he screams like a girl.

He began a decade of traveling when he left his native New England for college in Wisconsin, then journeyed west, where he walked from Mexico to Canada on the Pacific Crest Trail. From Canada, he kept going, traveling extensively through the U.S., Europe, and Asia.

After surviving Y2K, he decided to get serious. Between April 2000 and September 2002, he moved to Los Angeles, got a good corporate job, got married, bought a house and a dog, and had his first child. He now has two children, two dogs, and a bigger house.

In 2014, he began writing. In earnest. He has completed manuscripts for a novel, a memoir of that Pacific Crest Trail adventure, many short stories, and a chapbook of poetry. He is writing like his sister's hair is on fire. He is writing before he forgets.

Gary Campanella writes fiction, nonfiction, and poetry. His work has appeared in many print and online publications. He lives and works in Los Angeles.

A Tale of Two Jodys

The first person I look up to when I return to Milford on some business I'm conducting is my old best friend, Jody. I've been away and mostly out of touch for years, but he's the one guy from the old gang who's still around, just like I knew he would be. Jody is one of those guys who will never leave the town he was born in. He is one of those guys who likes it that way.

The first thing I notice about Jody is how he looks like the small town politician that always wanted to be. The second thing is how he is pretty much the same guy that I remember from high school. He's like a friggin' time traveler.

Jody is a talker, and right away, he starts talking about things that happened twenty years ago in high school. He talks about them like they happened yesterday. They're almost all things that I forgot about, but I nod and look interested. After a story about a girl who just got married to some guy we went to school with, I say, "Sorry man, I just don't remember them."

To which Jody says, "Petey, you don't remember Sherry Anderson? Dude, you went out with her once."

I say, "Sorry, man. I really don't." And I really didn't. Which I guess is also strange, if I really did go out with her.

Jody is a big Italian guy, about 6'2", and he's putting together this barrel-chested, pot-belly look that goes well with the three-piece suits he thinks are back in style. He's losing most of his hair, but not his booming laugh or his habit of buying drinks for anyone sitting within ten yards of him. That might not be the perfect image for a School Committee Member, which Jody currently is, but you have to understand that Jody is in this thing for the long haul. I call him the King of Milford.

As Jody tells me, between interruptions, the School Committee is just a steppingstone to bigger and better things, like Selectman or State Rep. He tells me a confusing story about waiting for someone's brother-in-law to step down, or run for something else, or something like that, so he can run for Selectman in the next election. This is when some guy comes over to us at the bar and buys him a drink for no reason. "It's good to be the king," I say, my own drink held high.

2.

My name is Peter "Petey" Flynn, and I don't come from Milford. I come from Charlestown, which is a small town inside of a big city, that city being

Boston. I'm not truly a "Townie," which is what Irish people from Charlestown are called, because my father moved us out to this awful Italian suburb when I was ten. I moved back to Charlestown later, after I quit school, which for me was two years of partying at UMass. Now I'm kind of a Townie with an asterisk. Like Roger Maris. Though, I'd rather be dead than be a Yankee.

My grandfather and his father and so on, back a few generations, were Townies. They called Charlestown "the neighborhood." My father was the first to leave. He went "lace curtain" on the neighborhood, choosing not to be a cop or a fireman or a priest or a bank robber. He was a dentist, which to the neighborhood was pretty good, just a hair below those other jobs. He calls Charlestown "the old neighborhood." I grew up calling Charlestown "where I come from."

Where I actually grew up was Milford, Jody's town, which is a small town in the woods of Southeastern Massachusetts. Then and now, Milford is the start of the beaten path to Boston. Any further out, and you're too far to commute. It's where the Charles River starts too. It is the last outpost of civilization before you get stuck in the swamp towns of south-central Massachusetts or, even worse, Rhode Island.

Being back here doesn't feel great. I'm like a fish out of water. Everything seems small, and not just because I'm bigger, but because everything is really friggin' small. The roads, the buildings, the sub shops. The afternoon before drinks with Jody, I'm downtown between this tiny bank branch, a tiny insurance office, and the Town Hall that feels like a middle school. In between, I can't remember if I'm supposed to just jaywalk across the street, which I do and get beeped at, or wait at the crosswalk while hardly any cars go by, and I feel like an idiot. I've just got to get my shit done and get ought of here.

3.

Like Jody, Milford is stuck in the 90s, maybe even the 80s. It's Friday night when we meet up, and so we meet at a local bar where people play darts and listen to a DJ. The place is packed. The DJ is spinning classic rock records in the far corner. I meet Jody up at the bar where he shouts loud enough for everyone at the bar to hear over the music, "Petey Flynn, the wandering traveler returns!" He introduces me to the bartender, "Darbo, this is my oldest and dearest friend!" He buys me a double shot of Jack Daniel's. He tells the dozen or so guys at the bar about how I played high school ball for Milford, and that I once stole home in a playoff game.

I haven't thought about that in years. "I missed the sign," I say. "The coach chewed me out after the game, even though we won."

"That was Ducky, right?"

"It was. I wonder what happened to him?"

Jody knew, of course. "He moved to Florida. Died last year. Heart attack while mowing his lawn. You remember how fat he was. God rest his soul."

The area behind the bar has tables and chairs and is like another room. A half wall with fake plants hanging over it blocks it off from the rest of the bar and creates a little sound barrier. People sit and eat bar snacks and talk over all the Bob Seger. Jody leads me through the crowd, new drinks held high and greetings all around, to a table in the corner where sits a pretty girl smoking a cigarette inside the bar. This is Jody's girlfriend.

Jody's girlfriend's name is also Jody. Sparks fly when I meet her. Literally. She's smoking a cigarette inside the bar, and I smack my bar glass into it as I try to free up a hand to shake with her. Sparks and ash from the cigarette shoot high in the air and into my drink and across the table.

I strike up an instant rapport with my friend Jody's girlfriend Jody. I notice that this makes my friend Jody a little nervous, which of course, is ridiculous because I'm not going to hit on someone else's woman right in front of him. And I would never do that to an old friend like Jody. Besides, even if I would, I'm not in Milford to cause any trouble. I haven't been there in years, and I won't be coming back once my business there is settled.

4.

"You really make an entrance Peter Flynn."

"Call him Petey," Jody chimes in. "Everyone does."

"I don't know if I like that," she smiles.

"It's okay," I say. "It could be a lot worse."

"That's true."

"Yeah," Jody says. "Remember Horsenuts?"

I laugh and shake my head. "I don't think so."

Before my friend Jody tells me who Horsenuts is, or if I am Horsenuts, his girlfriend Jody says, "That doesn't sound like such a bad nickname."

We laugh, and my friend Jody beams, and I can tell he's into her. It's good. "I got a story about a nickname," I say.

"Do tell."

"We hired this new warehouse guy a few months back, and when I introduced him to all the guys, he said, 'My name is Kevin, but you all can call me Hawk.' And this guy, Bob, who works there, he's been there the longest and is kind of the leader of the crew. He doesn't miss a beat. He says, 'What'd you say? Cock? You want people to call you Cock?' And the guy gets flustered and says, 'Hawk. I said, Hawk. Everyone calls me that.' And Bob says, 'Cock? Okay. If that's what you want. But it doesn't sound like that great a nickname.'"

The female Jody says, "He's right. That's not a good nickname."

"I'll say. Everyone still calls him Cock. It just goes to show you that you can't pick your own nickname."

"I guess," she says.

"So, like I said, I'll take Petey any day."

My friend Jody had stepped away when I started the story, which is something he's been doing since high school. He tends to disappear when he's not the center of attention. But he soon returns with more drinks. He says, "I just talked to the DJ. He's gonna play Pearl Jam for you."

"Great."

"You remember driving down the Cape in the summer. I had that old Camaro. We used to blast that one Pearl Jam CD all the way there and back."

"I remember."

"By the way, did you check out Jody's car in the parking lot?"

"Dude. How would I know her car? Is it an old shit box Camaro or something?"

"That's funny—" she starts to say, but my friend Jody interrupts.

"It's the silver-blue Corvette with the T-Tops."

I, in fact, did see it. It was parked right at the entrance, under the floodlight. We're all sipping drinks pretty liberally by now, and I say, "Sweet ride. What kind of work do you do, Jody?"

The other Jody answers. "She's a Vet Tech at Milford Animal Hospital."

I keep addressing the other Jody. "They pay you like a hundred G for that?"

She laughs again. And again, my friend Jody answers. "Hardly. It's called savings, Petey. Being smart with money. Ever heard of that?"

"Can't say I have, old friend. Can't say I have."

5.

The drinks keep coming, mostly thanks to my friend Jody, a new one bumping into the old one before it's finished. Jody and I we are drinking VO and water, which is all he drinks, and which I think is hilarious. Vet Tech Jody drinks vodka and grapefruit, which also seems pretty retro.

After a few more, they talk me into playing darts. They both have their own darts, which I didn't know anyone had, with little wallets to carry them in, and extra "flights," the little feathers at the ends. They kill me, even after they explain the rules to me.

As expected, my friend Jody dominates the conversation, and for whatever reason, he decides that telling embarrassing stories about me is the theme of the night.

"Hey, Jody, did you know Petey once got suspended for calling the art teacher a bitch?"

"That didn't happen."

"It did. You don't remember it? Miss Black said, what did you say? And you didn't even deny it."

"I don't think that happened."

Or later, "Hey, Petey, tell her who you took to prom."

"I don't remember."

The female Jody jumps in. "Sure, you do. Come on." She's clearly enjoying all the badgering.

"Okay. Let me think—"

"He took his cousin. He had just broken up with his girlfriend Carla, the big love of his life, and so he decided to take his cousin, and she ended up meeting some guy there."

"I don't remember that part, Jody, but I do remember Carla. Whatever happened to her?"

"She married Bert Bertnazzi. You remember, the 'Nazi.' They moved to Worcester. Her parents still live in town. I talk to her dad all the time. Should I say something for you?"

"That's okay. It's ancient history, Jody. Ancient history."

After a while, we sit down again and have even more drinks. They are clearly watered down, but they're also taking their toll. The female Jody keeps smoking in the bar, and I want to join her, but I look around and notice no one else is smoking. I don't smoke a lot, but I can't resist when I'm drinking, so I asked her if she wants to smoke one with me outside.

My friend Jody says, "Sure. You guys go. I'll get more drinks."

Outside, I ask Jody how long she's been in Milford.

"A year. I had a bad breakup. I got the car out of it though."

The air outside is late summer cool, but it doesn't feel that way with all the alcohol in my veins. She says, "I moved here to be closer to work."

"You like work?"

"It's a good gig." She has a way of looking at you when she answers a question that's like she's asking a question back. It isn't quite flirting, but it's in the neighborhood.

Back inside, I slow down my drinking, but it seems like neither of them do. We stay until after the place closes. My friend Jody goes behind the bar and makes a pot of fresh coffee like he owns the place, and we talk with the bar staff until it's time for even them to go.

Out in the parking lot, I decide I won't even try to drive home. Instead, I drive a couple hundred yards to a motel. They want 150 bucks for a room, so I end up sleeping in my car.

Too early the next morning, I start driving home. I'm still a little drunk and definitely hungover, and I wonder why I do these things. Still, I had a pretty good time in my high school time warp.

I still don't get Jody and Jody as a couple. They don't quite fit together. They'd be reaching for each other's hands at different times or distracting each other with little surprise kisses on the cheek while the other is trying to talk. We are all about the same age, but the two of them seem to be different ages. The male Jody, who I grew up with, is an adult. He is an adult's adult, always trying to act like an adult, and he's been that way since we got out of middle school. In high school, he was the guy selling football betting cards and getting the questions for next week's test. He was also the guy who was never around when shit went down. It strikes me as typical Jody to learn that he now drinks only VO and water and that he doesn't tolerate the use of drugs in his presence. This last point is maybe prudent considering his ambition in local politics.

One thing I do remember is that when we stumbled out to the parking lot, Jody and Jody got into their car, and as I was walking to mine, I noticed that they were kissing in the front seat.

6.

There's a two-week span between my first encounter with Jody and Jody and my second encounter with the repetitive couple. As good a time as we had, I don't make the thirty-mile drive to Milford unless I have to, and my business doesn't call me out there again right away.

My business is to settle the affairs of my aunt, my mother's sister, who never married but followed her sister and my father out to this suburb years before. She was the only one who never left. She died and left me the condo, and so I am closing her accounts and cleaning up her stuff.

On my next visit to town, I stay for a week in the condo, cleaning, painting, finding new homes for all her stuff, and setting up for an open house. I also commute back into Boston for work, and so it is several days before I get around to calling my friend Jody.

When I do, Jody tells me that his girlfriend Jody likes me and that they want to set me up on a blind date with her roommate. Now I know from that first night that Jody's roommate is a biker chick who hangs around with Milford's biker crowd. I suspect it's the remnants of the same biker crowd I knew in high school when they first got their leathers, and none of them had motorcycles, and they all lived with their parents.

In my mind, I picture a plump chick in a halter-top, but I say okay because I am hanging out in town, and it beats watching TV. What the hell, I think, maybe she'll be cool.

7.

So, the night comes, and I go out with Jody and Jody from Milford, and their roommate, Siobhan. Right away, I see she's an odd choice for a roommate for Vet Tech Jody. She's a lot younger and kind of a punk, a small, thin kid with pinkish-red streaks behind the ears of her brown hair, which is cut short. She is somewhere in her twenties. When my friend Jody and I walk in to pick them up, she's curled up on their beige leather sofa, smoking a filterless cigarette and watching cartoons.

I think she's stoned, and so does my friend Jody because he introduces us with a stiff and out-of-place formality that I think is kind of hostile. Siobhan ignores him and sticks out her hand for a firm handshake. Then she sits up and offers up a place next to her on the couch. I oblige as Jody opts for the Lazy-Boy across the room, and we wait for his girlfriend to appear.

Siobhan is dressed in a sleeveless Nirvana T-shirt, a band I have seen live. I think she wasn't even born when Cobain offed himself. She knows them like I know friggin' Elvis.

I say, "Nice t-shirt," or something like that, and she reaches across the coffee table and flicks an ash into an actual ashtray and then blows smoke into the area between Jody and me.

She says, "They were pretty cool. I don't listen to them much, but when I do, I remember how great they were."

She strikes me as too young for me to even be in the room. I feel a little creepy but decide to go through with the date. I was recently in a club with a bunch of teeny boppers and told the friend who dragged me there that it felt kind of creepy being there, and he said the best way not to appear creepy is not to be creepy. So that's what I decide. I ask Siobhan what her favorite bands are, and she rattles off a few bands I never heard of.

She has a compass tattooed high on her left arm, by her shoulder, and she wears tight jeans and work boots and has a black leather biker jacket draped over the back of the couch like it's waiting for us to leave. "What's the ink about?" I ask her.

"It's in case I get lost," she says. I laugh.

Jody says, "A compass tells you where you are, not where you're going," missing the point.

And Siobhan says, "If where I am is lost, then at least I have a compass."

"Good point," said Jody, and he kind of rolls his eyes, and I have to remember that he's the one who suggested this thing.

8.

When the female Jody walks out from the bedroom, she's wearing jeans and a loose-fitting shirt with a light blue floral print that looks like the couch I just sold from my aunt's house. My friend Jody is wearing a suit, of course, but without a tie, while I wear my black jeans and black shirt and black socks and black shoes. We must have been quite a sight, thrown together like castaways. We roll into a chain restaurant and have cocktails and appetizers and make small talk about Charlestown, and Boston driving, and music.

Afterward, we return to Jody and Siobhan's apartment for a good old Milford night of TV and pizza. Jody and Jody recline awkwardly on the couch while Siobhan removes her shoes to reveal toenails painted red and sits on the carpet near me, against an easy chair where we split an ashtray. During commercials, she lightly interrogates me. She asks what my job is, and how I like living in the city, and if I have roommates. Like my friend Jody, she likes playing adult too. She is smoking her cigarettes in her own apartment without self-consciousness, and she pauses when she is talking to snuff them out consciously, hard and completely, before matter-of-factly returning to what she was saying. "You been to the Royale?"

"Not since it was the Roxy. You been there?"

"Not yet. Supposed to go in a few weeks."

She offers me a beer.

"Sure. We got a few minutes, I think."

"Yeah. Jody was just getting out of the shower when you showed up."

She tells me where they are in the fridge and to help myself. I say to Jody, who is ignoring us now, watching TV, "Dude. Get me a beer."

"Go fuck yourself."

So, I get up. "Anyone else?"

Siobhan says, "No Thanks," and lights another cigarette.

"Sure. I'll take one," says Jody.

Asshole, I think.

While we wait, Siobhan asks what it's like in Charlestown, and I explain that it used to be dangerous for strangers, but it's now pretty tame. She nods her head wisely, like she knows what I mean, though I know she doesn't. I like her. It's kind of like she's just getting used to being an adult, and she likes the way it feels. I think this is why she seems to rub my friend Jody the wrong way because Jody is the kind of guy who is scared that he isn't very much of an adult, or even very much of a man, so being an adult is a chore for him, a thing with rules, a thing to keep his guard up about.

Because of all this, there is some nervous tension in the room. It's like we all held our cards, but no one is showing. There is Siobhan and Vet Tech Jody entertaining two men in their apartment. There is my friend Jody, who is starting to think that he's found Mrs. Right. And there is me, less invested than the others but still kind of weirded out by being back in Milford and wondering what is on Siobhan's mind.

Still, we all have a fine time, thanks to the female Jody, who is basically a brat, and who likes to keep everyone laughing.

When we decide to order the pizza, my friend Jody, the big Italian, will only order pizza from one particular place, and that place doesn't deliver, and so he and Jody leave, and Siobhan and I are alone. There are a few minutes of awkward TV-watching silence, and I feel a little ridiculous sitting with her on the floor. During a commercial, I reach into my jacket and pull a joint from my cigarette pack. We smoke it outside on the landing, then laugh together like two little thieves for the rest of the evening.

We eat the pizza and later watch Saturday Night Live. Jody complains that the old cast members were better. Vet Tech Jody tells him he's like an old person.

Even though I decided that Siobhan is pretty cool, but just a kid and not for me, we all make plans to see a Grateful Dead tribute band at an outdoor rally for something or other at some fairgrounds out near Worcester. This is one of the female Jody's ideas, and it's happening in a few weeks, and though I'll be back in Charlestown by then, I say I'll go, and I want to go. The crew is fun to hang out with, even if we're all completely different.

9.

Two days later, I'm back in Charlestown, and a few days after, I'm out at the racetrack betting on the ponies with the usual riffraff. I'm watching a race that bunches up tight off the gate, and during the bumping, a horse and rider go down. The horses in the lead pack veer wide, and a long shot, I bet on broke from the pack and won. As it rounds the last turn, holding on just fine, my phone rings with a Milford number. It's Siobhan, calling to say hi and calling to see if we're still on for the rally thing. I say, "Of course. I can't wait to see you." She said "me too" in a way that isn't flirting, which is great. Then she says I better check with my friend Jody because she thinks they might not be going.

That night I call Jody, expecting all along that he'll cancel out. The Grateful Dead is not quite his style or quite the image he needs out there in the Milford public forum. There's other news, though.

He says, "Petey, I'm not going."

"You're no friend of the devil, Jody."

"Jody and I broke up."

"Really. How come?"

"Because of something you told Siobhan."

"Me? Jody, what are you talking about?"

"Did you tell Siobhan that I said that Jody was a bitch but otherwise was keeping my dick happy?"

I laughed. "Jody," I said, "I haven't even talked to Siobhan."

"Well, someone did."

"Well, it wasn't me."

"Well, I heard it was."

"Fuck, dude. What is this? High school? Jody broke up with you because someone said to someone else that you supposedly said something?"

"Yeah. Whatever. Someone's planting rumors, though. I wouldn't say anything like that."

"You would too. You say shit like that all the time. But who gives a fuck? That's no reason. Not the whole reason. I mean, Jesus, Jody, she's not nineteen. You didn't see this coming? You guys haven't been having problems?"

"No way, man. Not at all. You know, Petey, you always think you know what people are thinking, even when they tell you it's something else."

"I do?"

"Yeah. And, you're wrong. There's someone trying to fuck us up, and if it's not you, it's someone else. I'm telling you that."

"You've gotten a little paranoid in your old age, my friend. That's fucking crazy. How did my name come up, anyway?"

"It just did."

"It did, huh? Well, it's still ridiculous. I got no reason to cause no trouble. Trouble's the last thing I want. I'm a man of the people, my friend. I want everything happy. You know that."

"Listen, you don't know Milford people. You've been wandering around with your head up your ass for twenty years now. People around here like to start rumors and cause trouble. I know them."

I say, "Jody, I don't think you know shit. I mean, if you know them so well, why wouldn't you know that it's all bullshit?"

Jody doesn't answer. Jody hangs up. I freeze for a second. I can't believe he actually hung up the phone on me. Who hangs up on people? It's ridiculous.

I don't take it personally or very seriously, so the next day, I call him back. This time it's an even shorter conversation. I say, "Jody!"

"I can't talk right now."

"Then why'd you answer?" And he hang ups on me again. Unbelievable.

On Thursday, I call Siobhan and confirm our plans and confirm that Jody and Jody will not be going. Friday, I roll a few joints and buy a pint of vodka for my flask.

10.

Saturday morning is sunny and warm. I take old Route 16 out to Milford and play the radio loud. I arrive in Milford by 10:00 AM and take the two-dollar tour on the back roads, where I used to hang, up Silver Hill, passed the new housing construction, and then back down into town on Congress Street.

I cut down into the old Italian neighborhood, where local legend says that either Sacco or Vanzetti lived. It was the guilty one, but I forget which one that was. Then I cross the railroad tracks and pull into Siobhan's driveway at the foot of Bear Hill.

Siobhan and Vet Tech Jody live in a converted attic apartment in an old two-family house owned by an Italian family that still lives on the first two floors. They have a separate entrance in the back, up a rickety stairway that leads to a landing between the second and third floors. I climb the stairs and look out at the town's two Catholic church towers. The Italian church is on one side of the tracks and the Irish church on the other side. The town hall, oddly painted purple, is in between. I ring the doorbell. Ten seconds pass, and Vet Tech Jody comes.

I walk up the stairs behind her and look at her worn and torn blue jeans and yellow tank top, her blond hair bouncing on her bare shoulders. She's a chameleon. A pretty hot chameleon, I decide. I picture her yoga pants. I imagine her Vet Tech uniform. I have no idea what her "look" is.

I try to decide whether to mention Jody and the rumor that apparently broke them up when she spins around at the top of the stairs and announces, "It looks like you're stuck with me today."

"What do you mean?" She tells me that Siobhan is nowhere to be found. She had gone out the night before and never came home. Jody says, "I don't know. She must have found a good party or something."

I stand at the top of the stairs and say nothing. Jody says, "If you still want to go, I'd love to." And then she smiles, and I say okay, and we leave. Just like that.

On the road, I'm tense and weirded out. When Jody suggests we stop at Burger King, I overrun the drive-thru menu. The lady in the car behind me won't let me back-up to the goddamn microphone. It's immediately fucked up and stupid, and I don't want to give in, so I shift the car to park and go inside and buy the food. I come back outside to a three-ring circus of blaring horns, shouts, and Jody gamely defending the rear end of my car. We smile at each other and drive away.

The fair itself is one of those anti-marijuana laws, Amnesty International, Greenpeace things, with lots of grilled food and Ben & Jerry's ice cream and twenty-something hippie types. The music is good, though, and the sun is good, and lying on the grass and drinking vodka and cranberry juice with Jody is good.

To me, all live music is good, even if it's music I never listen to. We stake out a spot near the stage and listen. Jody dances while sitting, and I watch the musicians and the crowd. We can't hear each other, but we smile a lot.

At one point, I get us a bottle of wine from a wine truck, and we move our blanket well back from the stage to a small rise under a tree, where we can still see the stage, but it's a little quieter and less crowded.

Sometime in the late afternoon, after the fake Grateful Dead band set and during a set by the real Arlo Guthrie, I find myself kissing Jody. It's very tender and very sweet, and I'm not thinking, and I'm not stopping. We leave before the end of the show, and she falls asleep against the window as we drive my old car into my old hometown.

11.

I drive without the radio. Jody wakes up at a red light just outside of town, and I say, "This is kind of a weird situation, huh?"

And she says, "Yeah," and nuzzles her face into my shoulder.

We turn a corner, and the sign on the road says, "Welcome to Milford."

12.

Back at her apartment, I choose not to think about the whole situation. I don't care about the troubles this could cause. I take her to the couch and lay her down. I run my hands along her shoulders and down her arms and slide them underneath her tank top. She runs her fingers up my thigh, past my crotch, and pulls my zipper down. Siobhan climbs the rickety stairs and slowly opens the apartment door.

"What are you two up to, or should I say down to," she laughs.

Jody says, "Wouldn't you like to know," and she gets up and goes into the bathroom.

Siobhan asks me how the concert was. I say, "Good. You should have gone."

She says, "It looks like you had enough fun without me." She says it like she's happy for us.

"Where were you, anyway?"

She said, "Oh, I was at my girlfriend's house. When I called Jody, I had just got up. I've had a Mount Rushmore of a hangover all day. You shoulda seen this party we were at last night."

I say, "Good, huh?" but I'm not listening to her answer. I'm remembering how Jody said that she hadn't heard from Siobhan. And I realize how easily I've been played. And how I am, in fact, causing trouble in Milford. And how I am, in fact, getting too old for this shit.

13.

Siobhan says she's tired and goes to bed. Jody comes out, and we watch some TV, and pretty soon, we go to bed too, together. At about 3:00 AM,

I hear a car outside, and I go to the window just in time to see my friend Jody look up at me and drive away.

I'm a total shit. I think that unless he's also in on the plot to get me into this bedroom, I'm gonna have a helluva hard time easing his paranoia.

I stay at the window and stare at the Milford night. Familiar quiet. Stars and trees. It used to be my home. It's still my hometown, no matter how often I claim to be a Townie. Nothing else moves on the street. I talk myself into feeling vindicated by Jody's spying. At least he knows now. And I figure he still knows me well enough to know I didn't plan all this. I don't plan anything.

I eventually decide I don't give a fuck. I mean, he was a close friend a long time ago, and they did already break up. I move back across the dark room and watch Jody sleep. She's curled up on her side facing towards where I had been sleeping. She sleeps very quietly. I don't understand her.

A full moon comes out from behind the clouds and casts a long light through the open window I saw my friend Jody through. I kick any lingering guilt out of bed and wake up Jody, and we make love again.

14.

In the morning, Siobhan makes us breakfast, and we all sit down together.

"I love bacon. Don't you love bacon? Siobhan, this is really good bacon. What kind is it?" Jody is good at small talk, especially when it's avoiding big talk. I say nothing about seeing Jody in the driveway.

Before I leave, we have a little big talk about Jody, my friend. I say, "Jody's going to call me one of these days. What do you want me to say?"

Jody furrows her brow and scrunches her eyes and thinks about it while she finishes her eggs. Siobhan has left the room, and we're alone with each other, not under the spell of the concert or in bed together. She says, "Let's not tell him." And she squeezes my hand like we are co-conspirators.

I look right at her, and she looks right back. She says, "I don't want him to know because he wouldn't understand that this had nothing to do with him."

I could have and should have told Jody that he already knows, but I don't. Instead, I agree not to say anything and let it go at that. I figure I'll deal with my friend Jody by myself and try to keep her out of it.

We talk for a little while longer, and she holds my hand across the table. The mood is light. When I leave, we kiss, but we make no plans for seeing each other again. I'm not able to gauge the degree of guilt she's feeling, but I sense there's some. I want to talk with the other Jody before I talk about that with her. I want to see how much trouble I've caused. I don't mind a Milford affair, but I don't want a Milford soap opera

15.

During the next week, my correspondence with Milford is a series of missed connections. I call Jody, my friend, and get no answer. I call his parents' house, and his sister says he isn't there. I suspect she's lying.

On Wednesday, I called Vet Tech Jody just to talk. All feels pretty good, but she's in the middle of Vet Teching, and so the call is quick. She seems happy to hear from me and makes no mention of talking to my friend Jody. She suggests another concert the following week. I tell her I'll get the tickets.

On Friday, I call to let her know I got the tickets. The call goes like this:

"Jody?"

"Hi. I can't talk now."

"Then why did you pick up?"

"I'm sorry. I'm just busy."

"That's okay. I'm just letting you know I got the tickets. Doors open at six. It's Sunday, so there won't be traffic coming back into town. Can I pick you up at five?"

"Sounds good."

"What's the matter? You okay?"

"I'm fine."

I hang up wondering if this whole thing is worth it. There's trouble in her voice, and I want no more trouble than I already caused.

I also call the other Jody that night, and, again, I get no answer, and, again, I leave no message.

I get drunk on Saturday and talk to the bartender at Sully's.

16.

It's raining out. I enjoy it. Rain is like validation for depressed people. I don't consider myself depressed, but maybe I am. I climb Jody's rickety stairway and get a splinter from the railing. Fuck. I knock on the door, but I know the instant my knuckles hit wood that no one is home. I knock again. I look at the locked door. I know the affair is over. I knew it from the tone in Jody's voice a few days earlier, but I don't realize it until that moment. I have heard that tone before. I am immediately pissed off, mostly at myself, but fuck her, I think, and fuck all this shit, too. I'm getting too old for this.

Vet Tech Jody seems at once like a business deal I can't afford, and a pretty girl I've seen once or twice across a crowded bar and will never see again.

I go down to my car and get a can of spray paint out of the trunk. I don't want any trouble, but I don't want to just go away either. Fuck that. I write

Petey Was Here on her door and leave. Then I know I won't see her again. I know I won't be coming back to Milford again either.

17.

The next week, I accept an offer on my aunt's condo. I got six figures coming at me. The next day, I quit my job by not showing up. I have pretty much planned it all along but don't decide for sure until I get up. I drive to my aunt's grave in Quincy and pay my respects. I had planned to bring Vet Tech Jody with me, but that didn't work out.

My aunt was a hardworking woman who kept the same crappy job for 30 years. She never got promoted, or a big raise, or even a retirement party.

Still, she wouldn't like me quitting, even though I know I won't have trouble finding something else. As I leave the cemetery, I feel a little hungover and a little empty. My adventures in Jodyland have left me feeling like I don't have a lot to show for myself. I like my apartment and my friends, but I'm not tight with anyone, especially now that my aunt is gone. I haven't been in love in years, and I haven't seen my eight-year-old daughter in Arizona in more than a year. It's not important here to get into the particulars of that situation, but believe me when I say that I am not an asshole and have never shirked my responsibilities. Sometimes trouble just finds me.

My aunt's grave has no headstone yet. It had to be ordered. I sit next to the fresh dirt and think how hard it's getting to keep my vagabond lifestyle going.

The summer will be ending soon, and maybe it's time for a new Petey too. I look at my friends, with their offices and mortgages and home lives, and I am pretty sure that kind of life is not for me. I'd be terrible in the suburbs. I'd be a nightmare as a neighbor. But still, I think my style of living is causing me to miss out on some good things. I don't understand why my settled down friends do most of the things they do, but they do seem happy. And I think that I should understand.

Lately, I've been feeling like maybe I'm missing out on something important. And more important, it's feeling like I'm not making enough things happen for me and that too many things are happening to me.

For instance, two days after the no-show concert, I received a plain white envelope in the mail. Inside was a typewritten card that said:

Dear Petey,

Fuck You.

Jody

I don't know who sent it.

Terry Sanville

Terry Sanville lives in San Luis Obispo, California with his artist-poet wife (his in-house editor) and two plump cats (his in-house critics). He writes full time, producing short stories, essays, and novels. His short stories have been accepted more than 440 times by journals, magazines, and anthologies including The Potomac Review, The Bryant Literary Review, and Shenandoah. He was nominated twice for Pushcart Prizes and once for inclusion in Best of the Net anthology. Terry is a retired urban planner and an accomplished jazz and blues guitarist—who once played with a symphony orchestra backing up jazz legend George Shearing.

Tioga Pass

My mother never liked mountains. The tall ones scared the living hell out of her. She came from Philadelphia, from a narrow brick row house in the Kensington District with no mountains in sight. But during the summer of 1954, she somehow tapped into the silent spirit of the Sierra Nevada and changed our family.

My father brought Mom and my two-year-old sister west on the train right after World War II. They settled in Santa Barbara, on Calle Poniente, a dead-end street on the city's West Side. Then, I was born, and the fun really began. As an ex-Marine, Dad wanted to show me all the manly things that boys should learn: how to shoot a rifle, pitch a tent, build a fire, throw a perfect strike, and cut loose with long belches after chugging a bottle of Frostie Root Beer.

The Korean Conflict had ended, people bought houses, had babies, railed against the Commies, and stared transfixed at the flickering screens of their new rabbit-eared Zeniths. My Dad, who always had a strange design sense, bought a '51 Studebaker Starlight Coupe, a dove-gray car with a weird three-eyed front end and little curved windows in the back. I think Mom liked that two-door because once my sister and I got shoved into the rear seat, we couldn't get out and couldn't play with door handles, although window cranks stayed fair game.

During those *Father Knows Best* summers, our family took annual road trips across Western America. Dad clamped a roof rack onto the car and tied on a mound of camping gear under a green canvas tarp. The Studebaker looked like a disfigured shark being humped by a huge sea turtle. In August 1954, we drove to Yosemite National Park—from Santa Barbara heading south, through the Coastal Range, then over the Grapevine Grade into the sweltering San Joaquin Valley.

We climbed the Grapevine in stages. When the Studebaker's temperature gauge touched "H," Dad pulled over and waited for the car to cool. Pieces of exploded tires from cars and semis littered the highway. Once over the summit, the Central Valley's heat caused Mom's temperature gauge to climb.

"I'm hot. Why'd we have to come this way? Harry, do something."

She repeated this complaint in various forms every few minutes until Dad finally stopped the car along Highway 99 and retrieved a T-shirt from the trunk. He soaked it in water from the dripping canvas bag tied to a front bumper post.

"Here, put this on your forehead."

"Gee, thanks. We shoulda brought extra ice... or maybe bought one of those window coolers."

"You mean those streamlined swamp coolers? Those things don't work."

"It'd be better than this. My behind is welded to the seat."

Dad stared out his side window, trying to cover his smile and smother a chuckle at that mental image. Mom looked indignant.

As we headed toward Bakersfield, our trip took a turn for the worse. We got stuck behind a manure truck—the gutless Studebaker couldn't go fast enough to pass. My sister Cindy and I begged Dad to stop at one of the Giant Orange roadside stands and get something to drink. But Dad's diabetes wouldn't allow him to down that sugary stuff, and we had to settle for warm water from a battered canteen.

And then we had to pee. For Cindy and Mom, that meant a stop at a gas station. But for Dad and me, it meant standing on the highway's shoulder with one's back to traffic at the car's rear right fender. With the passenger side door opened to block views from oncoming traffic, we'd cut loose, sometimes peeing into the wind, with Cindy giggling the whole time and Mom scolding her for looking.

All of us felt road weary by the time we reached Yosemite Valley and found a campsite within earshot of the Merced River. In late afternoon, Dad and I hustled to erect our canvas tent, install everyone's Sears and Roebuck sleeping bags and air mattresses, and set up the Coleman Stove. While *we men* made camp, the women scouted the area, looking for restrooms.

Wood fires scented the breeze that carried bits of conversation from surrounding campers and music from guitars. Tiny aluminum teardrop trailers and one or two rounded Shastas looked out of place among the rag-tag military and umbrella tents. Clothes lines strung between trees displayed bathing suits and undies. Some folks just hooked an awning onto the side of their car and slept on the ground.

Mom and my sister returned with wrinkled noses, holding their hands out in front of them.

Mom started in. "Harry, the outhouses are disgusting, and there's no running water. We couldn't even wash our hands."

Dad turned to me. "Grab the bucket from the trunk and get some water."

I hustled away along the campground road. The shadows had grown long, and I remembered Dad's warning us about bears coming out in the evening to scavenge the garbage cans. Failing to find a faucet, I headed for the Merced River. At its bank, I looked for a good spot to dunk my pail but couldn't find one. I removed my sneakers and socks and waded in, fighting back a scream. The water felt like it had just melted from a nearby glacier. I found a clear spot, filled my bucket and hustled back to shore, my feet turning blue, my nine-year-old back aching.

"Why were you gone so long?" Mom asked. "And why are your pants wet?"

"I couldn't find water, so I got some from the river."

"The water faucet's right down there," she said, pointing in the opposite direction I'd gone. "See, where those people are standing?"

"Ah, sorry. Be right back." I wetted a pine tree with the river water and headed out.

Near my normal bedtime, we joined the other campers at an amphitheater in the middle of a moonlit meadow to watch the *Firefall*.[2] Burning embers spilled from the top of Glacier Point and fell to the valley floor, thousands of feet below. It looked like a crazy flaming waterfall.

Among the *Oohs* and *Aahs* from the crowd, Mom murmured, "Won't that set the trees on fire?"

"Don't think so," Dad said. "It falls mostly on rock."

"I think it's neat," I chimed in.

"You think rabbit turds are neat," Cindy said.

"Yeah, better watch your oatmeal. Those might not be raisins."

"Hush you two," Dad said but chuckled anyway.

That night, lying in the dark tent, I felt Yosemite's giant granite monoliths towering over us, standing silent guard, cold, inhuman. I dreamed about gliding off the edge of Glacier Point, high above the valley floor and floating on the wind to land softly in a meadow filled with bears. Wait! Bears?

I woke to the sound of someone yelling, "Bears, bears!" and banging on something metal. Gray daylight streamed through the open tent flap and mosquito netting. Mom and my sister groaned and sat up. I pulled on my jeans, then ducked out of the tent. Dad stood in his boxer shorts and T-shirt, banging the butt of his World War I bayonet against the bottom of a pot. A mama bear and two cubs perched on top of our car. The mama had peeled back the roof rack's canvas cover and had found the loaf of bread. She opened the loaf and handed her cubs individual slices, like a mother serving breakfast.

"Come on, start yelling," Dad hollered and waved his bayonet at me. That thing looked like a short sword and had razor-sharp edges. Dad kept it in the tent at night and shoved into the Studebaker's armrest during the day. When gas station attendants saw the bayonet as he opened his car door, they gave him really good service.

Some of the neighboring campers joined us, yelling and beating on various pots and pans until the bears became bored and lumbered off toward the meadow.

We spent almost a week hiking trails that bordered the Merced River and extended into side canyons. But the minute a trail started to climb, with steep drops on one or both sides, Mom would stop and go no farther.

"I'm not killing myself just to see a waterfall. The river is pretty enough for me."

Even as a kid, I knew something about what frightened her. Just looking up at Yosemite's granite monoliths made me a little dizzy. And on narrow trails where one wrong step could send a hiker tumbling into the abyss, I moved carefully with trembling legs, my heart pounding. Dad and Cindy acted sure-footed as mountain goats. Consequently, Mom and I spent afternoons on the rocky shore next to the river, she reading and me riding an inner tube downstream, then hiking back and doing it over and over until I got so cold I couldn't feel my knees.

On our last day in Yosemite Valley, we broke camp right after breakfast. Dad and I hauled our collection of canteens to the water point. The family in the next campsite had also packed their car, and the father stood filling grungy canvas bags at the faucet.

"So where are you folks headed?" the man asked.

Dad answered, "We were gonna go south to Kings Canyon. But I really wanna go east and see Mono Lake."

The man grinned. "Yeah, that lake's really somethin'... kinda strange out there in the desert. But are ya going over Tioga Pass?"

"Is that a problem?"

"Well, at least the snow's gone. Ya know, it's almost ten thousand feet high. Some cars get vapor lock[3]. "

"So... so what's the road like?" Dad asked.

"Never been on it myself. But I hear they're still building parts, and it's really narrow in spots. Ya know, it was an old wagon road that served the silver mines."

"I didn't know that. And thanks for the warning."

On our way back to the campsite, Dad gave me the look that meant keep your trap shut and say nothing. He checked the Studebaker's water and oil levels, squeezed its hoses, and ran his hands over the surface of each skinny tire. We piled in, my sister and I ready for a new adventure.

"We've got plenty gas to make it to Lee Vining," Dad assured Mom.

She gave him a quick glance and smiled. She seemed happy to be leaving the land of the granite giants.

The road out of the valley seemed reasonable enough, two lanes, paved. We climbed steadily, passed through an arched tunnel made of stone, and into Yosemite's high country of alpine meadows, lake-filled valleys, gray looming peaks, and stunted pine forests. The air stayed cool as we pushed upward. I peeked over the front seat at the Studebaker's temperature gauge and watched it slowly sweep toward the dreaded "H."

When it read hot, Dad pulled the car onto a turnout. We all piled out. The turnout had no guardrail and the near-vertical slope dropped away from the road to a far-distant canyon floor. I backed up from the edge and leaned against the car, waiting for the ground to stop swaying. Mom had a death grip on the door handle while Dad and my sister kept busy pointing out features of the distant landscape.

"Harry, did we have to stop here?" Mom complained.

"Sorry, but the car heats up faster the higher we go."

"Maybe... maybe we shouldn't... try this route."

"Ah, honey, it's only a few more miles. We'll be out of the mountains in no time."

In the thin air, we continued to climb. Trees disappeared. The sky burned a brilliant singing blue, the sunlight white and piercing. It felt like we drove closer to the scattered clouds.

"Harry, I'm not feeling good," Mom complained. "I think it must be the altitude."

"Just hang on, Elaine. We'll be down soon."

Just like our passage over the Grapevine, Mom fell into a pattern of complaints, her voice raspy, her breathing loud. At each stop to let the Studebaker cool, Mom rolled down her window and sucked in the cold mountain air, eyes closed, concentrating. But she wouldn't leave the car. I felt I had to follow Dad and Cindy to the road's edge and take in yet another impossible vista.

Along certain stretches, the road narrowed to a little more than one lane wide, and gravel replaced asphalt. We slowed along a twisting section with no guardrails that cut across the face of a mountain. The stench of boiling radiator water filled the car. Rounding an uphill curve, we came head-to-head with an idiot driving a Chevy pulling a boxy vacation trailer. Dad braked, yanked the Studebaker's three-on-the-tree transmission into low gear, then turned off the engine. He pulled the emergency brake, tugging so hard on the handle I thought it would snap off in his hand.

"What the hell are you doing?" Mom croaked.

"Just try and relax, Elaine," Dad said in a soothing voice.

The Chevy had also stopped, and Dad and the other driver got out and stood in the middle of the road talking and gesturing. Fortunately, no other cars came by. A high mountain wind shook the Studebaker, and Mom let out a low moan. My sister and I stared at each other. This was not good!

Finally, Dad returned, shaking his head. "Well, that fool shouldn't be on this road to begin with. And the law says that uphill traffic has the right-of-way. So, he should back up and find a turnout. But he'll never back uphill with that stupid trailer."

"So... so, what are you gonna do?" Mom asked, her voice low and shaking.

"I'll ease us down the mountain to that wide spot we passed."

"Are you crazy?" Mom's voice rose in pitch. "You're gonna kill us all... drive off the cliff and... and..."

We were on the cliff side of the road and had to back up about a hundred yards to reach a slightly wider road section.

"Now, Elaine, I want you to tell me if I'm getting too close to the edge. Can you do that?"

Wide-eyed with trembling lips, Mom nodded. Dad started the engine, put his foot on the brake and clutch and released the emergency. When he eased his foot off the squishy brake pedal, the Studebaker fell backward like an elevator out of control.

Mom screamed. "Stop, stop," and pressed her feet to the floor so hard I thought she'd punch a hole in it. Dad pumped the brakes and stopped the car.

"Take it easy, Elaine. Take it easy. Now... how am I doin'?"

"I... I can't see the road," Mom said, her voice rising to panic levels.

I pushed Cindy aside and stared out the side window. Sure enough, the mountain dropped straight down into a deep valley. The Studebaker's tires must have been inches from the edge.

Dad white-knuckled the steering wheel and stared into the tiny rearview mirror, eyes wide, lips compressed into a tight line.

"Harry, you've got to stop this," Mom screeched. "You're gonna kill-"

"SHUT UP, ELAINE!"

In an instant, the drama shifted from going over the cliff to the insult inside our Studebaker. Neither my sister nor I had ever heard Dad tell Mom to shut up. We kids were told never to use those words. If we lived through that mountain passage, there would be consequences, serious consequences. Mom had jumped when Dad yelled at her. She sat red-faced, tight-lipped, staring straight ahead, as if daring our father to finish us off.

Dad eased the car farther down the mountain. The smell of burning clutch added to the stink of hot radiator water and fading brakes. Finally, he steered onto a slightly wider stretch of road and pulled as far over as possible. If we had tried to get out the right side of the car, we would have fallen to our deaths.

Dad leaned on the horn and the Chevy pulling the trailer crept toward us, the driver pumping the brakes, jerking his rig along a few feet at a time. As he passed us, his side view trailer mirror glanced off our mirror, his right side mirror smashed against the mountainside with a tinkle of glass. The screech of the trailer's sheet metal scraping against granite sounded like fingernails scratching a blackboard.

"Serves 'im right," Dad muttered.

Mom said nothing.

We must have stayed there for a half hour, letting the car collect itself. Nobody talked. The only sound came from the buffeting mountain wind and the grind of engines from the occasional passing vehicle. We stayed quiet for the rest of the mountain passage, over Tioga Pass without incident, then the drop toward Highway 395 and the Town of Lee Vining. Dad apologized to Mom several times but got no reply.

That night we stayed at a fleabag motel and ate dinner at a greasy spoon. Nobody talked. Cindy and I waited for Mom to explode, to pin Dad against the wall of guilt and poor decision-making. But it never happened. She stayed silent, rebuffing Dad's attempts to make amends.

The next day we headed south, crossed the Sierra Foothills at Tehachapi and dropped into Bakersfield on our way to Santa Barbara. We never explored Mono Lake. Mom stayed silent the whole way home and for some days after.

During the following years, Dad always went over the routes for our summer vacation with Mom, would change directions at her discretion, avoided sketchy mountain passes in deference to flatter valleys and coastal plains. Although I sometimes missed the drama of the High Sierra and Rockies, I learned to recognize the power of silence. My wife and I use it on occasion—passive retribution being worse than direct confrontation.

And I've learned that the phrase "silence is golden" has multiple meanings.

[1] Father Knows Best (1954–1960): a family-friendly CBS television program starring Robert Young and Jane Wyatt.

[2] The Firefall occurred nightly, beginning in 1872 and ending in 1968. The Director of the National Park Service ordered it stopped because the overwhelming number of visitors that it attracted trampled the meadows.

[3] *Vapor lock* is a problem caused when gasoline changes from a liquid to a gas while still in an engine's fuel lines. Gasoline can vaporize when heated by the motor, by the local climate or due to a lower boiling point at high altitude.

My People

Scientists say that earliest childhood memories form at about age two. They're wrong. I remember my parents wheeling me up and down Calle Poniente on Santa Barbara's West Side in my pink stroller before I could even walk more than a few steps. I think they wanted to show me off, saying, *Hey look, we can do this too. We've joined the club.*

Mom told me decades later that she and Dad had been trying for over three years while nearly all the other ladies on the street had already shared stories at the weekly coffee klatch, about two-day-long labors, breech births, C-sections, stretch marks, teething, and never again wanting to have sex with their husbands—until they did and all felt right, well almost.

When I turned five in 1952, Judi was my first best friend, lived six doors down and had frizzy hair with white freckled skin.

"Donna, you wanna make mud pies?" she asked one summer's day.

"Ugh, that's icky."

Judi put her hands on her hips, her rag doll stuffed into the waistband of her dress. "So, what do *you* wanna do?"

"Let's go in there." I pointed to the Nolans' garage where her father spent most afternoons making lots of noise and drinking beer out of red, white, and blue cans. I still remember the pop of his church key punching through their metal tops, such a satisfying sound.

Judi shuffled her feet. "We'll get 'n trouble. My Dad won't let me in there."

"Ah, come on, we won't touch nothin'. Jus' wanna see."

Judi and I had been friends since nursery school. We'd already confirmed, via anatomical exploration in back of my dad's tool shed, that we were both female. But Judi acted girlier than me, always wanted to mess with dolls, playhouse and act the mama part. Me? I didn't know what I liked.

Machines filled the Nolans' garage, some with jagged-looking blades, some with screw-like limbs. Strange tools hung from one wall.

"Don' touch nothin'," Judi warned. "My Dad cut himself on dat thing." She pointed to a metal table with a silver blade sticking out of it. "Had to go to the hospital, got stitches."

I stepped forward and touched the circular blade, expecting to see blood. "Yeah, sharp." I reached for the on-off switch.

"DON'T," Judi said. "Makes too much noise. My Mama will hear."

I let my trembling hands fall to my sides.

I loved garages: the smell of old grease and laundry detergent, wall hangings of camping gear, garden tools, broken toys, shelves with rusted half-full paint cans, old carpets slung over the rafters, and workbenches textured with saw cuts, drill holes, chisel marks, and stained with solvents and lacquers.

In the low light, I stepped on something and stumbled, almost turning my ankle. "Ouch, that hurt."

"We better get outta here," Judi said, fidgeting.

"What's this stuff?" I pointed to the floor littered with small blocky pieces of wood over a bed of sawdust.

"My Pop's buildin' somethin'."

I bent and inspected the wood scraps. They seemed somehow fun, useful. I wasn't sure why.

"Can I have these?" I asked.

"I don' know. Come on, we gotta go."

"All right, all right. I'll jus' take some."

I found a crumpled paper bag, collected a bunch of wood ends, and we hightailed it out of there.

Mom called me in for lunch, her voice echoing down Calle Poniente. She probably had the loudest call in the neighborhood. I hustled home and brushed past her into my bedroom, hid my prizes in the closet in back of dust-covered suitcases, and forgot about them.

*****

By age nine, I'd become some sort of freak, and I didn't know why. I didn't like dolls and hated skipping rope because I always tripped and skinned my knees. I also detested how other girls wanted to dress up in their mother's clothes, play hopscotch, or help fix supper. And I wasn't much of a tomboy. Sports made me tired and seemed stupid. I liked reading and had struggled through half of our Encyclopedia Britannica before my eyesight blurred and dimmed, and I couldn't even read newspaper headlines. I thought blindness would overtake me and had already read *My Eyes Have a Cold Nose* by Hector Chevigny.

"You've got astigmatism in your left eye, poor vision in the right, and you suffer from eyestrain," Dr. Campbell said and prescribed glasses, thereby completing my ensemble as our school's chief nerd. The boys called me "four eyes," and the girls made fun of my Buster Brown shoes and chopped off stringy brown hair.

But Miss Adams, my fourth grade teacher at Dolores Catholic Elementary, never made fun of me or anyone else. At the end of a Friday class in the doldrums of February, she cleared her throat and stood. "All right, students, enjoy your weekend. But remember your art projects are due Monday."

A chorus of groans sounded. I liked Miss Adams because she encouraged me, and I did well in math, science and art. A "real Renaissance girl," she called me, whatever that meant. The kids made fun of her double chins, huge belly, and flabby arms, called her the "Atom Bomb" behind her back. Maybe we were both nerds but for different reasons.

I hadn't even started my art project, had thought about using my box of 100 Crayolas to draw a stained glass window, like the ones I stared at during Sunday mass as the priest droned on in Latin. But everybody would be using crayons to do their project. That night, when I tossed my shoes into the closet, one of the suitcases fell over and there sat the crumpled paper bag with its wooden scraps.

I cleared off my desk and turned on the gooseneck lamp. The blocks were squares and rectangles. But many of them had ends cut off at angles. I arranged them in patterns, stacking some. I liked the way they cast shadows, their shapes creating spaces between them that looked solid but held nothing but air. I played with the blocks for hours, moving the lamp to various angles until I had created this crazy village of shapes and shadows. On Saturday, I borrowed a piece of sandpaper from my father's stash, worked the wood smooth, then painted them a dull black with primer Dad used on the hotrod he'd been working on forever.

When I arranged the blocks on my desk again, I couldn't tell exactly where their edges stopped and shadows began. I squinted my eyes, and they became mini sculptures with the spaces as sharp as the blocks themselves.

I took off my glasses and rubbed my eyes. *Maybe it's just how I see.* I turned off the lamp and hurried into the kitchen where my mother cooked dinner.

"Mom, come look at somethin'."

She shook her wet hands over the sink and stared at me. "Can't you see I'm busy?"

"It'll just take a minute."

"What is it?"

"I finished my art project. Don't know if it's any good."

"I'm sure it's fine, Donna. I'll look later."

"Ah, come on. It'll just take a second."

She sighed, dried her hands on her apron, and followed me into my bedroom. I moved to my desk, turned on the lamp, and stepped back.

She stared at my creation, mouth open. "What... what is this?"

"I don' know. But I like the way it looks with the light."

"Yes, I can see that. It reminds me of Stonehenge. You remember reading about that in the encyclopedia?"

"Nah. I've only gotten to 'M'."

"Huh."

"So, do ya like it?"

My mother always told me the truth about my schoolwork. I think she knew that glossing over problems didn't help.

"I'm not sure what to think, honey. It's definitely different and all those shadows…"

"So, you can see 'em too."

"Yes, and the way you've painted whatever those things are makes my eyes see funny… funny spaces."

Not praise, but at least she saw what I had tried to do.

"Ya know," she said, "if you glue them onto a piece of cardboard covered in butcher paper, the shadows would be even sharper."

"Thanks, Mom. Great idea."

By late Sunday night, I had finished my project and carefully slid it into my laundry bag along with my gooseneck lamp. The next morning at school, I set it on the shelf in the stuffy cloakroom next to my sack lunch. Mom had packed an over-ripe pear, and I knew it wouldn't last until noon before soaking through the bag and falling out. She always made me eat fresh fruit.

Miss Adams had art period right after lunch. I barely made it to recess without peeing my pants. Would they like my project? Would they understand what I had tried to do? Did *I* understand? Would they laugh? And most troubling, what would Miss Adams think? What kind of dumb thing had I done, anyway?

Each of us had to go to the front of the room, show our artwork, tell the class something about it, and answer questions. Over the next hour, I sat through presentations of Crayola portraits of dogs, cats and a hamster with bulging eyes, boats sailing in Santa Barbara's harbor, cave-art tracings of brightly colored hands, drawings of various flowers, and an exploding volcano that Jimmy Maddox made out of pottery clay and baked in his father's kiln.

When my name got called, I stood on wobbling legs and moved to the front of the class, holding my project in its cloth bag.

"What have you got for us, Donna?" Miss Adams asked. "Don't be bashful; show us."

I set the bag on her desk, took out the lamp, and plugged it into the wall outlet. Titters of laughter filled the room.

"All right, class. Settle down," Miss Adams said.

"Can, ah… can they come up here to see?" I barely got the words out.

"Of course." Miss Adams motioned the class forward.

With a rumble, the fourth graders encircled her desk. I clicked on the lamp and pulled my project from the bag.

"I... I don' know what to call it," I said and positioned the light at just the right angle. "But I... I liked how the shadows kinda blend with the... blocks... and make their own... I don' know... space."

"It's jus' a buncha blocks," Sally Markowitz muttered.

"That's enough," Miss Adams snapped.

"If you move around the thing, you can see how the shadows and spaces change."

The class crowded in close and began to circle.

"Try gettin' down at eye level. I like making believe that I'm walking between 'em... that they're towering over me."

I stared at the faces of my classmates and saw mostly confusion. The boys seemed to get it better than the girls, maybe because they'd played with blocks as tiny kids. But they all muttered to each other with short bursts of giggling.

"That's very... very creative, Donna," Miss Adams said. "Where did you get the idea?"

"Don' know. My Mom said it reminds her a little of Stonehenge. But I don' know what that is."

"Yes, I can see her point. We should talk more about art, just you and I."

"That'd be great, Miss Adams." I let out a deep breath.

The rest of the school day flew by. Waiting for the bus afterwards, Jimmy Maddox sat on the bench next to me holding his clay volcano. Everybody seemed to admire the volcano.

"I like your blocks," he said.

"Your volcano's neat too, 'specially the red paint for the lava."

"Yeah, my Pop and me went to Hawaii last summer... saw the stuff movin' 'cross the ground. Scary."

"Yeah, I can imagine."

Jimmy grinned. "I can make believe that your... your blocks are towers under a stinkin' hot sun. I'd like their shade. Sittin' in the shadows drinkin' cold root beer would be great."

"Thanks."

*****

Through grade school and high school, there always seemed to be one or two kids like Jimmy Maddox who got what I tried to do. But even they wouldn't hang out with me, afraid that my cooties might rub off on them and they'd turn into some kind of dork.

I grew breasts, had periods, fought against the onslaught of pimples and raging hormones, and fell in love with boys who wouldn't give me a second glance, not that they could see much under those high-necked and below-the-knee Catholic school uniforms. My mother even let me wear makeup my senior year, a touch of lipstick and a little blush on my pale cheeks. But I just got strange looks from the girls, and the boys didn't seem to notice.

So I curled up inside myself and drew, painted, and sculpted. My family's garage filled with art projects in various states of creation or decay, which annoyed my Dad because they encroached on his "car guy" space.

Meanwhile, Mom worried about what I would do after high school. I had zero homemaking skills, and going to college for more book learning seemed boring and way too expensive.

Miss Adams kept in touch with me long after I left Dolores Elementary and started high school. She'd invite me out for dessert at McConnell's Ice Cream Shop on State Street at Mission. Over butterscotch sundaes, we'd talk about art and my life.

On the Wednesday afternoon before Thanksgiving of my senior year, we hunched over a tiny table at the back of the sidewalk, spoiling our dinners and talking.

"You need to find your people," she told me.

"My people?"

"Yes, the ones that get excited about the same things you do. The ones you can talk with, share your feelings, fall in and out of love with."

"I guess they've been hiding from me. I'm pretty sure not even my parents are 'my people.'"

"Yes, my folks are the same, own a lemon ranch outside of Goleta. I was an only child too, first to go to college."

"So, who are 'your people?'"

"Good question." Miss Adams took a stab at her sundae and spooned a huge lump of ice cream into her mouth. I watched cars pass by on State Street in the autumnal light.

"I guess, the other teachers I work with," she answered, finally. "But I think the children are more my people than anyone."

"Do you have, ya know, your own kids?"

She laughed. "You have to have a man to have children. Not too many want this." She waved her swollen hands in front of her bulging front.

"Yeah, I know what you mean."

Miss Adams scoffed. "What are you talking about? You just haven't found your style. This is 1964. Things are starting to happen, to change, the clothes, the crazy music, the politics. It's gonna be exciting for you."

"So why do I feel so... so adrift?"

"You just need a push in the right direction." Miss Adams reached into her capacious purse and grabbed a packet of papers bound by a rubber band. "Here, look these over and we can talk later."

"What are they?"

"Art school brochures."

"But you know my folks can't afford it, and my grades aren't good enough to get a scholarship."

"Don't worry about the money. Just look at what they offer. Some of them are not that far away, and we can visit their campuses if you want."

"I don't want to bother you with my—"

"You're my people too, you know."

"Thanks. I don't know what to say."

"Say 'next week' and we'll talk some more."

*****

I called them my "studio days," and I loved each and every one. The College of Art's main workspace had a bank of clerestory windows that let in golden afternoon light and sea air off San Francisco Bay. Each student had a small space to do his or her work, not much bigger than an office cubicle. But we spent more time in the common area, talking with each other about our studies, projects, girlfriends or boyfriends, parties, crazy music, and the problems with the Vietnam War. We drank God-awful coffee, sucked on cigarettes, and felt serious as hell about our art and the world in general—until somebody smuggled in some grass, rolled a thumb-sized joint, and hell seemed far away and irrelevant.

Miss Adams had helped me fill out the college application materials and take photographs of my art: paintings, sculptures, and mixed-media work, including a spiffed-up version of the blocks I'd submitted to her in fourth grade. With a partial scholarship, an allowance from my parents, and wages and tips from my part-time job at a greasy spoon in the Tenderloin, I could make it.

I loved life in the City. When I wasn't struggling to finish a project or working the graveyard, my fellow art students and I walked Haight Street, hung out in head shops, and marveled at the psychedelic poster art on display. Or we'd take in a free concert in Golden Gate Park. One afternoon, I sat on the sunlit grass next to Javier as the Grateful Dead played to a stoned crowd.

"So, you gonna, ya know, stick it out at school?" he asked while the band took a break.

"Yes, I love the classes. Besides, jobs for 3-D artists aren't happening."

I could talk with Javier, a Hispanic with homemade tattoos who had accepted my nerdiness ever since we met as freshman.

"But you can draw better than the rest of us," he said. "Your graphite work is as good as Kautzky's."

"You're sweet, thanks. What about you? You gonna stick around?"

"I don't know. I like it here, but classes bore me… and my grades are for shit. I might take a semester off and hit the road."

"You can't leave school," I said. "The draft will get you."

"You don't need to remind me."

Javier took my hand, and we kissed. It wasn't our first. He left a nose print on my glasses. Somehow, out under that winter's sky, in the sea air with the first wisps of evening fog curling in off the bay, a piece of me felt grounded, planted in that particular space and time.

Later that semester, Javier vanished. He'd talked about fleeing to Canada to avoid the draft. But a lot of guys talked that way. All of us studio rats missed his ability to see the beauty and value in other peoples' artwork and to describe it so eloquently. Then I got a letter from him during fall term of my senior year, from a hospital on Long Binh Army Base, northeast of Saigon. He'd been badly disabled during a firefight in the Central Highlands and was headed back to the States. He wanted to reconnect with me, with art and the life. But my life and the City had changed, the hippies were leaving the Haight, and President Nixon stumbled through the fog of war, searching in vain for an honorable and just peace in Vietnam.

Miss Adams, she wanted me to call her Adele, but I never did, visited me during Christmas break. She looked older and walked slower than I'd remembered. I took her to Chinatown, to Lands End, to my third-floor walkup off Oak Street. I asked her to sit for an oil portrait that would take me years to complete. Sometimes I think I never have. She'd gotten thinner, and I didn't know what woman to paint—my fourth-grade memory or the new older version.

Miss Adams died the next year of complications from diabetes. She'd never told me, always steered our conversations away from herself and toward my art and the future. I wondered about all those super-sweet ice cream sundaes we'd downed. Did I help her hurt herself, to feed some sort of addiction? Or did she sacrifice herself for me, to allow us to talk intimately? When I stare at her portrait, I sometimes apologize to her for not knowing, for not paying close enough attention, for being so self-absorbed with my own adolescent issues.

After graduation from art school, I continued to waitress and scrape by. My life as an artist seemed to wane quickly, like the song mentions a moment's sunlight, fading on the grass.

Eleanor, a watercolorist I admired from school, came into the restaurant one day, and we gabbed at the counter about our studio days.

"So, what are you doing now?" she asked. "Got any commissions?"

"Are you kidding? I'm still taking money from my parents."

"Yeah, I know the drill. If I don't find something soon, it'll be back home to Modesto. My Pop always said an art degree was a waste of money."

"My father feels the same... but he would never tell me."

"So, are you still living on Oak Street?" El asked.

"Yeah, I like the neighborhood. It has quieted down a lot."

"How would you like a roommate? We could split the rent, and I hardly have any stuff that'll get in the way."

"Why do you need to move?"

"I was living with my boyfriend. We broke up. It's his place, and I couldn't afford it anyway."

"Sorry."

"Hey, not the first time. Not the last."

Her talk about boyfriends made me feel guilty about how I'd treated Javier. I'd never written him back, not knowing how to deal with a disabled soldier and shying away from the reality of war. I'm still not proud of how I acted.

El became a great roommate. Pretty, sociable, and easy to talk to, she got a job with a local ad agency doing layout work, setting copy, and doing paste-up. But when they needed original black-and-white art, I'd get the work. Poor El couldn't draw worth a damn.

A couple times a month we'd invite the remnants of our graduating class over to talk about art, jobs, the lottery, and how the guys had escaped the draft. And we'd connect with those that had left the Bay Area—long letters and phone calls, Christmas cards with photos showing dogs, babies, and telling stories about how they'd been hired by Allstate Insurance or Shell Oil, drove trucks, or applied their artist's hand-eye coordination as dental hygienists.

Dead students at Kent State and Vietnam War headlines morphed like a melting water bottle into the Disco Era. The music became equally as plastic, its message content drained away. I'd been working graveyard for ten years, began to feel like Flo, the aging foul-mouthed waitress in *Alice Doesn't Live Here Anymore*. El had moved out, married one of the ad agency's execs. Then Mom called.

"Your father died."

"What... when... how?"

"Last night, heart attack. I found him in the garage working on that damn hotrod."

"But... he never..."

"I know. Always claimed he was strong as a bull. So, can you come home and help with the arrangements?"

"Of course, Mom. I'll take the first bus out."

"I wish you'd come home to stay," she said. The sound of her soft crying echoed over the scratchy phone lines. "You could use the garage as your studio, live here free."

"We'll talk more when I get there, Mom."

I moved back to Santa Barbara, got a job at the 101 Café working breakfast and lunch. I spent most evenings in my garage studio, the faded odor of old grease reminding me of my father. I hung the portrait of Miss Adams over my workbench next to my framed art school diploma. Once again, the garage filled with my works. On commission and to keep my hand in, I did pencil portraits of rich people's houses in Hope Ranch, Montecito, and Santa Barbara's Riviera.

Then, in my early forties, I entered an international 3-D art competition, recycling one of my old projects. I won and got a handsome prize and great publicity for my efforts. A rancher outside of Denver noticed and commissioned me to design and oversee the installation of a light and shadow garden, made from giant granite blocks quarried on his property. A six-figure commission and more publicity sent me on my way.

I quit my waitress job after twenty-five years of refilling coffee cups and deflecting advances from horny truckers. I'd dated a few of my customers over the years but could never find one good for the long haul.

Well-heeled patrons, big-named critics, Hollywood types, agents, and educators banged on my door, phoned me up asking for interviews, wanting a piece of the action. Yet none of them were really my people. They seemed more like the Remoras that attach themselves to sharks and feed off remnants of food captured by their host, a group not to be confided in, but marginally tolerated.

I can now afford to move from my humble home, even in high-priced Santa Barbara. But I love Calle Poniente. I love walking the oak-studded hills at the dead end of the street or talking with the newest generation of mothers as they push their babies in strollers past my house.

In late afternoons, after school lets out, some of the neighborhood kids sneak up my driveway to my open garage door and spy on me while I paint, draw, or build a model of a 3-D installation. I invite them in, give them paper, wood blocks, glue, crayons, pencils, old artist brushes and crumpled tubes of Liquitex, and let them have at it. I show them tricks of the trade and ask each to present their artwork when they're done. Miss Adams would approve.

My surviving college classmates stay in contact: long phone calls and letters, and now e-mails, Skype, and Zoom. But after so much time, my people are scattered throughout the world and beyond. Yet somehow the portrait and memory of Miss Adams still connects me to them, and to her.

Masha Kamenetskaya

Masha Kamenetskaya is a writer, an editor, and a publisher. Originally from St. Petersburg (Russia), she's been living in Budapest (Hungary) for 6 years, where she publishes and co-edits a literary magazine *Panel*. She writes both in Russian and in English.

Short stories in English have featured such publications as *Verses of Silence, Flying Ketchup Press (the anthology "Tales from the Dream Zone")? 45 Magazine Women's Literary Journal, Budapest Local.* The collection of short stories "On The Set" was published by Duck Lake Books (USA) in 2020. The story *Unhold My Hand* is part of a new collection "Forgotten Dinner," which is focused on family; Masha believes that family is one of the most fulfilling, inspiring and terrifying journeys in life that one can only take.

Unhold My Hand

"...red dress it is. I am here for the red dress. The YSL red dress. It's Queen. My name is Queen. The dress smells of Chanel and Clive Christian. Of both. Now it presumably smells of a dry cleaner. I don't need this dress. Shall I pick it anyway? I'd give it to you, but you are much bigger than I am."

It was two o'clock in the afternoon, when Mrs. Queen showed up at the dry cleaner. Usually it's a quiet time—an hour break before the "I ruined my suit, and it has to be cleaned by tomorrow" customers. I'd just had my chicken noodle soup, when Mrs. Queen stormed in.

"You've got a noodle thing." She pointed at my chest with her index finger. "You might want to clean it."

I'd never seen Mrs. Queen before. I knew her clothes though: fitted coats, cashmere jackets, fit-and-flare or knitted dresses; all expensive, all neat, pastel colors—at some point, I thought she was a time-traveler. Every month, I get something to dry clean for her—her assistant brings them in.

Mrs. Queen turned out to be a sparrow woman—with light brown hair, a tiny nose, and a paper bag of snacks which she occasionally dipped her hand into.

"I told my husband to come and pick it up, but he never did. It's Queen."

"Have you got a receipt?"

"Do I look like a person who's got a receipt?"

If I actually had to answer this question, I'd have said—no, you don't.

"This is a red YSL dress. It smells of Chanel and Clive Christian. Used to smell, yeah. Now it smells of a dry cleaner."

She cringed.

The kettle was boiling in the closet—I'd meant to have a cup of tea with homemade apple cake from the pastry shop next door.

Mrs. Queen's red dress was crammed in the back. Two weeks and three days had passed, according to the tag on the sack.

While I was checking on the dress, I heard Mrs. Queen talking on the phone.

"...'age suits him well' type, yes. I know that. I know all, dear. This doesn't make him less of an asshole."

We're a good and expensive dry cleaner. Customers trust us with their most precious items in life.

"It's been here for a while," I said, having got back to Mrs. Queen.

"Tell me what I don't know."

I handed her a white sack.

"Here you go."

She gripped the bag with two fingers.

"Am I supposed to drag this down the street?" she asked. "In a white sack? On the street? The dress I don't need anymore?"

"If you want, we can make home delivery, I'd need just..."

She interrupted with a gesture. "I need to pull myself together." Mrs. Queen sat down.

"Take your time," I said with intense cheerfulness.

She tapped her foot on the floor.

"Is it so difficult just to pick up a dress?"

"Excuse me?"

"And now I have to take this horribly unpleasant journey... Down a one-way street."

"Would you like some water?" I offered. Oh my, she's old, I thought.

She nodded.

"We were about to go out for a reception when I realized he hadn't picked up the dress. My favorite, my beloved dress. I've been wearing it for... twenty years. I asked my husband to do that, I told you... So, we were about to go out. To one of those receptions, where no one, no one shows up alone."

She was drinking water greedily, and, while looking at her, I gagged a bit.

"I loved to hold my husband's hand."

Mrs. Queen tilted her head, as if it suddenly got tired of sitting straight on her neck.

"I belonged," she said, clenching her hand. "I held his hand and belonged. There are only few things I am so-o sure of."

Another customer came in—a young lady with a fleece overcoat in each hand.

"When you enter a ballroom, you have to have a partner by your side."

The young lady glanced at Mrs. Queen and smirked.

"Separate receipts, please," the young lady said. "For me and for the... other coat's owner. Things are pretty erratic these days."

"Got it," I said.

Mrs. Queen was daydreaming.

"So, I just asked him to pick the coat," she started over again. "I realized I didn't have the dress an hour before we had to leave."

The young lady rolled her eyes.

"And the other name will be..." I asked.

She hesitated for a second, then said, "Just put Bauer."

"Bauer?"

"Yes, Bauer."

I put this 'Bauer' on the receipt, though I probably misspelled it.

"He didn't apologize. He said: you've got plenty of stuff, just pick something, and let's go. After thirty years of marriage, I was still not sure of my choice: he fucked other people; I once did, too. I chose a lilac-brown dress he'd brought me from one of his business trips. Fuckers like him know how to please with dresses and shoes."

The young lady flinched, then got her separate receipts and finally left.

I was trained to handle elderly customers with a spoonful of empathy.

"Was it a good reception?" I asked.

"It was a room with bright lights, and music, and champagne." Mrs. Queen closed her eyes. "Such a place where you can't really tell where you are—in heaven or in hell. But with such la joie de vivre in every moment…"

"Perhaps you can work it through," I said very politely. "With your husband. I mean, things happen."

Mrs. Queen looked at me as if I were an idiot.

"Death happens only once," she said. "He's dead."

Oh, well. How was I supposed to react? "Really?" I said.

Mrs. Queen blinked at me.

"Didn't you know that?"

How on earth would I know?

"Heart attack."

"I am so sorry."

"Isn't he a traitor?" Mrs. Queen looked at me like there was an answer in my mouth.

"Probably not," I mumbled.

She didn't hear.

"Keep the dress," she concluded. "I've had enough of it."

We're a special, expensive, and trustworthy dry cleaner. We don't have too many regular customers, but those that we have, they pay well and come back. Unclaimed items are displayed in the very back of the shop. We call that part the "museum." The red dress found its peace among others like it.

The rest of the day was quiet.

Once I saw Mrs. Queen through the window. She was leaning on a walking stick.

Melissa St. Pierre

Melissa St. Pierre teaches writing and rhetoric at Oakland University in Michigan. Her work has appeared in *The Blue Nib*, *Ponder Savant*, *Panoply*, *Valiant Scribe*, and *Elizabeth River Press Literary Anthology*. St. Pierre has also performed her work in Listen to Your Mother, a literary nonfiction storytelling showcase. When she is not writing, she is making construction paper art, playing with her daughter, or both.

Sublime

It was about $70.00. I think. He could have lied.

I said "sure" instead of "yes" because the future seemed like a long way off. And it was.

I had zero. Zilch. No. Aon cheann. Intentions of actually getting married to this guy.

He was a fun boy I dated because, well, he was low stress, and I was an intense student. School was (is) my happy place. My zen garden. My.... I am. I am. I am.

But being low stress to me was important because I had "the things" to do.

I didn't think he would ever pressure me to sleep with him, and, to his credit, he never did.

He was a fun boy I dated between high school and college.

That is all. Nothing more. Nothing less.

I began college and knew I was "home" in the sense that I was in a place I could not only shine, but I could be a supernova.

I loved everything about school, which was good, since "school" eventually became my career choice. But my university has one big problem: parking. And if it weren't 2021, and we weren't (still) facing a global pandemic, it might be the one thing I bitched about on the daily.

We came to a point at what I'll call "the great annoyance."

He was in a band, and they were, I'll admit, pretty good. They weren't going to win any Grammy awards, but they were "Michigan good."

I hated going to their shows.

Hated it.

Not because I hate music. Quite the contrary. I love live music.

Not because I have a thing against musicians. Again, definitely the contrary. (Wink, hey Pete.)

It was him.

He must have hit himself while playing because his head swelled six times too large after every show and "oh my gawd, you're so talented... "swoon, swoon, gag" wasn't my gig.

Good musicians don't need their girlfriend to say, "Yep, Bonham ain't shit."

They're just good.

So, I stopped going. I also lamented the fact I ever started dating him. But, he was a fun boy I dated between high school and college.

The band played a local gig, read: that played a fair in our hometown. I went for exactly ten minutes. Then the annoyance set in as did his, "I'm so good, why aren't you fawning? Blah, blah."

I went home and picked up my mom and dad to get some dinner. Our house wasn't air conditioned and it was a 1,000 degree July day.

He called nonstop, and I had gotten into the habit of not answering. I turned my phone off and watched Buffy (again) and felt no guilt.

I eventually came around to the fact that I was going to have to break it off.

The tipping point came when I had a voicemail with "I know you're here. I found your car." I was in my zen garden, the place where I still go to contemplate. I was in my university library in "my" spot.

My university has a parking problem.

As in, there is not nearly enough of it. And at the time that he went out of his way to stalk me, it was worse.

We finally sat down across from each other at my favorite local diner.

"This isn't going to work out," I said, as nicely as I could. I told him the parking thing was weird, and it was really what told me we were in two different places.

I didn't place any blame, and things went as well as they could.

He lavished me with gifts and refused to take them back.

I drove home with a pile of useless junk.

He quickly went from "fun boy I dated between high school and college" to arch nemesis number one.

He buddied up to my best male friend and soon they were inseparable. I'm not sure exactly what kind of bullshit rumors they started, but I have ideas.

That was the worst loss.

My friend believed an "ex" with an axe to grind.

I hadn't hurt my former boyfriend, not really. His growing ego wasn't tainted by the dismissal from his (academic) rockstar girlfriend.

I'm sure he had an "oh my gawd, you're so talented... swoon, swoon, gag" type soon after.

What stung was my best male friend taking his side. His "side"? I hadn't even drawn battleground.

But, I guess it was a "bro" thing?

I took the gifts he gave me, and I ran them over with my car.

I lined my driveway with the car as fast as I could safely go, pummeled the items into junk limestone.

What I didn't grind into dust, I gave away. With great big smiles, I watched this stuff disappear.

This is significant because I keep everything. From the first Christmas card I ever got from a boy to the necklace that very same boy gave me at thirteen. Those things mean something to me. He means something to me.

This was different.

I took the ring I had been given and left it on the edge of a sink in a heavily trafficked building on campus. I hope it brought another girl joy.

Sublime might have said it was forty ounces to freedom.

No, it was about $70.00.

Freedom.

Landré Bendaña

I am a 22 year old struggling writer who has been writing since I was 16. I am born and raised in the Philippines. I found my interest in writing when I read a short story dating back on my early college days.

And as an introvert who loves my alone time, I decided to write what's on my mind. Little did I know that I've been creating a story little by little. Ceiling, keys, and coffee partnered with frustrations, every sip has been my companion. At the very least, I just want to pacify and validate my thought, and one way of doing so is by writing. Because in writing, I am the creator. And being a creator gives me the satisfaction every time that I finished a piece, I am in control. I am free to do everything within the worlds that I create.

Words are powerful. And as an aspiring author, I want to contribute my words to the world. I want someone to feel they are understood and validated. I want to tell more stories that have never been made. That way, I will leave something—my legacy—to this world.

Audrey

Your time is up," I said as I gallantly pointed my scythe onto her neck. You could see her calmness despite the fact that I came here to take her life. On the brink of dying, she was composed like I was just a customer ordering a cup of espresso in the coffee shop she was working at.

Without a glimpse of fear, she asked me, "Are you the one they called *Death*?"

As the breeze passed through us, I claimed, "I am."

It was a windy night on a rooftop. The sky hazy, it was obvious rain might fall anytime. Rooftop was good for watching. Having myself from such a spot made me observe the people from below as they rushed to go home before the rain caught up. City lights also fetched my attention because it complemented the shady horizon. Observing the scenery gave me a brief hiatus.

"So, you can recognize me, and you're not even flustered. Aren't you afraid of me? You know I came here to take your life, don't you? I can't sense a trace of fear," I said. She lowered my scythe as she walked in front of me.

"Not flustered? I am. 'Death' appearing in front of you while drinking coffee in the breeze, who would not be flustered? I am afraid. A skull-head in a black hooded robe with its scythe pointed at me to take my life, who would not be freaked out?"

"You're afraid, and you still come near me. And you dare to pertain to me as 'its,' like I am just a mere thing." I forcefully batted my scythe's staff on the floor. I wanted her to think she was an inferior. After all, she and her kind are just life forms capable of dying when their time runs out. And her time will soon be mine.

"Don't fret. If you're not a thing, then, what are you? You aren't human, are you? Your voice sounds like a man, but it's too hefty that I nearly consider you as a whale giving birth to deformed sextuplets."

She walked to the deck. It had a small garden with sorts of flowers and a pleasant couch, a table for two with an umbrella attached upon it and a fiberglass roof. The flat lighting provided a solemn mood.

"Come sit here, mister," she invited. "Rain might fall anytime soon. Be my guest,"

Not only was she insulting me, she was completely ignoring 'Death' in her front. It was humiliating, but I got the hang of it. After all, she was a sardonic biological being.

"Are you into black or creamy coffee?" she asked.

"Let me have both. I'm not into coffee, but I want to talk to you, and I bet cups of coffee will fit the bill."

"Is death always that pensive? I'm surprised," she impassively said.

She lacks emotions—those that my past preys have shown when I approach them. Emotions are what distinguish humans from other life forms. It is an easy read that they display emotions too often. You can clearly see what they feel. Both yield a positive and negative outcome. But most of the time, it can be a hindrance. It precedes oneself until actions are done and words are said.

"Am I? What do you think?" I asked.

"Well, given the condition that you are just a concept for me before, and that concept abruptly showed and now having a coffee talk with me, I don't know. Death really has a physical form, as they've said. My mind's in shambles."

"A concept. Everyone thinks of me that way. But I am an entity like you people," I addressed.

"Here. It's not the same as those I make in the coffee shop. I don't have my ingredients. Still, that should be fine. But how will you drink my coffee? It will just spill. Is that nose even working? What's beneath that robe, anyway? Are you a pure bone from head to toe?"

"Humans really are mean. That's why you often make misunderstandings. You tend to make your own mistakes… always. And as a result, you put the blame to others for what happened, yet in the first place, it is you, yourself, who should be held accountable," I said. "And by the way, your coffee is great."

"By 'you,' are you referring to just 'me' or 'us' in general? Yeah, humans are foolish. They make things worse. They seem to help you, but they're just curious. If they have nothing to gain from you, they'll leave. It's like everybody is just manipulating everybody else to have their way on things. I sometimes wonder why they're defined as rational beings when they make the worst judgment. Some act like they're your friend, but they aren't. They're your foes, your destruction, and your vanity. You know what's worse? They rule this world. They're cretin."

Her notion aroused my interest. At that moment, my thoughts about humans became turbid. Who would have thought that a mere human like her could seize an entity like me?

"You don't recognize yourself as a human? It seems that you despise them," I said as I was about to sip my coffee.

"I am a human. That's the fact. Or I was. I am a life form—a creature, but I no longer deem myself a human. I guess I failed at being one. I don't mean that one must succeed to be a human; it's just that… they're a mess. I neglected humanity in me long ago."

"Then, what do you think you are?"

And with a tear in her voice, she claimed, "An unknown entity."

Drizzle moistened the surrounding. Thunder started to rumble, indicating the incoming rainfall.

"Can I be vulnerable with you?" she asked after finishing her first cup.

"Of course, you can," I said as I laid down my scythe on the floor. Of course, it can be intimidating.

Trying to be tough outside but slowly dying inside. She is a human, after all. She's also foolish. She's just making it hard for herself. That's one interesting part of their nature.

"Thank you," was all she managed to say as tears rolled down her cheeks. And before I knew it, it was already raining. I thought that the sky might know the history of this lady; that's why it accompanied her in her anguish.

We kept silent—listening to the raindrops plopping on the floor. I couldn't fathom how an emotionless lady created an atmosphere that was heavy enough for me to lift back and bring this one to an end. Those words she said, she's broken, abandoned, and damaged. Upon watching her working in the coffee shop, I can see her struggling to cope with life. Wearing a curve on her face to cover up the torment that was condemning her as she was taking orders from their customers. It seemed that I was bound to listen to her; after all, she was the only one who made it this far on talking with me.

"I don't feel sympathy towards humans. I only see them as my livestock. But I am obliged to listen to what you have to say. I may not be able to shed a tear or satisfy your emotional needs, but I will listen," I asserted.

The ambient fall of the rain was wistful together with the feelings she was emitting. She couldn't utter a single word for a while. I believed it was her first time crying for a long time. Wiping your tears using your hands signals a gloom that no one is there to wipe them away for you. Fighting your outer self while your demons are slowly devouring your insides is the same as burying yourself to the verge of rotting.

"It's mortifying—opening up to someone, you know that? They don't deserve to know me of what I really am. Of what I am made of. Of what made me this way. I'm afraid they might not see me as an equal again. It's not good that you're being defenseless against a variety of humans when all you want for them is to understand you. It's uncomfortable, really, especially if the one you're opening up to is someone who has his scythe lying on the floor, dressed to kill—ready to slay you anytime."

"Just think that you are doing yourself a favor. Allow that weight to diminish until you can easily breathe. Think of me as anything so that you'll never feel uneasy."

"Then, I will think of you as a prop at a Halloween party."

"That will be... just fine."

Rain continued to fall. It was compulsive to presume how these cups of coffee gave us warmth she needed as compensation for the years she lived in the cold isolating herself.

"Life is a cliché," she began. "Everyone lives in a stereotypical way thinking that there is all there is to it. The moment you realize that there's more to life than living, it's too late.

"In my case, I failed at trying. Or I already failed before I even tried. That's a simple wordplay, yeah? Then, let me make it intricate. I am trying to have a life, but life doesn't let me. It always keeps me on edge. People don't let me. They're all a bunch of users craving for their own satisfaction. Everyone has a mindset that they're all difficulties to test you as a person, and you have to overcome it in order for you to become stronger. That's too mainstream. But how can you know if 'too much' is too much? That's only an excuse they've been using to stay positive disregarding the fact that everything is messing them up, that everything is a decoy for a better tomorrow, that everything isn't under their control, that everything belongs to those who strive, and nothing belongs for those who slack. Sometimes, you just get fed up by these peoples' principles. It's toxic. Just because their ideals don't suit mine doesn't mean I am rejecting it. It's just that... after all I've been through; I don't know what principles I should implement to myself anymore because life controls me. Life owns me."

"I see. I am staggered. You've always been wanting to say that, but no one was... no one will be able to comprehend. Let me tell you wordplay, too: Everything happens for a reason. No. People just give reasons to everything that happens."

"I like that wordplay. It does make sense," she broke in. "Everything happens... for what reason? A mother died giving birth to her child for that child to feel desolation all her life? That's absurd. Really."

She blankly looked at the rain.

"You see, I am that child. I was in third grade when my father told me what caused my mother's death. It was me. My parents had a hard time deciding whether to have a child or not because of my mother's health condition. My mother told my father that she wanted to give him a child, saying that it wasn't a family they were making if there was no child to raise, and it was the least she could do for him. My mother died giving birth to me. All that left were a mourning husband and a daughter delusively treated as disaster by her father. You know what it feels like being raised by your own father knowing that he only sees you as his wife's murderer?

"I was nine years old when I tasted my father's wrath. It was a cold December night. The living room was effusive with the smell of cigarettes. The table was filled with bottles and cans of liquor. He was obviously drunk watching his and Mother's favorite movie. I approached him saying that he already had enough; he should rest because tomorrow is another day. What I said might be what triggered for his rage to suddenly flee. He took one bottle and smashed it on to my head. While crying in my blood, I perceived him as a demon. The words he said still cling to me until now. I am a misfortune. I am a killer. I am nothing but a tragedy waiting to happen. I often think and hope that they should just kill me so that I am not the one who's suffering from what kind of mistake I am that they've made. My grandparents took my custody. It was hard at first—having no parents that were supposed to be with me on Christmas and watching the fireworks on New Year's Eve. But I got used to it. I got used to everything that a child is yet to experience."

I wanted to feel her. A child that age normally would just dream of what he or she wanted to be and enjoy the caress of his or her family. But her fate doesn't allow her. Life doesn't let her as she said. "I already failed before I even tried," —how can someone afford to live—how can someone attain life if those who gave them to you abhor you the peak of their conviction? And she has been carrying them alone since she was a child. It's no wonder how she has grown into a strong and independent woman.

"How about your grandparents?"

"Oh, them." She looked at me and smirked. "I am grateful to them because they taught me that Santa isn't real, and they're squeezing my father's wealth out of me."

"I shouldn't have asked."

"It's okay. Before you cast judgment out of this unknown human-shaped entity, I might as well cast my abomination to this world. That isn't bad, is it? So that my decomposers will not be able to taste the misery lingering upon me."

"Go ahead. I am listening," I assured.

She poured another cup and sighed after showing me the scars on her palms, both with deep embedded scars. You could see a still-fresh wound caused by laceration. She was self-harming.

"They said that high school was the best part of life. Friends... friends and a lot of them. I believed that I would finally be able to have them. Those whom you can say anything without the fear of being yourself. Without the fear of having them by your side, knowing that they've got your back. Eat with them. Study with them. Even ditching sometimes. I had the best time of my life with them until a simple joke that was meant to cheer me up ruined everything.

"A simple joke that inflicted me to self-harm. 'Your parents love you, that's why they work abroad to support you.' That was a joke. That time, all I thought was my father holding a broken bottle of liquor. I accidentally slapped her. I wanted to say sorry, but instead, I ran away. That was better than explaining yourself. I never told them my secrets. I told them lies to protect myself. Weeks passed that I was alone and longing for a company. I wanted to approach them, but I thought that would just make things worse. That's a girl thing, you wouldn't understand. Anyway, another month passed, and I decided to give them a letter stating that I was so sorry, that I didn't mean to do that and sorts. Eventually, they responded. I felt happiness. I envisage that everything will be back to the way it used to be. I told them everything. I told them 'me.' I revealed myself to them. Everything turned out fine for a while. Just for a while. Then, everything went wrong. They said I became too dramatic. I became another person who sought attention. I wasn't the old me that they knew. That I had changed. Like, what on earth? After knowing the real me? After knowing how twisted I was? From that point, I've been inculcating myself this: Don't let anyone know the actual you because you are giving them an edge to destroy you. And if that happens, you'll just feel lost."

Looking her in the eye, I concluded the way she showed me her scars meant that she wanted me to take away the pain. The pain that she couldn't describe using words.

"You are forsaken. I understand why you are self-harming. But why on your palm?" I curiously asked. "So that it would be easy to hide it?"

"That's one thing. People say that we, who are self-harming, are crazy, dangerous and attention seeker. We are not. It's our way to cope up with feelings like sadness and emptiness. It can be very compelling because it puts a certain pleasure to what I feel inside. It's a way to have control over my body because I couldn't control anything else in my life. It is a cure. Emotional cure converted into scars. You asked why on my palm? It is because when I cover it with my fingers, it will form a fist—telling me to fight. To keep on living."

The coffee became cold just as the rain fell harder. Tears that flowed from her eyes connoted that she finally freed herself from years of misery that imprisoned her.

"Are you still listening, Mr. Grim Reaper? Where are Billy and Mandy, anyway?" she sneered while wiping her tears. "You are Death, sitting in front of me. So, am I literally experiencing a 'near-death experience'? You get the pun?"

"If mocking me helps you feel at ease, I will not stop you. Cry all you want. I am here. I won't leave."

"Don't fret. It's my way of retorting. I just opened myself to you. I made myself an open book. That's the least you can do."

"If that's the case, then—"

"If high school had the best of me, my college life was well-aware, and I am certain it witnessed just as the opposite. There were two sides of me saying that if I want to start anew, now is the right time and the one saying that being alone doesn't mean you're lonely. I was not alone at all; I had sadness deep within me. That's when I thought that I was just continuing living a miserable life if I let myself depend on my feelings. 'Nothing is too late if you try'. With nothing to lose and something to prove, I gave myself another chance to experience this 'one shot at life' only to experience the worst.

"I needed someone to talk to. Someone who will take the risk of picking up the shards of me just to heal me. Someone who will sail through the storm to dive to my deepest ocean. So much for the sugar-coated words. I fell in love. I fell in love with a pretentious predator hiding behind a look of a shepherd who preys on my flesh. It's erroneous to depend on your happiness that was given by someone, especially if he or she only thinks of you as his or her pastime."

I witnessed everything that happened. Death flag of a person is being raised shortly after he or she has reached the critical point of discerning that he or she wants to die. It will make their time to stop—giving way for the lost time to emanate. That tells me if a person will die. But if he or she accepts life once more and opposes the reigning of his or her lost time, that person is bound to live his or her life again. I witnessed everything. And I can't do anything but to watch.

"Consumed by the stress and pressure because of the acads, I decided to loosen up. He invited me to his place saying he wanted to help me. And there I was, a foolish sheep, hoping to eat more grass became an easy meal to a hiding wolf. I fought. I screamed. I resisted with every ounce of strength that I had, but the more I resisted, the more pleasure and satisfaction that he had. Using me against my will to feed his satisfaction, it was like my soul, being the only remnant of humanity left in me, abandoned me.

"Despair enveloped me. The 'someone' who was supposedly the one to heal me... just breaks me. The shards of me scattered. The storm of feelings turned into a calm of abyss. Everything turned against me to the point that I just couldn't feel anymore. I want pain. I want more pain because it tells me if I'm still alive. Although I am living, I feel numb. You know you're hopeless when you're inviting more pain to heal the numbness. That's the purpose of my life—to feel unending pain."

"You might not feel pain anymore," I said after I took my scythe. I stood up and fetched some rainwater on my hands. "I witnessed everything."

"And yet, you did nothing."

"I can't be involved in the way a living dies. It's against my directive."

"Yeah, right. Your duty is to let us die. To watch us die. How cruel."

"Death exists because life exists. Life is a beautiful lie, while death is an ugly truth. All that lived will meet their end—me. I am a paradox. I am death, myself, but I feed on people's lost time for me to exist. Lost time is the span of one's wasted time upon searching the meaning and purpose of his or her life not knowing that the purpose of life is to live; you find the meaning of it by living. People are my livestock. They are my lifeline. Would you call me vicious if I want somebody to die? That's why I, death, am hated and life is loved. And I have nothing against that."

I walked near her and washed her bleeding hand.

"Life is beautiful." I looked her in the eyes as I caressed her palm. "You just have to make a good use of it. In your case, life seemed to cast a curse on you. You hated life because of that."

I turned my back on her and faced the rain that was washing the city.

"And if life despises you that much… just remember that I am waiting—right from the time you were born. People are more than accepted to my realm. The condition is they just have to give their lost time to me. Would you call me selfish because of that? All I wanted is to welcome them when life gave them the reason to feel outcast. I am giving them a place to belong where suffering and pain will never be felt."

"That was a grandiose farewell advice. I am moved," she admitted. "Pain and suffering no more... because they're dead."

Death has been considered a sad occasion. But she stared at me telling me death wasn't a bad idea given the conditions she had. It's hard. Taking their lost time. Just thinking that someone has only one shot at life, and I am the one who steals that chance. But that's my directive. If someone is destined to die, then be it. I willingly accept the responsibility of enduring the sorrow.

I faced her and hovered my scythe above her.

"I don't want life to control me anymore. I already gave life its last chance, and I can't accept it any longer." She stood up and earnestly walked through the rain. Gently, she offered her weight on the palisade.

"Make a good use of my lost time," she said as she was slowly vanishing in the cold air.

***

It was a windy night on a rooftop. Rain stopped just as I finished my second cup. The noise caused by the heavy rainfall was replaced by the commotion of the people from below as they were clustering in a circle, making a hushed street into a crowded and uproarious one. The siren of the ambulance followed.

I am waiting. I am inevitable. Don't bother, for I will take all lives with no exceptions. I may not be able to shed a tear or satisfy your emotional needs, but I assure you that I will listen.

Steve Saulsbury

Steve Saulsbury writes from Maryland's Eastern Shore. When asked who his writing might appeal to, the answer was readers of both Anne Tyler and T. Coraghessan Boyle. His flash fiction, "Quicksilver," will be published in an upcoming issue of Thimble Literary Magazine. Previously, he has been published in MudRoom and U-Rights Magazine. In addition to writing, Steve enjoys shaking loose ideas on the occasional 5-mile run. He spends free weekends exploring with his wife Cathy and dog Zeus and visiting his grandson.

The Yellow One Was Actually A Cowboy

1970, Linthicum Heights, Maryland.

I collected plastic army men, green and blue, indistinguishable. A handful might be Nazis. My favorite guy, the yellow one, was actually a cowboy. He held a pistol, like my cap gun. Detailed chaps. Boots.

I had boots from Sears.

***

Ray and I were partners in a self-defense class. It was hard not to glance at that rubber foot of his. The old prosthesis reminded me of animal erasers I had collected as a child in grade school. Like a yellow dolphin marked gray with pencil.

"I was on the cover of a book once," Ray was saying, as we gathered our stuff after class.

"Really? I'd like to see it."

He brought the promo placard next time. On the poster, Ray carried canvas equipment bags from each shoulder. Tucked up in his right armpit, a rocket launcher. He gripped a standard M16 in his left fist. Boot raised, mid-stride.

He leads a trio, the other two fearlessly flanking, as if posed. A perfect shot. I was fascinated. Vietnam, to me, was mostly abstract. Childhood army men. Movies. Songs.

"Nice shot," I said.

"Book editor found it. I look pretty good."

I wanted to know more, but class began, and we went to the mat. Deflecting his punch, I tumbled Ray gently to the floor. His rubber foot was knocked askew. Ray murmured something.

It sounded like, "Thank God."

Then gone. A dry throat swallow click.

Ray smiled at the ceiling for a moment before I pulled him up.

***

1970, Binh Duong Province, South Vietnam.

After jumping from the chopper, Ray and his men started across a field. He stepped on a toe popper. The mine took most of his foot off.

Lying in the blood and grass, he craned his neck to see down his leg. His fingers found a piece of shredded boot leather.

"Thank God. Now I can go home."

***

185

The men didn't stand up in the grass too well. I took them inside, to the upstairs landing and set up the two sides.

The fighting was intense, but the good guys took the windowsill, with heavy casualties. The bad guys retreated, making a final stand by the doorway to my sister's room. A few of the good guys saw the most action. He'd been knocked down, but the yellow cowboy was still a hero.

He always lived when I got the men out.

John Tavares

Born and raised in Sioux Lookout, Ontario, John Tavares is the son of Portuguese immigrants from Sao Miguel, Azores. After graduating from arts and science at Humber College in 1993 and journalism at Centennial College in 1996, more recently he earned a Specialized Honors BA in English Literature from York University in 2012. He worked as a research assistant for the Sioux Lookout Public Library and as a research assistant in waste management for Sioux Lookout public works department and the Northwest Ontario recycle association. He also worked with persons with disabilities for the Sioux-Hudson Association for Community Living. His significantly earlier journalism was published in community print newspapers and trade publications in Toronto, and his early fiction and creative nonfiction have been published in Centennial College's campus newspaper. His short fiction has been published in an eclectic variety of print and online journals and magazines in the US, Canada, and internationally.

Following a longtime fascination with economics, John obtained certification in the Canadian Securities Course. His many passions include journalism, literature, writing, reading, and coffee, and he enjoys hiking and cycling. He is also an avid photographer, and, aside from significantly earlier photojournalism for community and trade papers, his images were featured in The Writing Disorder and on Flickr's popular Explore.

COMIC BOOK COLLECTOR

In Yonge-Dundas Square downtown, Dan observed Lori seated in a comfortable lotus position, sketching, drawing, and even painting, reading from an art history book or a volume or paintings of photographs, taking photographs with her camera, but he didn't recognize her from their hometown. Lori sometimes saw him in the square, wearing a suit, reading the business section of the Globe and Mail or the Wall Street Journal, drinking a takeout coffee from 7-11 or Starbucks. Then she did her research on social media and asked to meet him.

Her call came unexpectedly; he possessed fond memories of her, although he always remembered her as a girl from the time he was classmates and school friends with her sibling. She remembered his drawing ability, which fascinated her, as he drew pictures for panels in the comic books he produced with her older brother. Dan wondered why she called him, but Lori insisted on meeting and invited him on a date and suggested Burgermeister, a choice of restaurant which surprised him, since he expected she, slender, was into fine dining or vegetarian cuisine, not huge servings of burgers and fries. She told him the flagship restaurant was nearest to the apartment building she lived downtown, and she felt comfortable walking there at night. Still, Burgermeister was usually the last kind of restaurant Dan associated with any young women he knew. He never noticed her in the place; he was friends with the night manager at the restaurant. He even made friends with the manager's sister, who transferred to the downtown Yonge Street location to replace him, until she, too, died unexpectedly. He was a frequent late-night customer, since he lived nearby in a recently constructed condominium building on Gerard Street. He found Burgermeister's hours and location convenient and amenable for late night research on equities.

Still, having grown up in the same town, Dan felt anxious to meet Lori. So, they decided they would meet at the Burgermeister. Lori told him she had moved from Schreiber to Toronto. She was studying education and art at York University, hoping to become a high school art teacher. When he Googled her name, dozens of news articles about her father surfaced. He thought she would never live down the experience. Possibly, she could change her name, but the Bickle family of Beaverbrook always possessed an excellent reputation. The Bickles were renowned as pioneers in the town. If you stayed and lived in Beaverbrook, there were definitely advantages to being a Bickle.

At the anointed hour, he met her downtown at the Burgermeister restaurant, where she was drinking a coffee. Dan asked if she wanted to order anything to eat, but she said she enjoyed the coffee they served. He told her he was a regular customer at Burgermeister and even became acquainted with the manager, who became a friend and invited him to his apartment for his infamous patio barbecues, which usually roused the ire and annoyance of his high-rise neighbours and involved close to a dozen Hispanic men drinking imported beers and eating Tex-Mex food. A hedonist, Ricardo loved food and drink, and he was a large man. Ricardo passed away several months ago from a myocardial infarction, with undiagnosed diabetes and coronary artery disease, which might have been controlled, his sister said, if he bothered to see a doctor and moderated his smoking, drinking, and eating. Lori told Dan she was sorry to hear about his friend. Then he told her he had gotten to know Ricardo's sister, transferred from a midtown Burgermeister on Eglinton Avenue to manage the downtown restaurant. He didn't say he got to know Ricardo's sister so well they became romantic partners.

Then, several weeks ago, she chased after a Tesla driver who stole his takeout meal from the takeout window for Burgermeister. Running down Yonge Street after him, she was struck by an unmarked SUV, belonging to a private security company, hired by an association of downtown merchants, which responded to a call about a disturbance in the neighbourhood. Later, she died in the hospital from the injuries she sustained. Police tried to identify the takeout thief from DNA on the fries and hamburger he tossed out the front window of his Tesla electric car on Yonge Street.

Lori joked with Dan about legions of Tesla drivers dining on takeout orders from Burgermeister and dashing. When the joke failed to arouse any reaction, she told him she was sorry to hear. He felt relieved she was not disturbed by this revelation.

"It's kind of tragic," Dan said. "She died chasing a customer who didn't pay for his burger and fries. But she was that kind of person, devoted to her work, with a strong sense of justice." He did not say Isabella's sense of propriety was not traditional or conservative, despite her strong religious beliefs, since they first became intimate after her brother's funeral. Dan told Lori he was sorry to hear about her father. Her father was his favorite high school teacher when he was growing up in Beaverbrook. The password and security question on his different online accounts was the same, he said, which was the name of his favorite high school teacher, her father.

As Lori bit her knuckle and tried to restrain her tears, he coughed and sputtered on his coffee. "About that, I think I'm in total agreement." Dan looked around the restaurant interior, the hard rigid plastic, the artificial wood, the gleaming surfaces. "But those we're different times and we—people—hardly talked about these things, or they talked differently."

He took out a case, which contained a gift ballpoint pen. He remembered to bring the pen before he left his apartment to meet her. "How did he die?"

Her eyes started to tear over. He realized he inadvertently touched upon the taboo topic again, or maybe he deliberately wanted to touch a sensitive nerve.

"I don't want to talk about it," Lori said. She stood from the table and went downstairs to order food, an order of Caesar's salad. He insisted on paying for the salad. Dan followed her to the front counter and asked if she wanted anything else, a Burger, a poutine, a pulled pork sandwich, but she insisted she was satisfied with the salad. She insisted on paying for her own food order, as she counted the money amidst the charcoal, paintbrushes, and coloured pencils, and the sketch pad in her handbag. He became determined to provide some consolation and solace to her somehow. She sat back down at the table and looked deeply into his eyes, so deeply she left him disconcerted.

"Remember that time you came into the house, and I was just a kid all alone in the basement."

"I hadn't expected you to be at home because I thought you went grocery shopping with your mother while your father and Larry went fishing."

"But why did you come downstairs?"

"But why do you ask? It's kind of ancient history."

"Because I'm trying to work through a few issues with my therapist. She recommended I ask."

"Sure, if it helps, and I mean you're justified to ask because, after all, it was your house. I went there to pick up my special edition collector's issue of *Superman versus Spiderman*. I lost it—I mean, Larry borrowed the issue from me without asking. I wanted my comic back. If I remember correctly, he said he returned it, but he hadn't. I went to your house to rescue my comic book commando style. I guess I practically broke in the house."

Larry and Dan even worked on a comic book together, as a school project, drafting and writing the media project in Larry's basement bedroom. Larry provided the storyline and dialogue, while Dan drew the pictures. Dan remembered how Lori watched intently as he drew, admiring the intensity, skill, and concentration. He thought he caught a glimpse of infatuation as she hovered over him, marvelling at his sketching and drawings of the figures for their comic book. But the comic was not about superheroes; it was historical, based on a real-life figure—The Mad

Trapper. Larry joked there seemed a certain obsession in how Lori watched him drawing the comic book figures and panels.

"But it wasn't like you were a burglar. I mean, you were a guest in the house so many times before."

"Still, it was kind of shady. But it shows you how ardent and serious a comic book collector I was. Comic books meant more to me than people, friends, even friend's feelings. Like maybe money means more to me than people these days."

"That's awful."

"Truly awful, but, until I got into that conventional mindset, I wasn't going anywhere career-wise."

Lori became short-tempered—disappointed at how he changed. "Forget about it. I didn't come here to talk about comic books. But what exactly did you say to me?"

"I didn't say anything. Trust me: the memory has plagued me a bit ever since: I behaved badly, in the name of my precious comic book collection; it was such a creepy thing. But you were, like, totally unfazed. In fact, you said: 'I want to show you something.'"

Hurt, Lori frowned. "I wanted to show you the house I built for my Barbie doll collection."

"Then I was so scared I took off."

"But didn't you... touch me then."

He noticed she phrased the question as a statement. "Touch you?"

"Inappropriately?"

"Absolutely not."

"That's not what I remember."

"I went to find my oversized collectable comic book, and then I left. Then it became the comic book war. I start arguing with Larry about it at school. Then, one afternoon after school, while I was riding home on my bike, after I complained to your mother and father, separately, and started bugging him at school, he caught up with me with his thuggish friend. They jumped me from behind, made me crash my bicycle and started beating me and kicking me in the stomach."

"You should have complained."

Dan laughed, remembering the crash of bicycles, a few blocks from the police station.

"Didn't you tell my parents?"

"Absolutely not. I didn't even care about the punches and kicks then. All I cared about then was my comic books. When I called him one last time, I pleaded with him to please return my comic books. Your mother was listening on the telephone, the extension telephone. I think your family was one of the few in town to have extension telephones then. She made

Larry return the comic book immediately." He remembered Larry's mother drove the family's Cadillac across the railroad tracks, across town, to his parents' house to return that collectable. "What kind of amazed me—he returned other comic books I figured he had, other comic books that disappeared on me. But I think she forbade him from seeing or talking with me because he hardly spoke with me afterwards. He never came over to the house again. He never invited me over to your place again."

"That time, though, didn't you touch me... inappropriately?"

Dan was not listening or paying attention; he saw another employee removing trays and remembered Ricardo. He wondered how a relatively young man, only in his forties, could have died from heart disease. He thought about Ricardo's sister... and her beauty. She unexpectedly offered herself to him, at a moment when he least expected, although he recalled numerous jokes about sex and funerals. Still, he did not think his memories were significant or even worth discussing, but she nurtured other ideas.

"But you touched me then."

Dan frowned. "Absolutely not. I can't remember that part."

As Lori started sobbing, Dan realized she was in some unhappy headspace. He pulled out the case with the engraved pen. "Anyway, I wanted you to have this pen. Your father gave this pen to me when I graduated from Beaverbrook High School. He must have given them to all his students. Anyway, I hung onto my pen. I thought you should have it, as a token of appreciation."

"I don't want it," she said. "He was an evil man."

Looking wounded, he nonetheless pressed the pen into her hand, stained with oil paint. She placed the shiny silver writing instrument in the pocket of her coat. He thought he should try to make the best of a difficult situation. He suddenly noticed how attractive she was—physically. He thought her personality wonderful, although he received the impression she had personal issues, but she looked physically attractive as well, something he never expected or remembered; she had become a regular at the gym and yoga studio.

"Can I take you to dinner next week?"

They agreed to meet at the Starbucks for coffee further down Yonge Street, but still downtown, in a week. She told him she was in the middle of term for fall semester at York University. A double major in arts and pedagogy in the faculty of education, she planned to become an arts teacher once she graduated. She insisted she needed to study for her midterm exams. They agreed to first meet at Dundas Square the Starbucks, a block south of the Burgermeister on Yonge Street. He seemed disappointed she did not want to meet for dinner. The Starbucks, though, was more spacious. Then he mentioned how sometimes smaller restaurants made him feel claustrophobic. She agreed to meet him in Yonge-Dundas Square at night, when the pace of city life had slowed. When he met her later at the Starbucks at King and Yonge, large and spacious, she said she was relieved. They could have an intimate conversation.

Eager to open up, Lori confessed her actions may have led to the death of her father. "I killed him." When she saw how shocked and appalled he appeared, she explained: When her father was first charged, he wanted her to help him kill himself with a cocktail of his heart, hypertension, diabetes, and pain medication. He had done his pharmaceutical research and determined the precise dose, just over the prescribed amount, that would lead to his death. He repeatedly asked her to assist him in his own suicide, which he wanted to make appear the result of natural causes, but she refused. When the news became public, the latest versions of the stories sounded more scandalous. She could not bear the pressure of being the daughter of a sexual predator, living in the same house and even the same hometown as him, to say nothing of his victims. Even their mother moved out of the house, back to her original hometown on the West Coast, and abandoned him. Then Lori mixed up his medications, peeling apart the capsules, emptying the powder, grounding and pulverizing the tablets with a mortar and pedestal in the laboratory of the high school chemistry class.

"You have to understand," Dan said, "he was suffering from a sickness, an illness."

Lori sobbed again, as she drank a second latte, which he got the impression was the only nutrition she had received that day. "If you're telling me that to make one feel better, you need to know it's simply not true. It was evil, pure evil." She took a paper napkin from beside his coffee and laptop computer, wiped her eyes, and blew her nose. "But I need you. I need someone. Do you think I could stay with you?"

The perennial Toronto problems: rents; places to stay. "I can help you with the rent, if that's an issue."

"Don't we have a bond, an affinity?"

He was finding her more attractive each time he met her, after knowing her as a girl and a teenager, bullied by her older, bigger brother, who even choked her in front of him, including in his impersonations of Darth Vader, which he tried to prevent. He didn't feel that strong an attraction— yet. A stronger sense of attraction came later, when it was too late, maybe because it was too late.

"I don't think I'm ready for that—yet, but if you need any financial help—"

"No!" Lori shouted. She slammed her balled fist on the table, spilling her coffee, staining and splattering the beverage on the keyboard and screen of his laptop, which he wiped clean with paper napkins. While he apologized and asked her if everything was all right, Lori gathered her backpack and left the restaurant. He felt lost, abandoned, and rejected. He realized she trapped him, caught him, in some mysterious attraction. When he tried to call and message her, she didn't reply. He tried calling and emailing Lori again, but she didn't answer the telephone, and his e-mails returned to his inbox as unsendable. Dan realized Lori blocked his e-mails and blocked him on social media.

Late at night, Dan boarded the subway train from the high-rise King Street offices of the brokerage firm where he tried to calm investors panicked over the selloff in oil and natural gas stocks after Saudi Arabia led the cartel of oil producing nations into waging a price war. In the subway station, underneath Yonge Street, Dan saw a woman, who resembled Lori, wearing a red coat. She frantically paced the southbound subway platform. Dan could not identify Lori for certain from where he stood, partly because the fur-lined hood of her coat and scarf obstructed a view of her face. The young woman's figure resembled Lori, though. Her face frozen in a mask, she grimaced as she muttered, her hands ominously clasped in what appeared like prayer. Dan wondered if Lori sought and followed him but dismissed the possibility. He called across the sets of tracks to the southbound platform, empty of commuters on this chilly, rainy night.

"Lori, is that you?" Dan asked her if she needed to talk, but the woman looked away and covered her face with her scarf. Then the unthinkable, which he somehow expected, happened, as the roar of a southbound train flooded King station. As the train sped into the subway station, the woman leapt in its path. He managed to stay calm and keep his senses, since this wasn't the first jumper he witnessed, commuting on the subway system. Spotting the blue light at the end of the platform, he hurried to the power cabinet and punched the emergency button on the blue light box to cut the power. He called 911, but when the operator asked for personal information, he hung up the receiver of the pay telephone. He raced to the front of the southbound train, leaping onto the tracks, muddying his shoes and suit with dirt and oil. When he saw the blood and a mangled body twisted beneath the front of the train, he realized her chances of survival were remote.

Afterwards, he felt relieved he gave the necessary info but refused to offer his name when the emergency operator asked. He couldn't be the sole witness to a subway suicide when his work as financial advisor put him in a crucial position of trust. He hurried up the steps from the underground and walked along Yonge Street homeward bound. He hoped the victim he saw wasn't Lori; he dismissed the resemblance as a figment of his imagination, a function of his subverted yearnings.

Still, over the following days, he tried to contact her. He thought she simply refused to answer the telephone. Finally, he decided to try to visit her in her apartment in a rundown building on Dundas Street, but he knocked on the door and buzzed the intercom until he realized nobody would ever answer. Then he went downtown to the Burgermeister, but the place seemed empty without his friend Ricardo or his friend's sister, Estrella, and he longed for Lori. Late at night, no restaurants or cafes were open in the area, so he decided to buy a self-serve takeout coffee, in an extra-large paper cup, from the 7-11 downtown. He drank his coffee and read his newspaper until a few hours passed and searched for Lori again. He hoped to find her in the square, usually quieter late at night. Maybe he would spot her getting off the streetcar or climbing the stairs from the subway or reading an art book or sketching in her bound sketchpad. He reflected on whether the identity of the woman he saw leaping in front of the subway train was Lori. If it was indeed Lori who jumped, he wondered if she wanted him to bear witness, as accusation or retribution, making him feel her pain and turmoil.

Earlier, Dan told Lori the route he took on the subway from King Street, a station near his condo apartment, when he worked late, worried about a disgruntled client, or didn't feel like walking. As he read the Wall Street Journal and sipped coffee on a cement bench in Dundas Square, he wondered if Lori was upset at him. Then one night, as the night grew chillier, and quieter, and the drizzle turned to rain, he thought he saw Larry walking purposefully past Dundas Square, but he couldn't believe his eyes. Why would Larry be in Toronto, a thousand miles from home, in a city he despised, during the Sacred Heart School Grade Eight Toronto trip?

Why would Larry, dressed formally, in an overcoat, be walking along Dundas Street in Toronto? After all, he was a high school teacher in their hometown of Beaverbrook. But he recognized him from his awkward walking gait, his nervous tic, his squint, as he constantly adjusted the position of his glasses. Dan, pressed against the wind and the chill, hurried across Yonge-Dundas Square, following after.

"Larry, what are you doing here?"

"I'd ask the same, but—"

Larry was surprised to see him. Dan looked good—wasn't dressed as if he was taking a hike through the bush around Beaverbrook. He was actually wearing a pair of fine shoes, not scuffed, muddy runners, and a suit, which surprised him, although he had heard he was working in financial services in Toronto. They sought shelter beneath the pavilions and open air structures in Yonge-Dundas Square.

"I was talking to Lori, and she said—"

"Lori is gone. She ended her own life."

"What?"

"Listen, she was messed up, and it was bound to happen sooner or later."

"I got the impression she had personal issues, but she sounded like she was on the right track, back in school, studying at York U, working towards a career as an art teacher."

"After she says she killed her father, yeah."

"She mentioned your father passed."

"I told her to shut her mouth, but she insisted on a confession. I did the best I could to stop her from confessing to the police."

"You should have encouraged her."

"Encouraged her? You think?" Larry forced a laugh. "I just came from the precinct to answer a few of their questions. I had to sign for her body and belongings, etc. Listen, whatever she told you—"

"She didn't say much."

"Good. The sooner you're able to forget Lori, the better; it will mess with your head to think about her." He dug his hands into his overcoat and pulled out an engraved silver ballpoint pen. "Here. The police gave me this. They found it in her coat pocket. This pen has your name engraved."

"Your father gave me that pen—at our graduation. I thought he gave one to everyone."

"I don't remember receiving one. You must be special," Larry said, as he again emitted a forced laugh. "Now, if you don't mind, I have to clean her apartment and handle business with her landlord."

"Do you need help?"

"Definitely not."

Larry didn't need his consolation or companionship, and now Dan wondered what motivated him to make the offer. Meanwhile, Larry marvelled at Dan's transformation into a city slicker from a small-town life of drifting from job to job in northwestern Ontario, where he could never seem to decide if he was an Italian immigrant, like his father, or an indigenous Cree from the nearby reserve, like his mother. Dressed in funereal style, Larry walked through the night and drizzling rain and fog, striding along Dundas Street towards Lori's bachelor apartment in the inner city.

"I remember you choking her," Dan shouted. Larry turned around while he walked backwards.

"Are you talking about my Darth Vader impersonations?" Larry shouted beneath the street lanterns on the darkened sidewalk of Dundas Street East.

Dan realized it was a cruel and heartless thing to say, even if true; Larry's sister recently passed. The experiences to which he alluded occurred when they were children. "Sorry for your loss," Dan shouted.

Larry shrugged and turned around. "She really liked you—in fact, she loved you, but our father warned her against you. He thought you were a loser, a wayward Indian, and he ordered her to steer clear—wisely."

Rage overtook Dan, who chased after Larry. He tackled him to the ground and pummeled him with his balled fists until he split his lip and his nose bled. He realized his primitive emotion overwhelmed the better part of his nature. He apologized to Dan, helped him to his feet, and told him he was sorry for his loss. After he loaded him into a taxicab, he headed back down Dundas towards Yonge Street, through the rain and darkness, punctuated by the streaking lights from the bustling traffic downtown.

The memory of Lori lingered. Dan couldn't forget Lori as a child when he, a commando on a raid to rescue his collectable comic book, went into the basement. The image of her there and in the subway lingered with him. Whenever he rode in the subway in Toronto, whenever the train roared into the station, his heart and temples pounded and he was short of breath, filled with fear and self-consciousness. Dan felt afflicted—haunted by the image of Lori leaping in front of the speeding front car. He feared somehow the same fate would befall him. Public transit was his preferred mode of transportation, and he did not enjoy driving in the city. Still, although he bemoaned the expense, he bought an oversized SUV, with poor gas mileage, which the salesperson reassured him, had the best safety record.

Romall Smith II

Romall H. Smith II is an American science fiction and science fantasy novelist. A graduate of Full Sail University, he is currently on a quest to write the next great Sci-Fi epic or at least one that can earn him a ticket on the first commercial space shuttle.

Primetime on Primus V

It has been said that the greatest thing one can do is to give their life in the service of others. Out here on Primus V, the most significant thing you can do is live one more day.

Iontach stood at the edge of an ornate platform. The smell of ocean brine sprayed against him as it descended closer to the salt crystal-laden waters below. A silver sphere followed just above him. It moved about the air, its lens intent on capturing his every movement. He paid it no attention as his focus was elsewhere. Towering holo-stands hovered a few hundred meters away, each one filled with the opaque green images of screaming fans. All of whom had paid to see the greatest gladiator on the planet. Fireworks explode overhead, their bright lights reflected off the metallic adornments of Inotach's armor. The polyurethane gloves he wore warmed, and electricity sizzled as his grip tightened on the trident. The thunderous cheers of the crowd crashed against his ears. He barely heard the horn of battle blare but, hear it, he did. Iontach knelt, his gaze on a shadow in the water. The shadow appeared to grow in size by the second. He tapped a sensor on his breastplate. Layers of ablative armor extended out the collar and covered his mouth. A Selachimorpha, the size of a bus with an eight-foot dorsal fin, leapt out of the water. Its maw, wider than seven men, gaped open, displaying rows of blood-stained teeth. Iontach exhaled, then dove from his platform toward the waters below.

The city of Scogliera is one of the largest found on Primus V. That isn't saying much, however, as there are only three cities and a handful of villages scattered across the aquatic world. A collection of shanties, canals, and floating docks, Scogliera is a man-made island, unfortunate for Jericho of the Pescatore clan. He is not the biggest fan of the islands, water, or people, for that matter. Born on Earth, before the cataclysm, Jericho is among the few citizens of Scogliera that can't swim. He even takes pride in that fact.

"You gotta learn sometime; jump in," shouted Brin, his arms fanned out to stay afloat.

Jericho stared out at the water. The sapphire blue expanse stretched to the horizon. Its unreal depths were interrupted only by the neon indigo crest of the waves.

"Primus herself would have to pull me in," said Jericho. He stood up and walked along the edge of the fishing boat. "If the universe wanted me to be a swimmer, I would have been born to the Nuoto clan. Those guys swim like fish," Jericho said as he stopped at a small white box. His hand disappeared into the opening of the box.

"You know there were no clans back on Earth. Dive in, and I'll teach you how to tread water at least," said Brin as he bobbed in the water. "If dad were here, he would have just thrown you in."

"Maybe," said Jericho. He smiled. Dad would definitely have thrown him into the water and yelled, 'sink or swim.' Ironically, his dad would've also been the one to dive in and rescue him at the first sign of trouble. Jericho pulled a small cephalopod out of the cooler. Its tiny tentacles wrapped around each gloved finger.

"What happens if you fall off the boat?" Asked Brin.

"Well."

Jericho tightened his hand into a fist. A faint smell of ozone drifted through the air. The cephalopod released its grasp and retreated into a ball as electricity crackled and coursed across the gloves. Jericho pulled back his arm and launched the creature. The cephalopod unfolded and flew as though it had wings. A shadow appeared to give chase beneath the waves. The tiny creature smacked the water a hundred feet away. The cephalopod struggled. Its efforts fruitless as the paralyzed creature began to sink. Suddenly a fish jumped out of the water, its metallic dagger-like teeth sheared through the defenseless animal.

"Nature will take its course."

"That's one way to look at things, not sure it's the best way. One of these days, you're going to have to show me how you do that."

Brin began to swim towards the ship. Jericho walked back towards the stern. He stopped at a glowing blue pad on the ground, the heel of his boot clanged against it. Several beams of light emanated out of the deck. The beams searched the air for one another till they connected. One by one, each of the beams interlaced till a bridge was formed. The light bridge lowered into the water in front of Brin. He walked out of the water on the bridge and up to his brother Jericho.

"You two ready to head back to the city?" asked Ines as she walked out of the ship's cabin.

"We are ready whenever you are, Mom," said Jericho.

The deep lines of age around her mouth cracked and shifted into a smile.

"I'll go start the engines. You boys secure the ampoules. We have a storm coming in, and I can't afford to lose any of this shipment," she said.

Usually a fishing vessel, The Amelia had been modified for a different purpose. Atop her weathered deck sat four large polished silver ampoules. Thirty feet long and eight feet tall, each was capable of holding ten thousand gallons of Indigo muon. A scarce and addictive substance, Indigo muon can be found only on Primus V. The two-teenager moved quickly to secure their precious cargo.

"You ever wonder how different life would be back on earth?" asked Jericho.

"Are you kidding me?"

"I am serious. You ever wonder where we would be or what we would be doing?"

"Well, I doubt we would be running muon for one."

"That's true, and Dad would probably still be here."

The two went silent for a moment. The only sound audible was the hum of the ship's repulsors pushing against the wave beneath them as the craft accelerated. It was a sound that seemed to grow and change more than expected. What started as a low pitch rumble began to grow into a high pitch whine.

"Something's wrong. We are moving too quick," said Brin. He held on to the side of the ampoule and moved to the aft of the ship. He opened a panel, flicked several switches, then pushed a flashing button. "Is everything all right, Mom?"

"Nope, we got something closing on us fast," Ines said, her voice hurried.

"Selachimorpha?" Asked Brin, his voice shaky with terror.

"It's a ship," Ines said. "Can one of you get to the bolt thrower?" she asked.

"On my way," Brin took off running towards the starboard bolt thrower of The Amelia.

"Everything all right?" shouted Jericho. He watched as his brother sprinted past.

"We got company; I'm going to man the bolter. Finish securing the cargo."

"I'm on it."

Jericho ran to the third container. His hand reached out to a keypad. He quickly tried to key in the lockdown sequence. His fingers froze just above the last digit. At first, it felt like a bee had stung him, then a myliobatid, but in just a couple of seconds, the pain stopped him cold. Electricity coursed through his body. Jericho's head seized as he tried to look down. Blood poured out of his side and down to the deck floor. A tingle went up his neck and tightening his jaw as he struggled to lift his head. Looking down to the end of the ampoules, there was a cruiser on fast approach. It's fore ship bolter lit up as it fired another salvo. He felt another sting on his shoulder, and the world went dark.

Sweat dripped and heat radiated from the mob. Two pillars stood atop a platform; energy arched and swirled between them. The air filled with the smell of dry paper as the fabric of spacetime between them ripped, revealing a blackness so dark even light seemed to disappear. Thousands of voices crashed together in the street like a raging river as the mob flowed into the portal. In the midst of the chaos, a small boy stopped. The world may have been coming to an end, but in that moment, it was silent for Jericho. He lifted his head to the sky and held up a card. The rolling cloud of darkness cascaded from one end of the horizon to the other, with flashes of blue and purple. Light exploded in the air, raining down sparks like fireworks celebrating the end of the day. Lighting arched from the sky.

"Jericho, wake up," said a man, his voice fading with the darkness.

The metal deck was cold against Jericho's jaw. In front of him lay Brin and Ines.

"What do you want to do with them, Captain," asked a burly pirate.

"Fighters, the whole lot. We either take them all or none," said the Captain.

"Can't we just keep the woman?" asked the burly pirate.

"She'll sooner slit our throats in our sleep. Do what you want, but secure the cargo and throw 'em overboard."

The burly man moved to grab Ines. Not in the best shape but still coherent, she resisted, pushing him away. The pirate slammed his giant fist into her face.

"Oh, you are going to be fun," he said.

Jericho screamed into the void, but nothing came out. Paralysis persisted as he tried to will his body back to life. A twinge of something shot up the back of Jericho's neck. He wasn't wholly unstunned, but the sound of cloth ripping echoed in his ears. Finally, a flood of adrenaline flowed throughout his body.

"Toilteanas," he screamed, the word half caught in his throat.

Several of the pirates turn towards him. The Captain stopped mid stride.

"Toilteanas," Jericho said again.

Like his father before him, he now offered his life in exchange for the freedom of his family. The Captain walked over to Jericho and kneeled. The old sailor's sunbaked face stared at the young man with curiosity.

"Boy, do you even know what you are saying?" asked the Captain.

Jericho steeled his nerves and stared back at the pirate.

"I challenge any one of you cowards to Toilteanas. I win, we go free."

The pirates each let out a hearty laugh.

"You lose, you die, and we keep them as slaves," said the Captain.

"I am already dead," Jericho said with adrenaline still surging through his body.

"Bring him to the ship," said the Captain pointing to the burly man.

The giant pirate lurched over to Brin. He effortlessly picked the boy up off the deck. He pushed Jericho, and the two walked to the pirate's vessel. Twice the size of the Amelia, this ship was meant for more than fishing. The ship was lined with metal plating and bristled with bolt throwers. Jericho caught a glimpse of what looked like a laser cutter at the bow of the ship. This ship is a fighting ship meant for raiding. Jericho and his family never stood a chance. The two men stopped at a small platform on the opposite side of the pirates' ship. Their Captain waved his hand. The platform beneath the two men hissed, steam released from its edges as it lifted into the air. When it stopped, small devices rose out of the ground. Jericho grabbed the two closest to him. Gripping the device, he squeezed till a burst of light emitted from the devices. The one took the shape of a shield. The other resembled a sword.

The large burly pirate took off his vest. The barrel-chested monster grabbed the weapon and left the shield.

"I, Qiknas, will be your challenge," said Qiknas pounding on his chest.

Jericho still felt the bolters' effects. Even as the world wobbled around him, he charged Qiknas. The man casually sidestepped. Jericho lost his footing, stumbled forward, and dropped his shield. The light deactivated just before it made contact with the water. The group of spectating pirates roared with laughter.

"You embarrass yourself."

Jericho gritted his teeth. The heat of anger rushed over his face and down his back. He charged Qiknas. This time, he feinted left, then stabbed right. The large pirate was not expecting the quick movements. Caught off guard, he allowed Jericho to draw first blood with the blow glancing off his pectoral. Jericho smiled; his mobility was returning. Qiknas winced, then launched a series of attacks against Jericho. Every swing was more thunderous than the last. Jericho's grip, not at full strength, couldn't hold against the onslaught. A powerful swing knocked his sword away. It slid to the edge of the platform, then Qiknas' blade pointed at Jericho's throat.

"Warning. Selachimorph fifty meters out," chirped the ship's computer over the P.A.

"You are better than you look," yelled the Captain. "Join my crew, and only the others have to die here," he said.

"Go eat a Tetraodontidae," said Jericho. His disdain and defiance saturated every syllable.

"Warning Sciliamorph twenty meters out," chirped the ship's computer.

"Okay then, now you can watch them both die," said the Captain. "Throw the boy over."

"No!" shouted Jericho.

One of the pirates picked up a barely conscious Brin and tossed him into the water. Jericho's chest ached, and his heart tightened. The taste of the sea air was washed away by the tide of vomit cresting in his throat. Jericho looked around, then his eyes locked on the enormous dorsal fin speeding towards Brin. The voice of their father echoed in the back of his mind.

Jericho knocked Qikna's blade away with his forearm. He turned and dove to the edge of the platform, his outstretched fingers grasping for the small device that was moments ago his sword. He rolled over the sword, then leapt off the platform. He gripped the weapon as though it were one of the cephalopods. Electricity crackled and burst out his gloves, consecrating the weapon he held, just as 30-foot Selachimorph rose from the water. Its razor-sharp teeth ready to feast. Jericho drove his blade through the top of the shark's head. The beast thrashed, bucking him off. Thrown against the hull of the ship, Jericho's world once again grew cold and dark.

"Jericho, wake up, my boy," said Hionach.

The tingle of electricity numbed his arms while the pain of fire ripped through his body in waves. Ines ripped off shreds of her shirt and handed them to Hionach. The smell of grilled meat and ozone filled the air. Jericho looked down at his body. Charred flesh and blood were everywhere. Brin poured water over the wounds. The ground trembled as if in fear of the inevitable.

"Ines, you and the boys have to go. They can help you on the other side," Hionach said.

"What about you?" she asked.

"We only have three passes left. The greatest thing I can do…"

Jericho watched them exchange final affections, unable to voice his disagreement or say goodbye to his father. Standing on the platform before the portal, Hionach handed him over to the guardians. He leaned down and kissed Jericho's forehead.

"Survive," Hionach said.

He watched his father fade as they carried him into the darkness.

It has been nearly seven years since he last saw his mother or brother. The pirates that day were a mix of Concorso Clan and Guerreiro Clan. Both of whom respected the Toilteanas or one's willingness to sacrifice. He lost that rite of passage, but with his bravery, he earned his family's freedom. The catch to losing a rite of passage is you lose your name and clan. That was the day Jericho of the Pescotore clan died, and Iontach "Shark Slayer" of the entertainer clan, Concorso, was born.

Sarah Kaminski

Sarah Kaminski writes stories dealing with love, loss, and other bittersweet moments. She loves a story that connects with the reader on an emotional level and explores the depth of the human experience. She teaches math in Kansas City, where she lives with her husband and two children. In her free time, she enjoys singing along with very loud music, telling corny jokes, and playing fetch with her rambunctious dog, Loki. Her years in the classroom have taught her that everyone has a story to tell. You can find her at www.sarahkaminskiauthor.com.

EMPTY SPACE

In art, the empty space holds meaning. Parts of the canvas are purposefully left empty, seemingly forgotten, void of paint, so that the rest of the piece shows through that much more magnificent.

Sidah hadn't been an artist for many years. She had gone to school for it, one of the most prestigious in the country, but when her desire to eat overpowered her desire to create, she had gone back and earned a more marketable degree in graphic design. At first, she told herself she could still paint on the weekends. She filled her studio apartment with canvasses and oils. When the girls at the office invited her for happy hour drinks, she made excuses and went home to paint, but over the years, inspiration became more difficult to come by. Worries about the meaning of life fell away, replaced with worries about paying rent. Soon, entire canvasses were filled with empty space.

Her mother, who had earned her keep in the seventies, had filled Sidah's head with ideas of women's liberation, no more needing a man. But she had hated every second of her workday, and now that Sidah was grown, she could hardly be counted on to lend a supportive ear. Once a week, Sidah called to complain, but her mother wouldn't listen.

"No one likes their job, Sidah."

"Every day, I feel my soul dying."

"Don't be dramatic. You've been there so long. Try making friends."

As if Sidah's lack of inspiration was a symptom of loneliness. Still, she felt she ought to at least put forth an effort. The next Friday, when Julie from Marketing stopped by her cubicle to ask if she wanted to join the gang for drinks, instead of her usual "No thank you," Sidah nodded and said, "Yes."

The weekly ritual of happy hour involved seven or eight single twenty-somethings walking to MacLaggen's, the only tavern in the city that served Midleton Irish Whiskey, which was the only whiskey worth drinking, according to Paul Clemons, the company's resident liquor snob.

The group peppered Sidah with questions as they walked. The who, what, when, where, and why of her life. Paul wanted to know what she drank.

"Vodka tonic."

"Damn," he said, "that shit's disgusting."

"But it'll get you drunk." And it had helped to get those creative juices flowing, in those not-so-long-ago days when she had still harbored ambitions to put paint on canvas and sell it.

Julie asked where she was born.

"South Carolina."

Beth, another graphic artist with a mediocre eye for color themes but a double D rack that more than made up for her ineptitude, asked her what brought her to the city.

"Delusions of grandeur," she replied. "Same as everybody else."

They laughed, then avoided each other's eyes. She had been too honest. A criticism she had heard often at art school.

Too much honesty.

"Art," she had argued, "is supposed to be honest."

"Yes, but you don't have to hit people upside the head with it."

Now she worked in advertising. There was no honesty in that. Only deadlines and tricks and bottom lines.

***

After eight years, she still worked for the company, still slaved away at her 9 to 5 with little to show for it. Her old boss, a humorless, emotionless woman only three years her senior—had been promoted and replaced with Mr. Barker. He insisted on being called "Mister" as if his first name was too good to be used by the likes of them. On particularly bad days, and she could tell they were coming by the way his gait changed from a general stomp into a rushed stumble, he questioned every decision she made.

"Why did you use this color?"

"Should the logo be at an angle?"

"What were you thinking shrinking it to 85% its original size?"

On good days, he ignored her. He passed her in the break room without even registering her presence. He said "Good morning" to everyone in the office, except her. Pointedly so. When she and Beth stood by the coffeemaker and waited for it to issue two mugs' worth of holy nectar, he glanced at both of them, then nodded to Beth. "Morning, Beth. Did you catch that game last night?"

He conducted weekly meetings where he praised the same six people for their work.

"Beth's web design on the Hoops-Craig account was superb. If you get a chance, check it out."

In truth, Beth's web design on the Hoops-Craig account was uninspired. Sidah could see that. She tried not to feel jealous of the praise Beth received, yet again, for sub-standard work, while she put together brilliant designs that went largely unnoticed. Mr. Barker never mentioned Sidah's name during the weekly reports. She had stopped expecting it, though she never stopped hoping.

"Why do I even care about what that man says?" she asked Beth over lunch at the café down the street.

"You shouldn't. He's an ass."

"I blame my father," she joked. "Doesn't everything come back to a Daddy issue? Expecting praise, breaking your back trying to impress a man who doesn't care that you exist?"

Beth shifted in her seat, poked at her salad, and said nothing.

Sidah went home to an empty apartment and stared at her empty canvasses and prayed for inspiration to come. She longed for the days in her early twenties when she could stay up all night painting and survive the next day with copious amounts of coffee. High off her own brilliance.

Now, instead of feeling inspired, she merely felt invisible. Disappointed in her lack of creativity. Exhausted. She worried that her brilliance had come and gone, and she had nothing to show for it except more empty space.

At happy hours, she told herself she wouldn't drink too much, she wouldn't reach that point when work frustrations came bubbling out and she started complaining. But inevitably she would consume two drinks in silence, until Julie made some remark about this or that, and Sidah's own laundry list of complaints came pouring forth. The chief of which:

"Barker hates me." She refused to call him "Mister" outside the office.

"No, he doesn't. Why do you say that?" Paul had long ago made it his personal mission to win Sidah's affection, after she stupidly brought him home one evening after happy hour, but his insipid insistence on being loved barely registered on her radar. Paul was harmless—one of those lapdogs who will gladly do anything you want in the sack but drive you up a wall in the morning.

"He doesn't even know I exist."

"Sure, he does."

"He never acknowledges me." Sidah finished off a third vodka tonic. Her tongue felt heavy. She should have slowed down. At least she lived within walking distance. "That Hoops-Craig account Beth did so well on? She kept coming to me with questions about a thousand times a day. I practically did it myself!"

She couldn't help but compare herself to Beth. Sidah's work was better. She didn't need confirmation to know that. Beth worked harder, but Sidah had natural talent. No amount of training could replace true talent. And yet, her work went unnoticed. She was given smaller jobs, fewer opportunities for promotion. She felt stuck. Applying for a new job was exhausting. She didn't have the energy anymore.

And it seeped into everything she did. She wore muted tones now, no more brightly colored tops and thick eyeliner. Sidah had switched to wearing beiges, grays and blacks. She blended with the walls, just like everyone else. When new hires came in wearing their personalities on their sleeves, she chuckled to herself, rolled her eyes, and watched them slowly die and disappear.

How much of herself had she lost in those eight years? When was the last time she picked up a paintbrush? Eventually, she threw out the empty canvasses, to make space in her apartment for an actual couch where she could sit and stare at the TV screen at the end of the day and become yet another mindless drone from the office. A couch where she could waste away the empty hours of her life.

She kept some of her art. The best stuff, but she had hidden it away in her bedroom closet. Instead, she decorated her apartment with kitsch, pretty things bought at Bed, Bath & Beyond that lacked any real meaning.

Days rolled into each other. Every one of them the same.

Every moment filled with meaningless empty exchanges.

"Good morning."

"Did you have a nice weekend?"

"Weather's turning."

"About time."

Her mind wandered away from conversations. She didn't need to be present to hold up her half of it. She could fill in the empty spaces.

"Pleasant enough, I suppose."

"We could use the rain."

"Yeah."

She ate her lunches with Beth in the break room. Most days she ate leftovers from the night before, or a ham sandwich, nothing special. She had long ago given up trying to cook the cuisines of the world. Macaroni and cheese was easier, and, if she had to be honest, tasted better too.

"You have any plans this weekend?" Sidah asked between bites of canned soup.

"It's our anniversary."

"So, ditching the kids?" Sidah suggested, "Dinner and a movie?"

Beth shrugged. "Yeah, I guess."

Mr. Barker walked in. His eyes passed over Sidah and landed on Beth. "I need you to come in tomorrow and finish up the Mapleton project." He turned and left before she could respond.

"What the hell?" Beth tossed her spoon down and pushed her food away. "I'm busy."

"I'll do it."

"You don't have to."

"I don't care." The work would fill the empty space that had begun to haunt her weekends.

Beth smiled and agreed. "Thanks!"

Sidah had to bite back her venom. She couldn't blame Beth, who hadn't asked for the extra responsibility. Still, when the Mapleton account was finished, Beth would get the credit, not her.

***

Sidah let herself sleep as late as she wanted on Saturday morning, because she knew she would be the only person in the office. She fixed herself a glorious omelet for breakfast, filled with spinach and sun-dried tomatoes. She ate slowly, savoring every bite.

At a quarter past eight, she threw on some old jeans with rips in the knees and paint stains from long forgotten artistic endeavors and an old hoodie from the prestigious art school, the one that still made her feel proud to know she had attended. Even if no one else cared.

Which they didn't.

She dawdled in the streets, stretching out each second to its max before she had to resign herself to working the weekend away in a cramped cubicle with only a framed 5x7 photo of her mother for company.

Eventually, though, the office building loomed ahead, and she resigned herself to the task. Perhaps she could finish it in an hour or two. How hard could it be?

But once she got underway, everything that could go wrong did go wrong. The worst of which, when she went to upload a file to the company's server, it crashed, and several hours' worth of work disappeared into the Internet cosmos.

"Mother fucker!" she screamed, slamming the palm of her hand on her keyboard, sending a string of jumbled letters and numbers across the screen.

She stood and stormed to the break room. The coffee pot, which at some point in time might have held promise, instead held day old cold dregs of weak coffee and soggy grounds.

"You have got to be kidding me." Sidah snatched the pot from its holder and began scrubbing. "Why am I always the one washing the goddam coffee pot every goddam day?"

No one answered. How could they? They were all out.

"It's not like I'm the only one drinking it!"

Except, that on Saturday, she was. She cleaned the mess and started a pot brewing, tapping her finger impatiently on the counter as it dripped. While she waited, she scanned the fridge for something to eat. Sometimes Paul left a spare sandwich in there, in case he got hungry or forgot his lunch.

Bingo! Turkey sandwich.

Not her favorite, but she was starving. She hadn't brought anything, assuming incorrectly she would be out by noon. She could always pay him back on Monday.

Equipped with caffeine and food, she returned to her desk to start the entire process over again.

The hours dragged by, until finally, the project was finished.

"Thank you, God," she said sarcastically. "And more importantly, thank you, me!" No one else in the department would thank her for her work. She might as well.

She stuffed the last bite of sandwich in her mouth. It had long ago warmed to room temperature, as she focused on her work and neglected her food. The bite was too large. She struggled to chew it. She worked her tongue around sticky white bread—Paul wasn't really the whole wheat type—and dried up turkey and cheese. She reached for the bottle of water she kept at the corner of her desk, but her hand slipped on the desk, and she fell forward, stumbling over her chair and falling against the edge of her desk.

The sticky ball of chewed up bread slid to the back of her throat, lodging itself firmly against her airway. She tried to draw breath and failed.

Her eyes went wide, and her hands scrambled along her neck, foolishly trying to pry the obstruction loose from the outside. She desperately tried to pull more breath, but nothing would come. She balled her hands together and pressed on her stomach, an ineffective attempt at the Heimlich Maneuver. The room swam, and she tried again, but she couldn't force the damn turkey out.

In one last, vain attempt, she threw herself onto the back of her chair, but the wheels slid out from beneath her. She slammed to the ground, unable even to vocalize an "oomph" with the food still lodged in the back of her throat.

Just before she lost consciousness, she rolled to her back, catching sight of her computer screen.

Dammit, she thought, *I didn't press send.*

***

Beth strolled into work a little later than normal, late enough that she snuck up the back stairs and in through the break room, where she made quite a show of making the coffee, as if she had been there all morning. In truth, she was a bit surprised that Sidah hadn't done it already, but occasionally Sidah stopped by a local coffee shop then spent the rest of the morning expounding on the importance of supporting small businesses and giving anyone carrying a Starbucks cup a superior eyebrow raise.

She tapped her fingers on the counter as the percolator did its thing.

She heard Mr. Barker's voice booming across the office before she saw him. "Beth! I need that Mapleton account, pronto!"

He stomped into the break room. "Did you send that account?"

"Oh," she scrambled for an excuse. "I'll send it now."

His expression softened. "Of course, you will." He knew he could count on her. He pushed past her to fill up his cup of coffee from the newly filled pot, then nodded once to her. "You make the best coffee." Then he walked out of the room.

Beth rolled her eyes, filled her own mug, and went off in search of Sidah. She didn't search long. Beth walked down the row of cubicles to the connected pair where she and Sidah sat. Halfway there, and she wrinkled her nose. "What's that smell?"

Paul peeked up from above his cubicle and gave a dramatic sniff. "I dunno."

"You're no help." She moved onward. As she turned the corner, she raised her mug to her mouth, sucking in the bitter drink. Her toe hit something hard, and she fell forward, catching herself against the cubicle wall but spilling hot brown liquid all over.

"Sidah!" she shrieked, looking down at the motionless foot she had tripped over. The mug slipped from her fingers. She knelt to the floor and shook the already stiff body. "Sidah! Sidah! Oh my God!"

Her screams attracted the people from neighboring cubicles, and pretty soon she had an audience.

Paul chivalrously attempted to lift the body, but death had made it heavy. He noticed the Ziplock baggie in the trash. "She ate my sandwich."

Beth glared up at him. "Are you serious?"

At least he had the decency to look properly chagrined. The commotion attracted the eyes of the boss, and pretty soon Mr. Barker towered over Beth as she knelt over her friend.

"What happened?"

"I think she choked on a sandwich," Beth replied.

"My sandwich." Paul put in, earning a smack on the back of his head from a coworker standing behind him.

"Hmm." Mr. Barker surveyed the scene. "When did this happen?"

Beth leaned against the cubicle wall and covered her eyes with her hand. "She came in Saturday to work on the Mapleton account."

Mr. Barker snapped to attention at the name. He stepped around the body to check the computer. "Well, at least she finished it." He attached it to an email and hit send. "Someone call the police," he muttered as he walked back to his office.

Daniel Hurley

Daniel Hurley began writing some time during adolescence, mostly song lyrics and dialogues which he sometimes received detention for when caught working on them in class.

He enjoys history, literary documentaries, books—both fiction and non-fiction—running in the woods, and forcing himself to got to the gym. He lives with his family on the coast of Massachusetts and has published numerous stories under different pen names.

Cleopatra

Roland and Trevor Henshaw stood in the sacristy. Roland had just asked Trevor, his best man, if he still had the ring, just making sure, when Trevor rubbed his nose a bit and looked him in the eye, wide-eyed, watery-eyed, slightly bloodshot, and told Roland his bride to be was a whore.

The organ had begun playing, and Roland could see her in the distance, at the back of the church, white dress—off the shoulder—and veil. She insisted on the veil. And she had sent him a picture of what she was wearing beneath to his iPhone. White lace and garter. Signed the text simply "Yours."

She was beautiful. Roland hadn't seen her since the rehearsal dinner the night before. Now everything was moving, everything had slowed down. He waited for the punchline, waited for Trevor to laugh, but Trevor wasn't laughing—just staring at him.

"A whore, man," he said. "Dude, I kid you not. She tried to do me. She wanted to, you know, take me to the tonsils, too. I'm so sorry."

Roland's mouth went dry, metallic, blood pumping. Everything suddenly on red alert. This couldn't be happening. Roland wanted to put his hand over Trevor's mouth, stifle him, and he wanted to throw him through the stained glass, watch his body slice into ribbons. *Why was this happening?* he wondered. *Why?* They had already made it this far, no big occasions in his family made it this far without something going wrong. Usually horribly wrong. Something crazy.

And now, he thought, *it was*.

Roland clenched his teeth, bared them. "Shut your mouth. I swear to God, Trevor, you need to shut your fucking mouth, or I will shut it permanently for you."

Trevor started to cry. "Dude, I'm saying this for you. I couldn't keep quiet anymore. It's not right. It's been killing me for like two years, keeping it to myself. Tearing me up inside. But she did it. She tried to seduce me."

Roland put his finger in his face. "I will kill you," he said. "I promise. I just can't do it right now. But after this is over, and I am back from my honeymoon, I will kill you. You are a dead man, you understand?" He could see Cleo's father now, too. Round and balding. Dressed in his Captain's outfit—he owned a boat, moored in the harbor, and had insisted he wear his captain's outfit, the white hat removed now that he was inside the church. He was holding out his arm for her, and the March was about to begin.

Roland hadn't seen his older brother Trevor for months. No one had seen him, and the most contact he had had was to hound him on the phone about getting his tux; Trevor had finally just picked it up hours before the wedding. He had been living somewhere in New Jersey, met a new girlfriend, and had been talking about buying a couple pieces of property, maybe opening a pizza place. The girlfriend had money, or that was the most anyone could figure as Trevor did not. And then after missing the rehearsal dinner last night, he had shown up with her this morning and the girlfriend had walked about showing everybody her ring. They had eloped in Atlantic City the week before.

Roland had done a double-take when he had seen Trevor's new bride. Trevor had just turned thirty, and his wife, although heavily made up and slim, still sporting a high eighties hair, couldn't have been a day under fifty-five, maybe older. Trevor, he heard, was husband number four.

"So, dude," Trevor had said to him earlier, a slight twitch to his lips after they had reached the church. "We've only been married five days," he continued, "so when you think about it, this is really my day, too. I think we should share it. Like a double reception."

"We've been planning this for over a year," Roland had said, taking a deep breath. Inhaling the stale air, tainted with old incense, at the back of the church. Sacristies sometimes seemed quieter than even an empty church itself. A quiet with a hum. Eyes Watching. There was a picture on the far wall of the Christ, his head slightly bowed, pulling open his robe, exposing his heart. "I forked out over twenty-thousand dollars," Roland had said to him. "And the Captain forked out thirty. It can't be your day, too. Not today. We can celebrate it tomorrow—before I leave. Maybe Ma will have a cookout for you or something. I mean, how long ago did you get engaged? Ten days ago? Twelve?"

And it was then that he told Roland that Cleo had once come onto him.

"We were up in your apartment," he said, "and we'd been drinking—me and her more than you. Dude—and you went out to pick up some pizza. And then she started. I didn't know what to do. I was on the couch, and suddenly she is next to me, and the next thing I know, she's climbing on top of me, trying to put her tongue in my ear."

Roland gazed out upon the church. Full. The entire congregation wore sunglasses. Old ladies, teenagers, toddlers. Only in Revere did the parishioners all wear sunglasses inside the church, but Cleo was from Revere; Cleo loved Revere, she wanted to get married in Revere. Wanted to stay living in Revere. The heat inside the church was rising, stifling, even with the ceiling fans spinning above. It was an evening wedding, but the temperature was still in the nineties. Mid-July. Cleo had insisted they get married in July. "I was born in July," she said. "I'm going to get married in July, and I'm going to die in July. I even lost my virginity in July. I think."

The priest motioned for Roland and Trevor to step out onto the altar.

Roland turned to Trevor and bared his teeth, clenched. "You keep your mouth shut. You keep your fucking mouth shut, see if you can do that, and maybe, just maybe, I won't kill you later."

Cleo wasn't Cleo's real name. It was short for Cleopatra. But Cleopatra wasn't really her name either. It was Helen. She had told Roland that she wanted to be named after a famous woman, a beautiful, historical woman—and had thought about calling herself Greta, but there were already too many Gretas—and so she had changed it. Roland had started to say something about the name Helen, the words on the tip of his tongue, but then thought better of it. She was happy with Cleo, and he wanted her to be happy. When she was happy, things were good. Besides, she kind of looked like a Cleopatra. Jet black hair— "I swear it's always been that color even when I was little. I'll show you pictures," she'd told him—and wide blue eyes. Heavy eye shadow and thick mascara. Just a few freckles.

When they met four years earlier, she was just out of college, and subbing at the high school where Roland taught history and coached a little baseball.

"I don't want to be a teacher," she had said. "Fuck that. But it's not bad money subbing for right now, and I can kind of pick my hours, you know what I mean?" They had eaten lunch together a few times in the break room, and then she had shown up in Roland's classroom after school, asking his advice on an assignment she was supposed to cover. Roland had begun looking over the teacher's plan book, Cleo crouched next to him behind his desk when he felt a hand on his knee, then moving inward, up his thigh.

Less than a minute later, she was backing him into the closet. Her tongue going in his ear, her hand on his package. She took off her shoe and began to drive the spiked heel into his shoulder as they kissed. And then she dropped to her knees, tugging at his fly, and hurriedly pushing him in past her lips. Wet, sloppy, and loud. "I've been waiting to do this since the first time I saw you in the cafeteria," she said. "God, I love it."

She moved into his apartment two months later. A fight with her mother and her sister. "I can't live there anymore," she said. "I'm too old, and besides, those two are acting like a couple of cunts. I love them to death, but I can't stand them, know what I mean? All I did was borrow my sister's car for the night while she was away on business, and she comes back and starts having a tizzy fit. She gets all cunty whenever she has to travel for business. So it has a couple little dents in it, big deal. The car is a piece of shit, anyway; I couldn't even get the Bluetooth to work."

The apartment was small, and it was a mess. It had been a little bit of a mess before Cleo, but nothing like it ended up being after. Food smeared on the sheets, the couch, and kitchen chairs, counters covered in dirty clothes. Empty pizza boxes and dirty dishes everywhere. Vodka and beer bottles and ashtrays piled over with cigarettes. And then the anxiety when she was unable to find something. Walking about with her mascara smeared, topless, in nothing but a thong, smoking cigarette after cigarette, and throwing anything in her path over her shoulder.

And then somehow, before they went out for the night, she would pull it all together. Roland couldn't help marvel at how she would pull it all together. Suddenly beautiful. Tantalizing and sexy. How often did he enter a room, a club, look around, and realize he was escorting the sexiest, prettiest woman in the room? And then three drinks later, she might lean up, nibble his ear, and whisper, "I can't wait to get home so you can stick your tongue inside me and do me from behind."

And no matter how much they fought, yelled—sometimes her pulling his hair and sometimes, well once, him throwing dishes—the sex never stopped. Even now, three years later, the sex hadn't stopped. It was therapeutic, she said. And sometimes, she said, it even made the fighting worthwhile because once they made up, they could "fuck it all away."

Roland pretty much doubted they would be able to fuck this one all away, though. Not if Cleo got word of it. It would be Mount Vesuvius all over again. Her temper was explosive, and no matter what she said, did, you were either with her or against her. No in between. How many times had she told him that? And the people who were against her? "Dead to me," she said. It didn't matter how close they had been, or how long it had been since the infraction. "Dead," she said. "They can fucking rot in hell or rot right here on earth for that matter. I'll watch them. I don't care." The list of dead was long: Eight to ten friends from high school, six from college, her cousin Veronica, neighbors on either side of her parent's house who had turned her in for having parties in high school, Roland's sister Lucy just because she was a nosey, fucking bitch, Cleo said. The guy at Dunkin Donuts. Her grandmother—her mother's mother—that windowsill apple-looking old bitch could stick her gold and amethyst ring up her wrinkly old ass for all Cleo cared; she didn't want it anyway.

And now, Trevor was going to be dead to her. Roland had no doubt. There was no way around it. She was going to hear about it. Roland loved Trevor; he was kind of smart—although not even close to as smart as he thought he was—but he had no brain to mouth filter. If a thought came in, that thought went out. Right out the lips.

And then something worse occurred to him—*What if it were true?*

Roland's own thoughts were moving quick, and he was beginning to sweat, trying his hardest to freeze his smile, his mind running over every scenario, any time he had possibly left Trevor and Cleo alone, any time it could possibly be true. But in the past three years, there was nothing. He was sure of it. Trevor was crazy. Cleo didn't even like him that much; she said his eyes were funny. It couldn't be true. And Cleo *was* beautiful. Roland looked at her again now as the organ picked up. Taller than her father, the Captain, in her four-inch heels, and taking such dainty steps with her bouquet before her. Shining in her moment. Happy. She had wanted the organ player to play *The Way You Look Tonight* halfway down the aisle, but the church wouldn't let her—save it for the reception, they said. That had burnt her ass, but wasn't she good? She asked Trevor. She didn't say a word. But that priest was dead to her now; she would let him know after the ceremony.

Now she smiled wide, seemingly oblivious to what had just transpired in the sacristy. And Roland knew he had to keep it from her, at least for now. He couldn't ruin her day. He needed to keep her happy.

It didn't work.

Roland's hands were shaking. From the corner of his head, he could see the priest's bald head shining beneath the lights of the church, the slight pungent smell of booze diluted in aftershave, slipping from his pores, as they recited their vows. Then they were kissing, the crowd was clapping, and Trevor just staring at the floor of the altar, and the ceremony seemed to go off without a hitch. And Roland had begun to hope that the rest of the night would, too. And it had, at least until they reached the lawn overlooking the sea to take the pictures. A white gazebo bedecked with flowers on a green lawn, white ribbons tied to the posts and blowing in the breeze. A string quartet playing before them. And Trevor, the best man, now, happily, nowhere to be found.

Cleo's mother marched up, her face red and her own bouquet by her side. Looking left to right. She had been doing so for the past ten minutes, looking for Trevor. The rest of the wedding party—all sixteen of them were crowded on the lawn, whispering.

"I don't want him in the pictures, Roland," said Cleo. She put a cigarette in her mouth, leaned over so her sister could light it.

"He's the best man," Roland said. "He has to be in the pictures."

"Fuck that, Roland," said Cleo. "He told my mother I was a whore. Five minutes after we walked out of the church. Fuck him."

The woman looked at them. Small, dark eyes, suspicious, and loose pale skin, Cleo's face hiding beneath a face morphing into something quite severe. Roland could see it there. Layers of time built over what had been her youth. And he could see Cleo now in thirty years. Twenty?

"He did," the woman said. "I couldn't believe it. Climbed into the limo and says, 'You seem like a very nice woman, but your daughter's a whore.' I kicked him right out. Right out the door."

"But we're going to straighten this out. It will all blow over, and then we'll regret it if he's not in the pictures," Roland said. "We'll laugh about this someday."

"Fuck that," said Cleo. She ground the cigarette out with the heel of her shoe. "I won't laugh about anything, and I won't regret anything. But you'll regret it if you have anything to do with him again, Roland, I swear to God. *I* tried to fuck *him*? Really? Are you kidding me? Oh, please. If I was going to fuck anybody, the last person in the world would be Trevor."

Cleo looked up and smiled at the camera.

"I think he's sick. I think he needs help," Roland said. "To be honest, I'm starting to feel kind of bad for the guy." The photographer started adjusting his camera again. One more shot of the couple alone in the Gazebo. Roland looked back at the wedding party. Waiting. Getting restless. The bridesmaids all in purple. Roland's older sister, Diana, eight months pregnant, looking ready to pop. His younger sister, Lucy, towering over her. And his two younger brothers, Stephen and Roger. Roger, the youngest, 6'5" and just getting bigger, taller every time Roland saw him. Roland swore to God. He was just getting bigger. He had to be. His tux looked three sizes too small for him, and he looked as if he were going to burst right out of it, one lone button holding it tight together in the front, over the cummerbund that was riding up his belly, but that was all impossible—he had just been fitted for the tux less than a week before; it had to fit. Trevor had been the one they were worried about—he had to phone in his measurements after three months of phone pleadings from Roland to just go to Mr. Tux and get it done.

"Dude, I will," he had kept assuring him. "Listen, I have a plan. I want to lose another ten pounds first, so it makes no sense to get fitted now."

"That doesn't matter," Roland had said. "They can just adjust it when you go to pick it up. They can do that shit in a second, believe me."

"I don't have the cash right now anyway," Trevor had said.

"You put down like twenty bucks, and you don't pay the rest until you pick it up. And if you don't have the money, don't worry about it. I got it. No big deal."

That had been the last time they had spoken. Two weeks before. And no one had been really sure whether Trevor would show up or not. He had mentioned the girlfriend but didn't say anything about getting married. He was just racing a little on the phone, and Roland wondered if he had started doing coke again, maybe speed. He just said his girlfriend was awesome, called her his savior. "And she's loaded, dude," he added. "Loaded."

Now Roger sauntered over and asked Cleo for a cigarette. His pupils were dilated, and his eyes looked loose in his head. Roger looked like he was probably off his meds again, and Roland began to say a silent prayer that he was not. Things were bad enough with Trevor right now. And Roger off his meds was not good. Last time he went off, he had attempted to murder the inside of their parent's Honda with a butcher knife, and the time before that, he'd shown up at the rectory of his mother's church with nothing on but a Red Sox visor. He had been hospitalized for two weeks after that one.

"I've been thinking a lot about quitting smoking lately," he now said to Cleo.

Roger leaned over, and Cleo pulled a lighter from her small white purse and lit the cigarette.

"I told myself I have to the end of September," he said, "and then I'm done. That's it. I quit. Last month, I quit for two days, and I thought that was pretty good. And then I started reading that book again by Cormac McCarthy—*No Country for Old Men*—and I started thinking about the sheriff and his uncle and those dogs shot up in the desert, and I don't know, something, something, just went off like a bell in my head, like I could see it all, and then I saw Cormac McCarthy the following day outside the Tobacconist Shop at the Mall—I swear it was him—and he had the book sticking out of his back pocket, and I knew somehow that it was just a sign, so I went in and bought some cigarettes. I know it doesn't sound like it makes a lot of sense, but I don't know. It was very clear at the time, crystal clear. I'm just not explaining it right. When I meditate, it's that much clearer. I think I need to go back to church. Celibacy. It's all about celibacy. That's my problem. I don't want to be celibate—even though I know I should be—and I still am." He shut his eyes for a moment. "Celibacy in perpetuity," he whispered.

Cleo puffed. "Your brother Trevor is a fucking asshole, Roger," she said. "He's a fucking lunatic."

Roger puffed. "I have not had the opportunity to adequately assess that situation. Microscopically, I mean. Is that the word I'm looking for—microscopically?"

"I'm going to assess it with my fist up his ass if he shows up again," Cleo said. "Calling me a whore. Wanting to fuck him? Are you kidding me? Who the hell would want to fuck him?"

"I know. He apprised me of that situation some time back. And quite honestly, I did not know what to think. I didn't believe you tried to seduce him, but he usually doesn't lie, so I could not fathom—fathom? Is that that word I'm looking for?—why he interpreted your advances as an attempt to do just that. If you made advances at all, I mean. Maybe they weren't advances, but conversational pirouettes of some sort. Pirouettes, I think that's what I'm trying to say. You look beautiful, by the way. Stunning. Absolutely stunning."

Cleo stepped on the cigarette. "Thank you. You are so sweet. That piece of shit ruined my wedding, though. Fucking bastard."

"He can only ruin it, if you let him," said Roger. "All life is about free will. I read all about it in Saint Augustine. Our... our greatest gift from God is free will. To do as we please, when we please. Anything." He shut his eyes. "Anything," he muttered.

Stephen was pacing about, his hands pushed down in the front pockets of his jacket to keep them from shaking, shoulders high. He wore small oval glasses, and his long hair pulled back in a ponytail. Pasty skin and big chapped lips. Bloodshot blue eyes from less than three hours' sleep the night before. He was tall and slim, and he hadn't eaten in over three days. A waitress came by with a tray of champagne flutes, a strawberry in each, and he reached out and grabbed one. "Give me one of those things, will ya?"

The waitresses were all dressed like French Maids at Cleo's request. This one was short. Big chest and big brown eyes. Dark hair. Stephen smiled at her after he took the flute. "Do you got a cigarette? I'm dying for a cigarette."

"I can't smoke on the job," she said.

"That's kind of silly," he said. "I mean, I know smoking's bad for you; it's dumb. But if you smoke, you smoke, you know what I'm saying? I've been smoking since I've been nine years old. I'm not proud of it or anything, but it is what it is. Some people smoke, and some people don't. I can tell by your eyes that you're probably a Capricorn. Are you a Capricorn?"

"Cancer," she said.

"Well, I was close. *Tropic of Capricorn. Tropic of Cancer.* Those books were fucked up. Old Henry Miller. He was a pervert for his day. A wicked fucking pervert. I'm trying not to be a pervert, but it's tough. Henry loved the word 'cunt.' I've never read anyone who used the word 'cunt' so much in a book. The shit was crazy. Listen, I've got to find a cigarette, but maybe we can get a drink or something after this thing is over. Do you live around here? I don't have a car, but maybe I can borrow my mother's or something."

Roger had stepped away from Cleo and Roland so the photographer could get another picture. Stephen grabbed him by the sleeve. "Give me a cigarette, will ya?"

"I only have thirteen left," Roger said. "Normally, I would say that is a lot of cigarettes, but I figure at a wedding, drinking, it might not even be enough."

"Thirteen is an unlucky number." Stephen smiled. "You don't want to bring bad luck down on the happy couple, do you?"

"My fear is that Trevor already has," said Roger. He pulled out his cigarette pack, and Stephen grabbed one.

"That shit is fucked up," he said. "Who tells that to somebody on their wedding day? I mean, she tried to fuck me once, too, but you don't see me going running up to Roland to tell him. Not today. I wouldn't do that shit, man. That shit's fucked up."

"I was not aware that she tried to fuck you, too," said Roger.

"Crazy. It was crazy."

"When did this happen?"

"I don't know. It must have been five or six years ago."

Roger stopped, thought on this a moment. "I don't believe we knew her five or six years ago."

"Well, it must have been less than that then. It was all fucked up." He blew the smoke out of the corner of his mouth, looking Roger head-on. "Maybe it was two years ago, I don't know. I haven't eaten since Wednesday, and I'm starting to have visions, you know what I'm saying?"

"I know exactly what you're saying."

"Anyway, I could have fucked her, I know I could've—she was all over me—but I took a back seat to Big Role. I'm not about to do that to him—not unless he wanted me, too, I mean, you know, some guys dig that, like watching—he's the best."

The tent accommodated over two hundred and fifty people and overlooked the harbor. The Boston skyline in the distance. Sailboats moored, others moving against the glow on the horizon, and chartered ferries, pleasure boats, heading in and out of the city. Rowe's and Long wharfs. Small islands covered in green brush glowing golden beneath the setting sun. It was a wonderful time of year. Roland and Cleo had their own separate table—a table for two, away from the bridal party. Roland had argued against this at first, but now he was thanking God he had given in. A little time away from everybody was exactly what they needed. A little time for Cleo to compose, de-escalate. She had been introduced on her own. The band playing—Exile's *Kiss You All Over*. She took small steps, her bouquet held with two hands in front of her, and she was smiling so wide you would never have guessed any turmoil was going down. She raised her arms wide for Roland to meet her in the middle of the dance floor.

Now at the table. "I'm glad to see you looking so happy," he whispered to her.

Cleo drew back and smiled even wider. "I'm not going to let that fuckwad ruin my day. I'm going to ruin his life, though. I can promise you that. Just watch."

"Well, I don't think we should focus on ruining people's lives. Not on our wedding day. It's probably bad karma, you know what I mean? We don't need any of that."

Cleo took a bite of her potato. "Maybe," she said, "but if you ever have anything to do with him again, I'll divorce you."

Roland smiled. "That's funny."

"I don't think so," she said. "I don't think it would be funny at all. But I'll do it." She sipped her wine—white. She didn't want her teeth to be purple during her wedding, she said.

"No one talks about getting divorced the day of their wedding, Cleo," Roland said.

"If you ever have anything to do with that fuckface again, they do. He should be in jail for what he did. He's lucky he's not in jail."

"You can't go to jail just for making stuff up," said Roland.

"Yes, you can," said Cleo. "It happens all the time. Trump lies, and they want to put him in jail."

"That is different. That stuff deals with our national interests; this is just crazy talk. I'll tell you what I think. I think he's just jealous because he got married and no one knew about it, and no one cared. That's all it is."

"No one cared because she's a wrinkly old bag. Yuck."

"Well, maybe, but he didn't invite anybody or even tell anybody or anything, so there's no way anyone could've known, and now he's pissed because he sees what a beautiful day we're having. And he's jealous, that's all. I kind of feel bad for him to tell you the truth."

Cleo glared at him then. "I better not ever hear you say that again."

The DJ—a Revere local dressed in a white tux, open shirt, and gold chains—was out on the floor now. Mike in hand and calling for the dance with the father of the bride.

Cleo swept over to the Captain's table and took the Captain by the hand. The Captain put on his cap before standing, and she led him to the floor. Dancing to *Muskrat Love*.

Roland gazed over at his mother, Loretta, and Loretta gave him a big smile and a big, exaggerated wave. Still in her chair, she kicked her feet up and down in excitement. Roland and Loretta were next. Loretta had worn a white dress—and according to Cleo everyone knew that no-one but the bride was supposed to wear white, and she was pissed—and she had her hair done up high, and she looked medicated. Glass eyed. Loretta had wanted to dance to some Polish song that Roland had never heard of before, but he talked her into Barry Manilow's *Even Now*. Barry Manilow songs were a little gay, probably, he figured, but Roland liked them anyway. He was very comfortable with his gay side even though it didn't really exist, because at the end of the day there was nothing gay about him, but even if there were, it wouldn't bother him, not even a tiny bit, he liked to tell people.

Loretta looked ready to lunge from her seat even before the father of the bride's dance was finished. She sat between Roland's father—hooked nose and completely bald—and her mother. Roland's grandmother was almost ninety years old, and someone had dyed her hair a fresh blue for the wedding. Her skin was translucent, and you could see the blue map of her veins beneath. Hooded red-rimmed eyes. They had already asked her not to smoke inside three times that Roland had noticed, and the old woman had huffed and given them the business.

She was handicapped, she kept reminding them, and unless they wanted to carry her outside, they better let her smoke.

Now she smiled at Roland, sly. "Your mother's been waiting all night for this dance. You better not embarrass her."

"I've been practicing for months, Grandma," Roland said. As soon as they hit the middle of the floor, Loretta did some little maneuver, spinning around and waving both hands like she was in a vaudeville show, twice, and then she clapped, and then she settled in.

"Where is your brother?" she asked.

Roland decided to play coy. "Which one? There's like four of them. Last time I checked. Two of them are shitfaced and probably going to get kicked out."

"The best man," she said, her face still locked in a smile. "Your best friend."

"Oh, him. He called my wife a whore, and then he took off. We didn't give him much of a choice, actually. If he stayed, I was basically going to make sure he went home unrecognizable."

"He's your brother," she whispered.

"Not anymore, he's not. He called my wife a whore. Who does that? At a wedding? Seriously. I think he might be mentally ill, that's what I think."

Loretta made her thinking face. "Hmmm...There's a lot of mental illness in the family. I had an uncle who thought he was Rasputin."

"Yah, well at least he didn't call his brother's wife a whore at her wedding. That's like unforgivable."

"Hmmm…" whispered Loretta, exaggerating her thinking again. "Well, maybe he misread things. She does like to dress quite provocatively and flirt a bit. I think maybe she's just one of those 'touchy' people. Sometimes women go into heat, and they just can't help themselves. You see it all the time. Look at your sister Diana and all the trouble she got into when she was young, with that… that… asshole. Pregnant at seventeen."

"Mum, stop," Roland said.

"I'm just saying. I've never known your brother to lie."

"He lies all the fucking time—I can't even keep up with it—and this is a big one."

"Don't swear, Roland. I'm a mother, and I need to protect my children."

"Protect him from what?"

"Outsiders. People outside the family. People that might hurt him. Families need to stick together."

"Ma, Cleo is my wife. She is part of the family now."

"Well, there is how shall we say… a trial period."

He looked down at her. "You need to stop, or I'm ending this dance."

Loretta stepped back and took both his hands just as the song came to a close. "Thank you, my love."

Roland was almost back to his table, everyone clapping, when he noticed, out of the corner of his eye, someone talking to the DJ. He did a double-take. Almost shocked, if he could be any more shocked today. But he didn't think that was possible. And he was seeing what he was seeing. Trevor. Back again. Bow tie loose and vest open in the front.

Roland froze up for a second. The last he had seen of him, outside the church, Trevor, eyes dilated, had just said something like "I'm right. I'm not lying, dude. You'll see." And then he had been spotted, taking his own new bride by the elbow as he led her off towards their car, and now he was back, trying to pull the microphone away from the DJ. The clapping had stopped, as had the music. The room silent. As far as Roland knew, most of the guests were unaware of what had transpired, but his mother knew, a few of his siblings knew, and Cleo's mother knew, and word traveled fast. Especially, he thought, in a situation like this. People loved drama; people loved dirt.

The DJ kept reaching for the mike, and Trevor wasn't giving it back. Stepping away, he just held it high above his head. "Dude," he said, "I'm the best man, you're not going to stop me from giving a toast at my brother's wedding. This is ridiculous. Now go pick out some of your best ABBA or something. This will just take a minute."

Roland started towards them. Trevor caught sight of him and held up his hand. "Dude, before you attack me or anything, hear me out. First off, I want to apologize. Seriously, I want to say I'm sorry."

Roland stopped. Not sure what to do. He was the groom. This was his wedding. And if he got involved in a scene at the front of the room, if he put hands on Trevor, that was all anyone was going to remember. And Trevor was his brother, and there was something wrong with him, he knew there was. There had to be. And if that was the case, he bet Trevor knew it, too.

"This is your day," Trevor continued, "—just like it was my day just last week—and I should never have done anything to make it any less wonderful than it can be for you." His Adam's apple began going up and down in his throat, his lips twitching a bit, and his voice began to shake as he struggled not to cry. "You're not just my brother, you're my best friend. And even though you're younger, I've always looked up to, always loved you. We've gone through everything together. Sports. Friends. Psychotic nuns. Psychotic relatives. Parties out in the Stetson Shoe field. Everything. We even banged some of the same chicks." His face froze up for a second, second-guessing his words. "Back in the day, I mean. I'm not talking about today." The tears came now. "Anyway, you deserve better. And I mean that, you deserve better."

Roland felt something beginning to stir inside him. Something small, but growing. The seeds of forgiveness, he thought. Already? But he did love Trevor, and they had been through a lot together.

A plane passed overhead, low. Trevor was still talking, but for the moment, Roland couldn't hear him. "If I had been any kind of brother," he continued, "I would have told you about this a long time ago, and not waited until today. If I had any kind of balls, I mean. But Dude, I fucked up, and I'm sorry. I fucked up so bad that my own wife already took off somewhere. Took a cab. I think she is leaving me. I don't know where she went—she doesn't even know where she is. But I came back because I couldn't leave it like this. I had to tell you I was sorry, and I love you. I'm sorry for me, and I'm sorry for you. And I'm sorry your wife is a whore. But if I don't tell you now, we'll both be even more sorry later."

Roland heard Cleo let out a squeal. She called Trevor a fucking bastard and threw something at him. Trevor ducked.

"Dude," Trevor said. "See what I mean? Classy chick."

Roland was now seeing red. He charged them. Trevor dropped the mike, the bang amplified as it hit the dance floor, and then he was sprinting off across the lawn, off towards the sunset, breaking in reds behind the city, the cliffs. Roland turned to Cleo and said he would be right back, it wouldn't be more than five minutes, and then she threw her champagne at him, and he ran. Trevor was already out past the gazebo, a small silhouette against the horizon. There for a second and then gone. Descending the cliffs down towards the water. Roland was running, fast, but not as fast as he could run. He could run very fast. He wanted to catch him, and yet he did not. He heard shouts from behind him, sounding like Stephen, sounding like Roger.

By the time he reached the edge, Trevor was already down on the beach. Holding up his arms in surrender. Roland started hurriedly down the path through the beach grass, sliding in the sand. He was going to have sand all in his socks, all in his shoes.

Roland could hear voices behind him. Stephen's. Roger's. The waves were breaking on the beach, a small beach, mostly rocks, small pebbles, the tide coming in, and the sun glowed red on the water. "Don't make me do this," Trevor called up, his eyes wide—the Trevor look of amazement. "You're backing me into a corner, and I don't know how to swim." He started walking backwards. "You know that, Dude, I don't know how to swim."

Roland reached the bottom of the trail and broke back into a run, and as soon as he did, Trevor turned and headed towards the water, arms held above his head as he splashed in. About twenty yards out, up to his chest, he turned around. "Don't make me do it," he called out.

Roland stopped, pointed. "I can't get my tux wet. Now you get your ass back here on the beach, so I can kill you."

Trevor began backing up some more. "No, you need to cease and desist, Dude, or I'll keep going out. I swear to God, I will." He was up to his armpits now. "And then you'll have both a dead brother and a fucked up marriage to a cock loving tart."

"That's it," Roland yelled. He pulled off his shoes and jacket and charged into the water, and as soon as he did, Trevor turned and dove into the surf.

"If you drown before I can kill you, mother fucker, I'm going to drag you out and kill you again!"

Trevor's head suddenly bobbed up in the surf for a moment, gasping for air, and then a wave passed over him. Roland lunged, arms out and reaching. He caught hold of what felt to be Trevor's jacket, but then Trevor twisted and was gone again. When Roland came up—he was just about up to his chin, spitting sea water—he looked to see Trevor, now somehow in between him and the beach, and Stephen and Roger sliding to the base of the cliff. Roland dived forward and swam until he was almost up to his waist, and then he grabbed Trevor by the shoulders, pulling him backwards.

Trevor landed on top of him, still struggling and shouting. "You can't kill me, I'm your fucking brother!"

A crowd had gathered at the top of the bluff, shouting down to him. His mother. Father. Sisters. A few of his friends. Cleo's mother. The Captain. Cleo. And the DJ.

Cleo was holding the DJ by the elbow with one hand, her bridal bouquet in the other. "You better let him drown, Roland," she called down. "Or that's it! This wedding is over! I mean it! Do you hear me?"

Roland tried to pull Trevor to his feet, grabbing him by the front of his shirt, to drag him closer to shore, and as soon as Trevor began to catch his balance, he hauled out with a roundhouse, catching Roland in the jaw. Roland stumbled backwards, and Trevor began attempting to run again, this time towards the shore, but he had barely taken two steps, lifting his legs high, when a black shape, an enormous black shape, broadsided him, knocking him again back into the surf. Roger. Eight inches taller and a hundred and fifty pounds heavier.

Roland's face broke the surface, spitting out some sea water. The world was spinning. The bluffs, the sky, and the sea, memories of the past, and his brothers wrestling in the surf. Trevor crying. His brother Stephen, standing on the beach, smoking a cigarette and calling out, "We got this, big Role. We got this! We'll straighten his ass out! Mother fucker owes me twenty-five bucks, anyway! We got this!"

And then, stepping back away from the cliff, Roland could see a white silhouette against the oncoming night. She was standing facing the DJ, close, her face less than six inches from his as she held a cigarette to her lips, looking for a light. Her other hand still held his elbow, and then as he lit her cigarette, she moved it lower, her fingers circling his wrist.

Kevin Finnerty

Kevin Finnerty's stories have appeared in *Eclectica Magazine*, *Me First Magazine*, *Rathalla Review*, *Variety Pack*, *The Westchester Review*, and other journals.

The Party People

Morgan arrived first and grabbed the table nearest the window. He placed his gabardine jacket across the two seats opposite from him and draped his rainbow-colored scarf over the chair beside him. He waved to nearly half of those who entered the coffee shop but did so without affection and said no more than "Hey" to anyone.

He pretended to be nice to people because he believed most only pretended to be nice to him. People now recognize gays as fellow human beings. (Big concession.) It was no longer acceptable in most parts to openly abuse or tease them as once had been common. Those with any sense of decency understood they had to be respectful and act as if they were treating Morgan like their equal. Morgan knew it was an act for many. Straight people knew he was different, and they still didn't treat him the same.

Sprout entered twenty minutes later. She was still ten minutes early for the first gathering to discuss the annual party, set for three months to the day into the future. She opened her white down coat and threw it around Morgan to hug him inside of it.

"Where you think you are with that thing? New York?"

"It's winter."

"There's no such thing here, no matter what the calendar says."

Sprout removed her ski cap with a puff ball on top and tossed it onto the table. She wore a large flower-shaped bow on the left side of her head. Today's was red—the colors changed daily—but it was gaudy and cheap like all the others because it represented her effort to slum down her appearance.

"You order anything yet?"

"I was waiting."

"I'll get it. You seen Mitch?"

"He'll arrive ten seconds before the time we agreed to meet. And he'll want the largest cup of the darkest roast they have."

Sprout shimmied out of her jacket and let it fall to the floor. She kissed Morgan on the cheek. Morgan glanced at the coat, then at Sprout bouncing her way to the queue. He waited a few seconds before concluding he couldn't leave the jacket on the dirty floor.

Sprout returned with a box containing three hot drinks, some pastries, a banana, and some yogurt, just as Mitch entered the shop.

"Why you sitting so close to the front?"

"What's it matter?" Sprout handed him his drink.

Mitch scratched two days' worth of patchy stubble with the back of his hand and shrugged. He frowned as he removed a tablet from inside his leather jacket.

"Morgan likes to keep track of everyone."

Mitch turned on his tablet and looked around. "It's easier to talk about potential guests if we don't have to worry about any of them sneaking up on us."

Morgan grabbed the yogurt. "Paranoid much?"

"Relax. Everyone knows Morgan and I are the catty ones, not you."

Sprout raised her frothy drink, but neither of her companions followed her lead. "Has it really been a year?"

"Almost to the day." Mitch scrolled through a spreadsheet on his tablet. "What you got there?"

Mitch resisted Sprout's attempt to pull the device away. "Notes."

"Guess the first thing we should think about is where we're going to hold the party this year." Morgan continued to glance at the door and offer entering patrons a false smile even while he spoke to Mitch and Sprout. "This way, we'll have some idea about how many people to invite."

"No need. My father already offered us his boat."

Mitch and Morgan both abandoned their focus to stare at Sprout.

"Yeah, he thought the bill was too big last year. He said there's a sunk cost on the boat's overhead. Something like that."

Morgan uncrossed and re-crossed his legs. He wore the sort of colorful, checkered pants one might expect to find on a croquet lawn in England. "We going to go out on the water or stay at the dock?"

"TBD."

Mitch nodded and began typing. "So how many guests can we invite?"

"As many as we want, I guess. How many we have last year?"

"Invited 202. 104 showed."

The group commenced the process of developing the new invite list by reviewing the names of those they'd considered the previous year to determine if they should receive the same ranking—"+", "-", or "0"— depending on whether the group believed the individual would add to the party, subtract from it, or in no way affect the party positively or negatively.

"Ty Wilson." Mitch shook his fingers. "I guess I need to loosen up for all the notes for this one."

"Can't we just change him from Plus Plus to Minus Minus and be done with it?"

Sprout elbowed Morgan. "No reason to put it in writing. We all know he's my Ex now. But what's the etiquette for that?"

Mitch took the last sip from his cup. "He's not invited."

"Really? He loved these."

"Honey, we don't need the drama."

"I don't care if he comes."

"Because you broke up with him. But what if he's not over you yet?" Mitch asked.

"I don't think he is," Morgan said.

"Why'd you break up with him anyway?"

Sprout waved her hands as if they had the power to ward off the question. "Where are we at with the tally so far? It seems like we've downgraded way more than we've upgraded."

"Happens every year. The longer people live, the worse they get."

"Or the worse we judge them." Morgan reached over and pulled Sprout into him. The two rocked in their seats.

"C'mon," Mitch said, "we still have to discuss new people."

"Oooh, sounds like someone's anxious," Morgan said.

"No wonder we've been flying through the dead wood this year."

"Why don't we jump ahead and talk about the one we can't even name?" Sprout placed her chin in her palms and her elbows on the table.

Morgan ripped the tablet from Mitch and turned his back to him. "My oh my, don't we have lots of information on her. Likes gymnastics and foreign films. Lives in the Gardenia Apartments. Birthday, November 12. You've got where she went to high school and college. It goes on and on. Funny, we don't have these sorts of details about anyone else."

Mitch walked around the table and stood over Morgan until he relinquished the tablet. "She's a Plus."

"Not a Plus Plus?" Sprout asked.

"Not yet."

"He hasn't slept with her yet," Morgan explained.

"Sometimes that leads to a downgrade," Mitch said.

"Not for you two."

Sprout and Mitch quickly looked at each other and then Morgan.

"Oh, come on. Neither of you had to tell me. I know you guys have fooled around a couple of times, so what? You don't have to put that in your little database. We're all friends here."

Mitch hit the table with his fist in rapid succession. "All right, who should we discuss now?"

"Ellington."

Sprout scowled at Morgan's suggestion. "He thinks he's so smart."

"He is smart." Mitch added the new entry.

"He thinks he's smarter than everyone else."

"He is."

"You like that?"

"We should invite him," Morgan said.

"Agree."

"You guys think he's a Plus?" Sprout asked.

Mitch looked up from his tablet. "He's not a Zero."

"And it's hard to envision him as a Minus."

"I'll put him down as a Plus for now. We'll see, I guess."

Sprout licked the rim of her cup. "What's his first name?"

"I thought it was Ellington," Mitch said.

Morgan shrugged. "That's all I know. Everyone calls him that."

"What about Devo James?"

"Not another bad boy."

"Definitely a Minus," Mitch said.

Sprout reached out and grabbed Mitch's hands so he couldn't type. "You think so? It's okay to invite a few Minuses, right? We always have. Makes things more interesting."

"What're we going to do with him if he causes trouble on a boat? Especially if we're out on the water."

"Tell him to step off," Morgan said.

"Dad said he's going to provide security, so things don't get out of hand."

Mitch resumed typing. "I'm putting him down as a Minus. We can decide later how many of each group to invite."

Morgan waved at a young female with straight brown hair who entered the cafe. She responded by barely twittering her fingers.

"What's her name again?" Mitch asked.

Morgan and Sprout respond simultaneously. "Kelcey Kramer."

"What do we think of her?"

"Must be a Zero."

Morgan and Sprout again spoke in unison: "Not going to add to the party but won't take anything away."

"Sounds like we won't know she's there."

While Mitch recorded Kelcey as a Zero, Sprout pulled out a sheet of paper with various names to discuss. Morgan recalled a number of others from memory. The group laughed frequently as they debated the new potential invites. Involved as they were, they failed to notice a group of four until they appeared in the middle of their conversation.

"Hey, it's The Party People." The speaker was an athletic figure with broad shoulders.

"Hey, T.J.... Mark, Ashley, Amber."

The others nodded at Sprout.

"You're planning it right now, aren't you?" T.J. spoke more to his group than those they'd accosted.

"Three months out."

"I sure hope we'll all be invited."

"You will."

Morgan tried to kick Sprout but hit her chair instead and brought unwanted attention to himself.

"Yeah, we wouldn't want to miss it." Ashley had an overabundance of teased, blond hair. Her sarcasm wasn't as subtle as T.J.'s.

T.J. led his cohorts towards the door. Sprout got to her feet and practically shouted that this year's party was going to be held on her father's boat, but no one turned to even acknowledge her.

After a minute, Morgan pulled Sprout back into her seat. "Why'd you promise to invite all of them?"

"T.J.'s cool."

"Mark's an asshole," Mitch said to his tablet.

"And Amber's a b-i-t-c-h." Morgan whispered but peered about to see if he'd been overheard.

"I don't think so." Sprout looked to her companions for support but received none. "They're not so bad."

"Mark is."

"What's so wrong with him?"

Mitch shook his head.

"What?"

"I wouldn't trust him. He might drop shit in girls' drinks. Or pee in some guy's beer. Who knows what else."

"He can't be like that; he's really popular," Sprout said, "and good looking."

"Believe him. And the rest aren't much better. It's no wonder they found each other."

"Then why's T.J. friends with them?"

Mitch typed more information into his tablet. "Maybe he's like them too and just disguises it better."

***

After four hours, The Party People decided to invite 248 people they knew to their third annual party. They hoped 150 would attend. In less than two minutes, Sprout's father disrupted the plan before any invitations could be sent.

Sprout thought it was so unfair. She didn't ask her father for anything, even though he had everything. Sure, she accepted whatever he gave her, and her father made sure she had all the comforts she could desire, but she never asked for those things. Not for her birthday. Not for Christmas. Not at any time. Just for a party one night each year. She only asked that she be allowed to entertain her friends.

Sprout wanted to plan the entire event—the people, the place, the entertainment, everything. Her father had let her do it the first two years, but now he wanted greater control, veto power. And he exercised it.

He told her it was for financial reasons, but Sprout wondered if it was really because of her decision to break up with Ty after two years.

Sure, he was nice and all, but she didn't want nice. Or she didn't want only nice.

She texted Morgan and Mitch and told them they needed to reconvene. They did so a couple of days later when they'd been scheduled to evaluate a potential band for the party.

"Now I know how these guys got your attention." Mitch opened his tablet on the drummer's empty case while the band called The Pre-Millennials played a cover of *Buddy Holly* in the local university's sound room. They followed that with a non-original version of *Beverly Hills*. "Why don't you just ask your Dad to pony up and actually get Weezer to play at the party?"

"Because he's being mean." Sprout sighed and rolled her head into Morgan's shoulder. "He said the boat can't hold anything close to as many as we wanted."

Morgan kissed Sprout's forehead. "Did you tell your father what percentage accepted last year?"

"He said we can't go by that. He thinks more will want to come this year. Plus, he reminded us we have to count these guys, servers, bouncers, etc. He said we can invite more if not enough accept initially."

"The problem is not enough respond until really late. If at all." Morgan leaned into Sprout and Mitch and lowered his voice. "These guys don't look like they belong together."

The band of five consisted of a singer, guitarist, bass player, keyboard player, and drummer. Two of them sported goatees and wore flannel shirts; two had long-hair but were clean-shaven; the singer appeared more boyish than the others, with short hair and an ironed shirt. They had set up a small stage in the middle of the room.

"They cover all sort of songs from the '90s," Sprout said.

"You guys play any Backstreet Boys?"

The group had just begun a version of Hootie's *Hold My Hand*, but the singer nodded to acknowledge Morgan's request.

"The good thing is Daddy said if we agreed on the number, he'd let us take the boat out on the water. He's really concerned about the amount we spend this year. It's a down year for the markets."

"Which markets?" Morgan asked.

"All of them, I think. Daddy's at least."

"Must be nice when dropping half a million just leads to some belt tightening." Mitch reached behind him and pulled a beer out of a backpack. He cracked the top and took a long swig. "You guys want one?"

"I don't think you can drink here."

"Why not? I'm a graduate."

Sprout shook her head. "Let's go out for a drink after."

"How you hear about these guys?" Morgan asked.

"The singer knows Melanie Mason who told Ali Sanchez who told me. I think they really want our gig."

"Must know the guest list will provide good exposure. Get one or two weddings out of it and cha-ching."

Mitch held up his sweaty aluminum can. "Not mine."

"I need to marry rich," Morgan said.

"You guys don't have to worry." Sprout looked back and forth between her companions on each side of her. "I'll take care of both of you. You guys know that."

She grabbed Mitch's beer and took a large gulp, then crunched her face. She offered it to Morgan.

"And look as pretty as you? No, thank you."

The Party People quietly listened to The Pre-Millennials' slightly mocking mash of *As Long As You Love Me*, *I Want It That Way*, and *Everybody*.

"What do you think of these guys?" Sprout asked.

"How about some grunge?" Mitch's shout triggered the commencement of the opening rift of *Smells Like Teen Spirit*. "They've got something for everyone, anyway."

"Should we check out anybody else?"

Mitch and Morgan shook their heads.

"I'll just go for a drink when this set starts," Morgan said.

Mitch scrolled through his database. "We were planning on inviting 14 Minuses. Even if we eliminated all of them that wouldn't be close to enough to satisfy your father."

"How many Zeros we have?" Sprout asked.

"Too many." Mitch looked up. "Think about it. How many people really make a positive contribution? Most people are neutral."

"Sprout should decide; it's her party."

"No, it's all of ours. Let's go through the names one-by-one again. Each person says yay or nay and majority rules until we hit 100."

"I think we can tell these guys to stop playing." Mitch got to his feet and made a slashing motion across his throat while The Pre-Millennials neared the end of a rocking *Even Flow/Not For You* mix. "You got the gig."

***

The Party People arrived three hours before anyone else. Sprout's father's yacht, named Buffett, occupied an entire section of the dock by itself. Inside, there were granite countertops, chrome fixtures, and original artwork.

"Seriously, I don't care what he does. How can your Dad actually afford this?" Morgan asked.

"He has a lot of money."

Sprout provided the tour and explained the plan. Guests would come aboard, as they had, on the main level. Food and drinks would be available there in the largest room, where The Pre-Millennials would start playing an hour after departure. A smaller bar and food station would be located on the top deck. The forecast was for a mild and clear night.

The lower level was generally off-limits. "That's where the problem children go," Sprout said.

Morgan held the door open and looked down into the darkness. "I hope there won't be any for a change."

"We've got two bouncers if there is. One will go down below to guard."

"Probably preferable to having them walk the plank," Mitch said.

Once he had fulfilled his pre-party duties, Mitch positioned himself near the entrance to be present the moment the first guests arrived. When they did, he offered some a brief friendly greeting but mostly gave them a half-smile or raised eyebrow. He recorded the arrival of each person, usually adding a note about their demeanor or appearance in his database.

Mitch anticipated only spending a half hour with the bouncer who looked to him to confirm those who sought entry had been invited, but the guests were slow to arrive. Most significantly for Mitch, The Obsession was late.

She was short, not much taller than five feet, with wavy hair with red highlights. Certainly pretty, but not the sort of woman who would stand out at this party or in this city. But Mitch thought there was something special about her. At least for him. Her smile, maybe. It seemed more real, less fake, than most of the young, single women he knew. Or perhaps it was her wit. She had a dry sense of humor. More like a guy. Said really funny things with a straight face. Who knew what it was exactly. Mitch just knew. Or thought he did.

As the hour Sprout had decreed the boat would leave the dock approached, Mitch fretted The Obsession had decided not to come, despite her RSVP. He opened the sheet of information he'd compiled on her and stared at the screen. He began ignoring those who boarded and his assigned role until he saw two bare legs before him. Before he looked up, he knew.

The Obsession wore a pink blouse, a short black skirt, and heels that didn't elevate her nearly as much as the shoes most of the other female attendees wore.

"I see you got your tablet as always." Lacey was a platinum blond who was almost as tall as Mitch. Always the center of attention, she was flanked by The Obsession and a light-skinned African-American named Angel.

Mitch ignored the comment while he looked at and through The Obsession. Not to imagine what lay beneath her clothes but because he believed he could see more than her mere physical presence. He imagined he could see her essence, her soul.

After a minute, Angel took The Obsession's hand and pulled her friend past Mitch. "You gotta blink, man."

"No stowaways, okay." The Obsession lightly tapped Mitch's shoulder as she passed.

Mitch half-laughed and half-coughed before he turned and offered a broad smile. "Don't encourage him," he heard Lacey tell The Obsession as the three women entered the main room.

Mitch remained at his post for another five minutes but found himself unable to complete his duties once he knew The Obsession was nearby. He asked his burly companion if he would mind handling the security on his own.

"I thought I already was, Kid."

Mitch was momentarily offended. The authority figure didn't appear that much older than him—he was probably in his early thirties—but his voice and presence certainly conveyed a maturity Mitch lacked.

"I mean, keep out anyone who doesn't belong."

"I wouldn't know who you invited, would I? But you run along and don't worry. I got this."

Sprout and Morgan stood off in the corner of the main room like they were uninvited interlopers at their own party. They called to Mitch as soon as he entered the room.

Mitch immediately saw them but pretended he didn't to give himself time to scan the rest of the room before heading towards them with a frown. "At least you could have gotten me a drink."

"Want mine?" Morgan offered his friend his martini.

The glass appeared full, but Mitch noticed a lip imprint on the rim. He saw Sprout was three-quarters of the way done with hers. "I'll get something in a minute."

"How we doing with guests?" Morgan asked.

"About two-thirds. We probably should delay shoving off."

"We can't. It's been announced," Sprout said.

"The best plans account for unforeseen variables." A skinny figure, at least 6'4" saddled beside Sprout. He held a glass of Scotch in his hand and twirled it continuously. "Though in this instance, reality was far from unforeseeable. Wouldn't you agree?"

The Party People silently stared at Ellington but offered no response, so he turned to his companion. "Jack?"

Jack was almost a foot shorter and a hundred pounds heavier, but both men wore khakis and a green sweater. Ellington's was forest green, while Jack's was more emerald, but the more significant difference was that Ellington wore a solid while Jack's had horizontal black stripes.

"I would say the odds of full compliance were ridiculously small."

"Of course, that might have been Sprout's intention all along."

"We built in some leeway time."

Sprout had barely spoken the words when the boat's captain sounded the horn as an indication the yacht would be leaving port.

"We'll see, dear Sprout, won't we? Why don't we head to the top deck to see how this plays out?"

The group proceeded towards the stairs but were pushed aside by five young men in t-shirts and worn jeans just as they arrived.

Mitch shrugged. "I never saw them come aboard."

Two men untied the ropes that held the boat to the dock just as the group arrived on the top deck. The yacht soon eased itself away from the city and its skyline in favor of the vastness of the sea.

Ellington held out his arms and turned in a circle. His wingspan was enormous, even for a man of his size. "To stand at the fulcrum of mathematical perfection of the universe and the inevitable randomness of human behavior."

Mitch tapped Sprout's shoulder as two couples ran along the pier and yelled for the boat to wait for them. The men in dress shoes raced ahead, leaving behind their dates, who held their shoes in their hands and jogged along barefoot.

Sprout used Morgan as a blocker and partially ducked. "Leah's going to kill me."

Morgan waved at the couples in the mechanical manner of a bored flight attendant.

"Do you know if your father has seen my paper on temporal market chaos?"

Sprout remained in her squatted position even as she looked over her shoulder. "I have no idea what you're talking about."

Ellington bent at the waist and lowered his voice. "I know. You really need someone to take care of you, don't you?"

Sprout began to crab-walk towards the stairs but stopped and jumped to her feet when a bottle crashed onto the floor a foot before her. "What the hell?"

Everyone on the top deck ducked when a second bottle crashed against a railing. They discovered the objects were not thrown at them by Leah or her friends but by two guys wearing leather pants further down the pier.

"We didn't invite them, did we?" Sprout asked.

"Abe and Cleo, the dynamic duo, no way." Morgan threw his arms around his friends.

"So, why did they think they could come?"

"We see you, Sprout, you cunt, and your faggy boyfriends as well." The slurred speech indicated early evening intoxication.

"I stand—or squat—corrected." Ellington shuffled beside The Party People. "Perhaps an early departure was a wise decision after all. Though one wonders about your circle of acquaintances."

"We do too." Mitch ran from the others. He took the stairs two at a time as he raced to find the security worker. Upon reaching the main level, he heard sirens blaring. He looked out a window and saw the bottle throwers in flight.

"Little shits don't even have beer courage."

The entrance security guy had found his partner, who was even taller and wider. They brushed through Mitch and the rest of the crowd like a moving wall. Mitch wondered if he should follow but quickly recognized he wouldn't add anything if he did. Better to leave the problem to those who could resolve it.

He looked across the room and saw The Obsession alone with a drink in her hand. Or so he thought. He walked towards her. Only when he was almost on top of her did he realize not only was she not alone and that not only were Lacey and Angel nearby, but so were three guys seemingly confident about their place in the world. Mitch simply hadn't seen any of them at the outset of his trek when The Obsession was his sole focus.

Mitch attempted to compensate for his error by trying to isolate The Obsession and remove her from her pack. He did so with a series of smiles, shuffles, and changing body angles.

"Did you see the commotion?" he asked after he'd guided The Obsession into a corner and positioned himself, so his back was toward the rest of her group.

"I heard something. Were you the target?"

"One of them, I expect."

"I don't get it. You guys are nice enough to hold this event. I can't imagine how much it costs."

"A lot." Mitch smiled and waited for The Obsession to say more. When she didn't, he felt the need to fill the void. "Actually, Sprout pays. Well, her father. I'm pretty poor."

"Oh, me too." The Obsession reached out and grabbed Mitch's arm. He stared at the physical connection. "I met Lacey and Angel when we were in college together. They've always been nice enough to bring me along to events I couldn't otherwise afford. I've got a real job, you know? Not just volunteering."

"Hey, you want to dance?"

Mitch observed The Obsession withdraw her hand and her light fade.

"To the music in your head?" Lacey intruded upon their conversation.

Mitch turned and observed the sad truth. The Pre-Millennials were still in the process of setting up their equipment. Guests were still getting food and drinks and chatting chit.

Mitch internally punched himself for not just simply asking The Obsession about her work. Or college. Or anything else. Things had been going well until he blew it, he thought.

Angel reached out and grabbed The Obsession. "We should mingle."

"I'll see you later, Mitch." The Obsession glanced over her shoulder in his direction while Angel pulled her rather forcefully.

Lacey stood before Mitch with her hands on her hips and her mouth open as if she were ready to slam him. He began to crouch to lessen the blow, but Lacey simply shook her head and laughed. Mitch thought he heard her use the word "creep" as she abandoned him.

The Party People toured the entire boat, briefly stopping to say hello to most of their guests but eschewing all lengthy conversations. They discovered another group of interlopers and asked security to bring them to the hull, where they were soon joined by a couple of drunks who had begun to wrestle on the top deck.

Following this latest episode, Sprout abandoned her companions. She draped herself off the stern as if she were considering leaping.

"Don't do it." Morgan ran ahead of Mitch and grabbed her waist.

"Nothing magical has happened. What are all the Plusses doing?" Sprout asked when Mitch arrived by her side.

"What do Plusses do?" Mitch asked.

The Party People stood in silence with the light of the stars stronger than that of the city, unable to come up with an answer until they heard a roar of excitement and cheering beneath them. They raced down the stairs and saw Lexi and Cora, two Plusses if there ever were any, in the middle of the dance floor wearing nothing but body paint.

Lexi was a tiger, orange in back, white in the front, striped all over; Cora, a lion. Her breasts were its eyes, her navel its nose, and the mouth further below.

When The Party People arrived on the scene, the two ladies occupied the center of the dance floor, the rest of the attendees having backed away and formed a ring around them. The Pre-Millennials initially played a few notes of *Hakuna Matata* before apparently realizing that was not what the audience feeding off the energy and alcohol wanted. They began playing louder, faster, quickly moving from one song to another—Chumbawumba, then, *All Star*, *Song 2*—while the party's attendees swarmed around Lexi and Cora.

As the evening progressed and the boat got closer to its point of return, the room even accepted The Party People into its penumbra so they could dance with, not just on the outskirts of, the group.

The Obsession appeared beside Mitch, unaccompanied by Lacey or Angel. They danced together without a word being spoken, not that any could have been shared over the music.

Later, those who had been escorted below appeared at the far end of the room, dancing with or at least near members of the security team.

"Here's to your hosts!" the lead singer of The Pre-Millennials shouted before they began their last set.

"TPP!" the group responded in unison.

"I said here's to your hosts!"

"TPP! TPP!" came the shouts as The Pre-Millennials covered Naughty by Nature.

It was a Plus night, all would agree. But it was soon over. The boat returned to port. The music and dancing stopped. People rushed for one last drink, though many had passed the point when they should. For most, the drink, by then, was a minus. But that's what happens to those who chase the ultimate plus.

Security returned the captives down below for appearances' sake if nothing else. They would be the last to disembark, other than Sprout, Mitch, and Morgan.

A fleet of taxis waited at the pier to drive guests to their homes or elsewhere. Sprout had arranged this in advance. Not that the guests acknowledged or even recognized the courtesy. Few said thank you. Or even goodbye.

Lacey, Angel, and The Obsession were among the first off, failing to offer the hosts even a wave or smile.

There was a brief moment after security removed the riffraff and before Sprout's father returned with the muscle to inspect the boat when The Party People occupied the yacht alone. They'd returned to the top deck to watch the final departures, to see their guests disappear into the mist and darkness, happy, for the most part, with how things turned out, but wondering if it was enough to sustain them for an entire year.

The Party People had delivered for the third year in a row. Sure, none of them were Plusses in their own right, but one night a year they added something to the lives of many. Was it so wrong of them, standing together and alone, to expect something in return?

Rie Sheridan Rose

Rie Sheridan Rose multitasks. A lot. Her short stories appear in numerous anthologies, including *Killing It Softly Vol. 1 & 2*, *Hides the Dark Tower*, *Dark Divinations*, and *On Fire*. Her poetry appears in numerous venues, including *Speculative Poets of Texas, Vol. 1*; *Texas Poetry Calendar*; and *Illumen* to name a few. Her photographs have been in *Ghostlight Magazine*, *The Passed Note Review*, *Thoughtful Dog*, and *Constellations*, as well as on the covers of several small press volumes. She has authored twelve novels, six poetry chapbooks, and lyrics for dozens of songs. She tweets as @RieSheridanRose.

Liberty

Bellina Corvacae stared out over the pseudo-Grecian columns and terraced roof gardens of Orion 6. Her fingers played restlessly with the streams of her water harp as she contemplated another dull afternoon as the pampered only daughter of wealthy First Citizens.

"Bellina!" Her mother's imperious voice rang out in the still morning like a claxon. "Where are you, girl?"

Bellina cringed. What now? Endless hours standing like a statue while the insipid dress-maker pinned yards of cloth to various parts of her body and scolded her for slumping? Another boring afternoon listening to her mother whine about her lack of a suitable gentleman caller? By the stars, she was only fifteen! Why couldn't she just be left alone?

Not today. She just couldn't take it today.

Setting aside the harp, she tiptoed to the balustrade and stared down into the city. Unlike the ivory towers of the First Citizens, the Lessers lived in low-slung dwellings with open shop-fronts attached. The sounds of bartering and laughter rose to her thirsting ears. Tantalizing odors were carried on the wind. They seemed to be having so much fun down below.

She wished that her ancestors had come on one of the later colony ships. Then she might be allowed to go down to the streets and walk amid the Lessers without a train of servants. She hated being a First Citizen. The first seventy families to reach Orion 6 on the Liberty Launch had grabbed the hilltops and built New Athens. All other colonists were looked down upon, deemed "Lessers." As if there were anything special about being on the original ship besides better alarm clocks on launch day. All the colonists on all the ships had been first come, first serve besides the crews. Only Captain O'Hara's family and those of the babysitting officers who had watched the cryo-tanks deserved special recognition. The rest of the First Citizens just had better timing.

Bellina stepped up on the balustrade, walking it like a tightrope. She didn't watch her feet—she'd done this a thousand times, and even if she fell, the force net would catch her before she hit the ground—instead, she continued to watch the streets below her. The Lessers going about their business.

They were so much more interesting than the First Citizens with their endless soirees and afternoon teas. The Lessers ran businesses and created things more useful than ballgowns and baked goods. She would love to do something meaningful like that.

Something caught her attention, and she froze. There he was again. The boy with the golden hair. She had been watching him come and go for months now. He seemed to be about her age, but he had the well-muscled frame of someone who worked for his living, unlike the pampered First Sons her mother was forever foisting on her.

He glanced up and smiled when he saw her. Waving, he gestured for her to come down.

She shook her head sadly. "Force net," she called to him.

"It's damaged. Look." He stepped to the wall surrounding the lower garden, and stood on tiptoe, reaching up over his head.

She could see his hand sweeping the air in a circle. The hand was moving above the level defined by the force net.

Her eyes widened. Could it be true?

She had talked to the Security Chief occasionally from sheer boredom. She knew that the net was created by several localized sensor arrays. If one had gone out, there might well be a hole in the field... a way to escape... at least for the afternoon.

"Bellina! Where are you?" Her mother's voice rang out again. "Come inside at once!"

She was running out of time. Mother would come looking next, and she would be trapped.

Darting a glance over her shoulder, she made up her mind. Heart pounding in her throat, she spread her arms and dove off the balcony onto the force net.

It caught her just above the tops of the trees in the lower garden. It was like falling onto a firm mattress. Most fun she'd had in months, actually. She struggled to her feet and picked her way carefully across the net to where the boy still stood beside the garden wall. It reminded her of a trampoline she had played upon as a child.

"Bellina Celestine Corvacae! What in the name of the Six do you think you are doing?"

She glanced over her shoulder to see her mother's horrified face above the balcony wall. She almost relented... it was bred into her to obey... but this might be her only chance to see the world below her wall.

No! She would not lose this chance. Whatever the consequences.

The boy reached up and helped her to the ground. He was taller than she had thought—towering a good half span over her. His eyes were the bluest blue she had ever seen.

"Run!" she commanded, taking his hand and heading away from the Tower.

He followed without question.

They ran until Bellina had to stop, gasping at the unaccustomed exercise. Leaning against a wall, she fought to catch her breath. "She'll be raising the Guard," she panted. "I'm sorry."

"We'll just have to make the most of the time we have. I am Sten," he said, smiling shyly.

"Bellina," she replied.

"Ah. I've heard of you." The grin grew wider. "You're a First Citizen. Should you be fraternizing with a lowly Lesser?"

She made a face. "Do you know how boring it is to be a First Citizen?"

He threw back his head and laughed. "I can imagine. Would you like to see what life is like for the rest of us? While you still can?"

"May I?"

"I'd be happy to show you. But first, let's do something about that dress." He cocked his head, taking in the filmy, diaphanous cloud of chiffon and silk billowing around her. He wore a long coat over worn leggings and simple shirt. Slipping out of it, he held it out to her. "Put this on. It'll make you less conspicuous and might buy us some time."

She did as requested. "My Father is away in New Babylon on business, so we have that bit of luck. Mother doesn't have the command of the Guard she thinks she does. Still, there will be some hue and cry after me. Keep a watchful eye for Security."

Nodding, he took her hand again. "I'll keep you safe."

The rest of the afternoon passed in a blur of new sights and sounds. Sten showed her the shops that clustered around the base of New Athens. She whirled, trying to take everything in at once. The vendors cried their wares:

"Knives ground. Scissors sharpened."

"Fire flowers five for a credit. Old Earth roses a dozen for two."

"Books for sale. Paper and plasma. All makes and models."

"How can you take it all in?" Bellina breathed, clutching his arm to ground herself amid the chaos.

"It's home," shrugged Sten. "I don't know what you mean."

She giggled, drunk on sensation.

As they wove their way through the maze of streets, she was overwhelmed by smells she had never experienced before. Perfumes in blown glass bottles; spices, both native and brought by the colonists; cook fires and their contents—they wove together to create an aromatic blanket.

Once they saw a Guard questioning a vendor and ducked behind another stall to avoid detection. Several other times, they heard shouted orders and turned to run the other way.

The danger of discovery added a spice to everything. Colors seemed brighter on fabrics coarser than the silks and sateens she was used to, but the materials were more sensual to the touch. Her eyes were dazzled by the variety and quantities abounding. She wished she dared buy one of the cotton shawls or brilliant skirts to take home, but her mother would simply confiscate and burn it.

Why couldn't she stand up to the woman? Just once… it would be such heaven. Though maybe she had by making this escape. At least she was doing something on her own.

"Here, try this," Sten encouraged, turning back from a cooking stand and handing her a stick with a courtly bow.

She took it gingerly. "What is it?"

"Taste it."

There was a strip of meat impaled on the stick. With trepidation, she nibbled the corner of the meat. "It's the most delicious thing I've ever tasted!" she breathed, savoring every morsel, and then licking her fingers. What ecstasy!

They wandered on, and somehow, again, her hand found its way into his. It felt right there.

A band of musicians stood on a street corner, playing for the passersby with a basket on the ground in front of them collecting tips. One of the young men strummed the streams of a water harp not too unlike her own, and Bellina stopped, entranced. The music was beautiful.

"May I?" she asked, unable to resist the urge. She reached for the harp.

The musician nodded and handed it to her.

She played several songs with the group, and the crowd surrounding them applauded. The approval lifted her spirits. In the salons of the First Citizens, her playing was considered an amusing little diversion that a girl could use to please her husband, but nothing special. The crowd of Lessers appreciated her talent as a gift. She lost herself in the music, forgetting their danger if the Guard spotted them.

Suddenly, a shout rang out, "There she is!"

She came to herself to see a squadron of Guards running toward them. Thrusting the harp at its owner, she turned to flee. Before she had taken more than a dozen steps, she heard the sound of a scuffle behind her and, looking over her shoulder, saw Sten struggling in the grasp of a half-dozen Guard.

All fight went out of her. "Don't hurt him!" she ordered, slipping off his coat. "Let him go at once!"

The Security Chief frowned at her. "I'm afraid I can't do that, Miss Bellina. My orders are to bring him before the Council for trial."

"Trial? For what?"

"Kidnapping."

"I came of my own free will!"

"I have my orders, Miss."

Despite her continued protests, Sten was manhandled through the streets of the market toward the Corvacae Tower. She trailed behind them, pulling at the Security Chief's arm and trying desperately to convince him to release Sten.

All too soon, they arrived at the base of the garden wall. Bellina was marched up the interior stairs, straining all the way to keep an eye on what was happening to Sten. But once they turned the first corner, she lost all track of him.

"You must let Sten go!" she commanded. "I will take the consequences of my actions, but he is innocent! I was not coerced to follow him."

The Security Chief shook his head grimly. "Not my call, Miss. The Council will judge."

"First Citizens! What right do they have to judge a Lesser?"

"Not your concern, girl." The Chief was beginning to lose his hold on his temper. He shoved her before him into the Tower proper.

Her mother was standing in the center of the Great Hall, arms folded across her chest, foot tapping impatiently on the marble floor. "There you are!" she burst out as soon as she caught sight of Bellina. "Where in the Seven Quadrants have you been, girl? Are you hurt?"

"No, Mother. I'm not."

Before the words were completely out of her mouth, her mother was speaking again. "I was horrified when I saw that person man-handling you. Well, he won't get away with it. How dare he put hands on a First Citizen? He'll get what is coming to him, believe you me!"

"Mother! It wasn't like that—I went with Sten of my own free will!"

"You've been traumatized, child. Go to your room and rest."

Bellina stamped her foot. "I am not a child! I am old enough to make my own decisions as to who I spend time with."

"You mind me, girl!" Her mother slapped Bellina across the face.

Stunned, the girl stepped back, hand on her cheek.

"You have no idea the trouble you have caused me today, you ungrateful little baggage. You were a disgrace to the entire House of Corvacae," she hissed. "You have a place to uphold on this world. You can't just run around willy-nilly doing whatever you please. Your father and I have worked too hard to maintain our position as First Citizens for me to allow you to throw it all away. Do you understand me?"

"But why must I be a First Citizen, Mother?" whispered Bellina. "I didn't ask to be. I want to do something with my life. I don't want to be some hot house flower up here in my Ivory Tower. They really liked my playing…"

"Children's games! None of us get to live our dreams. There is a way to the world, and we all have our places in it. Yours is Daughter of House Corvacae. Learn to live with it."

Realizing that nothing she could say would sway Lady Corvacae, Bellina lowered her head. "Yes, Mother." Peering up through her lashes, she stood meekly until her mother swept out of the room.

As soon as she heard her mother on the stair, she darted the other way, heading for the Security Center beneath the Tower. The Guards would have taken Sten below. Perhaps she could persuade the Chief to let her have a moment alone with the boy. Even if he wouldn't, she would find a way to speak to Sten.

There was no one in the Guard Chamber except Sten, slumped inside one of the force-warded cells. Bellina drew in her breath with a hiss. Dashing across the room, she searched for the forcefield controls. She keyed off the field and knelt beside the boy.

His eye was blackened, and he favored his left wrist.

"They've hurt you! I am so sorry."

Sten shrugged. "It wasn't your fault, Bellina. I knew what I was doing when I called you from the wall."

"It isn't fair! You've done nothing wrong."

"Lessers mustn't mingle with the First Citizens. We are taught that from the time we can walk. I knew I was breaking the rules we live by. One day, Society may change... but for now... this is our world."

Bellina knew in her soul that he was right, but she wished he weren't.

Sten took her hand in his good one. "Come with me. We can go to New Babylon... or maybe get a berth on one of the Spacers. Find a new world to explore."

She shook her head. "Thank you for giving me this day to remember, but I must stay here. I will give you the time you need to make your escape from here, but I have an obligation to my family. I must marry well, raise children, and continue my bloodline. Like it or not, it is the way of my world. But now, I will always know that there is more to life than the First Citizens. I will know that there is more to life than the Ivory Towers.

"I will make it my goal to learn our laws, so that I will be able to champion the Lessers, to try and bring some equality to the world we are all creating here. Give me time to become the woman you see in me." She ran her hand down the side of his face. "To be worthy of the man I see in you."

"Every day, I will come to the garden wall and wait for you."

"You mustn't. It is too dangerous. The force net will be repaired by morning. I won't be able to leave again."

"In that case..." He leaned over and kissed her. "Have that to remember me by as well."

Her lips burned at the touch. She felt her cheeks flame. "Thank you," she whispered. "For making me realize the world is bigger than my back garden. I'll never forget it."

Rising to her feet, she checked the hallway. It remained empty—apparently the Guard trusted their forcefield to hold the prisoner with no difficulty. She signaled to Sten and led him to the front of the Tower.

"Go as far as you can. They will be looking for you. I couldn't bear it if you were hurt any further because of me."

"I'll go. For now. But I will send a message once a year until you are ready to meet me again. Look for a fire flower on your doorstep on this day."

"And when you receive it back from me, you will know it is time. I will send it to the shop where you bought me the meat stick by the end of the same day." It was a sketchy plan at best, but it was better than none...

***

Ten years of fire flowers... Sten was regular as clockwork.

On the eleventh anniversary of their meeting, Bellina plucked the blossom from the step of the Corvacae Tower, brushing it across her smiling lips, inhaling its sweet perfume. Then she stepped out of the lower garden and walked through the streets of New Athens' Lesser Quarter. Head held proudly, she nodded to shopkeepers and vendors as she passed.

Behind her, she heard excited whispers. "That is Lady Corvacae! She's the one who authored the Lesser Equality Law. They say she has vowed to champion integration of the classes. She's younger than I expected..."

Bellina fought to hide her smile. It had been a long decade. She had thought of her day with Sten, every one of the intervening hours. It had kept her focused on her goals—breaking the barriers between Lessers and First Citizens; creating a world that she would be proud to live in.

And now, with the passing of the Lesser Equality Law, that world was one step closer. She could return Sten's fire flower at last.

She stepped up to the booth where they had shared that meat stick so long ago. Her heart was pounding in her chest. They had been children all those years ago... separated by so much... That afternoon had meant the world to her, but had it meant anything at all to him?

"I have been waiting for you..." came a soft voice from behind her.

She whirled. He was taller, slimmer, but his face was just as she remembered.

She handed him the fire flower. "I made you a promise."

"So, you did."

"The Lesser Equality Law isn't perfect, but it is a step in the right direction," she said softly. "I read something in my studies. It reminded me

251

of you. It talked of 'life, liberty, and the pursuit of happiness.' I decided that those were words I could live by."

"What about your duty to the bloodline?"

"My mother had a son the year after we met. Now *he* can carry on the bloodline. As soon as my brother was born, I told my parents I would be a lawyer, and I would see the barriers come down. They resisted at first, but I can be most persuasive." She smiled. "You taught me the importance of liberty. I've come to claim mine."

Robbie Sheerin

Robbie Sheerin was born and raised in Oban, Scotland but now lives in the United States. He moved to the Boston area when he was twenty-three years old. Married with one daughter, a snobby cat, and a crazy dog, he has worked in the aerospace manufacturing business for fifteen years and is now a quality inspector.

Robbie enjoys spending time with his wife Rebecca and daughter Lilly. He also enjoys gardening, woodwork, golf, classic sci-fi tv and movies, and writing. He is a whovian.

The 42 year old is a fan of *The Twilight Zone* and *The Outer Limits*. He has been inspired to write by such writers as Asimov, Bradbury, Serling, and Dan Brown. He has been published him *AHF Magazine* and also *The Abstract Elephant Magazine*

He writes every day and looks forward to releasing a collection of short stories in 2021. Robbie writes Sci-fi and General Fiction.
Robbie can be found on LinkedIn and Medium.

http://linkedin.com/in/robbie-sheerin-welcometocrumville-dot-com-blog-ab9b35196

https://medium.com/@mywords1900

Just Ignore Me

I have been at this computer all day, typing away and staring at this screen. My eyes feel like they are on fire. I'm not sure who is more uncomfortable, him or me, at least I'm sitting in a chair. He's been sitting on the floor, with legs crossed all day. Three more hours till I'm out of here.

"Will you stop that clicking noise?"

"I need to type. It's my job. I'm a writer."

"Seems super boring; click, click, click."

He is so annoying. He sits around all day doing nothing except watch me and follow me around. Sometimes it's good to have him around, someone to talk to, someone that listens to me. But other times, he is like a nasty rash that you can't get rid of. Not that I've ever had a nasty rash. It's just what people say. Although I think I would rather have a nasty rash than him. With a rash, you know it will eventually go away. Him? He's been there my whole life.

Okay, focus.

...in these critical times... or complex times? no, critical, I think... *investors and banks need access to financial funding that is not....*

"Will you stop that? I'm trying to write!"

"I feel like singing. Just ignore me."

"I can't just ignore you when you're singing Adel in that awful cat-like squeal. Just stop, please."

"You used to love me singing."

"Yeah, when I was a kid, and I didn't have to work and hit deadlines."

"Remember that time at Disneyland we were singing so loud in the hotel, and your dad went ballistic?"

"Yes, I remember; it was kind of funny."

I'm starving. I didn't eat breakfast. I think I will eat that salad.

Needs fewer onions. But it's still good. I think these tomatoes are the best I've ever had.

"A salad, again?"

"Shut up!"

"I mean, you flip flop back and forth on these ridiculous diets. One minute you're bingeing on cheese puffs and candies. Then you're starving yourself eating crackers and water."

"I know. I know! What do you want me to do? Nothing seems to work."

I hate him.

"Exercise, exercise, exercise. You can't do one and not the other. You need to eat healthier AND exercise."

He's right. "You're right, I know."

"Let's walk home tonight instead of riding in one of those dirty cabs. Come on, finish clicking, and let's go."

"I need to finish this article for Friday's paper."

"Work, work, work. I don't see what all the fuss is about. I don't work; it's no big deal."

Ok, so where was I... *restricted by governments outside of….*

"Do you overeat because Mom and Dad judged you all the time?"

Aaaaarrrrrrr, I'm never going to get this finished.

"What?!"

"Mom and Dad… not my mom and dad, your mom and dad; they were always making comments about you not being good enough. Dad never hugged you or told you how much he loved you. Mom always had that condescending tone to her voice, didn't she? Is that why you overeat? To spite her?"

"I don't know, maybe."

"Every cheese puff you eat is a slap in the face to Mother, right?"

He always does this. Now my mind is running. I'm getting emotional. He's right, though. Mom would hate me eating junk food.

"Yeah, I guess."

"Yup, I was right. I'm always right."

"I think I also eat because I'm sad. So, I eat junk food because in that moment it makes me feel good about myself."

"You know, you are the nicest person I know. And I know a lot of people. You need to be at peace with yourself. Don't listen to Nelly."

"Who's Nelly?"

"Eh, negative Nelly."

"Okay, okay. I'll try."

"Come on, let's sing. 'I wish nothing but the best for you, too'"

"Don't forget me."

"Yessss!! Don't you feel better singing?"

He's right, "Yes, you're right."

"You finish clicking away, and then we can sing while we walk home. But I'm going to sing now. Just ignore me.

Charles Cooper

Charles Cooper is a program manager, systems engineer, the owner/operator of Elizabeth River Press, and an artist/author who has written and published eleven volumes of poetry, two novels, and five non-fiction books. During the daylight hours, he pursues the design and creation of large, innovative systems for Airbus in Herndon, Virginia. He is the recipient of American Poetry Society's Best Poet Award for 2002.

Cooper received his PhD in International Political Economy from Kings College London. From 2017 – 2019. He was both a judge and editor of the Atlantic Economic Journal. He also has an LLM from American Military University, an MBA from Villanova University, and a bachelor's degree in Information Management from Palm Beach Atlantic College. Cooper is currently pursuing the creation of a new series of books based loosely around his experience in government contracting and the international intelligence arena.

Operation Cheget Domcheck

0143 Hours M.S.T., 27 Dec 1991
Sidreriya Pub
Saint Petersburg, Russia

On an icy night in Saint Petersburg, two days after Boris Yeltsin took the reins of the Russian government from Mikael Gorbachev in Moscow, the Sidreriya Bar, or Cider Bar, in Saint Petersburg had no customers again. What little cider they could procure, sat in the stone jars behind the counter.

Irina Yahantov looked at her partner, a tall, strong blonde woman, who was sitting on a stool at the bar with a rag in one hand, the other cradling her head as it lay on the counter. Irina groaned, "Elizbieta, now is not the time to be sitting. For God's sake, there is work to be done if we want to get out of here sometime tonight."

Elizbieta rolled her head to the right, looking at the woman. "What do I clean? No one has been in here since two days before Christmas. All the men have gone to Moscow and for what... To be butchered by KGB? I tell you the country will burn before the party surrenders an inch."

Irina was clearly disgusted. She curled her nose. "I tell you this; until it burns, it will be clean. The next man who enters will not find cobwebs here. He will see that we two women have a clean and upright establishment."

Elizbieta sat up. "Dare to wish... I will leave with the next man who enters here. You can have this fucking bar for all it's worth. I would trade the inheritance of my ancestors for a man's weight on top of me right now."

Irina smiled and giggled. "Da, da. Please, just clean. No more of this father was a czar bullshit. You and I are sisters. Your father made it so. This is what we have, and what we must do." A tear came to her eye, but she brushed it aside. She looked at the counter more intently, scrubbing harder. The wood, already smooth and shined polished by four hundred years of use and wear, needed less tending than Irina. Her soul was brittle and hard, tarnished by twenty-five years of cold and fear.

The front door opened, and a bell tinkled. Both women turned, startled at this late arrival of customers. Two men entered, a black man and a Russian. The black man led the other into the room. His hand flashed to his mouth, where one finger brushed his lips in a sign that is not a universally accepted request for silence.

The Russian man, seeing the black man's gesture, rolled his eyes. He raised his fist to within an inch of his face with his thumb tucked between his index finger and middle finger, the Russian sign for silence. The two women were Russian, however, and they did not need the translation. There were only two reasons men burst into a closed pub at two in the morning, and they both required immediate silence. As these men were definitely not Soviet Security, then they were running from them.

Elizbieta heard footsteps outside. She waved to the men. Under her breath, she said, "Here," in English.

Silently, Irina waved her arms in protest, but the men were already inside, right behind Elizbieta as she opened the door to the building's cellar.

Quickly and silently, the men dropped down into the hole in the floor. She closed the door behind them. Then, she tugged a tattered rug over the door. Irina, who knew her part well, was already placing a table onto the top of the rug. Before either woman paused for breath, two chairs were in their proper place next to the table.

A heartbeat later, the door to the establishment opened again. A bell tinkled. Two men in long black canvas overcoats came through the door. One of the men looked up at the bell and flicked it with his fingers. Everything about them said they were state security. NKVD, KGB, GRU, it didn't matter what you called them; everywhere they went, they carried an air of ownership over life and death. It didn't help that the coats did little to hide the Yarygin Pistols in their shoulder holsters. The holsters were standard issue, which was clearly too small for these men. Each man was roughly five feet, six inches tall, and where the shoulder holster cut into their chest, the bulge of flesh was evident beneath the coat. While they were the same height, one of the men was nearly double the width of the other. Neither man had exercised recently enough to remember the feeling. The men stopped moving, and their eyes surveyed the place like a video camera, recording everything to be used later.

With characteristic Russian impassiveness, Elizbieta said, "May I get you some cider? We are closed, but we are, of course, at your service."

In a low growl the smaller man said, "Yes, you are."

Elizbieta was behind the bar pouring glasses of cider. The larger of the two men sidled up close to Elizbieta. She could smell turnips and body odor. When he leaned in close to her, it took all her power to suppress her gag reflex.

The man said, "I don't want to draw this out." He ran his hand over her body, as though checking for weapons, but he was slow, and drew out his touch at those places he knew she would feel it most.

Elizbieta set the drinks on the counter. Irina pulled out the two chairs at the table covering the door to the cellar. The smaller man sat down. From below, a small thump could be heard. The man's eyes shot to Irina, "What was that?"

"There is a cat which sometimes lives in the cellar. It comes and goes."

The man nodded his head, as if accepting what she was saying, but he continued looking at Irina with hawk-like eyes.

Seeing his stare, Irina said, "Don't you want to search me? You have checked my sister for any danger, but I have not yet been checked."

The man smiled. He took a long drink of the cider. He said, "This is good," and raised the glass.

The larger man stopped molesting Elizbieta and raised the drink from the bar. "Za zdarovye; *to your health.*" Both the women and the other man echoed his toast. They drank.

Then the larger man turned back to Elizbieta. "So darling, I know we are having an amazing time, and I hate to dampen the mood, but I must know, have you seen two men? One a Russian. The other is dark as night. Both men are very dangerous. This negr, is American, he goes by the name, Henry, Henry James."

Irina said, "Like the American biographer." Perhaps realizing she had made a mistake by revealing what she knew about American writers, she added, "Zloy capitalist, *damn capitalist.*"

The smaller man, sitting at the table next to her, eyed her suspiciously but nodded his approval. "Da. Zloy kapatalist." He continued looking at Irina, but still, he made no attempt to touch her.

Elizbieta said, "No one has been in here since Christmas Day. We are happy to have guests when they can pay." She looked from one man to the next, silently asking the question, *who is paying for the cider?*

A low laugh escaped the man, whose hands had only recently retreated from her bodice.

The man sitting next to Irina rose. "Is this true?"

Irina replied, "Da, no one since Christmas Day."

He rose and looked at the other man. They turned and walked straight to the door. It closed hard behind them.

The two women sat at the table and nipped at the cider. Irina said, "You should have warmed the cider."

Elizbieta said, "I wish I'd poisoned it. Those assholes think they can have whatever they want."

The two women laughed under their breath as though they were hiding from an emotion, which might be, if interpreted correctly, determined to be harmful to the state. Elizbieta and Irina, like all Russians, believed the security organs of the newly minted Russian State were listening to their conversations, even possible assigning emotions to their tone and inflection. In Russia, even feelings were punishable by death.

Irina said, "Do you think they are gone?"

Elizbieta stood, appearing quite regal. She said, "To tell the truth, I don't care. If they kill me, I won't have to listen to you anymore."

Irina uttered one word, "Suka, *bitch*."

Together, the two women pulled back the table, rolled back the rug, and lifted the door. The black man was the first to climb out of the cellar. He turned and offered his hand to the Russian man.

Elizbieta said in English, "You are the one called Henry James?"

The man looked at her, then, death in his eyes.

She said, "OK, OK. I only want to know who I am talking to."

Henry, still eyeing her warily, said, "Blagodaryu vas; *thank you*."

Elizbieta looked at the Russian man, seeing his tattoos. He was Bratva, the Russian mafia. Addressing Henry James, she asked in English, "Who is this?"

Henry responded in Russian, "Drug russkago naroda; *a friend of the Russian people*."

Elizbieta laughed. She said, "More like a murderer."

Then, the Russian man said in English, "Call me Vlad. But Henry here is wrong. Tonight, we are a friend to the world."

He handed a large case to Henry. When he took it, Henry gave Vlad a plastic wrapped wad of cash. Henry said, "You know where the rest is. If you ever come state side."

Pocketing the money, Vlad said, "You know this isn't necessary. What you did for my mother and my brother is enough for anything, anywhere, anytime."

With cold, businesslike precision, Henry said, "I've been told. If it's all the same, I'd rather we kept this even for now. My government gave me money for this operation. It's best I don't return home with it still in hand." He paused looking at the half empty mugs of cider on the table and bar. "Besides, I don't trust anything that's free. Where I come from, free has strings." Henry proceeded to set the canvas case on the table and open it. Inside were three identical black Samsonite suitcases, each with a gold lock securing them. He asked, "The Cheget?"

The man clapped Henry on the shoulder and said, "Da, I am Russian. I understand strings, and yes. All three cheget. Replaced with identical, useless simulations."

The two women looked at each other, then at the men, unsure of what was happening.

Abruptly, the door opened. The two security men burst into the room. One of them shouted, "Zamorozit'; *freeze*!"

Henry drew a silenced, Walther PPK from his coat and put a bullet precisely into each man's trachea. A barking dog was heard outside the pub, and there was a shout from some distance down the street.

Irina said, "Hurry." She opened the trap door. Vlad went first. Henry followed with the case of suitcases. Irina was near to letting the door slip shut when Elizbieta put her hand on the door.

She said, "I told you sister, I am leaving with the next man who walks through the door."

Irina groaned, "Which one?"

Elizbieta smiled. The two women embraced. "I love you, beautiful one," said Irina.

Elizbieta said, "I love you too, sister. I am sorry to leave. You know where I'll be." Then she slipped through the door.

Irina carefully composed a puzzled look on her plump Russian face. She closed the door, turned toward the two men lying dead on the floor, and screamed for everything she was worth. In Russian she cried, "Pomoshch', ubiystvo; *Help, murder.*"

In the cellar, Elizbieta took a metal flashlight from the side of the wall. She said, "Follow me. Quickly." In the Southeast corner of the cellar, there was an unlit wood stove. Motioning to the stove with the light, she said, "Help me." Then she took the right side and began to pull. Both men joined in. Soon, the stove slid away to reveal a tunnel.

"Follow me," she said.

Henry stepped into the tunnel. Vlad asked, "Where does it lead?"

Elizbieta said, "Not to a KGB torture chamber."

Looking back, Henry said, "Come on, she makes a great point."

The three slipped into the tunnel.

****

0215 Hours M.S.T., 28 Dec 1991
Piskaryovskoye Memorial Cemetery
Saint Petersburg, Russia

Elizbieta said, "Just one more push should do it."

Henry and Vlad both got down in a crouched position, backs against the stone wall before them and pushed with their legs. The flashlight flickered. Elizbieta slapped the side of it. It came back to life. The two men groaned as the wall seemed to move a tiny bit.

Elizbieta said, "Stop, stop. I forgot something."

Henry stood up straight. "This needs to be interesting. This wall ain't moving."

Referring to the American, she said, "I am not sure you will appreciate it. We are in the tomb of Mikhail Mikhailovich Zoshchenko, the writer."

Vlad laughed, "You mean the dissident."

"Some say," said Elizbieta. "I think he was very funny."

Vlad said, "He's been dead 30 years. What relevance has it to this moment?"

Elizbieta smiled in the darkness. The two men could not have seen it, but they heard it in her voice. She said, "I have just made a proper Soviet joke to honor him."

The men groaned.

"You see, a Soviet must try everything the hard way and work day and night to toil in the service of the workers."

Interrupting her, Henry asked, "So what's the joke?"

She took two steps to the left and began feeling around on the wall of the tomb. "The joke is," she said, pressing on one of the tiles. There was a click, and the tile popped out a centimeter. She turned it to the right until the top right corner of the tile was pointing down. After a pause, she turned it back the other way in a complete circle twice. She giggled.

Henry growled, "What is funny?"

Elizbieta said, "This was another soviet joke. I turn the clock forward and then back twice."

Vlad laughed.

"The joke is a soviet would work twice as hard as needed, but there was an easier way to do the work." She pressed the tile in again and it locked back in place. A click sounded. Henry frowned and rolled his eyes. This time when he pushed on the door of the tomb, it slid open easily.

Henry said, "Remind me not to attend a Soviet Comedy act."

Vlad said something in Russian. Elizbieta laughed and smiled.

Henry asked, "What? Oh, never mind. Let's just go." He took the light from Elizbieta and turned it off. It was a full moon, and the snow on the ground was a foot deep. Henry lay on the ground and waited a moment for his eyes to adjust. He looked to the right and the left. Then he held his breath, listening. Behind him, in the tomb, he heard Vlad whisper and Elizbieta giggle softly. He waved for silence.

Elizbieta lay down next to him. She said, "There is an abandoned farm nearly 60 kilometers outside the city. It belongs to my family. I still visit there occasionally. It has been kept up, and there are supplies. We can go there."

Henry said, "It's exactly what we need right now, to lay low for a while."

Elizbieta interrupted him. "You are already on the ground. How low do you wish to lay?"

Henry groaned. Behind him, he heard Vlad give a soft chortle. Henry cleared his throat. "Vlad and I accomplished our mission, but we aren't safe. I expect a little vacation is just what the doctor ordered. How do we get to this farm?"

She said, "Follow me. I know where there are horses."

She rose, trekking through the snow. The Piskaryovskoye Memorial Cemetery is roughly two and a third kilometers across. It holds many memorials of state heroes and soldiers, as well as the occasional satirist who was executed for the crime of speaking the truth about the state. In the Northwest corner of the cemetery, there are stables, which house twelve specially bred Clydesdales. The horses, which are kept to pull the carriage holding the caskets of the most important state heroes, are considered an invaluable asset of the state.

The three fugitives approached the stables. Henry waived the two behind him, but Elizbieta strode around him proceeding directly to the caretaker's dacha. She motioned for the men to follow her. Hesitantly, they did. When she arrived at the stable, she walked over to the caretaker's apartment door and knocked.

Henry's eyes bulged. Urgently, he motioned to her to hide. Under his breath he said, "What are you doing? I thought we were going to steal horses."

She looked back at him and smiled. "Who said anything about stealing? These horses are the property of the Russian people." She motioned, once again, to the men to come join her.

Vlad stood up straight and walked over to Elizbieta.

Henry hesitated. He shook his head, exhaling hard. Finally, he stood up and walked over to where Elizbieta stood. In a whispered tone, he said, "We need to be careful."

Then, Henry heard a voice he did not recognize say in heavily accented English, "Who is we?" A tiny man appeared in the doorway, shotgun in hand. The man, who was perhaps four feet six inches, stood in the doorway of the caretaker's apartment.

Elizbieta said, "Uncle!" The two hugged. After releasing him, she stood straight, as if she was a pupil in grammar school. "Uncle, *We* is the title of the classic novel of Yevgeny Zamyatin. A story of today set in the twenty-first century."

Then, the man said, "And how did you come to read it?"

"You shared a copy with me, when I was only eight years old. Even then, I saw the truth."

"And what is the truth?"

"If We leaves me alone, they can do what they wish."

The man laughed and hugged her again. "My sweet girl. You are grown so tall."

****

Chapter 2

0415 Hours M.S.T., 28 Dec 1991
Sidreriya Pub
Saint Petersburg, Russia

"Your name is Irina? Perhaps, this is good. My name is Alexi. I like the name Irina. Irina Yahantov, this is a simple process. You tell me what happened, and you go to sleep. I create a mountain of paperwork, and I will go to sleep. This sounds very good, yes?"

Irina nodded her head. Her eyes closed and then opened slowly. "I am very tired. Can I rest? I have answered these questions four times with four different men. Please."

Alexi said, "This pleading does not become you. I cannot put such a silly story in paperwork. The men at the station will mock me. A man cannot have this, you understand. So, you and I, let us make some changes."

Irina said, "I can only say what happened."

"Irina, you understand what will be said if two security personnel, such as these men here, were cut down so expertly by a chernomazyy? They would look like fools. In turn, I would look like a fool." Alexi rose from the table. "I am too old for this. At twenty-eight, my father was already a Captain in the Red Army. I should be further. Listen, let me make some breakfast. Perhaps with food, you will feel better, and we can tell the correct story."

Irina looked at him desperately. "There is not enough for all these men."

"I understand. They will go, when it is there time, and each will procure their own breakfast. For you and I, we will eat now." Alexi stoked the fire in the wood stove. "Where is your food?" he asked.

Irina rose from the table and walked over to the icebox. She withdrew five eggs and a lump of lard. Pulling a cast iron skillet from a cabinet, she placed the lard into it and set it on the oven to heat. She pulled her apron off a hook in the corner of the room and tied it around her. "If you would be a proper man, please? Wait at the table, and I will serve you."

Alexi reached past her and pulled down the second apron which belonged to Elizbieta and tied the strings behind him. "Who says I am a proper man?" He bumped his hips into her, moving her out of the way. The lard sizzled in the pan. He began one by one, cracking the eggs. He set the shells onto the counter.

She eyed him up and down, and in spite of herself, laughed. She said, "Razve ty ne ocharovatel'nyy, kto tebya etomu nauchil; *aren't you charming; who taught you this?*"

"Mamoolechka; *my dear mother.* With my father in the glorious Red Army, her three sons were all taught to fend for themselves. She used to say, Muzhchina dolzhen byt' samodostatochnym, inache on umret; *A man must be self-sufficient or he will die.*"

"Such a maternal thing to say. She must have loved you."

"You don't understand; my father died in Afghanistan of food poisoning. My mother blamed the Red Army's cooks."

"I am sorry."

"Many people died there, gloriously, for the Soviet Union. Some of their children learned to cook."

Irina laughed and raised her glass. "Salyut Krasnoy Armii; *a salute to the Red Army.*" She took a drink of the cider.

Alexi searched for a glass but found none.

Irina brushed past him, close enough to feel the warmth of his body. She opened a cabinet door. "Do you mind?" she asked. The glasses on the second shelf were beyond her reach. The taller of the two sisters, Elizbieta, had placed them there to insure she would always be tending bar instead of cooking or waiting tables.

Alexi moved to help her, deliberately making as much body contact as he could. He stretched out and removed a glass. The heavy glass was etched with the crest of the Romanov family. Alexi turned it in his hand, eyeing the etching.

Irina drew in a sharp breath. "It is my sister," she said. "She is consumed with Russian history."

Alexi said, "Sometimes, I wonder what has become of the children of Czars?"

Irina looked at him carefully.

Alexi nodded, in the way that a person does, when they are trying to communicate they are giving something careful consideration. He handed the glass to her, their fingers brushing with the exchange.

Alexi smiled and laughed. "You know this new Yeltsin. He proclaims a return to the imperial Russia. Only now, the people will vote for their Czars." Alexi laughed aloud. He turned the eggs, removed them from the pan and placed them onto two stoneware plates. "Can you imagine, voting for a tyrant? Have you heard of this man, Boris Yeltsin?"

Irina said, "I knew a Boris once, but I was very young. He was obsessed with the story of Peter and the Wolf. He could recite the entire poem by heart."

"This is true?" Alexi pitched it as a question, but the undertone of unasked questions was present in his eyes.

Looking directly into his eyes, Irina said, "I don't care for poetry."

"And we arrive at the truth of the matter," said Alexi. "Boris was not the man for you."

"This is definitely true." Irina straightened her apron, arranging it so a glimpse of her bosom was noticeable.

Alexi took the plates to the table where the two had previously been setting. The tattered rug under it slightly off center to the table's placement.

Irina brought two drinks from the bar which she had spiced with a pinch of cinnamon, impossible to get in 1991 Soviet Russia, and a dash of Schnapps. She placed the glass in front of Alexi, sitting down next to him. "So, tell me, how will you catch these men?"

In between mouthfuls of eggs and cider, Alexi said, "A magician never reveals his secrets."

Irina replied, "And a maiden keeps hers just as close."

Alexi looked down, noticing for the first time the woman's breasts. They were proud and firm. "It is an interesting question you ask. You have witnessed this violence, so perhaps you deserve to know more. These are no ordinary criminals." His head swiveled left and right, as if to discern who was listening. He nodded when he noticed that all but one policeman had left the building. The bodies had already been efficiently removed. The only evidence of the early morning violence were the dark stains on the hardwood floors where the blood had pooled under the men. Alexi put his hand on Irina's. Then he stood.

He addressed the lone remaining police officer, "Junior Sergeant Maxim, I have no plans to arrest this lady. She knows little. Please return to the station and begin to compile the paperwork until your shift is ended. I will be verifying the contents at the beginning of this evening's shift. Go now."

The policemen shrugged and left the building. Alexi walked over to the window and took the sign which read Closed and hung it in the window.

Then he resumed his seat at the table. He slumped in his chair a bit and sighed. "Kuda delas' eta strana? Otkrytost', podchineniye zapadnym tsennostyam. Teper' my umrem ot korruptsii. My tak dolgo borolis'. Rabochiye budut pravit', kak oni skazali nam, i my osushchestvim slavnuyu kommunisticheskuyu revolyutsiyu. Vot my, my s vami, sidim v dvukh futakh ot togo mesta, gde agent Soyedinennykh Shtatov Ameriki ubil sotrudnikov KGB. *Where has this country gone? Openness, surrender to western values? We have fought so hard, for so long. Now, we will die of corruption. The workers would rule they told us, and we would bring about the glorious communist revolution. Here we are, you and I, sitting two feet away from the place where an Agent of the United States of America has killed members of the KGB.*" He looked her hard in the eyes. "Eti lyudi, etot chernyy chelovek i russkiy, rabotaya vmeste, ukrali vsyakuyu nadezhdu partii, na budushcheye Rossii. *These men… this black man and a Russian working together have stolen any hope for the party, for Russia's future. Who would think such a day would come where a Russian would betray their own mother?*"

Irina shifted uneasily in her seat. The intensity of his gaze was unnerving. In the pit of her stomach, she felt uneasy. His eyes were a milky blue, like the waters of the winter palace. *I could get lost in those eyes*, she thought, but did not say.

Then, he put his hand on hers and rose to his feet, pulling her with him. Alexi embraced her, burying the woman in his arms, his warmth, his protection. He said, "Whatever comes, comes, but I will be here defending your beauty, Irina. I have seen too many days of violence, but to see you, this violence which has brought us together. This is all that matters. We are together."

Irina was stunned. A tear slid down her face. She said, "To be desired so…"

His hands reached down to cup her face. She looked up at him with pleading eyes. The two kissed. As he drew back, she moaned a single word, "Yes."

ARZONO Publishing Presents The 2021 Annual

POETRY

Keeja Fisher

Keeja Fisher is a writer of fantasy and supernatural literary fiction. She specializes in using the abnormal to bring relatable issues to life and creating characters capable of finding unique ways to solve them. She is very enthusiastic about fantasy fiction and enjoys creating magic as she brings her stories to life.

Keeja works in multiple media forms, including short stories, novels, and poetry. She focuses primarily on books and flash fiction pieces and saves poetry for her downtime. Her current projects include the novel *A Promise of Magic: A Raven Kyndred Novel* and the flash fiction anthology *For the Eyes of Innocents See Nothing to Fear.*

Keeja was born in Jamaica and emigrated to the United States at the age of 13. After high school, she enlisted in the United States Navy and traveled the world as an enlisted sailor before an honorable discharge in 2016. Since then, Keeja has received a Bachelor's degree in English from Arizona State University and a Master of Fine Arts degree in Creative Writing from Full Sail University.

Keeja lives in Montana with her two children and their dog Apollo where she encourages them to read and find the magic in words.

Pretty for A Colored Girl

"You're pretty for a colored girl."
Yes, that's what he said to me.
It could have almost been a compliment.
"You're pretty for a colored girl," He said.
"Not like them other ones, no. They're too ugly."
His words should not have meant anything
Right? I mean, times are different now
Aren't they? But as I looked at him
I saw his age; I saw his skin complexion.
I tried not to judge because the cover
It does not tell the whole story hidden within
And yet, I could not help myself
And I fell into the trap he laid for me.

"You're pretty for a colored girl."
The words banged around my head
Like a congo drum, like bullets from a gun.
As I looked at him, his smile reminiscent
As he looked at me in awe,
As if because of my skin color
I should have been insufficient
As if because of my skin color
My eyes should have been lackluster
As if because of my skin color
My smile should have been crooked
As if because of my skin color
My beauty came as a surprise

"You're pretty for a colored girl."
His words took my breath away.
Not because I was rendered speechless
From his eloquent compliment,
No, my rage had consumed my words
And hijacked my thoughts
Because he looked at me and determined
That my beauty was limited to my melanin.
Like he had snuck up on a unicorn
And he was in awe of it. My blood pulsed
like a river through my veins; his words,
A cacophonous ring in my ears,
Reverberated through my consciousness.

"You're pretty for a colored girl."
I smiled at him that day.
Though my blood boiled, and heart raced,
I smiled. I smiled because any other response
Would have left the shadow of every stereotype
A lingering stigma over my reputation.
Though his words stung like venom,
I smiled because I was more than his perception
Of whom I was or who I should have been.
I smiled because if I cried,
I would knock an old man from his chair,
Because age did not concede to ignorance
I smiled because his words did not define me

I am not pretty despite my blackness
"I am pretty because I am a colored girl."

The River

Time, like water, had eroded the rough edges of my anger.
Yet, the lines of my imperfections remained visible
as I cracked under pressure to contain it all.
I had sold myself into a lie, gave my heart away to love,
and walked away with regrets. A hard lesson
I should have learned never to repeat.
Love has a way of skewing things.
Twisting it and corrupting it until it is unrecognizable,
even to itself. It is a forever long journey
that never truly has a happy ending,
just happy moments that usually float away with time.
Love is not always light and hearts and laughter.
Love is also that indefatigable darkness
that cannot be tamed, that eats away at what could have been.
But I still fight for it, only in all the wrong places.
I forget about loving myself,
seeking only the love of others,
burying my heart and my dreams in the darkness.
I wander through my life, wishing for what was
and what could have been, never in the now.

So, I ran headfirst into love or the idea of it,
ready to be swept away.
It was when I began to drown that I realized
it is not what I wanted. My dreams were floating away,
and I was sinking. Burdened by the responsibilities
and dragged down by the chains I had linked to myself.
I had a plan not so long ago. One that required sacrifices,
but it was my dream. To use words to paint pictures,
like the strokes of Picasso's brush. To wield my pen
like a magician's wand and tales filled with wonder
I remembered it there in the depths as I sunk.
I could see it at my fingertips as if it were mine to hold
if I would just reach for it. It was a life raft
sent to save me from myself.
It was not too late; I had time.
Time to let go of the burdens I carried.
Time to cut the chains that held me tethered
to a life I wanted to rebuke. I was not down so deep
that I could not see the sky.

David M. Harris

Until 2003, David M. Harris had never lived more than fifty miles from New York City. Since then, he has moved to Tennessee, acquired a daughter and a classic MG, and gotten serious about poetry.

His work has appeared in *Pirene's Fountain* (and in *First Water*, the Best of Pirene's Fountain anthology), *Gargoyle, The Labletter, The Pedestal*, and other places. His first collection of poetry, *The Review Mirror*, was published by Unsolicited Press in 2013.

The Murderer's Hat

Look at the old pictures of city crowds,
men and women all in hats, from festive
decorated toques to summer boaters,
children and workingmen in soft cloth
caps, Never a baseball cap. Of course,
gentlemen took off their hats to greet a woman
or go indoors. When Tom Polhaus
wears his hat into Sam Spade's apartment,
we know trouble is coming with him.
Homburgs, fedoras, bowlers, porkpies, hats
told us about the men beneath them.
A man in a New York office with a ten-gallon
was Maverick; he followed the rules
when it suited him. Dangerous but
charming. Or just a weird non-conformist,
posing as Maverick. Then came Kennedy, hatless
at his chilly inauguration, a different manliness,
and car headrests pushed the felt brims down
our backs, until only guys with old pickups
could drive while wearing a Stetson. It was ball
caps, or keeping your hat on the seat while you drove.
Hipsters wear porkpies, but they don't drive.
And ball caps took over for function and style,
in the car or the office. Pledges of allegiance
to school or team or supplier of whatever is
needful. Borrowed identities. Some wear them
backwards, like catchers, but the bill is useful
facing forward.

Bill asked us, from the jail,
that his stuff, everything in the apartment, be made
useful, not just Dumpstered. He was never going
to see any of it again, never leaving prison,
but didn't want his life with Sandra thrown away
as he had thrown her life away. And we, somehow,
were in charge of cleaning up. I took a 5-wood,
Judy took some books, and we filled the car
with goods and possessions that could
find new lives. One last sweep through

the kitchen. I found the hats. The Indians cap
had to have been Sandra's; she was from
Cleveland. The stack of White Sox caps
had to be Bill's. I've changed planes in Chicago,
but that's all. Comiskey is alien territory
to this Yankees fan. I've seen my New York teams
at home, and the Red Sox, the Orioles,
got caps for the home teams.
Add all those schools where I studied
or taught. Why not add to the collection one
green cap with a white logo?

The Too-Examined Life

Gnothi sauton was the high school motto.
"Know thyself." No unexamined lives
allowed. What did she mean by that? Am I
understanding correctly? At all?
What did I mean by that? We picked up
the habit. Do I want the burger
or the grilled cheese? Why? What are
the ethical implications of
the cheeseburger? Fried onions?
We evolve, if we are unlucky
in our introspection, from Socrates' questions
to Descartes' universal doubts. Everything gets tested
and explored, explicated. Too many
questions, too many answers. Every answer
is another question, a bright four-year-old
with a shaky grasp of Freud, forgetting
Occam, forgetting that those fried onions are sometimes
just fried onions. But when? Another question.
Take a breath. Take several more deep ones.
Say "Om." Say it again. Shanti. Learn not to ask.

Anissa Sboui Ben Mohamed

A University teacher, poet, and Ph.D. research scholar, Anissa lives in Sahloul Sousse, Tunisia. She has two cute daughters, Nada and Sara Ben Mohamed.

The author of five volumes *Rebirth* (2018), *Transcend* (2019), *Number One* (2020), *The Co-Avid Breath* (2021), and another collection of poems in Arabic, entitled *Sunrise and Sunset* (2021).

Follow her on her Facebook @ https://www.facebook.com/Anissa-Sboui-Poet-238301153420495

Bill is Ill

Bill is ill
Fuses heat to chill
Mixes sweet with sour
Still

Bill is chronically ill
Peels dates,
Garnishes the grill
With pinches of a high shrill,
Kneads the argil
Waters the clay pot
With buckets
From the Nile,
Rears beavers
On a bookcase
As wooden as China steel

Bill is terribly ill,
Hunts oyster
On that hill
Cleans the laundry
Using home-made Prill

Bill is shamefully ill,
Surfs the latrine
E-mails his successor
On the bog roll
Refuses to surpass
The Gates to massive quill
The micro encroaches
The soft touch of the numeric character
Of the sleeping pill

Arab Lives Matter

What puzzles me today
At the age of the pandemic
Is the spread of dangerous minds
And contagious policies
Infected
Defected
Not well perfected,
Step back the West's frame
To mourn the Arab lands
To champion the *kibbutzim*
Behind the crooked scene,
Confirmed cases, subjected to
Celebrate ready meals,
Impulsive plans of crazy clans
With tons of champagne cups
Sweeping across the deal craft
Arabs have crossed the globe,

But,
Like a dear vulnerable deer,
Surrounded by famished
Destitute,
Cruel,
Wild Wolves,
Can't wage
War on
Acres of
Areas …
The tale is told
The secret is unfold
Of bronze, not gold
Forever within the Normalization Deal mold
Disqualified Libyanon, Palesyem[1]
An amalgamated bouquet of treason
Has announced how our territories
Are being cheaply sold.

[1] I joined the names of five politically unstable Arab countries: Libya, Lebanon, Palestine, Syria and Yemen.

A Letter to Covid-19 Pandemic

Dear Covid-19,
Where have you been?
We've not heard of you
Since the 1918 flu
We awaited you
While you were hidden somewhere
Where exactly where?
Cos before you bubbled up
The health crisis,
The detained symptoms,
The cramped cities,
The small gatherings,
The suffocating masks,
The growing death toll
Have been missed
From winter to fall

Bad Boy

The thought never crossed her mind
At nightfall Susan heard the owl, howling
She stopped crying in shower cell
Left the cellular in the oven
Cold-blooded she was now
To safeguard her dignity,
She knew well the key to serenity
This happened when his bubbles
No longer mattered to her
His calls, she didn't scroll down when asleep,
Cheating on her was a lovely game,
He played so many times
Covering his mean character
And her patient style of life.
Peppering, salting or sugaring her
Wouldn't block Susan from growing up alone
As a strong beloved
If this is costly
Goodbye bad boy!
Bye bad boy!

She was done
Being your property,

She was done
Being the bathmat you stepped on
She was done
Being the painting
You clang against the smashed mirror
She was done
Being your far-fetched virus vaccine

She was done
Being your sleeping pill
She was done
Being your lunch box
She was done
Being the guest room
She was done
Being the mushroom
She was done
Being your tamed fox
She was done
Being your domesticated Chinese box
She was done

Being entombed in a silly cave
She was done
Being your sex slave

She was done
Being your sentimental storyteller
She was done
Being the bullied belly dancer
She was done
Being the croaking voice
And the defunct instrument.

At daybreak she heard the first birdsong
And said:
"Carry your dirty surgical mask,
Your sanitizer gel,
Your rotten morals and flee, bad boy"

The Curfew

The curfew in 2020
The world's sun rises from the far East,
Filling in the earth with the contagious beast,
Its first beams itch the backs of the entity.

The curfew in 2020,
We have loved ones,
Infected by the deadly pandemic
Like a death-winged spear,
It darts the frightened hearts,
The trembling lungs,
The suspended veins,
The coffins' breath ceases, too
Setting back the moment of woe,
As the curfew will be swinging to and fro

Until 2022

Subhrasankar Das

Subhrasankar Das, born on 1st May 1986, hails from Tripura, India. He is an award-winning poet, a translator of distinct repute, and a passionate composer. He is a Teacher by profession.

Das authored three books of Bengali poems ('Tontukit', 'Baul Molecules', and 'Sfotikchapa Phosphorus'), and an e-book of English poems ('Zebracrossing').

His poems, short stories, and reviews have appeared in numerous periodicals, editions, anthologies, and webzines nationally and internationally. CDs of his recorded poems have been published by Eastern School of Publication and Souharda Kolkata.

He is the recipient of the ' Binay Padak', ' Banani Shahitto Somman', and 'Tobu Ovimaan Sommanona'. Das has been interviewed by All India Radio and popular TV channel Akash Tripura. He edits Shadowkraft (the 1st international and multilingual literary webzine from Northeast India) and Water (the 1st international and multilingual video-magazine from Northeast India).

He has translated some of the significant literary pieces of Shyamal Bhattacharya, Larissa Shmailao, Mario Santagostin, Linda Pastan, Trishna Basak, and others.

https://linktr.ee/SubhrasankarDas

THE CAP OF A MISSING PEN

An embrace can either love or kill you..
Still I believe the picture of darkness is more
graceful, pure and mysterious than any other picture of the world.
In the dark,
one can easily act on his infatuation with his darling sleep.
Is it true that optimistic people are more prone
to insomnia than others?
Adorned with the garlands of their prosthetic pain,
They rush towards the light like insects,
take off their husks like snakes..

They are not eager to know
whether the layer beneath the bright cover
is of a cloth or paper.
They fold the corner of the page,
underline themselves with a blunt pencil,
and wish to have an intercourse
with their favourite characters
in the gutters of the book.

The face is safe in the drawer.
The pen is missing.
The cap is somehow protruding from the pocket to cherish
the apparently beautiful world.

They are never disturbed by smell or nostalgia

POST OFFICE

1.

The curd-seller is dead.
The flower-girl has changed her profession.
The boy who used to wait for the curd-seller
peeps inside her window, tries to identify
kings, crowns and peons till she scolds him
...What the **** are you doing here?!
He runs in haste,
breaks the letter-box and
smiles at the dogs running towards the parliament

2.

The 1st floor is full of artifices

The ground floor has a divine garland and a pair of trembling hands

The doorway has a family of lizards locked inside the letter-box

STAIRCASE

The way U halt at the staircase,
cover your face being teased by a butterfly,
the way U flap your eyelids
being bathed by an anachronous shower
and sit at the table like a frozen storm
and a silly splash of wind titillates the drowsy curtain
spreading your fragrance around the room
when the filtered sunlight is busy in
fondling with your eyebrows...
I feel this frame holds the color of my existence.

Years ago my feet were stained with henna yet to be dried

Since then, I hate rains like a cat
Since then, like a gruesome seaweed,
the shadow of your impeccable body has been growing on my skin.

Stella Samuel

Stella Samuel is a women's fiction author whose credits include her novel *34 Seconds*, a short story compilation, *Stories South of The Sun*, as well as several short fiction pieces published in various literary magazines. Stella has been an Alliance of Independent Authors Author member since 2016 and earned her BFA in Creative Writing for Entertainment from Full Sail University, graduating valedictorian. As sole owner of ARZONO Publishing, Stella strives to uplift new writers and help authors create and build their portfolios. With the release of *The 2020 Annual,* she embarked on an annual adventure bringing authors and poets together. When she is not busy publishing and writing fiction or screenplays, Stella freelances for agencies and other authors, offering editing services and coaching. She's also created, developed, and taught a children's writing class for elementary and middle-grade children. Writing or not, Stella is often poolside with her chocolate lab and a notebook.

Gone

The pain comes in waves as life's breath attempts to heal.
Once there
Now gone.
Never a thought passed of content, only passion and promise.
~ Inhale.
Soak it all in, nurturing the soul and lighting the path to the future.
Exhale. ~
Every particle of sustenance takes pieces of soul away.
Move forward.
In the darkness of the halls filled with memories fighting gravity pulling
downward.
Memories.
None horrible. Only bliss. Constant challenge, but the good kind, like
hitting the pavement before a marathon never needing to be run.
Laughter.
Will it ever sound again?
Tears. Sobs. Disbelief.

Don't take love for granted. For it may not always live here.

She's gone.
This heart won't heal.
Breathing hurts.
Not breathing burns.
Forcing decisions of independence brings strength.
Unwanted foundations of life's blood and fire rips through the soul
again...
Sending signals of reminders to keep going.
Fiercely independent is sexy.
Relying on the drowning inferno, sucking souls, ripping mates apart at the
seams.
Kindness and calm are practiced routines.
Bring them back to the world before it ignites.
Come back to the souls meant to touch within the forces of reality—
forever.

Don't take love for granted. For it may never live here again.
That won't stop me from fighting...
Because her love was the most beautiful thing ever to cross this galaxy.

Molly Neely

Molly Neely is the author of the Paranormal novel, *The Sand Dweller* (Black Opal Books), a contributor to the *Fall into Fantasy Anthology*, 2017 & 2019 (Cloaked Press), a contributor to *The 2020 Annual* (Elizabeth River Press & ARZONO Publishing) and her short story, "An Heirloom Spirit," is in the collection, *CEA Greatest Anthology Written*, which is a contender for a Guinness Book of Worlds Records title.

Molly's poetry can be found in anthologies from Z Press, Literary Alchemy, and Animal Heart Press.

When she's not writing novels, Molly enjoys Pre-code films, preparing for the zombie apocalypse and eating pretty much anything with bacon in it. Molly lives in the San Joaquin Valley with her husband Lyle & their Whippet Devo.

~Insanity Remains Intact~

All my madness
Is self contained
Pandemonium
Roads to nowhere

A countryside
Dotted with
Landmarks of
Frailty
And jealousy
Bitterness
And doom

Bring on the
Dancing horses
The follies of devils
In brightly colored
Paper wings
Leaving pastel
Vapor trails
Behind bloodshot
Eyes

Dizzy and busy bees
Scramble already
Rambling brambles
Tightly woven

Consciousness
Into knotted
Stones

Light struggles through
Hacking away
At common sense
And decency
The machete of
The mind

Gremlins fall in
Like so many
Soldiers
They try to
Weave it back
Together
With threads
Made from doubt
And deceit
Wearing a smile

Insanity remains intact
So please don't
Walk on the
Grass

~*Long Gone Girl*~

The purity she would once exude
Still peeks out from behind her lids
With salted, swollen eyes
Who she was
And what she's become
Stand glaring at each other
From either side of the mirror

Innocence and naiveté
All lost to the winds of
Depravity and gluttony
Where she went
And why she left
Reach out across a concrete sea
An ocean of adult intention

The memory of her is torn
Brittle and faded by time
Who she was
And what she's become
Have merged with discarded gum
And the flyers of forgotten bands

Anonymous on the wall
Her time capsule left unsealed
Where her truth hides
Is why our faith dies
Abandoned to unfound rights
Absorbed into seedy nights

All that remains is glue
Crusted, tacky and weak
Where her soul clings
While her heart beats hollow
Echoes of life unfulfilled
Drowning in the moans of the street

~The Sun Compels Him (Van Gogh, Haystacks)~

Your muse gets no rest
you hear the voices
from lips only you can see

your craft is wholly unique
you capture the images
no one else bothers to chase

your passion is never starved
you eat from the vine
too high for others to reach

your demons forever peddling
you pay for deranged advice
no one else can afford to buy

your genius is hard to deny
you suffer for your skill
for the sun compels you

~*Solemn and Black*~

We follow a path against the grain
A speechless trail we carve amongst
The shapes in the clouds
Homeless winds pass on our left
Unlawful and
unwilling to be led
Just like us

I can't remember a time
When we weren't hated for our voice
Or questioned for our choice
Feared for our color
Solemn and black

We fill in spaces between the light

Escape is what we do
To flee the misunderstanding
and pray for the misfire
We take our pay in bottle caps
While hiding our hoards deep

Wolves of the witches sky

As you see
My murder and me run free
We glean the farmer's field
And preen our havoc without yield
With so much dust left behind

A scourge we plant in your mind

All outcasts are them and I
An ominous omen in the sky
Plagues me and my kind
We rise above it all
Literal, because we can

For we've whipped up a tempest
In the soul of man
That's solemn and black

Stef Gibson

Stef Gibson is a young, queer, anarchist writer from Dublin. Born to a British family, he has spent his whole life in Ireland. Stef writes primarily about his struggles with mental illness, love, loss, and universal human experiences. He began writing poetry in 2019 on his blog, EcklebergPoetry and quickly found poetry to be an outlet for pain.

Despite loss and trauma, Stef continues to write about his life experiences in a way others can relate to. In 2020, he took a break from writing but was thrown back into it again with the end of an important relationship. Stef is not only passionate about writing but also politics. He believes there is a better world out there and often takes part in activism to try and move towards this goal. Although Stef mainly writes poetry in English, he has also written a few pieces in German in the hopes of improving language skills over time. Stef mainly uses his blog to share poetry but also posts his writing on twitter @EcklebergPoetry

Confessionary Writings from a Loveless Poet

Sometimes confrontation is easier.
To be met with direct speech
of guilt or honesty,
preventing your pondering over
truthful confessions and risky decisions.
To hear shouts of his knowledge
versus anxiety riddled murmurs,
that disturb your sleep and feed your
insomniac infatuation.
Persisting still that I did not know in time.

November was the month where cupids
swarmed on me like flies to sweet
strawberry jam,
Propelling me towards a conclusion
of falling over the familiarity and kindness
you showed me.
The gentle smiles and dreams you held,
dreams that you offered to me
without hesitation.
Falling in love with what you said
we could do.

I watched you wish future plans
into existence upon shooting stars whom
you knew each by name.
I made one wish in exchange,
purely to become a plan of yours,
travelling on starlight towards better days.

You must believe I did not see myself fallen
til I reached the base of your rabbit's hole.
Feeling tiny and giant all the the same.
So when I said "The Other" was my first,
I am sorry to have lied.
Take it only as fear that you would know

how deeply I had tumbled for you,
because truly it was you all along.

I had prepared to tell you
under the eyes of fairy lights and stars.
Palms full of empty surprises that now
sleep on your bed,
in a space I could have held.
On academic grounds I held my tongue
tightly between bared teeth,
Weeping with the pain of tightening clamps on tender skin,
I made my way home.

I watched you drift away with
Miss Summer Smiles and Gentle Eyes,
Holding joy for you both but
pain in my heart alongside this burning sun.
I was forced to realise you had held me
like the rest,
and the spark was simply my own.

I still miss those days of texts that
you give now to someone else.
If I had not taken for granted pillow kisses
and tight squeezes,
perhaps I would be more at peace
with my own timing.

I had not known till moments passed
but I understand the answer as no.
Still,
I long for the relief of that answer
all the same.

Thomas M. McDade

Thomas M. McDade is a 75-year-old, retired resident of Fredericksburg, VA, previously Connecticut and Rhode Island.

He was a programmer / analyst for the last twenty-three years of his working life. He also labored at a good many blue-collar jobs that have that have found their way into poems and short stories.

He is a 1973 graduate of Fairfield University, Fairfield, CT. He holds a Library Technical Assistant Certificate from Capitol Community College but has never worked in that field outside of a semester internship.

McDade is twice a U.S. Navy Veteran serving ashore at the Fleet Anti-Air Warfare Training Center, Virginia Beach, VA and at sea aboard the USS Mullinnix (DD-944) and USS Miller (DE / FF-1091).

His poetry has most recently appeared in Dress *Blues*, *Beliveau Review*, *The Last Call*, *Chinaski Anthology*, *As Loud as it's Kept Review Magazine*, and *Spitball.* A number of short stories were published in 2020, among the presses involved: *Writer's Egg*, *The Rail*, *Flashes of Brilliance*, *Oddville Press*, and *Blue Nib*.

McDade has been published in all fifty states and DC and abroad in England, Ireland, Portugal, New Zealand, Australia, Mexico, Canada, Africa, India, and Philippines.

Eagles and Birches

A birdwatcher strolls
Into the Pegasus Gallery
(This is not a joke)
He claims to know the artist
Whose work is on display
Where are her eagle canvases
Why just common birches
He lodges his complaint
In the guest book pausing
Many times two fingers on forehead
I suppose seeking bon mots
He walks to the door twice
But returns perhaps
To dot an I or cross a T
After he has flown
I check each dappled tree
Trying to locate a hint
Of his majestic birds
Maybe camouflaged
But the lost limb scars
Are cruel mouths calling
Me a silly horse's ass
And why not
This is the bailiwick
Of the white
Winged mount and
I imagine Bob Frost's boy
Launching off one
Of these swaying trees
As the A/C kicks in
With a whoosh fit
To mimic the flight
Of equine, raptor or
Birdwatchers'
Collective gasps

Philosophy 101

A bearded guy who lasted
longer at RI Jr College
than I managed to do
sits across from me
at the horseshoe counter
in Joyce's restaurant.
Both hands embrace a mug
of freshly brewed coffee as if
the heater's not on full blast.
"Do You Know The Way
To San Jose" is barely audible
on the radio and as he sniffs
his A.M. boost an old TV show
comes to mind, a detective
questioning a senior citizen
living in an apartment
shabby and small.
Trying to be hospitable
the fellow says sometimes
the tap water gets hot enough
to make a cup of instant.
Joe lawman declines.
I put the tenement dweller
in that java sniffer's place
and sense his delight
sipping or inhaling
that round of Joyce's
high octane.
That's as deep as
I go on the matter
since Philosophy 101
is one of the courses
I left in the dust.
My former classmate
surprises me by weakly waving.
I imagine being bid adieu.
Splitting for California.

Thomas M. McDade

Doubloons

A goldfish pond near
a slated path surrounded
by a low picket fence
and lush grass in front of
a fancy house is a place
for a kid like me to stop
to wish that (no way tossing
a penny) the darting
carp that pass for
doubloons with my eyes
in a skilled squint are
small enough to fit in
a net just shoplifted
at Woolworth's but what then?
stick the prize in my pocket
down my pants
beat death to the swamp
full of trash, damned, even
a Cadillac grille and fender
a stove and washing
machine but still
full of life home to
snapping turtles
catfish, huge frogs
yeah bye-bye
easy life
you're like me now
living on the edge
but better off
than I am because
at least you're not
a fish out of water
like bullied me
in Federal Housing
in a heap of trouble
because I outran
a floor walker who saw
me as clear as your
old pool water
lift a cheap assed
aquarium net.

Weight

I use a needle
To nudge stitches
From the bottom
Of drapes to swipe
The anchors
That look like
Toolbox washers
Except they are
Made of lead but
There is a small
Bar across the hole
As if to warn
No screws allowed
But oh so perfect
So grey and severe
To serve as buttons
On mortician wear
Hinting their weights
And measures trade
Also helpful keeping
Expired eyelids shut
Now the kind

Keeping movie
Curtains in place
Must be substantial
No way to steal them
But how about breaking
Into ritzy homes
What would those
Fancy hems hold?
Ah, scrape and scrape
What's in hand
On sidewalk cement
Over and over
Into the size
Of a two-bit slug to vainly try
To trick a vending machine
In the end discs work well
As sinkers while fishing
For bottom feeders
Then the drape cleaning
The crime uncovered
Sewing those suckers
Back in just like a girl

Off to the Races

Benches, synthetic not wood sport
Plaques, some brass, some not
"She came here in '44 and raised 7 kids"
"A woman of remarkable courage"
"Adventurous spirit, generosity
And love of the sea"
One just a name and under
It "REMEMBER ME!"
A couple of surfers out
Waves barely strong enough
Magnificent shoreline homes
This stretch once called
"The Irish Riviera" after
Wealthy New York
Hibernians summering here
No doubt, they owned race
Horses and guaranteed
Enjoyed Monmouth Park
A shore tradition since 1870
The moneyed
And the memorialized
Slip my mind right quick
Etta's Current & Music
Consort in their place and
Both are scorched
in the ovals of my mind
Lengths ahead at finish lines
Safe from the salt and wind
Safe from the vandals
And the collectors armed
With sneaky screwdrivers
Until Current and the Music
Etta and the Consort mix
Ettamusicconsortcurrent
Memory limping, bucking
And finally fading
Like a rich or poor
Fair Dubliner's tan

Sabìnah Adewole

Sabìnah Adewole is a member of the Barking poetry group, the National Poetic library UK, a member of the Society of Authors UK, the Haiku Society of America and the Christian independent Publishing Agency - CIPA. Some of her poems appear in the Stripes magazine; she won the International Poetry contest. She also featured in the Havering Daily Mail and also in the Write on magazine.

About the Author:
She has been greatly inspired by the gift of poetry and writing. She was gifted the gift of poetry while sitting on a park bench in Gidea park in May 2018. She has continued to write daily and has created over 500 poems some Children Poetry books, A Childs Journey Through Poetry Volume 1 and 2: A Journey of a Childs Faith -Volume 1 - Faith book and Adults inspiration and Transformation poetry. She has also co-authored in four Anthologies and one Poetry Anthology -Poetica 2. She is grateful for those friendships and continues to work on building positive support networks. She has six published books, three best sellers and four she self-published.

Sitting on the Fence #353

As I walk past each time
It reminds me of Marbella
The fences in the Guadamila estate
I went in May last year
The image very vivid
The area is green and very affluent
Reminds me of Humpty Dumpty
Sitting on a wall
And the birds named Peter and Paul
Reminds me of me sitting on the fence sometimes
Can't make up my mind
Or at work sometimes can't make a decision
Of what to do and not what to do
Some units we have to make a leap of faith
What if you were on the fence and an animal was to attack
Would you carry on sitting or would you jump off the fence
That's what we have to do we cannot carry on sitting on the fence
As we have to move for things to move
Sitting on the fence

Composed in the bank in Stratford Inspired to write about the fence on 22/06/2020
Copyright reserved by Sabìnah Adewole

King Solomon asks for Wisdom #23

Why did Solomon ask God for wisdom?
Do you remember a time you prayed to God
A time you asked God for something specific
Specific as a time as the Coronavirus
Coronavirus did not affect children initially
But suddenly when the Pandemic hit Britain
It affected Children in different ways
Children as young as babies contracted the virus
From their mothers' womb
I have asked God for direction
Once God gave me an insight to write a faith book for Children
This happened in church and
I received confirmation at the same time
Solomon asked God for wisdom in-order to rule the people
"as who is able to govern this great people of yours"
The fear of the Lord is the beginning of wisdom
If we possess the wisdom from God in our hearts and believe it will never perish
Moral Message King Solomon asked for wisdom so he can make good decisions for his people.
That is very reassuring in the Pandemic season

Composed at home on 29/04/2020 Inspired to write about Wisdom
Copyright reserved by Sabìnah Adewole

Joe Sonnenblick

Joe Sonnenblick is a Native New Yorker who was a regular contributor to the now defunct *Citizen Brooklyn* magazine. Joe has been featured in publications such as *In Parentheses* for their 6th volume of poetry and *The Academy Of The Heart And Mind* and *Impspire Literary Review*, *The Bond Street Review*. Upcoming publications include: *Aji* for the Spring 2021 issue and *Ethel* for the June/July 2021 issue.

The Lost Generation

Raised up on cigar smoke in geometrically defunct rooms
How can four guys in a pool hall feel like a packed Madison Square
Garden?
Danny Rocco, making collections
Eddie Stix, running numbers…
Feels like I imagined it,
As my grandpa Dan was being lowered into the ground
As they handed my mother his American flag from the war
I remembered the abuse she and my grandmother took
From a beer swilling, gallivanting, hero of the German theater,
I'd spit on his grave now
It's too far though, Calvary cemetery is a two-hour drive
That's how I'll remember the man,
Not even worth a drive.

Every Man

A snuff film is always just an awkward stay away,
I misunderstand nothing
Shamed in public,
A lack of interest in humanity... Your humanity,
Sobriety, volunteering, community harmonium
I don't give out merit badges
Picking the leather coat out of my childhood home's closet with the dried
blood caked on,
I turned around on a windy Long Island City evening
Lit a bogey and my compassion went up in flame
Seeing a buddy on the concrete, just a puddle…
I'll cry on the coldest days,
It has nothing to do with the squall.
Be patient
Be patient,
Be ready.

A Visitor

Peering eyes through white hexagonal fence slats,
"What are you writing?"
"Poetry. Who are you?"
"I'm you."
I tip my hat,
Going back to scribbling about women, horses, loss, and misgivings.
Nothing to see here.

A Junky Ending

You are this façade facing the clouds,
Staring through a sea of grey topcoats with no features
Wanting a moment of silence, a cold one, a warm one, or no one...
You proceed to the agreed upon corner
Shaking hands with someone you don't know,
Retrieved is the baggy of indiscriminate relief
Like a pinball machine, you go off, lit up.
The one day you are too much
Taking one dose too many,
Frothing at the mouth
Doing the no doze Charlie on Delancey street
Gyrations to a sun god that has betrayed you so many times.
Fornicating with myself in the Port Authority restroom
That's how I wanted to be remembered,
Just how I lived.

Intolerance

On the mantle,
Dogs, parents, the past…
Ground into a fine powder
Plant a tree with it
Show it tours of your home
Let women who infiltrate the cavern know the history.
I could be anything
I chose this,
To make you aware that you aren't aware
Reconciliation is not an alternative
This is the sweetest fruit from the most thoughtless of trees
Ask your local produce person
"Where did you set such a ripe piece-"
With a hand to their heart they'll say the truism of all truisms
"He knows his harvest, he knows his crop, you are the idolator just eating
what he bore."
I didn't tell them to say it
Just one of those intellectual so and so's
Who got it right,
For once.

Fabrice Poussin

Fabrice Poussin teaches French and English at a small private Liberal Arts University. Author of novels and poetry, his writing has appeared in *Kestrel, Symposium, The Chimes,* and hundreds of others. His photography has been published in *The Front Porch Review, Foliate Oak Magazine, San Pedro River Magazine,* and hundreds more. Living in Northern Georgia, USA, he often travels to Europe. Always working on a project, he hopes his endeavors into another dimension of photography will be appreciated by the viewers (a mystery for now). When not photographing, he expresses himself in poetry.

Contact

It was ages ago when the masses began in motion
nebulae of colorful rainbows in the deep
a darkness thick as molten lava.

Strange lines traveled faster than origins
crossing realms of thinnest membranes
while a gentle symphony played on.

Minimalistic bodies swam through space
cold as if made of ice sharp as diamonds
infinitely small but all powerful.

Miraculous they were conscious of a goal
made of beginnings of so many lives
a multitude of dreams racing through time.

Today they stand atop a giant world
enlaced with every cell like a kiss
waiting for lighting so they may flee once more.

Dreaming in the Dark

Swimming in a dark ocean
remembering the silence
warm and snuggly
unaware of a boundary.

Feeding of life and growing
lonely for yet a little longer
little boy can't wait to chase
the ball he can almost kick.

Gentle Star

Galloping at the speed of a winged stallion
dressed in her somber coat
she brandished her scythe with a grin and a groan.

I imagined Goliath rushing to his puny foe
fate growing as a thick storm brewed
and the flesh was assailed by razor sharp hail.

Determined as she was in her grim intention
it was midday in the August sun
she could not shun the light of another day.

An icy breeze pierced the bones of the frail frame
uncertain of what may come next
yet I persisted brave in my weak defiance.

It is time she clamored through the thunder
I shrugged those shoulders laden with glee
for she may cut the thread of this brief moment
I will soar to the eternal brightness of my chosen star.

Laugh all you want in your moment of victory
goddess of our saddest days
it is eternal joy we win at your expense.

Hands of Mystery

Few still resist the temptation to relax their footing
and slip below into the infinite darkness
of an oblivion which may well hide a rebirth.

The most resilient rest upon the solid rocks
of those mountains risen before the invented hour
their collective hand on deepest mysteries.

Covered in the pallid shroud once joyful
bluish veins scar the ancient statues
flesh hard as marble ready to collapse.

Timid owners of the intimate legacy
their cavernous entrails recall a smile
when ecstasy was yet a safe enterprise.

Jealous of the envied possessions
they keep the secret coffers from thieves
a warmth only few can still preserve.

Origin

A little piece of the universe trembles under a gentle breeze
but whence does it come at such a late hour of the creation?

Oaken ancestors respond in syllables borne to boundless realms
a shuddering vibration sakes the foundations of all things.

Leaves of noble branches take notice of the quiet message
bleeding in their veins the lives of eternal souls.

Far from the tumult of ancient cities fallen to ash
history travels to change the world in a silent melody.

A lone spectator left behind contemplates the scene
reaching with the desperate hand to plead for a chance.

He once stood atop the peak of this known world
but can only kneel now in the humblest awe.

Gently wrapped within the ever-expanding shroud
he must surrender to the unknown beginning of the wind.

John P. Drudge

John is a social worker working in the field of disability management and holds degrees in social work, rehabilitation services, and psychology. He is the author of three books of poetry: *March* and *The Seasons of Us* (both published in 2019) and *New Days* (published in 2020). His work has appeared widely in numerous literary journals, magazines, and anthologies internationally. John is also a Pushcart Prize and Best of the Net nominee and lives in Caledon Ontario, Canada with his wife and two children.

Spinning Time

The click
Of the wheel
Steady and sure
The echoing rhythms
Hypnotic against cold stone
The tallow
Of sweat and sadness
On hewn and broken hands
Keeping time
To the temptation of dreams
Strung into baskets
Of folded space
Redemptive in the weave
Of new creation
And relieved
By the steady spin
Of time

Sahara Secrets

Along the song lines
And dream tracks
The trails that lead us
To deliverance
Beneath a wandering sun
In an oasis of hope
With miles melting over
Long dried rivers
And the arid salt pans
Of death and slim rebirth
I search for
The lost answers
Of you
Among the endless dunes
Of golden nothingness

Alfama Nights

Another late night
In Lisbon
The quiet of the hills
Broken only by laughter
From the last of the cafes
Hanging
Onto the short hours
Of morning
Good friends and good wine
In the warm
Alfama breeze
As light from the cathedral
Spills onto the street
And summer sings
Into the surrounding
Darkness

The Hard Part

The hard part is over
So everyone says
But they don't see
Inside my skin
The hard part is moving on
Scarred and scared
Thwarted by things
Unmentionable
The hard part picks at me
Everyday
Like worms turn in the mud
And disappear
Beneath those uncertain things
That are left unsaid
The hard part
Is tomorrow

P.J. Douglas

Originating from Hamilton, OH. P.J. Douglas has held variety of careers and traveled the world collecting experiences and expanding his consciousness. He is a retired educator living between the southwest United States and abroad. An advocate for DIY musicians, young people and artists, P.J. promotes anti-racism and the elevation of the sovereign and collective consciousness.

The Little One Inside You

Let me into your inner child,
I want to tell that little person
something.
I love you kid,
It's not your fault.
You have done nothing wrong.
You are amazing.
You are beautiful.
I love you little child inside.
Your shell may be old now,
You are stressed and broken.
Hopeless at times,
You need a break,
But you don't need anyone's
permission,
To reach down inside,
And hold the hand of that little
child.
They deserve a break,
Just like you,
Reach inside and love them,
Love them with all your heart,
Love them like you should
yourself.
Right now.
If you can love the little one in
you.

You will forget how the world
has wronged you,
How they all let you down,
How they hurt you,
If you love that little one,
The little one inside you,
You can love you too.
Then you can forgive them all.
You can meet new people and
look in their heart.
You can look in at the inner child
of theirs.
Hold your hand out and love them
too.
And tell them it isn't their fault.
You have done nothing wrong.
You can tell them how amazing
they are.
How beautiful they truly are.
You can love all the children,
locked away,
Inside the sad adults, we've all
become.
You can love all the children,
But start with yourself.
There is one inside you,
Waiting for your hug for so long.
Like a cherub on a cloud waiting,
Heaven is there, hold out your
heart, and love it so.

Something Nineteen

Something nineteen.
The best thing to happen to me.
I have waited for this.
For so long you see.
I love the end of the world.
Everyone knows how to be sad now.
I don't have to be around those fake shiny people.
Plastic participle.
The world burns and people are still dick-riding politicians.
Enjoy the end of the world with me.
You can do it.
Throw yourself into the end.
Insert yourself in the rapture.
God isn't coming back.
Maybe his consciousness will.
Maybe we will all die and finally, be together.
Nothing can stop us now.
The great big collective conscious,
In the ever after,
Looking down on our ruin.
Gaia celebrates.

Nayanjyoti Baruah

Nayanjyoti Baruah, a trilingual poet, essayist and translator is pursuing Master of Arts in English Literature from Gauhati University, Assam, India. He's written about 150 poems in Assamese, Hindi, and English languages. His poems have been appeared in state, national, and international magazines and journals such as *Tayls*, *Rasa Literary Review*, *Felicity*, *Akhore*, *Meghali Budhidrom*, *The Fiction Project*, *A Too Powerful Word*, *Necro Magazine*, *Litterateur*, *AMASHIWII JOURNAL*, *Dovelyisi Magazine*, etc. He has been nominated as the Writer (Artist) of the Month three times. He's the co-author of ten anthologies. Ten of his poems will be published in USA in 2021. He's written two essays and five short stories. Currently he's writing his first novel. He's 22 years old.

If I Were All

If I were a smith
I would hammer you on an anvil
Until all the hates'd smash from your heart
And I would shape a new one
Where there would only place for love
To me and for me
And the sparks of feelings'd rise from that heart.

If I were a poet, a true romantic poet,
I would write thousands of poems for you;
About your ups and downs, left and right,
Apply all the chances to demonstrate
Which would make you a lover of mine
And the rest would know our bonding.

If I were a carpenter and you the wood
I would cut off the bark
And would produce you in a new form
That would figure you to be beautifully cute.
And you would be praiseworthy to the world.

If I were the make-up materials of you
I would always tie to you forever;
On your cheeks as powder,
On your lips as lipstick,
On your eyes as eyeliner.
I would always be with you forever.

If I were a phoenix and you too,
I would fly up above the world with you
And would live there in tranquility;
We would birth a happy lonely life
Where there would be no people to interrupt.
The deafening world wouldn't hear us.

If I were a singer
I would sing all the nineties' romantic songs;
Songs of true lovers.
I would sing songs if you got bored
That would make you to fall in love.

If I were a painter
I would capture you on the canvas;
Your tiny happiness, cries, amusement,
And would hang you on my bedroom wall
To see you every single moment.

If all seasons were winter and you the coat
I would walk around the world if necessary
And would buy the costlier one
That would put on unto the last.

If I were a son of the government officer
Who had money in each pocket,
I would win you as my beloved
And would marry you without any violence.

If I were a doctor,
I would scan my heart
That would tell you about my pain; my facts,
You would then know me well
And would accept me as your husband.

If I were a plastic
My love would take decades to decompose,
The world even wouldn't collapse me by burning.

If I were a mirror
You would come to me to look yourself
And you would share your secret with me
Then I would know you better than before.

And if I were an astrologer
I would know whether you lied to me or not
Then I wouldn't disturb you for a second
And would run off from your life forever.

But if I were all!

Twenty Twenty

I overhear the unspoken songs of citizens;
They sing two songs together;
They sing two songs, songs of bitterness,
The singers are neither in the studios
Nor on the stages, they're on multiple lands
They're not smiling, they're crying of no tears,
Groups of helpless singers sing songs of suffering.

Twenty Twenty you're the cruelest year;
You encourage me to state my country; my world felt wound.
Scattered of bloodstream in the plain streets of those penniless workers.
You must have lost your eyes to notice, you're so harsh.
Few feel for them because they're human.
A few dig up the country like a rabbit,
They're brutal businessmen of resources.
But you're a real mirror of reality that visualizes other's reality.

I overhear the unspoken songs of citizens;
Two long songs with no rhythm
No melody in their voice yet I can feel it, feel it perfectly.
Songs of miscellaneous voices all over the nation.
"O my lord, are you breathing?
Look at us, the insignificant commodity
We are born to serve them with toiling, sweating hands
Is the lone incentive we have in mind.
O my lord, are you there?
Do you identify me and my overused colleagues?
What did we do? Are we guilty of Pandemic?
Look at my wife's feet; it's injured.
You must have died centuries ago
Or you must have lost your perception of seeing.
We want to dwell, we want to go home, we want to be pleased."

My country cries of real blood;
Even caves are not impregnable for all.
I sit back with my shield
But do I think for countrymen who walk with nude feet?

No fare, no water
No money, no objection
No advantage, no Tata safari.

Only miles to step with holdall
With sons and daughters and wives.
Does anyone remember my friends who died on the train road?
Does anyone remember my friends who died unconditionally?

Like clock moves, like day passes
Like human gets old and old people evaporate,
Resources end, animals slaughter,
We become voracious, immoral
Seeker of power, money & pleasure.
Will the earth remain after these?
Whom will you rule if there's no human?
Will there be left to be proud if there will no resources?
You will live with the sins you committed.
I overhear the unspoken songs of citizens;
"O my lord, are you there for blessing us?
Stop digging us up, we are innocent as babies.
What did we do? Stop cutting off our trunks
Stop annihilating us. We feel equal pain as you feel.
Stop merchandising your own glory.
Do plantation us more, propagate more new breeds,
Don't forget you exist because we do live."
A strange man wanted to perish
And born again as animal,
When I asked him the logic behind it
"There's only peace to live" response came from him.

We inventors not only of
Dynamite, gun, bomb, missile, nuclear,
We invented pillager officer, politician
To loot us, our neighbors
Our States, our countries, our Cosmos.

Yourselves objectify the consequences now
The entire world is under threat now
The heritage of wildlife is havoc now
Because your elected great people prove wrong now.

Twenty Twenty you're such a cruel year;
No sympathy, no serving hands.
Supreme creature is in exposure,
Halt not to ruin rest too.
We harvest only pain, suffering, death now.
Isn't it the world war three?

Mohamed Fouad Oodian

Mohamed Fouad Oodian is a writer, author, and researcher with a focus in spirituality, science, and religion who studied with the Writer Bureau from England. Mysticism is Mohamed's favorite passion used frequently for speeches and writings on spirituality and mysticism.

BIRTH AND DEATH

No one knows the decision of the hour.

It is as the twinkling of the eye or even quicker.

It is God who begins the process of creation; then repeats it, and then shall we be brought back to Him.

So, what is time?

The coming is always joyful but the departure is always a distress.

The receiver laughs but the mourner cries.

All is doing by the twinkling of the eye faster than the travel of the light.

A white star coming from the depth of the sky is quickly surrounded by other stars of the same color.

It is guided to a particular place, how he got to this destination only himself knows.

He then changed like a comet and crossed the time.

Has it undergone the trial of fire?

He penetrated the terrestrial atmosphere, the sky was reddish, and the transformation started.

He took the form of a white bird of a rare species and passed behind the mountain in the darkest night.

He crashed into the ocean, calm and black speedily.

He travelled on the sea like a ball bouncing here and there.

His travel ended on the beach and got his real form.

Who is the woman who will bear him yet again?

Kathryn Sadakierski

Kathryn Sadakierski's work has been published in *Capsule Stories, Critical Read, DoveTales, Halfway Down the Stairs, Literature Today, NewPages Blog, Northern New England Review, Poetically Magazine, seashores: an international journal to share the spirit of haiku, Silver Stork Magazine, Snapdragon: A Journal of Art and Healing, Songs of Eretz, The BeZine, The Voices Project, Yellow Arrow Journal,* and elsewhere. Her micro-chapbook "Travels through New York" was published by *Origami Poems Project* (2020). In 2020, she was awarded the C. Warren Hollister Non-Fiction Prize. She holds a B.A. and M.S. from Bay Path University.

Pocket Change

If I could, I would stay
In the sunshine forever,
I wouldn't slip this moment
Into a back pocket
For me to forget,
Like ticket stubs or spare change,
Though when you reach far back,
Into these memories,
You find them, a happy surprise,
The kind that sounds like serendipity,
A song that comes on the radio in the car
When you need it the most,
Summoning a smile
As the sun rests on your shoulders,
Ribbons of light braided through your hair
When the colors of sunset
Glimmer through your sunroof,
Nothing keeping you
From feeling it all,
The glow of hope
And the color of spring,
Like a row of glass bottles
Catching the glance of sun,
A rainbow stretched across the windowsill.

Spring evening

Silver spools,
Cloud curls,
Dangle like a waterfall of tresses,
Sterling chains of hair,
Streamers from a child's bike handles,
In the violet sky,
Woven through with tree branches
Like straw plaited into a basket
Of twilight horizon,
Flowers like fallen stars,
Dusky gold petals dusting the garden,
Vines enfolding their arms around each other.

The lanterns rise,
Pink, orange, red
Rose trellises climbing up through the air,
As though it were just a ladder
Leading up to the tree house
Where you lie back and dream
About the world above,
Before the colored lights fade again,
Arms stretched above in a dance
Brought to their sides again,
Moon covering what was once gold
In a web of white.

embers

the mountain range is pink with its own fire,
gold-rimmed in the necklace of embers
from orange sun and sky
that fringe the farms, and latent snow
still clinging to the yellowed grass,
quite desperately
as the clouds whose frayed edges,
like worn button-down shirts,
latch onto faded swatches of blue,
like paint samples,
at the perimeters of the heavens,
where the geese shoot through,
an arrowhead, in their v-formation,
swimming across the rim of world,
dauntlessly,
fluid as fish,
anyone who veers outside of their crest,
regal as a fleur-de-lis,
realigns quickly,
all moving together, as one unit,
a necklace of embers,
gold from the sun
reflected in the shallow pools of light
created by what was once snow,
water furrowed like wrinkles
in the dirt, combed in streaks
from car tires,
at the farm by the road
that wavers on like the geese,
orange sun and sky framing it all,
our faces reflected in the car windows,
glass hearts of the vehicle,
this engine,
holding some of the fire,
a spirit that won't quit,
a voice like flaming light,
pocketed in the clouds,
that just won't be quieted.

The Diner

The smell of pickles and frying meat
Mixed with the rubbery vinyl seats
Ripped, red patches bursting with foam,
Plates clanking, cooks shouting,
A music of their own.

Dinging of a timer,
As stomachs growl fiercely,
Waking up the tiger
Amid a sea of grease,
The ephemera of a dream.

Hot fumes,
Ovens toiling,
Water boiling,
As pies, roiling, complete their slow rotations
In glass cases,
Ballerinas, or the planets around the sun,
The same dance when dinner is done.

Galaxies

over our heads,
beyond our belief
the stars, in their endless seas
far away,
outside the scope
of the things we deeply know,
earth beneath feet,
sand through fingers,
heart inside that continues to beat,
our own inner galaxies.

over our heads,
beyond our belief
the stars, watching over us,
everlasting confidantes.
children press their faces to the window glass,
counting stars, with faith in the possible,
connecting the dots,
whispering their wishes,
not waiting for the stars to fall
to make them come true.

over our heads,
beyond our belief,
destinies seem immutable.
luck and fate are the lightning bugs
we just can't catch,
evading our grasp.
but the same lights glimmer
everywhere,
in blankets above,
reassuringly
over our heads, always
affirming our belief
that this is the air we breathe,
the stars around us, in us,
nature's reflection of beauty,
one that we know
in the heart that beats inside,
everything,
radiantly alive.

LAL Kelly

LAL Kelly is a British Writer and Author of *Surviving Bleak House*, as well as this memoir, LAL also enjoys writing poetry, and has featured in the *Lockdown Lit* anthology.

When LAL is not writing, she is also a radio show host and producer, and has a love of music from all genres.

LAL is also a busy mum and loves family get-togethers with films and board games.

LAL is also an advocate for positive mental health and has a holistic approach to life, winning her the Bizmums Inspirational Mum of the year Award in 2017.

Still the Waters Flow

Across the meadow
The chirps of a bird
Near silence is all around

Still the waters flow
Through ancient brooks
Gently babbling with sound

Calm is the feeling
Of the stillness of the day
Sitting in long grass to daydream

Still the waters flow
With ebbs and soft trickles
Through the countryside stream

Time will march on
Pondering the hours away
Dusk nears, soon the time is gone

Still the waters flow
Glistening with the last light
The straits catch the edge of the
sun

You leave natures garden
Your presence forgotten

Wind gently blows and leaves
quiver

Still the water flows
Not knowing life comes and goes
Unbeknown is the flow of the river

Round bends and rocks
The sound of a journey
The essence of life that seems free

Still the waters flow
Towards a pool of sameness
The waves and the strength of the
sea

Sheer vastness of water
Depths to explore and delight
In time we will leave this land we
hold dear

Still the waters flow
To this serene place of greatness
The oceans of eternity will still be
here

Under The Tree

I always felt stuck in this place, compelled to stay. The silence always seemed so loud, I could never hear my thoughts, though I never was a big thinker anyway. At sixteen I was impulsive, I lived in the moment, I was free as a bird. This place though, under the tree, this was my forever place. This old oak tree, at least three hundred years old, with its knots and ridges, was my grounding force. I always saw the changing of the seasons here in the leaves and it kept me alive. It wasn't always so serene, sometimes I felt heavy here, if I wandered I felt gripped, by some long cold fingers, an invisible force that I imagined to be breathing down my neck, I felt suffocated. If I stayed under the tree it left me alone. I saw many people here, mostly nice, but some who would wish to hurt me, and would, if I wasn't under my tree. This was the best part of the cemetery anyway. I had the best marble headstone, though a little dusty now, it reads Mary-Anne Powell, 1704-1720, taken from us too soon, now free as a bird.

John Grey

John Grey is an Australian born short storywriter, poet, playwright, musician. Has been published in numerous magazines including *Weird Tales, Christian Science Monitor, Greensboro Poetry Review, Poem, Agni, Poet Lore* and *Journal Of The American Medical Association*. His latest books are *Memory Outside The Head* and *Leaves On Page* available through Amazon. Has had plays produced in Los Angeles and off-off Broadway in New York. Winner of Rhysling Award for short genre poetry in 1999.

FOUND IN RANDY'S APARTMENT WHEN HE PASSED AWAY AT 53

There's a poster for
Porky's II,
a collection of plastic cereal-box toys,
a lava lamp
that no longer works,
a Pachinko machine,
a chipped coffee mug
with a Pisces fish sign
on the side,
a yellowing copy of Rolling Stone
with Janet Jackson
on the cover.

No ex-girlfriend
wants these for a shrine,
no local college
has expressed interest
in creating a special collection
is his name.

Maybe an anthropologist
but he or she
isn't born yet.

RETIRING TO FLORIDA

You wake to the gentle flop of waves on sand,
the air embracing, temperature, humidity
perfect - except for that ache in your
right shoulder. Breakfast on your balcony
brings scrambled eggs and ocean,
sea gulls and buttered toast —so why
can't the clavicle fall in line
with the loveliness.
You slip into something slight,
stroll the beach, pick up shells
and put them down again
but, for all the sun's bright massage,
it can't get to that kink in the rotator cuff.
Paradise boasts small waves that run up
to your sandals, tickle your bare toes.
But it also has a rider clause, small print -
when there's a human body involved,
a limit is placed on the available pleasure.
Then it's time for a swim.
The water's refreshing —for the fish at least.
One darts away from you. It may
be fearful but it doesn't suddenly grab
its arm or reach for the piscine painkillers.
Tune to walk back to your beach-house,
admonishing yourself with the likes of,
"Be happy. There's people a lot worse
off than you." Except, once again,
there's a caveat. "Those worse off people
didn't necessarily start out that way."
You spy a neighbor, a man in his early sixties,
bearded and brown-skinned, hands as
rough as yours are soft. When you first
moved here, the possibility of romance
had crossed your mind. But no longer.
He's nice enough but with more quirks
than your set-upon right limb.
You talk ten minutes or so. You mention
the twinge in your shoulder. He doesn't
volunteer to rub lotion into it. It wouldn't
do any good. Men, like the world, have a flair for
the demonstrative but a history of not helping.

KING DREAMER

In my dream, I'm a phenomenon.
I can leap thirty feet,
I can face up to the bullies.
I can adore or be adored back
by whomever I choose.

Head on the pillow,
eyes closed,
if you could see inside my head
I'd be a huge surprise to you.
Enigma, first class.
Marvel of the comic book kind.
Nonpareil...how I love to wrap
that word around my dreaming tongue.
I'm daring and divine,
dangerous to know
but heaven to hold.

Night after night,
I don't just offer my imagination
to this fabulous world,
I rule it.
I'm a king on his throne.
I'm the emperor of lands
farther than any third eye can see.
I can even be God
as long as I believe in me.

So is it my fault
that I have to wake in the morning.
Bed-sheets, mattress, sun through the window,
status quo awaits.
I'm back to who I really am.
You still love me
but it's a close run thing.
Ah...if you only knew.
Then I would never have to prove it.

Prentice Wright

Prentice Wright is a 24-year-old poet from North London. As the oldest child of four, he was very much influenced by his friends. Inspiration came from his peers as well as books, poems, films, video games, stand-up comedy, and the internet. He was the sort of kid who had a few books on the go but could also be found skateboarding or hanging out at a local park. Although he wrote his first poem in primary school, he first became serious about writing at the age of 16. He graduated from Goldsmiths, University of London in 2020 with a degree in English Literature with creative writing. He is currently working towards teaching English as a foreign language in China. At the moment, he sees writing as first and foremost a way of life as opposed as a way to open doors or achieve specific goals. He hopes to continue to share ideas with and enjoy the work of creatives of his generation - considering them as equally important as the artists studied at Universities.

Untitled

There is beauty in the dark,
pleasure and pain in equal parts
For without it how would I have known
my love was throat exposed, unarmed
See, all the bits of you amiss,
the intonation of choice favourite phrases
ride like petals in my chest
and cut the world I knew to shreds.
Every day I dreamt with you,
the life we carved out in our minds,
The children that you'd sometimes
breathe to life with words
will die with time.
"I'm good thank you,"
"I love you darlin,"
your silly laugh
all make me weep.
You stroke my hand,
you tidy with haste
In *these* words.
In these words you haven't gone.
In these words our love will live,
and we can wake up tomorrow
side by side.

Hooked up the Night

"You are..."
with vanilla candle drawl
With fire turning wax lighter
Thoughts made of generalisations
bouncing across the rim
drips harden.
Nothing like salt waves
washing grrrr from frontal-lobe
Nothing alike, most friends
not for rainy days
Stand alone like parakeets,
assume posture
apparently stable.
Of all the trials and tribulations
mapped out in sepia
– with your advancing red line –
Not one gifts the
Lion's share of credit.
Get down to brass tacks
and erode away,
Once gone you'll have
nothing to be afraid
of in your life
ever again.
I love you.

Trying to find home

Every pleasant accident
was preparation, training,
wood shavings spiraling off
increasingly deep and intricate grooves,
making you whole.
Or instead,
an old letter you kept
is nothing but a letter,
cause and effect.
Who cares?
I could have sworn
inspiration struck you
like a dust shockwave,
multiplying cellularly and
creating genuine belief in ingenuity,
drawing anatomy,
that has never been seen before.
You're like fucking da Vinci!
Apparently you can cheat death
by counting every card in the game,
so that, to your pleasure,
the fancy words from university
fizz and dissolve,
replaced with beautiful, imagined futures –
Postcards burn into the retina,
their different pigments bending around each other
like a line on a cardiograph.

A rainy motorway - 2004

Transmission towers loom over the M4
and so, the Jedi running beside the car
and jumping over the highway lights,
the Loch Ness monster
weaving in and out of the road,
splashing up damp, ricocheting rain,
all these things are made permissible,
are supervised by these gigantic robots.
Strangely enough
today I still wait for permission.
I still wait for the word
to float above the roads
and up into the sky.

Ancestors

The dust of ancestors in front of us,
a rich ochre shimmer
 as we run to meet them,
slowly disintegrating in turn.
I feel myself breaking up,
you know?
concerns shifting once again
like a kaleidoscope.
I see flashes of pubs,
T-junctions, old faces,
things and people
no longer in my life.
Reminders of what's to come,
of what has been happening.
Sometimes it's like the exact beer
tingles on my lips,
the specific pressure of air
from forgotten nights
kisses my skin again,
Eyes that used to be common
stare back, pulsing.
Sometimes you'd swear
the configuration of streetlight
is exactly the same.

Heartbeat.exe has stopped working

Targeted ads for aftershave,
set the mood.
This day is musk and citrus.

The maths doesn't add up –
How can I become a better person

with so much joy subtracted?
A YouTube video
by a balding statistician
with impeccable editing skills
supports these findings.

I still dream of taking my
children to school.
Their faces are rendered
from a face blending app.
It produces an amalgamation
of our faces, the kids don't have
the patches facial hair
that the software fails to edit out.

Cortana, for how long does
heartbreak leak into pleasure?
The answer cannot come in a
succinct paragraph.

Infinite combinations of words
produce an infinite capacity for
suffering.
"Cheer up buttercup," says
Cortana.

The walk to peace of mind is long

but walking in tetrameter
makes the vibration.
heralding 10,000 steps
feel heroic in your pocket,
It shakes the very cell walls.
It changes the transcriptase
enzyme
to make an entirely new person:
He says, when the feelings
were no longer euphoric,
when my heartbeat ceased to
flutter
flew down to earth and pulsed
stoically,
Then I knew I was in love.

Acknowledgments

It takes a lot to submit to any publisher, so kudos to those who took the time to write, submit, wait, and especially those I was unable to host in this year's epic Annual. Do not fear rejection. Do not set boundaries with your writing. Keep going, continue to inspire and connect around the world through words and stories.

If this group of stories and poetry has taught me anything in this year following a world shut-down and incredible pain for so many, it's that we are all connected. Each of these stories and pieces of poetry resonated with me personally on some level. Some more than others. I read each one at least five times during the choosing process, editing, and then formatting.

One evening, home alone and a bit emotional, I got up as I neared the end of one particular story. I'd read it already and knew what was going to happen, and on this second read, I had to stop and walk away from my computer before reaching the ending I knew was coming. That's how powerful these stories are.

This past year has torn humanity apart on many levels... and it has also brought us together. Those of us willing to listen, to talk, to connect, we are here understanding our differences can bring each of us closer together if we only embrace one another for those differences rather than distance ourselves in spite of them. Our words have the power to inspire collective thinking on many levels. At the risk of reaching for more beyond support, I ask each reader to pause and reflect on the many themes in these words here and realize as writers from around the world, the one theme that keeps humanity going is love. Seated comfortably in love resides kindness. Thank you to each of you for sharing difficult moments, sadness, vulnerability, and love in each of these stories.

For my family... I know projects like this one take time, which pulls me away from you all and keeps me occupied for weeks on end. Thank you for your patience with me as I build a world of writers who know they can call Stella Samuel and ARZONO Publishing home no matter where their writing takes them. Creating a space of uplifting support is important to me because writing can be a lonely world. For my oldest daughter, Ladybug... as I write this, you are away again. These weeks have been the toughest for us all. We all miss you greatly. Please know we all love you. Sometimes love and support is disguised and nearly unrecognizable. This is the toughest love we can give. For my Butterfly... you are cocooning again, and I cannot wait to see what you become this time. Adversity challenges us all, sometimes to the brink of breakdown. Each time you face those difficulties, you adapt and evolve. I love watching you grow. To my son, the froggy who couldn't sit still... your strength is inspiring. I'm so often amazed at how you empower me to keep moving and still have enough energy to go-go-go yourself.

For the woman I still love, Jessica. When this book drops, just a few days after your birthday, we will likely still be apart, maybe having dinner as a family and bidding farewell as we go our separate ways again for the night. This year has been tough—for everyone. There is nothing I would change more than the pain it brought us. Our journey will be what it will be, and I will keep loving you... because yours was the best love to ever cross the galaxy. No matter where life takes you, my home will always be yours. I love you.

For my tribe... it wasn't until my darkest days I realized my tribe is spread around the world. Some I leaned on right away, others took me longer to reach as I allowed vulnerability to seep in rather than overtake me like a wave hidden in the undercurrent. Beth, I couldn't ask for a better sister. I love you for everything you are. You understand me, hear me, validate me, and put me in my place when I need that most, even when I don't want it. Anne, thirty years of friendship isn't something that happens lightly, or easily. No matter the paths we take across the miles, we always come together exactly when we need it. Thank you for all the laughs, the questions that remind me you care, and for checking on me precisely when I need it, even when I think I don't. Tina, in times of strife, you've been there. Every single time. Don't think for a moment your love goes unnoticed. I love you, my friend. Susan, I miss you greatly. This journey through motherhood, love and loss, challenging times... well, it's been up and down, but it's also been filled with love and laughter because of the connection we made many years ago. It might be weeks or months, but when we connect, it's bright and beautiful. I appreciate that you are still in my world. George & Marie, I've survived because you held me up. There are no words to say to a family I chose... one that also chose me... that could ever show the gratitude I feel for the two of you. Mom, Courtney, Heather, Ian, Joanne, Dan, James, Chip, Chuck, Ken, Nick, Melanie, Kristen... there are many others I should take the time and space to thank. You all have empowered me to be me, to find me, to celebrate me. Thank you all. I appreciate you.

Be well.
~Stella
April 2021